SIMONE KING

The God Key

First edition

ISBN: 978-1-3999-3113-7

Cover art by Natalia Junqueira

This book was professionally typeset on Reedsy. Find out more at reedsy.com

I can't be the only person who wanted this story - the world is a big place. So, here's to you.

Acknowledgement

Love and eternal gratitude to Melody, Matt, Mamma, Fabienne and Pete who were my first readers and patiently put up with my babbling nonsense in the process of writing this book. Special thanks also to Kerry and Ian.

I

Part 1: The Nightmares

1 - Isaac

Don't run.

Isaac froze at the command. He grabbed at the urge to run all the same, at the adrenaline in his limbs. Both vanished. Both were stolen. He settled back on the balls of his feet instead, hand clenched around his to-go bag so tight that his knuckles bleached white.

Gabriel's control had got even better; his touch was as light-fingered as any good thief's now.

Isaac's gaze landed on his knife.

Don't even think about it. Sit down on the sofa.

He released a shaky breath but, after a beat, moved over. He sank into the faded leather cushions, hearing them squeak beneath him. He kept one gloved hand on the strap of his rucksack. The urge to run was gone, but his heart still slammed. The adrenaline had plunged cold and clammy. He tried to think of nothing, to feel nothing.

It was impossible.

Gabriel pulled his door open only seconds later, the autumn chill and the sweet smell of rotting leaves chasing after his heels as he stepped in. He didn't even hesitate. He sauntered right in as if it hadn't been five years, as if he might swoop over and press a kiss of greeting to Isaac's cheek and enquire about his day. Even then, somehow, he looked like he belonged in Isaac's living room more than Isaac ever did.

Isaac hated him a little for it.

He hated himself, more, for staring. For drinking up the sight of Gabriel, cataloguing every change those five years had wrought, and collecting up every scrap of him that hadn't changed at all.

Gabriel De Vere: shorter than Isaac, though it never felt like it, with dark curls and a handsome face and a burn on his arm from that time taking pizza out the oven and— and he plucked the urge to run from Isaac's synapses almost as soon as it fired.

Gabriel's stare locked on him in turn. His brown eyes darkened with an unmistakeable hunger, with grief, with anger. With a dozen emotions that Isaac didn't need to be a mind-reader to figure out but which he didn't dare to try and unpick.

"Isaac." Gabriel's voice came out breathless, reverent. He strode across the room, hands rising as if to touch.

Isaac flinched back. He squeezed his eyes shut.

Gabriel didn't touch him.

He could feel Gabriel's telepathy more now, like a warm hand on the back of his neck. Familiar, soothing, controlling, propriety.

"I thought you were dead," Gabriel said, oh so softly.

"Don't." Isaac dug his nails into his palms, letting the sting of it ground him. He opened his eyes once he was sure he had his expression under control. Every muscle in his body locked tense. "Don't," he said. "Let it go. Let me go."

Gabriel's expression hardened in reply. He turned away and studied their surroundings instead, scouring Isaac's small cottage and plundering it of its secrets. The weight of his power didn't leave for even a second as he strolled over to Isaac's desk, rifling through the sketchbook on top with the same arrogant sense of right which he flicked through Isaac's brain with. He smoothed his fingers over rough lines of charcoal. He thumbed whichever memories interested him most and set Isaac's emotions down gently after he held them up to the light and – that day didn't come up.

Isaac watched Gabriel's back stiffen.

Gabriel turned to face him again, leaning against the table with a fake casualness. He folded his arms across his chest, one brow raised.

"Impressive, Isaac. How are you blocking me?"

"It's rude to prod at other people's thoughts without permission."

Gabriel huffed something that may have been a laugh, if it wasn't so utterly mirthless, so choked. He dragged a hand through his hair. The familiar tic made Isaac's heart stutter. Gabriel was tired – he *looked* tired. A soul deep bone-weary sort of tired. Had he not been sleeping?

"So that's what this is going to be like," Gabriel muttered. "Fine. Throw me the bag."

It wasn't a suggestion. Isaac lobbed the bag at his head as hard as he physically could, hoping its contents would fall and smash.

Gabriel caught it; pulling out Isaac's passport, emergency cash, change of clothes, his laptop, his burner phone. He set the laptop on the desk and concentrated on the phone first. "Tell me the passcode." He glanced up at Isaac, continuing before Isaac could give him the wrong one. "The *current* passcode. Of this specific phone. Now, please."

5

"0829."

Gabriel flicked through the phone for a moment, his brow pinched. No doubt he was searching the contacts list. He wouldn't find anything. Not on the phone.

God, Isaac had to get out of there. What had he been training for, for the past five years, if not to ensure that nobody would ever touch him without his permission again? If not to be prepared to face *him*? He considered his options.

"Are you here alone?" he asked Gabriel.

"No. But I wanted to talk to you alone. I –" Gabriel faltered and his jaw clenched. "You're coming with us. I need your help. *We* need your help. And I'm not the only person whose been looking for you. What you can do…" Gabriel looked at him then, with awe, like he'd never seen anything so perfect in his life.

Isaac looked down.

"You're too dangerous for me to leave you alone, Isaac," Gabriel continued, gently even. "I can't let you fall into the wrong hands."

"Kidnapping your ex makes you the wrong hands," Isaac snapped before he could stop himself. The fear reared in his chest, bolted acid up his throat, and he surged to his feet, breathing hard and— and the urge to run vanished. The fear vanished. Both left behind an absence, a fog, the sensation of a phantom limb grasping at something vital torn away.

Gabriel didn't even flinch. Of course he bloody didn't, he thought he was in the right. He thought he was *helping*.

Isaac steeled himself. However much he didn't want Gabriel to touch him, it would also be his best advantage against Gabriel's powers. A person's abilities never worked on Isaac when they touched him, but in return their power grew. That was Isaac's so-called gift. Whoever Isaac touched would become twice, three times, four times as strong. Isaac didn't know the limit. It wasn't something he dared to test. Still, Gabriel's telepathy, his ability to read and influence and even control thoughts and emotions, wouldn't work on Isaac when Gabriel was touching him. So he had to make Gabriel touch him.

"Stay out of my head!" he took a deliberate step closer and let distress drown out the sounds of more rational thought. "I can't bear it." He met Gabriel's eyes and landed on the magic word. *"Please."*

Gabriel let Isaac's emergency bag crumple to the floor in a flutter of bank notes and bits of paper, and in an instant his fingers caressed feather-light along Isaac's jaw. He made a soft shushing sound, as if to sweep all of Isaac's troubles away, unable to help himself either.

All of the power in Isaac lit up and up and up. His stomach rolled. His head went quiet.

He saw Gabriel's brown eyes turn as white and shining as moonlight, the reflection of his own usual shade. He heard Gabriel's breath catch at the surge of power. His touch grew more solid, cupping Isaac's head in his hand like a treasure. The weight of Gabriel's telepathic influence scattered in Isaac's mind, gone without so much as a trace and the panic came flooding back and the urge to run filled his body. He breathed past the instinct to flee as best as he could and held still. There was no point running until he could be sure that Gabriel wouldn't simply order him not to before he even made it to the door.

"You're alive." Gabriel stroked his cheek. "God, *Isaac.* You're alive, you're really alive." One hand moved down to shove Isaac's turtle-neck aside and fumble at his pulse, as if to make doubly sure. The raw emotion on Gabriel's face made Isaac want to close his eyes again; in short, Gabriel looked like all of his dreams had come true.

Isaac seized the opportunity to take a mental stock of his own feelings on the matter. Near Gabriel, when they were touching skin to skin was the only time that Isaac knew for sure who he was and what he wanted and felt. For all he knew otherwise Gabriel could have told him to forget the last hour of his life. He could tell Isaac that he was thrilled to see Gabriel again, no need to be concerned, no need to worry about a thing! And Isaac would be thrilled, and he would stop worrying, and he would let Gabriel lead him right off the edge of a cliff if Gabriel only asked him to follow.

However, his mood more or less matched up with the before and after of contact. That was good. Maybe it didn't all have to be a fight.

(Maybe he'd got it all wrong.)

"You can't make me help you," Isaac began. "The second you touch me—"

"You're refusing to help before you even know what the problem is. That seems a bit unfair, don't you think?" Gabriel replied.

Isaac twisted his fingers into the front of Gabriel's soft cotton shirt, torn between instincts. To shove away, to pull closer still, to love, to hate. His head spun, in constant danger of distraction. He couldn't remember the last time someone had touched him for so long. It made it difficult to think straight. No, he remembered perfectly. It had been Gabriel then too. Gabriel cradling his head like it was the most precious thing in the world, his hands stained by Isaac's blood, his body bent shuddering over Isaac's on their bedroom floor. Begging, begging, begging Isaac not to be dead. Not to leave him alone.

This was all too much, too fast, too Gabriel.

He felt so much more real beneath Isaac's hands than memories did. Isaac had forgotten what he smelled like, too, but with one breath it all came rushing back. It would be far too easy to lean in, for too tempting.

"I want you to leave me the hell alone." He could say it, even it came out hoarse and half a lie. He knew he was himself without muddied waters. "You have to. Please. Gabriel—"

"I told you, I can't do that," Gabriel said, before he could continue. His fingers kept their slow hypnotic trail of movement along Isaac's cheek. "There are people looking for you – bad people. People who would use what you can do for evil. I know you're scared, but—"

Isaac laughed, a cracked sound, shaking his head.

A flash of anger crossed Gabriel's face. "Would you rather it was one of them who found you, instead of me?"

"Better the devil you know?"

"I'm not the devil."

"How did you even find me?"

"How the hell did you manage to convince me you were dead?" Gabriel's head tilted. "How are you alive? How do you have a block in your mind that I can't get past?"

Isaac wasn't sure they could afford to start asking *those* kinds of questions, he wasn't sure that they would ever stop.

"Come with me," Gabriel pressed. "Please, I can explain everything on the way. Just hear me out. That's all I'm asking."

Isaac hesitated, floundered. Gabriel knew he was alive – there was no taking that back, whatever happened. Maybe they did need to talk. Maybe Gabriel could be reasoned with, he wasn't some supervillain. He was *Gabriel*. Isaac's Gabriel.

Maybe she wouldn't even know either. Why would she know?

Gabriel held his scrutiny, earnestly.

"I don't want to force you, Isaac. I know you hate having me in your head. But if you make me…"

Make him. *Right.*

The smack of anger was like a gulp of icy air. It cleared Isaac's brain and washed away all the good memories and longings and how much he'd stupidly missed the man in front of him. At least, mostly.

It did have to be a fight.

"Alright," Isaac said. He let his shoulders sag and got back on track with a plan. "Alright…" He let his guard fall from his features, let himself look as terrified as he felt and watched the utter *love* and protectiveness bloom on Gabriel's face…and he slammed his knee up into Gabriel's ribcage. He seized Gabriel's wrists and spun him, slamming him down face first into his desk. He snatched up his knife.

And then the vines shattered through his window and hurled him bodily into the wall.

2 - Isaac

I saac often thought that if he was a telepath, he would have been afraid of inflicting himself on everyone around him. Doubtful, always, of how much of his life was true and how much of it was something that he wished into being with the force of his powers.

An example: you love a person, more than you've loved anything in your life. Every inch of you reaches out for them, to hold, to connect, to have and to cherish until death do us part. The person reaches back. Loves back. How do you know it's not a subconscious command? A hoping for returned feelings so powerful that the whole world bends out of place to accommodate it? And how could that person possibly know where the lines were drawn?

Don't move.

As far as he could tell, Gabriel had never had those fears.

Isaac's body crumpled slack in the vines, the knife clattering to the floor. The vines kept coming still, binding tighter and tighter around him like the coils of a serpent. He strained, uselessly, for his muscles to work. Gabriel wouldn't fall for the same trick twice. He had to win. He had to run.

An example: you love a person; you want them on your side, by your side. You wish they'd never leave you, that you'd stay together forever. Does that mean they choose to stay? Or just that they cannot choose to leave? It wouldn't be purposeful. You wouldn't use the word 'force' if asked to describe your relationship.

Gabriel straightened up off the desk, wheezing. He cupped a hand to his bleeding nose.

A thought: you love a person, more than you've loved anything in your life. But is it them that you love when every kiss, every touch, gives you unimaginable power? Or is it just the power? And what, then, would you do to keep them?

Isaac didn't know anymore how much of what he and Gabriel had was real, how much his emotions had been his own. Five years on, he still found himself analysing it all scene by scene, searching for some proof one way or another, never able to be certain.

Gabriel—

His door burst open and two more strangers charged into his home.

Isaac had blown it.

The first woman, hand raised, clearly controlled the vines. They stretched out of the palms of her hand, hovering in the air like dark green tendrils. By the look on her face, Isaac figured he was supposed to be grateful that none of them came with thorns, man-gouging spikes or poison. She was a small Asian young woman made larger by the force of her presence. Every visible inch of her, except her face, bloomed with vibrant flower tattoos. Isaac's neglected potted plant perked up as she passed it.

The second woman was Isaac's height, maybe even taller, towering six foot something and built like a fortress. She was fair like Isaac was too, but far brighter and more golden in her natural colouring than his pale ashy version of blond, and far more gothic in her clothing choices than his muted attire. She stood out. He did everything he could not to.

"Are you alright?" She marched straight over to Gabriel. "Let me see." Her questing fingers brushed over his nose and the other slipped beneath his shirt, before retreating. It was hard to tell with the lingering blood, but Gabriel's face looked significantly less broken than it had been a few seconds before. Healer. Her ability had to be healing.

"I thought you said he wouldn't hurt you!" the first woman snapped. "You could have got yourself killed, you prick." Her vines squeezed tighter around Isaac, making him gasp out.

"Don't," Gabriel said. "He's fine, I have him."

"Yeah," the woman snorted. "You sure had him when he was about to stab you."

"Dahlia."

Dahlia sighed, but the vines loosened their grinding death grip.

Isaac hit the ground hard and groaned in pain.

"I didn't mean drop him," Gabriel said.

Dahlia shrugged. "Oops." She didn't look remotely sorry about it.

"Do you want me to heal his face?" the second woman asked Gabriel. She took a step closer to Isaac without waiting for a reply, and he couldn't even tense after Gabriel told him not to move. "Don't be scared," she told him with a sunny black-lipstick smile. "I'm Sanna. I'm not going to hurt you. Sorry about Dahlia! It's been – well, this week has been *awful*! You have no idea."

"Don't touch me."

At least, whatever else Isaac could say about Gabriel,

13

Gabriel's control had always been impeccable. He wouldn't lose control of his abilities when Isaac touched him and so Isaac didn't have to fear that with him…only what Gabriel might do with more control, power and premeditated intention. He had no idea what would happen if Sanna touched him and lost control as a result. Healing required moving bones, didn't it? Isaac imagined all of the bones in someone's skull shifting when she tried to fix his nose and used far more power than she intended to. Bile clawed up his throat.

"It doesn't hurt," Sanna began again, reaching out, before her hand froze.

"You can't," Gabriel interrupted. He took a step closer, a merciful physical barrier between them, and gently pulled Sanna back. "Your healing won't work on him while you're touching him. Isaac, you can move providing you don't run or attack. Get some tissue or ice if you have any. Don't leave my sight. Then sit up against the wall and don't get up until I tell you to."

Sanna faltered, her brow furrowing. She pulled her hand back and eyed Isaac's lingering injuries like they were of personal insult to her.

"You should have said we wouldn't be able to heal him," she told Gabriel. "Dahlia would have been more careful!"

"Would I now," Dahlia muttered. "Thanks for letting me know my opinion on the matter."

Sanna turned a wounded puppy dog expression on her. Gabriel also shot Dahlia a look, warning and familiar.

Dahlia's spine straightened sharply. Her vines retreated back to her, shrinking down to small seedlings. She busied herself with scooping them back into her pockets, avoiding their gazes.

Isaac stumbled to his feet. He kept his distance from the three of them as he skirted the edge of the sparse space to get to the strip of the kitchen where he grabbed a wad of roll. His body ached dully. There wasn't enough air in the room. Fighting three of them without doing any real damage was going to be hard; though Sanna and Dahlia wouldn't know his tricks as well as Gabriel did. He doubted Gabriel was going to grab him again though, not when it meant Isaac could think unmonitored.

He'd goddamn blown it.

He could feel Gabriel picking at his thoughts again, sifting through the recent memories, monitoring intent and limbs like Isaac's body was an enemy territory he'd been charged with guarding. He searched for why Isaac had faked his death, why he was in the middle of nowhere. For so many things.

Isaac focused on one task at a time, keeping his thoughts narrowed as much as he could on 'fix your face' and, when that failed, 'pink elephants pink elephants think of nothing but pink elephants because apparently if someone tells you to not to think of pink elephants you have to think of pink elephants!'

Gabriel scowled at him.

"Tell me how you're still alive," he ordered.

He didn't say *now* so Isaac choked down the urge to speak and filed an answer for later, to be muttered quietly where Gabriel couldn't hear the response.

"Let me go," he replied instead.

Gabriel's head tilted again at the refusal, the seeming rejection of the command in Isaac's mind. His opened his mouth to say something, before closing it and rounding on his friends, followers, minions. Whatever they were.

"Sanna," Gabriel said. "His laptop is on the desk. Look through it to see what we're up against. This isn't right. Something's not right here."

Isaac would have snorted if he wanted to be cruel.

Sanna grabbed the laptop, before sitting herself down on the sofa and opening it up.

"What's the password?" she asked Isaac.

He didn't reply. He didn't have to do what *she* told him.

"Isaac," Gabriel spoke through gritted teeth. "Write down a list of every password or pass code you think I'd like to know and what they're for and then give it to her. You can throw it, no need to get too close." He tossed Isaac a notepad and pen off the table. "Write *legibly*," he added, as Isaac picked up the biro. "No tricks."

Isaac's fingers adjusted from their deliberately indecipherable scrawl. He could feel the stifling weight of their stares on his shoulders as he wrote, but kept his head bowed.

"…it's in, um, French," Sanna said. "I think it's French?"

Gabriel stared at Isaac for a moment. "I said no tricks."

"The French language is not a trick, it's a perfectly valid form of communication."

Gabriel looked pained.

"Again," he bit out.

The instructions that followed were meticulous, and Isaac could think of no loophole to the orders. So, that time, he handed his life over. His teeth gritted in turn. The panic drummed.

"What exactly are you hoping to find?" he asked.

"Answers you apparently don't want to give."

Isaac's fingers itched for his knife; it made him feel less vulnerable.

That time, Gabriel didn't take the urge to flee and fight away. He didn't snuff the fear or soften the anger. He simply ensured that Isaac couldn't act on it, shoulders squared in something absurdly like a challenge.

Isaac met his eyes, desperately, and tried another option.

Gabriel. I'm sorry, I am, and I know you want answers, but you have to let this go. You have to let me go, please. If I could have given you answers, I wouldn't have faked my death. Just let me go. For the sake of anything, everything, we had - please let me go. Are you listening to me? Gabriel?

The sound of Sanna's tapping filled the silence.

Isaac released a breath and dropped his head back against the wall to help with the bleeding, glaring up at his ceiling. His face throbbed.

"The Isaac I knew would never have tried to hurt me," Gabriel said quietly. "He wouldn't have – have faked his death, and let me believe he was—" Gabriel didn't finish. He looked at Isaac like he was a stranger then, like he was a monster instead of a miracle.

Isaac's mouth dried as he replayed his own mental thoughts back. He'd thought Gabriel had figured it all out, if he was there, that he must have done. Apparently not.

"Now you're worried that maybe you weren't the first to find me after all." There was an irony to that. Gabriel would never let him go if he thought he had to save Isaac from himself or anyone else. Isaac kept his eyes on the ceiling. He couldn't look at him. The genuine concern, the pain that would be all too visible on Gabriel's face, was more than he could bear. "You know, I wasn't actually going to hurt you. You said you weren't alone, I figured I'd use you as body armour."

17

Gabriel frowned at him again.

"You know I don't like knives."

"You know I don't like having my free will stolen from me."

"I'm not *stealing*," Gabriel protested. "I'm borrowing. And I wouldn't have to if you would be reasonable and not go for a knife."

Isaac felt another wash of anger at Gabriel's indignation, another flood of something uneasy and scared that squeezed cold in his stomach. Replaying the memories was one thing, Gabriel in front of him was definitely another.

"Maybe I should have tried to stab you." He looked at Gabriel again then, just because he knew the words would hurt, and smiled a vicious sort of smile that he knew Gabriel would hate. Maybe he would back off if Isaac could make him recoil enough. "I'm sure lots of people want to stab their ex-boyfriends."

"You *died*. You didn't break up with me, you—" Gabriel cut himself off.

Seeing Gabriel flinch really gave him no satisfaction; it didn't make Isaac feel any less powerless around him. It just made him feel sick for what he'd done.

"Wait." Dahlia's eyes widened. "You two…"

"Not now," Sanna said. "Or none of you get to go to Disneyland. Gabriel." Her voice was much too light, falsely chipper as the tension in the room grew more strained by the minute. "You're really going to want to see this."

They both glanced over at her.

Sanna's fear drained her strangely colourless, like a creature that had been left without sunlight for too long.

Gabriel's spine straightened. He must have seen whatever it was etched and echoed in Sanna's mind already, but he still strode over to see for himself first-hand. As if to be sure. Dahlia crossed to their side to peer at the screen.

"M," Gabriel said. "It's from M."

Dahlia's vines snarled thorns and turned on Isaac.

Gabriel. The thought, the plea, came without Isaac's permission and he hated himself for that too. He hated how easily he still directed his thoughts at the man, when he was in the room, as if five years alone could be obliterated in five minutes together. He raised his arms to protect his face. The vines hurtled in his direction. He couldn't stand, couldn't dodge. *Gabriel!*

"No."

The vines froze quivering an inch from Isaac's palms.

Isaac's stomach bottomed out in relief, if only for a second.

By the look on Dahlia's face, it wasn't by her whim. It wasn't Isaac's either – he would have preferred Gabriel let him move freely, but his command hadn't wavered. His control had definitely improved. The relief clenched bitter.

"You can't be serious!" Dahlia snapped. "He's – he's fraternising with the enemy! Don't *protect* him."

"Don't hurt him." Gabriel's face had gone tight, his features shuttered. "Bind him and put him in the car. We have to leave. Now."

Oh, Isaac. That time, he heard Gabriel in his head alone. *What have you got yourself into?*

19

3 - Gabriel

Isaac Morton was alive.

Isaac Morton had faked a suicide, let Gabriel find his broken body, and then continued to let Gabriel believe he was dead. Gabriel could barely breathe for it – he wished, not for the first time, that he could soothe his own emotions as easily as he bettered the emotions of other people. It was like Isaac had gutted him after all. He couldn't stop replaying the moments.

Four days ago, life had been normal. He and the others had been using their powers to stop a bank robbery when Ari had collapsed into one of her visions. She saw him meeting Isaac, a young man with white eyes, in a lonely cottage in the woods.

His first thought was that it was a mistake, some cruel trick to torment him with the impossible, to distract him from some villainous scheme. Then he began imagining all sorts of horrors – Isaac held against his will by some monster, locked in a basement for the last five years, to be used and abused for his magnifying ability. Had he prayed for Gabriel to come for him? Had he lost hope? He theorised that the body he'd buried could have been a shapeshifter, or created by someone who could form particularly realistic illusions.

Not really Isaac.

Perhaps it was selfish of him to find the reality worse. He'd always imagined that if he, somehow, ever saw Isaac again that Isaac would be *glad* to see him. He imagined that he would help Isaac get over the trauma of whatever had happened to him, and then the two of them would pick up where they left off at university and live happily ever after.

They would both be so happy.

Gabriel's throat locked tight.

Isaac hadn't seemed glad to see him at all. He hadn't seemed like he was being held in the cottage against his will either. So where did that leave them?

The morning after Ari had her vision about Isaac, Sanna found her withered dead in her bed with her eyes clawed out. There was a note on her chest, written in Ari's own hand.

> *This should be you, telepath. Stay away from him. –*
> *M*

After that, everyone in Gabriel's city began to fall asleep, like they were under a witch's spell. Except, no true love's kiss was enough to wake them and in sleeping they generally starved or dehydrated to death without assistance. The hospitals were overflowing. There weren't enough life support systems left to keep everyone hooked up. There weren't enough nurses or doctors to do the hooking up. As for the dreamers… well more dreamers led to more waking nightmares come to life. The streets began to empty as people fled to other unaffected places; those who had stayed and stayed awake gained an apocalyptic shuffle as time passed by, woozy with tiredness and fear.

21

There had been a message from M on Isaac's laptop too.

Isaac,
Meet me at Cambridge Market Square, Thursday, at
1 o' clock. Don't go to sleep before then. Something's
wrong. He knows you're alive.
He's coming.
M

"Do you think it's the same M?" Sanna cast a nervous glance at the darkening dusky skies and then at Gabriel like he had all of the answers in the universe for her. Her fingers tightened on the steering wheel. "Do you think M knows that we have him?" The car sped up, roaring down the roads towards Cambridge, towards home. "They did tell you to stay away..."

The radio blared obnoxiously loud in an effort to keep them all awake, and Gabriel had long since grown sick of the taste and smell of coffee. They all had. The threat of sleep lounged like a fourth member of their party on the backseat; panther-dark and predatory, as heavy and disquieting as a hand on the back on his neck that Gabriel just couldn't shake. Sleep was patient. Sleep, like death, knew that all things came to her eventually.

"It seems like one hell of a coincidence if it's a different M," Dahlia snorted. "Maybe M was trying to lure us out of the city." Despite her tone, her fear was a churning undercurrent in her mind, given all that M had already done in forcing the city to sleep. "Maybe they knew you'd do the opposite of what anyone told you."

Gabriel really wished she hadn't put that worry in his head – what if everyone and everything had fallen apart in the small time he'd been away?He balled his hands into fists.

"Maybe we should talk about something else," Sanna said. She glanced over at him sitting shotgun, wishing she could fix this pain like she did a bloodied nose.

Gabriel wished his pain wasn't so obvious that he was getting pitying looks. Was it really so obvious? He sent a wave of peace in her direction and tried to focus. He wasn't supposed to be what she, or any of them, worried about. He was supposed to be stronger than that. He rubbed his eyes blearily.

"He could be a nightmare come to life," Dahlia persisted, still on the topic of Isaac. "You did think he was dead, Gabriel. And he didn't seem very friendly."

"Dahlia!" Sanna said.

"What?" Dahlia asked. "You were thinking it too. You had to be thinking it."

Sanna was indeed thinking it.

"He's *not* a nightmare," Gabriel bit out.

They winced at the sharpness in his voice, of the telepathy behind it. Gabriel exhaled and smiled a reassuring apology.

"He's not a nightmare," he said, in a calmer, more rational tone of voice befitting of a leader. "He's real, I heard his thoughts. If he wasn't real I wouldn't be able to hear his thoughts." At least, for the most part, Gabriel had. There had been pockets of strange silence.

Surely, Isaac was real? He had to be real. But he'd been dead – Gabriel had watched him die. He'd felt him die. He'd held him, fighting to keep the blood in his wrists, even as it seeped across their bedroom floor. He'd never seen so much blood in his life, before that. The movies didn't prepare him. It was so silent. Blood didn't whisper like minds did.

"M would never give me Isaac anyway," he continued, quieter still. "He's too powerful." He was too precious. And, frankly, if he dreamed Isaac up he wouldn't have given him such a god-awful haircut. It didn't suit him in the slightest.

No, for what it was worth, and maybe it was worth everything, Isaac was alive.

Isaac was alive and he'd deliberately let Gabriel think he was dead. Gabriel buried his fingers into his hair like he could comb the nagging thought away.

Sanna and Dahlia exchanged glances while he wasn't looking; Sanna desperate still to make him feel okay, and Dahlia feeling hopelessly awkward with his 'relationship drama' and debating if it would feel less awkward if she hurled herself out of a moving car.

Gabriel took his hands away from his hair.

"Were you two…were you together long?" Sanna tried kindly. "It must have been difficult seeing him again."

"Are you going to go and see M in his place?" Dahlia asked. "Because even if he's not a nightmare, that doesn't mean he's not a trap. M literally gave us where they were going to be in that message."

Sanna blanched.

"You better not be thinking about going to see M," she said. "You're not, are you? Whoever they are, they kind of seem like they want you dead."

"Kind of?" Dahlia raised her eyebrows. "What do you mean kind of?"

"And you…" Sanna trailed off, looking at him, stubbornly ignoring Dahlia.

Gabriel's own powers didn't work on the sleeping, or the comatose. Something about both left his absolute control fuzzy. Their minds felt different. Nebulous, foggy things compared to the bright pinpricks of light he normally sensed them as. A normal dreamer's mind crackled in and out like a bad connection. And death, or near death…

If Isaac had died, was that why his mind had that strange block? Those unnerving empty abysses of silence where memories or at least feeling should have resided? Maybe resurrection left something behind. He didn't want to think what.

"I could go," Dahlia said. "I can sucker punch a dream just as much as a real person. I don't mind."

Gabriel tried to feel for Isaac's brain again in the boot, but there was nothing. A living person, even asleep, at least had something he could hear, even if that something was like static. Isaac's mind, in its silence, was like the mind of a dead man and yet Isaac was clearly not dead.

"Not until I know more," he said, trying to drown out Dahlia's eagerness in his head. "Like you said – it might be a trap." He couldn't ignore that everything bad started after he learned Isaac was alive, after all. He met Dahlia's gaze in the rear-view mirror, sensing her protest before she opened her mouth. "Your sister would kill me if I let you get hurt."

Dahlia reared, protesting anyway. "My *sister* may *die* if we sit around doing nothing." She leaned forward from the backseat, her fingers winding around the edge of his chair, her mistrust winding around his brain. "We can't just do nothing, and sit around hoping your ex tells us stuff. We might not get another chance like this. M's not going to just send us another letter, are they?"

"I said no."

"I'll be careful. I'm not scared of a bad dream."

"*Dahlia.*" He whipped around to face her properly. "Please. Trust me."

He considered making it a command, but he didn't think that would go down well.

She sighed and leaned back in the car seat, scrunching up near the window. In that instant she looked every inch the moody teenager that she had been not so long ago, and Gabriel had never felt so old or so tired in his entire life. He turned back to face the road.

Sanna gave him a commiserating pat on the knee.

The closer they got to Cambridge, the quieter everything became. Cars cut out; truckers parked up dozing as their exhaustion caught up with them. Some soft and unknown dread urged him to turn the car in the other direction. Gabriel braced himself.

Isaac's thoughts flared in the boot, reacting to that same soft and unknown dread. Gabriel smoothed the unease away, glad for something that he could fix, something to help keep him awake. It was odd having Isaac's mind so close again.

Isaac had always looked sharp, back in the day, all skinny limbs and jutting elbows. It used to make him look fragile, like a boy spun from glass. He didn't look – didn't *feel* – fragile any more. Isaac's mind felt dangerous. It snarled at him instead of melting and, though Isaac was still slim, he had a wiry toned strength now. The glass had become something else.

No, Isaac may not have been a nightmare or a trap, but...

Gabriel forced himself to focus.

"I know you're worried about the others," he said to Dahlia, in a gentler tone. "I know you're worried about Felicity. But

26

we haven't accomplished *nothing.* Isaac's powerful, and with what he can do...he's not someone we want in M's hands. If M has him, we've lost."

She said nothing.

"Do you want a magnifier in M's hands?" he pressed.

"I don't want a magnifier in anyone's hands, I think he's creepy," Dahlia said. "Maybe he's M. He's a magnifier. That starts with an M."

"Isaac can't put people to sleep. He can't bring nightmares to life either."

"He could be working with someone who can. Maybe that's why he got so skittish when he saw you. Guilty conscience!"

Gabriel wished he hadn't started the conversation. He'd only wanted to reassure her. Now he was imagining Isaac working with M, working *against him* and...well. He'd never imagined Isaac working against him before. Isaac not being on his side was a bizarre, painful sort of reality to consider. He'd thought they'd be on the same team forever, once.

He let the car fall into nothing but silence and memories.

And so, they drove.

***

They drove until the car breaks screeched, rubber squealing, and Gabriel jolted out of his thoughts. His mind lunged instinctively for those in the vicinity before he'd finished looking around with his own eyes. They hadn't arrived. They looked to be at the outskirts of Cambridge. Dahlia's mind was confused. Isaac's, confused and pissed off and still alive in the boot, Sanna...

"Oh god," Gabriel said. He followed her gaze and stared at the line of figures thick along the border of the city.

"What the hell—" Dahlia began, before she saw them too.

"Oh, *shit.*"

People lined the road. Young, old, female, male, all in varying states of dress. Gabriel fumbled for their minds with a sinking dread – silence. It was silence in the same way that Isaac was silent, not quite the dreaming that he was used to. And beside them – monsters. Some looked like children's drawings, dark and towering with a snarl of teeth. There were hairy spiders with gleaming eyes. A writhing mass of snakes. Bloodstained murderers. Ghosts.

"Is that a *zombie?*" Dahlia sounded disgusted.

There was everything that the world might be frightened of, and they were all blocking the way.

"M must be getting stronger," Gabriel said. He was proud that his voice was only a little faint.

For a beat, they all stayed frozen in the car, surrounded by the tinny sound of pop music and the rumble of the engine.

They couldn't go back.

They couldn't just leave.

So how were they going to get past them?

The nightmares were practically standing guard on the borders of the city. If Felicity was there – well, Dahlia's sister wasn't there.

Gabriel's insides plummeted.

Had they reached the house? Did they know? Surely the others were safe?

Everyone stay calm. Gabriel slipped the command into their heads, even as his own heart hammered nauseously, betraying him.

"I've got an idea," Dahlia said. "I can make the ground cave beneath them and close it up after that. They'd be swallowed. It would at least slow them down."

28

"You can't," Sanna hissed. "That sort of power will take too much—"

"—You can always heal me!"

"We have Isaac now," Gabriel cut in. He felt a giddy relief to be able to say that, to know that, at least. "That's not the problem. Power is not the problem. What about the people? We can't hurt them."

"I can bat them out of the way," Dahlia said after a moment, her eyes narrowed with concentration as she considered the problem. "Grab them with vines. If he's as powerful as you say, that should be possible, right?"

Yes. Isaac had always made him feel like he could do anything.

"The nightmares will notice us. We won't have the element of surprise. If they reach us…" Sanna's eyes darted to him and once again she didn't finish.

Gabriel was hit by her clinical, but rather visceral mental image of him being outnumbered and torn apart. The peculiar and unwelcome sensation of vulnerability followed. Why did it have to be dreaming? He could have simply commanded anything else gone. Stop.

"We don't have time to sit and come up with something better," he said, brushing away her concern. "Let's do it."

Both of their thoughts flashed to Isaac tied up in the trunk. Dahlia's brain bristled wary, given their introduction. Sanna was more preoccupied with her own unhappiness about kidnapping someone in the first place, let alone grabbing them and using them like a power battery. It brought back bad memories, flashes of needles and metal tables.

"We need to get back to the house," Gabriel looked at Sanna. "We don't have time." He placed his hand over hers on the

29

steering wheel as he nudged her concerns away. Subtle, of course, so she wouldn't notice and fight. Not that she ever fought his telepathy. She didn't want to. But Isaac was right, he'd worked hard, he'd got better. "Sanna."

"Shut up," she muttered. "I know. I don't have to like it. We'll put him in the backseat, we're not going to have a lot of time with Dahlia's trick."

"I'll get him." Gabriel eased the car door open, gaze fixed on the row of nightmares.

They paced, staggered, stalked restlessly. He imagined they hungered for more than the life they'd been allotted. He didn't know. It was horrible not to know, how did non-telepaths stand it? He pulled open the boot and looked down at Isaac, still frozen under his mental command.

Isaac glared up at him.

Gabriel felt a stab of relief that he was still there, even if of course he would be. He reached out, brushing his finger over Isaac's cheek again, just to be sure. Just to feel that familiar power rise. Alive. Warm. Good. He released a shaking breath as his power swelled and took the opportunity to run a mental check over Cambridge – counting the losses in their absence. More had succumbed to sleep. There was barely anyone left awake. He let that steel him and let go of Isaac again.

You right prick Gabriel De Vere. Let me go, I swear to god!

Get out of the car and sit in the backseat next to Dahlia. Don't make a sound. Don't try to attack us or run.

He'd left Isaac's feet unbound, though they'd debated it in case he kicked out a tail-light despite Gabriel's commands. If they tied his legs they'd have to touch him to move him. Isaac could take advantage; block their powers if he could get a scrap of skin in contact with theirs. Of course, with his ankles untied he could probably kick Gabriel in the ribs if he didn't keep guard.

Isaac straightened with a grimace and got out of the car, all of his joints clicking. They probably shouldn't have stuffed him in the boot. He was a bit big for it with all of his long limbs. They would have to watch him more in the backseat – he knew Gabriel well enough to exploit even the vaguest mental loophole. The two of them used to practice. Isaac had clearly not stopped practising.

Gabriel's heart clenched and he shoved that thought away too.

Isaac's gaze moved over the line of nightmares. *What the hell?* His mind plunged silent a second later, though the horror flickered plainly enough in his eyes still.

The nightmares made him silent. Gabriel's head tilted, noting that. It definitely had to be something to do with the nightmares, with how Isaac and M knew each other perhaps?

We're going to need to borrow your skill-set, he explained all the same. *Take your gloves off and give them to me.*

Isaac sat in the backseat a minute later, his muscles locked tense. He looked willing to kill anyone who touched him. It wasn't an expression Gabriel was used to seeing on Isaac's face, blazing and fierce from a man who – despite having been in a fight when they first met – more often went out of his way to do no harm and be as unnoticeable as possible.

So I just touch him? Dahlia asked, glancing at him, and then anxiously at the row of nightmares again.

Sanna's fingers tapped and skittered on the steering wheel. *None of your powers will work on him while you do.*
Will yours?

For as long as I'm not touching him, Gabriel promised.

31

Careful.

Of?!

He soothed her panic as best as he could, gritting his teeth. It was another reason to wish Felicity was there – she could always calm her sister.

When I say he magnifies, I mean he magnifies. You're not used to that amount of power and you may struggle to control or contain it. He will also find it frightening if you lose control or tug too suddenly at his energy. So, please be careful.

Her chin set with a grim resolve, her spine steeling. She thought of her sister, at home, and of the row of bad dreams that would descend and in all likelihood rip them to chunks if this didn't work.

Isaac shot him a pleading look, seeing as his glaring didn't work. His mind was full of ice and a dozen years of desperately trying to hide what exactly it was that he could do. Gabriel let the ice thaw and washed away the bad memories, the fear. Isaac's thoughts quivered in the cup of his palms like Gabriel was the only thing, as ever, keeping him together. It was an intoxicating feeling, it always was. Addictive.

He couldn't believe Isaac faked dying. The ungrateful prick.

Ready everyone? Sanna, wait. Isaac, hold still. Deep breaths. You're okay.

Don't make me do this, Gabriel, Isaac tried again. *You know I can't have people touching me.*

Dahlia hesitated a second, and then placed her hand on Isaac's bare one.

Her eyes turned white. The car rocked violently as flowers grew tall and with such force that they shattered the windows.

Not again. Isaac flinched visibly, but Gabriel's command didn't allow him to do much else.

Sanna yelped.

Gabriel lunged to soothe them all.

The nightmares noticed them. They were too far away to be made out properly, but Gabriel knew what he'd see. Black, empty eyes.

Dahlia stared at her hand, fingers trembling. She looked stunned. At least she wouldn't doubt him about Isaac's power now.

The spiders skittered towards them first, hurrying hairy and monstrous along the road.

Gabriel snarled and took control.

Dahlia, now! Focus. Grab the dreamers and use your powers to break the ground beneath them.

She grabbed Isaac's hand again, and the flowers began to grow. The earth shuddered, quivered, cracked. The crack sped wildly towards the line of dreamers, splintering off in this direction and that like the planet was rupturing. The vines shot up out of the earth, seizing groups of dreaming people and hauling them in the air. They held still with the slackness of the dead.

Gabriel's stomach turned. He waved at Sanna to drive, and focused on Dahlia and Isaac again, making sure that her powers stayed contained. His headache throbbed to life, the tiredness already sapping at him. Her power felt like something leviathan to wrestle under Isaac's gifts. Dark spots popped behind his eyelids. He closed his eyes, breathing hard. The urge to reach for Isaac grew.

One of Sanna's hands landed warm and healing on his arm, a line of strength to hold onto as it slid down. He curled his fingers gratefully around hers.

The car jolted painfully over the uneven road, lurching

33

over potholes, making Dahlia tighten her grip on Isaac to stay connected.

Gabriel forced his eyes open again.

The ground rumbled like some great monster in and of itself, before it gaped wide and swallowed the nightmares whole. They tumbled into the soil, among the writhing mass of vines and thorns clawing them down further into the earth.

Dahlia's breathing grew heavy. It wouldn't be that using her gift was difficult, when she was touching Isaac, but it would be harder for her not to keep going.

Isaac's mind writhed like the vines did, stretched taut in a way that Gabriel had so rarely got to see even when they were together. He'd heard Isaac describe the sensation – like drowning – but feeling it in his own head was different. Airless and desperate and *frightened.* Isaac was a buoy buffeted on every side, a creature drained and husked and scraped hollow. Gabriel itched to draw him close, to protect him from everything. Isaac's fear was so different to what it felt like holding him. Holding Isaac always felt like forever. Isaac said it didn't always feel like this to be touched. Gabriel had, over the years, held him aplenty.

Sanna squeezed his hand. "Focus. You're projecting."

Gabriel blinked.

The car roared over the border, across earth smoothing out inch by inch as fast as Dahlia could keep up beneath them.

The dreamers dropped down upon the tattered remnants of the road, unharmed, among a bed of petals of every colour.

Sanna whooped, Dahlia clenched her fist in triumph.

They drove.

4 - Gabriel

The windows of the house were as dark as he'd left them. The driveway, like the streets they'd drove through, were unmoving and empty. All wrong. Gabriel strained for the curls of un-belonging thoughts, and stumbled over the pockets of silence in the upstairs bedroom. Nothing. At least, nothing that Gabriel could see or hear or feel. If there were nightmares around, he wouldn't be able to sense them. He flicked a thought at Dahlia and Sanna to be on their guard and prayed to a god he didn't believe in that there weren't more.

"Come on," he muttered to Isaac. "Follow me."

Dahlia kept a wide berth from them, her fingers flexing. Her mind flittered with shock, fear, wonder. The expected Isaac Morton things.

Sanna watched them speculatively, uncertainly.

You should have dated a doll instead of a person. Isaac hurled the thought at him at him like a weapon. *I'm starting to think it would have suited you better.*

Shut up.

I'm not even allowed to think at you now?

I'm sorry – did you see a better way around the monsters? If not, stop bitching. They would have killed you too. Properly.

He left Isaac in his bedroom with the order to a) not leave, b) not damage anything be that the walls or his own knuckles and c) absolutely not to sleep. He'd also cuffed one of Isaac's wrists to the bed post for good measure. He hoped it would be enough. He'd have to mind him.

The thought ached in his chest.

He missed his Isaac who (just for reference, had hardly been some lifeless doll that he'd commanded as he pleased) had trusted him.

He faltered by the door of their bedroom instead. His heart lodged in his throat and he lingered outside longer than was courageous. His mind fumbled instinctively for their thoughts again, but, again, there was nothing but graveyard silence. All wrong. All wrong. All wrong.

Gabriel forced himself to open the door and step inside.

The machines in the bedroom beeped, hummed and whirred steadily, but didn't quite muffle the terrified breaths of his friends. Flicker, Pyrate and Viper were all lined up in a row on the beds like bodies laid out to rest. Occasionally, in the night, they had cried out for someone to save them. For Gabriel to save them. It was the only real sign he had that there was anything left of their minds inside their bodies at all.

Dahlia was already there, perched on the edge of Flicker's bed. She clutched her sister's hand like it was a lifeline, murmuring comforts that likely went unheard. She didn't look up. She didn't even seem to have heard him enter. No, she did. It was there in her thoughts; she was ignoring him. The vines, the flowers, had withered around her. She never summoned them sitting at her sister's side. She thought the heavy fragrance of them, the clutter, made the room seem too much like a funeral parlour or a hospital room. He privately thought the lack of them left her seeming oddly wounded, absent, as too-still as her older sister.

Flicker – Felicity – was able to move so fast that it was almost like teleportation. Normally, she was there one minute and gone the next. Instead of flowers, Dahlia had piled her bedside with the different tourist-crap shot glasses that Felicity collected in every new place that she visited. It was like a small city of glass.

He shut the door behind him with a soft click and moved closer. His team's dreaming faces twitched with distress; their muscles strained tight in their nightmares. There had been a steadiness to their breathing in the beginning, when they first fell, but more and more now the sound was hitched and ragged. Lost in their heads. At least in their dreaming they didn't seem to have summoned monsters in his absence. It was a pitiful sort of consolation. It wasn't, after all, like he'd been the one to keep their monsters at bay.

He hadn't been able to save Isaac, five years ago, no matter how hard he tried. He had to save his friends from their nightmares now, somehow. Otherwise what was the point of him?

So far, nothing he'd tried had worked.

Gabriel swallowed hard. He ached to reach out, to soothe the horrors but like shadows they all crept utterly out of his reach. The misted lights of their minds seemed darker than they had before he left. He couldn't find any grip in their heads. His fists clenched, nails digging into his palms hard enough to hurt.

"I don't know how much longer they'll last," Dahlia said. Her voice was barely audible and taut with fear, rage, too many things. She dashed a furious hand over her eyes to wipe away tears, still refusing to look at him. "Aren't you going to grab him and – you know – try and reach them? You put him in your room."

"It's not like that," Gabriel replied.

He crossed the space, sinking to sit between Pyrate and Viper's beds.

Tubes kept them all fed, watered, alive. Tubes made them look unbearably small and shrunken in their beds, compared to the vibrancy of their consciousness.

"What is it like then? Your magnifier is strong. Isn't that why you had us fetch him? He's *strong*, I felt it. God." Dahlia laughed without humour, running a trembling hand through her dark greasy hair. "You kissed that? I'm surprised your head didn't explode."

"He's not my magnifier." Not any more, it seemed. "And we're not discussing that."

What are we discussing? You didn't bother telling us he was your ex. An old friend, you said. Someone who could help. I suppose you didn't think that the ex-boyfriend part was relevant. I didn't even know you were gay.

Is it a problem?

Don't be a prick. You know that's not the problem. We're supposed to be a team!

Gabriel grimaced, but tipped his head to acknowledge the comment, even if he still had no intention of discussing the matter. He sighed.

"I don't know where his control is at these days. If he touches them…I don't know if it will make whatever M has done stronger, or if it will help them. If they're still fighting in there they might lose. Or – I don't know. There's too much that could go wrong. It's too reckless. We don't know enough."

"I could make him talk." Her mind writhed around him, prickling at him like her thorns might, protective to the point of violence. "If that's what you're waiting on."

"You could make him lie."

"Sanna could put him in so much pain he wouldn't be able to—"

"*No.*" It lashed out of his head and his mouth at the same time, and she winced at the force of it.

"Yup," she said. "Definitely not relevant that he's your ex. It's not messing with your head at all. You're just peachy. Very chill."

Gabriel clamped down on his annoyance and released a breath, reaching out a hand to smooth Pyrate's hair back from his clammy forehead. His skin was all too cool to touch.

Pyrate had a gift for flames. Real name, Jack. He much preferred Pyrate. He thought it made him sound like a swashbuckler of heat and swords instead of as pasty a ginger boy as there ever was. He said it made him feel like a superhero. Gabriel had encouraged him to think of himself as a superhero.

God, Gabriel hated this room. It was dormitory-like now, each bed no longer as cosy as it had once been after the initial bouts of nightmares. With the brightly coloured duvets he'd bought they looked more like mummified fucking children than the crime fighting allies he'd come to rely on. He half wished Dahlia *would* summon flowers – anything to mask the stale smell of cold sweat and terror.

"I'm just saying, if you need to talk to him before we do anything that badly, go talk to him." Dahlia looked up at him, and then back down to her sister. "Or I can talk to him if the fact he's your ex is going to get in the way. Like, I don't mean to be unsympathetic, it must suck. But we don't exactly have all the time in the world for you to work up the courage."

"No," he pressed on, softly. "It's not that. It's nothing to do with him being my—" he cut off. He didn't know if he wanted to say 'ex' or 'boyfriend'. "I'll have a better chance at talking to him once he's calmed down a bit. That's all. Trust me," he tried for a smile. "I know Isaac."

"Can't you just tell him to calm down?"

"I could," Gabriel said. "But then when I touch him he'll know that's what I did and he...well. This will go a lot smoother if I can get him to cooperate without using my powers too much. Just...stay away from him for now. You'll freak him out." He didn't make it an order, not yet. Hopefully he wouldn't have to.

Lucy Vale, Viper, lay furthest from the door. Her speciality was poison – she could spit it like cherry stones, and had learnt to whip up all the antidotes for her poisons too, with time. The kid was some kind of chemical genius. Viper's breathing was the shallowest, her pallor sickliest. She was the youngest too, at sixteen. Gabriel should have turned her away on their first meeting but he couldn't, the girl had nowhere else to go, and too many ways of getting into trouble. Perhaps anywhere would have been better than this. His saving people hobby, Isaac had called it once when he was feeling unkind. Collecting strays. Bile rose in Gabriel's mouth.

It had been two days with them sleeping now. What if morning really was already too late to save them? What if he killed them by waiting? Why had *he* been spared?

Two days. Had it only been two days that Gabriel had been

awake? It felt longer.

Sanna said that the longest a human had ever stayed awake, before the exhaustion killed them, was eleven days.

His vision doubled. He shouldn't have sat down; it was easier to stay awake when he was standing. He shoved himself back to his throbbing feet.

"What if he doesn't want to talk to you in the morning?" Dahlia's voice cracked. Her gaze lingered on her sister, to her entire reason for being in that house, with him. Felicity was the one who had wanted to stay, who had wanted to become a superhero, to join Gabriel's agency. Dahlia had wanted to go and study ecology and live in a rainforest. Her anger, her recklessness, her horror – it all mingled into one. It all smashed against Gabriel's mental walls like a wave crashing against the rocks, persistently eroding them with time. "It's not – he doesn't want to help us," she said. "He doesn't even want to be here! You forced him to climb in the boot of your car. I don't think he's going to be like, nah guys, it's cool! If I had an ex who forced *me* to climb in the boot of their car, took me home and locked me in the bedroom I'd think someone was going to find my body in a ditch a month later."

Okay. Apparently they were discussing it. Gabriel was tempted to wipe the whole thing from her brain, but his headache was worse than ever. He might hurt her. He couldn't help his dreamers, but she was still awake. He rounded the bed to kneel in front of her, taking her hands in his. He muted the roar of her emotions and watched her release a shaking breath in turn, her brain twitching between annoyance and a reluctant gratitude she didn't want to admit to.

"Isaac had plenty of opportunity to kill me when he was

41

dating me," Gabriel said. "We were together for almost three years. He knows me better than anyone. If he was on M's side, and wanted me dead, I would be dead already."

"I don't think that's as comforting as you think it is."

Gabriel sighed again.

"Isaac's mind is – something's wrong," he explained, as patiently as he could. "He shouldn't have been able to fake his death. Not from me." He should have been able to hear Isaac's thoughts on that day, even if the man found some way to falsify blood or muffle his pulse and breathing. Gabriel should have heard him thinking. "He's scared. Granted, scared is his default emotion, but it feels – different. I'll talk to him in the morning when he's had time to calm down, I *promise*, and *I promise* he'll help us. I'll make him help if that's what it takes. I'll fix this, yeah? It's going to be alright." He squeezed her hand and met her eyes with his best reassurance. "Felicity's going to be fine. I'm not going to let anything to happen to either of you."

Maybe that was a child's plea, a child's bargain. 'Everything will be better in the morning.'

It worked, at least a little. Her face lightened with the heavy trust that he would somehow fix everything, even if she would likely deny expecting it. Even the people who weren't overly keen on the idea of superheroes wanted one on a bad day.

"You promise?" She studied his face. "Don't bullshit me. I'm not a kid."

Close enough, he wanted to say.

"Cross my heart and hope to die," he replied instead.

The door opened behind them. Sanna stepped in, laden with a tray of coffees and some sandwiches.

Dahlia quickly pulled her hand away, lest anyone mistake

her as someone who needed comforting, and pushed to her feet. She cleared her throat.

Gabriel's head needled at the mere sight of coffee, but the interruption was a blessing. He rose to his feet again also and reached out for a drink.

"Did you know," Sanna shoved a cup into his hand. "That you can actually overdose on coffee? You'd need to drink over one hundred cups to consume a lethal dose though."

"Thanks for that," Dahlia said, "Clearly that's M's evil master plan." She turned back to Felicity. "Did you know that Finns drink the most coffee out of everyone in the world?"

"Of course I know that. Who do you think you're talking to?" Sanna grinned. It was a rictus grin. "Did you know—"

Gabriel said nothing, breathing in the bitterness. He took a sip.

Stay awake, stay awake, stay awake.

His vision fogged, flickered, and his brain seized. A hint of shadow, of scarlet curls, glanced in his mind. A glimpse of eyes shining like black glass, somehow familiar though he couldn't place them. Sleep yanked out of his grip.

He blinked awake still standing, startled. The coffee cup lay in pieces on the floor.

Sanna crossed the room to him and wrapped him tight in her arms.

If the longest anyone had ever survived without sleep was eleven days, then that left eight days at best. But, more likely, sleep or death was inevitable long before then. Certainly, sleep deprivation and accurately using his powers didn't go well together.

Isaac would help. He had to. And together - together they would fix everything.

43

But for that night, at least, the three of them kept their vigil.

5 - Isaac

Isaac willed himself to sleep.

Sleep had never been Gabriel's forte, and Gabriel had never slept well. Even when they were curled up in bed together, Gabriel had been prone to twisting and shifting restlessly throughout the night, his mind a flurry of sparks and nightmares lurking on the edge of his thoughts. He stayed up late and was up early in the morning, bounding.

If Isaac could just sleep, he could contact Mona. Fix the situation, or explain. Or, at any rate, have someone help him escape because he was getting the impression that Gabriel's lackeys cared more for Gabriel than Isaac's feelings about the moral dubiety of being kidnapped.

If he could just sleep, contact Mona, she'd kill Gabriel for getting close to him again.

Isaac's stomach turned. He rubbed his hands over his eyes. How had either of them even found him? He supposed dreams and minds didn't exactly go radio silent, however useful that would have been. Maybe he'd been an idiot for ever thinking he could truly disappear.

He knows you're alive: she'd tried to warn him. He didn't know what to think any more.

He tried counting sheep, holding very still, regulating his

breathing – the tricks of the insomniac. It didn't work. Of course it didn't. He hadn't slept well since he 'died'.

Isaac had always adored sleeping before he met the dreamweaver and he'd always slept well. Even as a child he'd slept later than most. Dreams, to him, had always felt like the best possible story. Anything good could happen, and if it was bad then all of his problems could be fixed by simply waking up. Life wasn't like that. He couldn't wake up to a new life if his old one was a nightmare, at least not without considerably more effort than squeezing his eyes shut for a moment or so. Isaac tried squeezing his eyes shut all the same. When he opened them once more, the room was still there. The ceiling was a pale, swirling middle-class white above him. He could still feel the handcuff biting around his wrist, too tight for him to slip even with a broken thumb. The panic gritted in his lungs.

For Gabriel to cuff him, instead of simply ordering him to stay put, he must have been truly desperate. It did nothing to make Isaac feel better. Desperate Gabriel was dangerous Gabriel, even more so than usual. Desperate Gabriel would throw him in a room and throw away the key if he thought it would save the world, even if he broke his own heart in the process.

Even without Gabriel's order not to, sleep seemed a world away, impossibly beyond him. The adrenaline had once again turned cold in his limbs, but his brain whirred still. It kept replaying all the looks on Gabriel's face, the slide of touch along his jaw, stroking his hair. Would Gabriel's lips have felt the same, pressed against his, as they used to? They'd looked chapped, gnawed down with worry.

Isaac sat up. He listened for movement, but the house was

quiet. It was a big house; he'd got that much of an impression coming in. It sounded empty. The room he was in was a suitcase of a room, stripped down to essentials and strangely placed as if its normal inhabitant was always ready to take off at a second's notice. Temporary. Most bedrooms had their signs of long-lasting life – the art on the wall, or the favourite duvet, or the sprawl of clutter along the desk. The only signs of preference, of personality, were the chunky black headphones and music player that coiled unobtrusively on the bedside table. Isaac looked away from them. It meant he wasn't in a guest room. He was in Gabriel's room. Isaac's heart flipped.

Gabriel had been wearing headphones when they first met, and Isaac had been quick to find them habitual. Gabriel kept them hooked around his neck for when the world and its voices got to be a bit too much and he needed something to focus him back into his own head for a while. Not that it ever seemed to occur to him to leave, to run, to go somewhere quiet and away from the scream of people. Of course not. Gabriel never ran away from anything, he merely occasionally retreated to the other room. He picked cities, despised country with the lack of minds close at hand. Isaac could understand being overwhelmed, but the staying had never made sense. If he was Gabriel he'd have long since become a hermit.

His palms itched with the urge to fling the headphones across the room, to go to the wardrobe and wrench out and rip fistfuls of clothes, to smash his fist into the wall plaster, into the windowpanes. Perhaps he would have, if not for the cuff both physical and mental. He dug his nails into his palms.

His mind flashed to the row of monsters – to how hurting, how frightened, Mona must be. His guilt curdled.

Would Mona notice, when he didn't visit her tomorrow? Or would she think nothing was wrong because Isaac turning up to anything was a long shot? The sick feeling churned in his gut even more. Worse, would Gabriel go and see her? There was no way that would be good, for either of them.

It was twelve or so hours until their meeting. Central Cambridge, lunch. Like they were actually just old friends meeting for a catch up. He had to persuade Gabriel not to go.

He wasn't entirely sure where they were, other than Cambridge, but the world outside sounded countryside quiet without any of the actual countryside. There were no crickets, no birds, no hooting owls. No distant roar of traffic either, no club beats, no patter of voices rising outside. There was nothing he would expect for a city, even a small one, let alone a university town. It was only quiet. It didn't seem the type of house Gabriel would ever stay at for any prolonged sense of time.

Unless, of course, it was quiet because the world was falling apart.

Dear Isaac,
   Meet me at Cambridge Market Square, Thursday, at 1 o' clock. Don't go to sleep before then. Something's wrong. He knows you're alive.
   He's coming.
   M

The bed was unslept in beneath him. Laundry crisp, lemony. Did Gabriel know what had happened? How much did he know?

Isaac yanked at the cuff, but it held fast, and any time he yanked too hard his brain blanked.

Don't try to leave. Don't go to sleep.

If Gabriel touched him again, maybe he could make a grab for the strings. Take control. Cut off his power somehow. It might be possible, with the element of surprise. And then what? Gabriel would inevitably come after him again because Gabriel clearly didn't know how to act like a normal person who didn't kidnap people. More likely, Isaac would magnify and magnify and magnify, and he wouldn't be able to do anything to stop it because he never could.

He still remembered when Mona first played that nightmare, that future, in his mind. It was so vivid that he woke up gasping and, for the first time, remembered to feel a prickle of fear when he looked at the telepath who'd made a home in his head.

Gabriel, back in the day, had never seemed like he should be a frightening figure. He'd never seemed like the kind of man who would kidnap a person and cuff them to his bed. He'd seemed like the only safe point in the whole damn world.

Isaac rifled through the drawers he could reach, through the songs on the playlist, with some nauseous hunger. Wanting to know, wanting to run, wanting to leap out of his own skin, wanting to feel safe. It was always easiest just doing what Gabriel told him to do. It couldn't be his fault, then.

In the drawer, there was a summons to power-registration. It was dated six months ago – ignored, abandoned. Gabriel clearly hadn't gone. Isaac hadn't gone either, though the summons had come through the post along with the catalogues and bills. As if he'd actually walk up to a government to tell

49

them he was uniquely cursed to make everything a hundred time's worse at all points. They would never have let him go either.

Under the bed, there was a box of Isaac's things left behind: an old green university hoodie, a sketchbook containing his playful doodles of Gabriel as the superhero Archangel, a bottle of the cologne he'd once wore. His throat locked. He couldn't breathe. He buried his face in the hoodie and tried not to think what it meant that Gabriel still had these scraps after so many years. He thought about it anyway.

Gabriel wouldn't have let him go, right? If he'd talked to him then? Isaac hadn't just been spectacularly cruel in faking his death? He'd saved them.

He'd first met Gabriel on his first day of university.

Isaac could taste blood in his mouth, that first day.

The boy – he hadn't caught his name at first beneath the ringing in his ears – had knelt before him in Isaac's tiny student bedroom, oddly out of place among the worn rug that might have been cream or even brown once but was left some murky shade of neither. The walls were a clutter of boxes unpacked in overcompensation, and art prints pinned to seem like the right type of artist, and a bottle of cheap vodka for if he got nervous talking to people, which was always.

Isaac's watched the boy's lips move, dumbly, before his head jerked back as the boy's hands rose towards his bruised jaw. "Don't touch me."

"Hey. It's alright." The boy took his hands back. "No touching."

Isaac felt everything in him ease, relax, and smiled back despite his swollen lip. In hindsight, that was probably

Gabriel relaxing him with his gift, smoothing his fingers over Isaac's brain in the same way someone smoothed out the cracks in a wet lump of clay.

"I'm not going to hurt you, yeah? I won't touch your skin again. I'm going to get you some ice. Just stay there, okay?" Concerned, intent, earnest.

Isaac watched him vanish, blinked, and he was back again with a dazzling smile of reassurance.

Gabriel held up a scrounged packet of frozen peas in a picture of triumph. "For you." He offered it out like a token, some age-old gallantry, with a smirk to say he knew it was so.

"Thank you," Isaac had managed. He took the ice, so cold that it burned his fingertips, and held it to the dull ache on his face. He still remembered that ice. So cold, when Gabriel and his smirk made his heart race and his stomach hot.

Gabriel sat back on his haunches, studying him, head tilted. "How the hell did you manage to get in a fight on your first day?" He'd laughed then, a little disbelieving as if he didn't already know. Warm, though, still. He'd said later that it was his way of asking if Isaac wanted to talk about it, without immediately opening with 'telepath'.

Isaac looked down at his lap. He'd moved to Norwich because it was the kind of city that was big enough for anonymity, and small enough that he wasn't going to be in constant physical contact walking down the street. It was the type of place he could quietly disappear into. The university didn't ask powered people to tell everyone their ability at the door. It had been a fresh start – he'd hoped. A place where nobody knew him or what had happened. He'd been wrong.

"I have a punchable face," he'd muttered. It was easier than

51

going into it.

The cheap vodka wanted to claw right back out of Isaac's throat. Too much vodka, too many people, too many nerves. A fresh start had always been a lot of pressure for any place. He'd had too many ideas of what university was supposed to be.

He could tolerate the non-powered humans, they were safe enough, even the ones who were suspicious of powered humans…but the powered ones made him feel like he'd been electric shocked and there were more and more powered humans every day. And they — well. There was too much touching on dance floors that he ached with the torn instincts of it all. Wanting, fearing. Pissed off with himself for both. A fresh start, but he couldn't quite bring himself to take it, hovering on the edge hoping that life would come to him. Or some safe version of it anyway.

"You have a goddamn lovely face," Gabriel said, after a moment. "It's a crime to punch it." He declared it as casually as one might announce the weather, or some other trivial and unalienable fact of life that didn't bear much philosophising over. Were people really allowed to go around saying things like that? Isaac hadn't thought so at the time. He'd stared at him, stunned.

Gabriel had stilled, for a beat, eyes taking a more guarded hint as he catalogued Isaac's reaction. Isaac remembered that guarded hint. It seemed odd to him now, when Gabriel must have known everything he was thinking. He'd known that a guy calling him lovely in his bedroom on the first night just wasn't Isaac's life. It was too much like a bad teen movie version of university. Or a good teen movie. Either way, not real.

The boy cleared his throat and straightened with a flash of something gawkier compared to the bitterly unfair confidence he'd shown so far. It had been the gawkiness that won Isaac over most; it had made him soften, long, desperate to hedge the gap because he'd been fumbling everything too and the boy wasn't the one with a bloody nose and a tongue too cowardly to say 'you have a goddamn lovely face'.

In hindsight, Gabriel must have done it on purpose. Deliberately been exactly what Isaac needed in that moment. Had Gabriel been planning, even then? Or had the scheming come later?

"I'm Isaac." He'd blurted it out, with the fear that the moment would end and the boy would vanish out the door and not come back. He would melt into some eager and faceless crowd and Isaac would never see him again, left sitting on an unfamiliar bed in a strange bedroom listening to other people having fun. His stomach cramped.

"Gabriel."

"You're joking." That had seemed funny too, charmed - guy called Gabriel rushed in to save him on his first night at university, that was definitely too much. "Gonna tell me you're my guardian angel next?"

"Witty, Isaac. I've never heard that one before. But I suppose you have just taken a blow to the face so I can't hold you to too high a standard." Still, the guarded look vanished and Gabriel gave him an easy grin and oh god, it was only ever going to end badly with a smile like that.

"Go around saving people often, do you?" It hurt to grin back, but Isaac couldn't stop. "Regular hero, aren't you?"

"Okay, now you're mocking me. That's just rude."

Isaac laughed.

Turned out, he'd lived in the flat above.

It had all seemed so simple, at the start, so good. He supposed everything did when it was just beginning, and nothing could have gone wrong or got tangled up yet. Gabriel had been a hero, the type who burst into a fight and dragged the guy up to his room to give him an ice pack. Isaac had liked it, then, the saving people thing. He'd liked the thought of being someone that Gabriel might save – the safety of it all, the not needing to be scared for once. Gabriel had made him feel so *safe* that Isaac almost felt sick with it now.

It was a bit awful, too, that it was the same saving–people instinct that got him stuck with a cuff clamped around his wrist, halfway across the country from his own home and unable to wipe the smell of rubber and car-boot from his clothes. Completely unable to run.

Gabriel had known everything about him during that first conversation and pretended not to. Isaac didn't know if he called that making friends, some kind of tact or courtesy because Isaac hadn't wanted to talk about it, or if it was just manipulation. Gabriel had given him answers but Isaac still didn't know. He wasn't the telepath.

One touch, and Gabriel's powers would light up again. What was he waiting for? He'd clearly had no problem having his friends use Isaac like a walking charger in the car. Admittedly, there'd been monsters then, but…

But Isaac didn't want to think about the monsters. Why would anyone want to put a magnifier around monsters? He didn't even know what he would do if he touched a nightmare come to life.

To hell with it.

"Oi!" he yelled. "Are you just going to leave me in here all

54

night? If you're going to bloody kidnap me, at least don't be so boring about it!"

Nothing from the house. A brush of Gabriel's power over his head, like the skim of a hand, and then gone again.

So, what, they kidnapped him and now he wasn't even worth the effort of talking to?

He saw Gabriel for the first time in five years, and suddenly he had nothing to say?

Outside, the night deepened.

His panic swelled.

He grabbed at the strings of Gabriel's influence and — for a moment, Gabriel's attention seemed to sharpen. He was all there, everywhere, larger than life and Isaac was drowning. His courage faltered; he dropped the attempt. He sat still, breathing hard, hands still fisted around his old university jumper.

He didn't try to run.

6 - Isaac

Five and ½ Years Ago

"Gabriel, what are you doing?"

Gabriel looked across from their small, shared kitchen. One of their housemates sat next to him at the table. They had been living with Liam since second year, and Isaac had never seen exactly that slack, vacant look on Liam's face before, as if someone had switched the lights off in his brain.

A chill slid down Isaac's spine before vanishing. He let his rucksack fall to the ground, thoughts of heading to campus to get some work done gone too.

It was afternoon. Spring sunlight uncoiled lazily through the window, spilling across the cheap blue carpeting, slashing across the familiar lines of Gabriel's body.

"Just talking," Gabriel said, with a bright smile. He patted Liam's shoulder and Liam seemed to snap out of it, flashing Isaac a slightly dazed smile too.

Of course they were just talking.

It wasn't the first time that Isaac had walked into such a scene over the years. He never caught Gabriel at it directly, but he was starting to have suspicions. Less from Gabriel himself and more from the vague comments here and there of other students, friends from class, or even friends of friends who he'd only vaguely seen in passing before.

"About?" Paranoid, perhaps, he shoved one of his gloves into the front pocket of his hoodie as casually as he could, disguising the lunge for mental protection as an affectionate gesture as he wrapped an arm around his boyfriend.

Gabriel's brow furrowed slightly at his tone and the action, eyes turning white, even as he leaned his head easily enough onto Isaac's hand on his shoulder to solidify the contact. His stare was abruptly intent on Isaac's face. "Liam, could you give us a moment?"

Even phrased as a question, Liam left. Isaac had once taken it as Gabriel's confidence, his general charm, or simply plain courtesy. Now he wondered if it wasn't some kind of mental command and hated himself a little for thinking so. For doubting Gabriel. He hated himself for feeling the need to grab hold of him, as if he might just make Isaac forget seeing the conversation. Gabriel wouldn't do that.

"I was giving him some relationship advice." Gabriel's voice lowered. "Namely, don't cheat on your girlfriend. I think he got the message."

"You mean you—" his hand caressed Gabriel's temples.

"Yes. Is that a problem?"

Isaac didn't quite know what to say. He supposed it shouldn't be. It wasn't like Gabriel could do more than give someone a mental smack on the brain, for all of his talents. It wasn't permanent. Merely a suggestion. Was it a problem? It wasn't like Liam didn't deserve it, if it was true, and it was probably true because Gabriel didn't lie about that kind of thing. Yet, something uncomfortable wriggled in Isaac's stomach, difficult to pin down.

Maybe he'd expected Gabriel to deny it.

"…do you do that a lot?"

"I wouldn't say a lot," Gabriel said. "I'd say I'm aware when someone on campus is about to do something stupid and requires a friendly intervention. Are you saying you would have told him to just go right ahead if you knew?"

"No. No, of course not." It felt like the answer he was supposed to give.

But Isaac didn't know. Isaac would never, could never, have known. Whereas Gabriel knew what everyone around him was thinking at any given time.

Gabriel caught his hand, pulling it to his mouth for a small kiss. "What's going on with you?" he asked. "What's this?" He gave Isaac's fingers a small squeeze.

"It's nothing."

It wasn't like Gabriel was running a crime ring with his skills. Gabriel would never. He would never get someone to do something *bad,* he had one of the fiercest moral codes Isaac had ever seen. The seed of doubt, the fear, refused to leave. It only spread like a weed, like shadow, hooking into him.

Gabriel's head tilted. "You know I'll know the second you let go of me, right? You can't lie to me. It doesn't work."

"Is that a threat? You could not look."

"Jesus, Isaac. Of course it's not a threat. So there is something?"

Isaac shrugged, not sure.

"No, sorry." He relented, a bit guiltily. Gabriel didn't deserve it. "Just people saying stuff. Be careful, yeah? With the head stuff? I think you're starting to piss people off. It's...er...slightly...I don't know. It's odd to watch."

Gabriel's expression cleared. "Ah."

It kept happening though, and people simply stopped talking about it. Once Isaac noticed it the first time, he seemed to see Gabriel's hand everywhere, pulling strings, nudging things along, arranging the sets of their life to what he liked best. When Isaac had success, he didn't know if it was because he deserved it, or because Gabriel whispered in somebody's ear.

Gabriel would never do something like that.

But, when he was alone, increasingly all Isaac could think about was that he *could*.

Five Years Ago

"You don't know me," the woman said by way of introduction. "But I know you."

Isaac stiffened. He liked the university library because it was quiet, and he could normally find an unoccupied section when he had to read or when he wanted to draw without the buzz of the studio. People didn't come to his table. It wasn't like the university café, crowded with laptops and group projects and the possibility of knocking elbows with other students. And people didn't start conversations like that. He averted his eyes – too obvious, too white, too visible a marker to pick him out.

"I think you have me mistaken for someone else." As if anyone ever did.

"Isaac Morton. Gabriel De Vere's boyfriend."

He'd been expecting 'magnifier' as his key identifier. It was no secret that Isaac had powers, though Gabriel did his best to offset anyone actually acting on that knowledge after the first day they met. Isaac paused, halfway to shoving his book skittishly into his bag. His jaw clenched. Something about her, undeniably, gave him the creeps. Physically, he towered over her, she was waif of a girl who looked like she could be scrubbed out of existence if not for the flame of her hair. She had to have a power of some sort. Isaac kept himself warily out of arm's reach.

"Right, and who are you?"

"Sorry." She blushed, shifting on her feet. "Er, I'm Mona. Mona Sanderson. I'm dreams. I mean – that's my thing. Dreams. And nightmares, I guess. I can bring them to life. Both my own and other people's. I wanted to warn you."

"...about my dreams?"

"And about De Vere's. I didn't want to say anything, lots of people have really loud nightmares, but yours is – I mean, you magnify. You sleep in the same room. You're both really loud. It's a bit tricky."

He stared at her.

"Can I sit down?" she asked. She had a cup of something that she set down on the table without waiting for an answer, even if they weren't supposed to have any food or drink in the library. None of the staff were in sight.

"I guess," he said, belatedly, seeing as she'd already sat down. Slowly, he eased himself down too, eyeing the drink. It was bright pink and shimmery. It didn't look real. Perhaps it wasn't. "You're not a friend of Gabriel's." He tried to place if he'd ever even seen her before. "He's not...he's not in trouble is he?"

"No," she said. "I'm in second year. I live down the street, number 52. I, er, overhear. Overdream."

"I haven't touched you."

"He's a telepath and he's touching you, which means he projects. When he's dreaming, at any rate."

Isaac's stomach clenched, his mind flashing to ice, to all that Gabriel might accidentally project. He wouldn't have the same control as he usually would when he was dreaming, would he? Isaac had been stupid not to think of it, foolish to think he could have that peace.

"Is Gabriel in trouble?" he asked again.

"He is trouble. Or in trouble. I don't know." She seemed to search for the best way to put it, spinning her cup round and round on the table. The pink drink turned blue and then pink again as it sloshed around. "He's tricky," she muttered again. "You're both tricky."

The library seemed too quiet all of a sudden, a humming quiet, like anyone could overhear them.

"He's got ambitions," it burst out of her. "You must know that."

Isaac knew about lots of ambitions, Gabriel's specific plans were nebulous and changed by the week. Charity work in Malawi. NHS Doctor. Superhero. Outreach to disadvantaged youth. Superhero. There was always some new idea. Gabriel liked being a superhero best. He imagined setting up a place for people with powers to gather, where they could work together to stop crime and use their skills to make the world better.

"What's the point?" Gabriel had said once, scowling over his much-loathed medical homework, "being a telepath if I'm not going to use telepathy? It's a waste. I've never met anyone

61

who can do what I do. At least not so well. Do you reckon I should talk to the uni about transferring to psychology? I bet I could write a critically acclaimed psychology paper."

"Has he…" Mona's hands stilled. "Has he ever mentioned anything called *The Archangel Project* to you?"

Isaac's mind flashed to his artwork, his final project, to that game of theirs. It was true that Archangel had been inspired by Gabriel, and that they'd once had the joking conversation of what their superhero names would be. He had a feeling she didn't mean his art project.

"No." He shoved his hands in his pockets and leaned back in his chair, feet tucked beneath it even if he couldn't touch her bare skin through his combat boots. "Spit it out."

"Okay. So. Basically, he wants to take over the world and make it better," Mona said. "He can do that with you. Or he thinks he can do that with you, because of what you can do. Which is something you're scared of. He scares you or, you know, at least some part of you, right? And he's scared that he'd get it wrong. All in all, lots of scared people, which is not a good combination seeing as he's planning to do it anyway."

Isaac's head reeled trying to get all that. He supposed that was certainly 'spitting it out'.

"I'm not scared of him," he said. "He's my *boyfriend.*"

The very thought was absurd. Yes, he had nightmares, but nightmares were just that. They weren't real. His nightmares were the worst versions of Gabriel, fragments and ghouls; they were nothing like the actual Gabriel who held him close and comforting afterwards in the dim light. His Gabriel. His Gabriel who always listened to what Isaac wanted, who protected him, who told Isaac that he wasn't a weapon he was amazing.

All of those nightmares were a re-arranged Picasso portrait of Gabriel's personality traits to make a monster, to make him the type of person who would manipulate and take advantage in the worst ways. It wasn't Gabriel. It wasn't even anything to do with Gabriel, it was just Isaac and his stupid fears.

"Yeah. I bring nightmares to life. It's causing a problem," Mona said. "It's already causing a problem. He's scared of being that, you're scared of him being that. I don't want to make that real but you're both kind of ramming it down my throat because he's a telepath and you magnify and it's a truly horrible combination and honestly I swear to god could you have picked a worse ability to date? You couldn't have picked someone without a gift? Or someone who, I don't know – did something harmless."

Isaac's throat closed up. He was amazed that she even had the breath to get through that spiel in one go.

Her blue eyes bore into him, anxious and fidgety and yet somehow cool. Remote from him. As if he wasn't real, exactly, but instead just another dream she had conjured up by accident.

"Gabriel isn't a nightmare," he said, a little hoarsely. "You can't - he's not a nightmare. He's not something that you've created, or whatever it is you do."

"No," she said. "Not yet. That's what I'm trying to avoid. But the stronger the dreamer, the stronger their dream, same if they dream something more often. He's a telepath. It doesn't clash very well with me. Even if I don't do anything," she laughed, not sounding like it was very funny at all. "Even if I don't, power corrupts and absolute power corrupts absolutely as they say. You're walking absolute power, aren't you? Do you really think that's good for anyone to be around?

63

I know you don't."

Isaac gaped at her. He wished Gabriel was there – he could find some snappy way of telling her that she was talking complete and utter rubbish, or at least to remind Isaac that other people's bad decisions weren't his fault, that he wasn't some contagion people could catch just by the mere mistake of his presence. It still stung.

"Gabriel keeps other people from getting too close," he managed. "That's a good thing. We're not the only people with nightmares. Maybe you should mind your own business."

"I'm just saying. I don't like the thought of world domination in the first place." She stared at him, flatly. "I like it even less when it might make him the worst version of himself. I won't be part of that. Will you? I wouldn't want to ruin someone I love like that."

"He's not planning world domination," Isaac snapped. "He's not – I don't know what you're talking about! Stay in your head if it bothers you, I don't know what you expect me to do about it."

Isaac's chair screeched as he stood.

"Remember the boy with ice," she said. "Is that what you want?"

Isaac froze. Then he shoved his belongings in his bag and walked away.

She had *no idea.*

And yet, he was more afraid than ever.

7 - Gabriel

Now

The night passed without nightmares. In recent times, even for the sleepless, that seemed like an accomplishment. The lingering darkness of autumn seemed lighter than before; the cold air sharp with possibility.

Gabriel used to love late nights and early mornings. They were the moments when most of the world was still dozing and its minds went quiet to him. Not gone – never gone – but they turned to a white noise like the rush of the sea on a beach. He never used to care about not being able to touch a dreamer's mind. It was a reprieve, a stolen beat to be alone in his own head without their thoughts and desires tugging him into a dozen different directions.

It took a lot of early mornings as a kid, and late nights as a teenager, and some combination of both as an adult, to begin unpicking what he wanted from the pull of other people's expectations. By the time he met Isaac, he knew for sure. Or maybe Isaac was the first thing he'd ever wanted so badly that it couldn't possibly be anyone else's. Everything else could still get tangled back then.

Nowadays, the quiet was nowhere near as comforting, the sleep of others less a reprieve from expectation and more the suffocating weight of one. But, god, he wished he could sleep, for once.

He'd spent the night considering ways forward instead, considering the note on Isaac's laptop, and spending far too much time remembering the past. He'd often wondered if he should have seen Isaac's suicide coming, if he'd done something wrong as a boyfriend to cause it. He didn't think he'd been a bad boyfriend; he'd always tried to make sure Isaac had everything he wanted, even the things that he didn't have the nerve to ask for. He'd never found answers for himself on what happened. Now he was even less sure.

He remembered too late that he'd left Isaac's old belongings in his room – he hadn't meant for Isaac to find them. It seemed embarrassing when Isaac had left him behind. Proof of how much he really hadn't got over it. Still, he couldn't blow it. Everything had all gone too wrong already, he needed Isaac's help whether he wanted to give it or not.

He made more coffee, and then he went to find him.

***

"Isaac."

Seeing Isaac again was still dizzying, despite the night that had passed. He couldn't get used to it. Even when they were together he couldn't get used to waking up next to Isaac in the mornings; the dawn picked out the pale strands of his hair and turned them the colour of spun gold, he was unguarded in sleepiness, and utterly breath-taking. Mornings made Isaac look warm in a way no other time of day did.

Gabriel still itched, damningly, to reach out and touch. To soothe bruised jaw and tension corded shoulders, to release

Isaac's chafed wrist from its cuff. He hated that cuff.

Isaac looked up to see him standing in the doorway and shot immediately to his feet, like he was going to start running. The urge to run certainly fired through his head.

Gabriel approached him slowly and held out the mug – a peace offering.

Isaac didn't take it. He eyed Gabriel warily, like he was trapped in a room with a tiger instead of his boyfriend. Ex-boyfriend.

"Oh, for god's sake," Gabriel said, wounded. "It's coffee, just coffee. You know I haven't drugged it. Even if I had, I could just tell you to drink it if that was the case." He set the mug on the bedside table next to his headphones, shoving his tentativeness away pointedly. "You know I can't let you sleep, so you may as well."

Isaac hesitated, before he took the cup of coffee with his free hand, bare of gloves still. He sat down again on the very edge of the bed and took a sip, then froze, looking up at Gabriel with wide eyes.

He remembered my coffee order, Isaac thought. *Of course he did.*

Gabriel felt his cheeks go hot. One sugar, no milk. Was he supposed to have forgotten? Probably. Probably, he was supposed to have long since got over Isaac, and found himself someone else. He always found himself comparing someone else to Isaac, as he'd known him.

Isaac cleared his throat and took another sip, focusing his thoughts on the steam and the heat to ground himself.

"Isaac—" Gabriel began, at the same time as Isaac did.

"You're exhausted." Isaac tugged at the shackle around his wrist, fingers flexing, gaze wrenched away from the mug.

Gabriel's mouth snapped shut.

"If you weren't," Isaac continued, "you wouldn't be using chains to hold me." A smile curled his lip, or something like it. It was that vicious smile again. It didn't suit him any more than the haircut did. "You can barely even stand to look at my arm in this thing, can you?" He gave it another tug, voice light. His eyes flicked up, as sharp as his knife had been. "Why aren't we sleeping?"

"You know why." It threw him off course. He'd had a plan. Stupid, really, to think he could have a plan around Isaac when even looking at him made Gabriel feel like he was bent over the ropes with the match bell ringing. "You probably know more than me."

Something crossed Isaac's face. Maddeningly, impossibly, it didn't reach his head. There was simply another blot of silence. Isaac set his coffee mug aside on the bedside table after a moment, mostly untouched. His stare drifted to the cuff once more, expressionless as he pressed against the cold bite of steel to bring up a bead of blood on his wrist.

Stop that.

Isaac's hand stilled and he shot Gabriel a look – the expression was easily defined, and he heard it loudly. Screw you.

He ignored it and knelt down to examine Isaac's wrist. It wouldn't be nearly so bad if Isaac could simply sit quietly and stop acting so dramatic – it wasn't like any of them were going to actually *hurt* him. He had to know that. When Gabriel glanced up, the position had put their faces level. Isaac was close enough to kiss.

All of the times they had kissed, all of the times they had been in that position in other circumstances entirely, flashed through Isaac's head too. At least Gabriel hadn't misunderstood everything about the relationship they had. For a beat there, Isaac wanted him so keenly that he could fill the entire city with longing.

"You said you needed my help," Isaac said quickly. "Why? What's happening?" He shuffled back on the bed to put distance between them, as much as the cuff would allow.

Gabriel didn't move. Judging by how twitchy Isaac was being it was in Gabriel's best interest to act as harmless and non-threatening as possible. So, he stayed on his knees and bit down on his lip in a worried little tic of movement that would only remind Isaac of the past again. He needed Isaac to remember. He needed Isaac to be on his side again. He needed *his* magnifier.

"Do you really not know?" he asked. He offered a reassuring smile. "If you've got yourself in some kind of trouble, it's okay. I can help you. I'm good at that, remember? It's what I do."

Isaac turned his attention to the wall, to the headphones, to anything that wasn't Gabriel himself.

"You're in my head," he replied. "You know I don't know what's going on. Or do you think I'm dumb enough to try and lie to you?"

Gabriel placed his coffee mug on the table beside Isaac's, and placed his hand on Isaac's knee, rubbing a soothing circle above his jeans, testing his reactions. Isaac's gaze snapped down to his hand. He stopped breathing for a few seconds.

"Your head keeps going silent," Gabriel countered. "You're blocking me. We covered that yesterday, though by all means if you'd like to share *how* you're doing that…"

"I'll pass," Isaac said, only a little hoarsely. He shifted his leg away, digging the heel of his palm into his knee as if doing so hard enough would replace the memories of touch. "I'm not possessed, you know. Or whatever you think is happening. All I want is for you to leave me alone. Let me go."

"I can't—"

"Yeah." Isaac rolled his eyes. "You can't do that. I heard the first time."

Gabriel searched Isaac's white eyes for any strands of malice, any un-belonging thing, but Isaac's eyes weren't familiar to him any more. He sighed and stood up, giving Isaac some space and pulling up a chair. He tried again as Isaac relaxed minutely.

"Look, I don't know what your problem is, Isaac. I really don't. But this is bigger than you and me." And maybe he didn't like looking at Isaac cuffed, but Isaac wouldn't be needling if he wasn't trying to make Gabriel recoil hard enough for it to constitute backing off. "Even though I assume 'he knows you're alive' was about me."

That stung too.

The silence blotted in Isaac's mind at the question, so whatever the block was, it seemed clearly linked with whatever was going on and whatever was making people fall asleep. He'd already established that. What he needed to establish was why Isaac was studying him with a careful terror that damn near broke his heart. Scared was Isaac's default emotion, it was true, but he was never supposed to be scared of *Gabriel.* When had that happened?

Gabriel itched to reach out again, to ease, but Isaac didn't want that. He was tempted to do it anyway. Isaac was shit at looking after himself.

"People have been falling asleep for days and not waking

up. Sometimes, the sleeping kills them," he said. "We're also seeing what we're calling living nightmares, or just nightmares, for want of a better word. It's like people's bad dreams are coming to life."

Isaac composed his expression, away from terror, away from anything. He stared back at Gabriel like he was searching out clues and truth as much as Gabriel was.

Gabriel continued. "I'll admit we don't know much, but we figure someone with power over sleep is behind it. Someone called M. You have a message from M on your laptop."

Isaac jangled the cuff, twitchy and restless and distinctly guilty looking. He moved to adjust his gloves and make sure they were securely on his fingers, an age old tell, before he seemed to remember he wasn't wearing gloves again. He shoved his hands out of sight.

"This all started about four days ago when I found out you were alive." Gabriel offered him a wry, 'you're not in any trouble, trust me!' smile next. "I would really, truly love it if you could tell me that I'm jumping to conclusions here and that you have nothing to do with anything this awful, but I don't think you can. So, your turn. I've told you what I know. Talk to me. I've read that's good in a healthy relationship."

He regretted the words, the jab, the second it left his mouth.

Isaac's shoulders tensed. His mind snarled.

"Don't you dare lecture me on communication – I told you to leave me the hell alone. And you're not taking no for an answer.What does your bloody reading on healthy relationships say about that? Apply that to literally any other relationship scenario. Apply kidnapping your ex to literally any other relationship scenario."

He should let the comment go. He should focus. He should

be, as Dahlia might put it, peachy and chill.

"I wouldn't have to be in your head if you'd just talk to me!" he snapped back instead. "And this isn't about us or our relationship and the fact that you'd rather die than talk to me. Because, you know, you didn't break up with me, Isaac. You died. Didn't even bother to leave a note."

Well, that went well.

Gabriel pressed to his feet, turning away, pacing to the window. He took a moment to catch his breath, to stare out into Cambridge with all of its unnatural quietness. He couldn't reach for anyone else's mind to calm him. Nobody in his general vicinity was even nearing being a safe space to mentally land. Still, it was a good reminder of what was important. He turned to face Isaac again.

The expression on Isaac's face had edged pitying, remorseful, something. Gabriel pressed that advantage however bitter it felt.

"You say you're not possessed, but innocent people are dying. The Isaac I know – the man that I *love* – would not willingly let people get hurt." Then again, the Isaac that Gabriel knew would not have taken his own life, so utterly without warning. So maybe he didn't know Isaac anywhere near as well as he thought he did. Maybe he was a failure as a lover, friend and telepath.

"I haven't done anything," Isaac said. "I've barely touched anyone in years. I've literally been in a cottage on my own, making web comics, pretending to be *dead*."

"And learning French." No. That wasn't the point. Gabriel didn't press the point that not acting in the face of evil was the same as enabling it either, not now, not yet. He kept his voice calm. "I just want to make sure no one gets hurt, that's all I ever wanted. You know that. I'm not your enemy, here. We want the same thing."

"No." Isaac dragged a hand through his hair and bowed his head. "We don't. You're not listening to me." Still, he sighed heavily and deflated. "I didn't know about this," he said. "I swear, I didn't. You have to believe me."

"Okay."

"But...I do know M. It's – it's what she does. It's her power, if M is who I think she is anyway. She can spin dreams and nightmares to life." He muttered a curse and lifted his head from his hands. "I don't really have a way to explain it. But I can't really explain what we do either, or what decides powers. I mean, if this was a fantasy—" Isaac caught himself. "Well, we've had that conversation."

When they first met, the two of them had spent a fair amount of time debating powers, and what force decided who got what, if any. Nobody had any answers. Not yet. They'd been among the first generation. Not enough conclusive research had been done.

Still, it was nice to have the confirmation of what exactly M did. Pity he didn't have the first clue how to get any of the dreamers to wake up. That would cut off her power source, surely? Slam the door shut.

"Did she promise to bring a dream of yours to life?" Maybe that was what it was. A simple misunderstanding. "Isaac, she's not – she was probably only lying to get you close. So she could use you."

Isaac's mind spiked and his face turned hard.

"Right, because there's no other reason anyone might want to be around me. Everyone in the whole world wants to use me except you?" Isaac pulled an expression of mock thoughtfulness. "Oh, wait. You do too, that's why you *kidnapped me."*

Gabriel held his hands up in a placating gesture and gritted his teeth before they derailed. Again. "What does she want from you then?"

"She wants me to stay the hell away from you!"

For a second, Gabriel frankly had no idea what to say to that. He didn't even know where to start. Of course, this had started after he'd found out that Isaac was alive, and of course M had warned him to stay away from Isaac but...*why?*

"She'll kill you," Isaac said. "If she sees you with me, she'll kill you. Or, she'll kill me. Whichever comes easier. So, you know, she'll probably kill me. And I don't actually want to die."

"Isaac..."

"So." Isaac's voice grew louder. "For the last time, shut up and let me go. It might just fix all of your problems, because god knows all I can do is make things worse. Are you still going to tell me that you can't do that?"

Gabriel paced his bedroom with a hammering heart and reeling thoughts. He directed his power, instinctively, two doors down the hall to Felicity and the others. His throat clenched. No, no he couldn't let Isaac go, not even for that, not even to save his life. Isaac, and what Isaac could do, was the only way that he could win against someone with power over dreaming.

He steeled himself, gathering up the scraps of his last resort like the shards of a broken mug.

"Do you know what the first thing I noticed about you was, when we met?" He moved across the room, organising his thoughts as he stared out of the window and to the eerily empty rain sodden streets below once more. "You were scared."

Isaac glared at his back.

"For as long I've known you, Isaac, you've been scared." He could feel Isaac's emotions, but that didn't explain them. It didn't neatly write out a list. He only ever got the flashes, the memories, to analyse and try and make sense of after. "I appreciate that you may be trying to protect me now, but with all due respect I think she wants us dead anyway. If you're running, it's not to save me or yourself, and I think deep down you know that. It's because you're too much of a coward to stand and fight."

"Screw. You."

"I think with me," Gabriel pressed, mercilessly, "was the only time I ever actually saw you stay and stand your ground for something. Anything. Even if only for a little while. And wasn't that better? You relaxed. You were happy." He turned back to look at Isaac. "Do you remember being happy, Isaac?"

"That's because you messed with my head!" Isaac snarled. "You literally forced me to feel safe around you! To *trust you.*"

What?

Gabriel waved a hand and swallowed his infuriation, his confusion, his hurt. It was a stressful situation; Isaac didn't mean it. Or maybe M had lied, twisted Isaac's memories somehow. He still didn't know how they actually knew each other.

"I gave you a few nudges, at best. Not as many as you would no doubt accuse me of – a safety net. Is that so bad?" He kept his voice soothing as he stepped closer again, like one might approach a spooked beast. "You needed one. You needed my help. Your mind was screaming for it, tripping over itself

75

nervous. That's not being a puppet, that's using a walking stick. I mean – god." He waved a hand in Isaac's general direction, the way he all but cowered against the table as if he wasn't the most powerful man Gabriel knew.

"It's not something you have a right to do, just because you can!" Isaac's composure splintered, completely, away from stony glares and silent hostility. Just like it had yesterday, at Isaac's middle-of-nowhere shack of a home. He lurched forward as much as the cuff would allow.

Gabriel was ready.

He pounced. He cradled Isaac's face so that he would stop feeling the press of his telepathy and power flitting around the room. So Isaac would feel silence and freedom and the possibility of it – even as Gabriel felt his telepathy open up and his abilities deepen like a bottomless well of power.

Isaac's breath caught.

Gabriel's mind washed over the silence of the dreamers down the corridor, but he focused on Isaac. For once, he stood taller. Isaac, with his silence and his secrets. Isaac who might be a trap, or a nightmare, or maybe just frightened.

"What if I promised to let you go?" he asked softly.

Isaac had the expression now of someone struck about the head, eyes wide and dazed. "What?"

"Help me defeat her," Gabriel said, caressing his thumb over the bruises on Isaac's cheek. "Co-operate with me. *Talk* to me. And once she's dealt with, I won't try and hold you and she won't be able to hurt you. I'll wipe all record of you from anyone's head so no one will know what you can do or what you once did, and then I'll let you go. The world will leave you alone. You'll never see or hear from me again, I promise." That was what Isaac wanted, wasn't it? More than anything.

Never let it be said that he didn't listen.

Isaac wavered.

A power like Isaac's, perhaps everyone wanted a piece, didn't they? Who wouldn't? Isaac Morton was the key that could turn a powered human into a god, with a touch of his hand. With Isaac, all of Gabriel's dreams and perfect futures were possible. Everything that he once thought bled out on their bedroom floor, with two slashed wrists and too many questions left unanswered. Isaac thought he didn't understand it – the fear of being used. He did. He got that, if little else. Isaac just didn't understand that sometimes the ultimate use was more important than the using.

"I promise." He held Isaac's gaze. "You'd be free of me, if that's what you really want. Free of all of it, no fake death required. I wouldn't try and save you and I won't let her kill you. But I…" He dropped his head, deliberately, and let his voice grow urgent. "I can't do this on my own, I can't save anyone, without you. Not against what she can do. My powers don't reach that far on my own." It wasn't a lie.

Blood and Isaac, dashed on the floor.

Blood and Ari, dead in her bed.

Viper, Pyrate, Flicker – graveyard silent, and him still fumbling to keep it all together, as if he could stop them from becoming ghosts too.

He couldn't let anyone else die.

He watched Isaac closely, without the benefit of his thoughts. He nearly had him.

"Help me, Isaac. *Please.*"

"Deal," Isaac said.

8 - Dahlia

Dahlia wasn't, technically, doing anything wrong by sneaking out.

Gabriel would only have tried to forbid her from going, and Sanna would have insisted on coming along if she didn't try the same 'stopping her' plan.

No one had actually told her *do not go meet the dreamweaver.*

They had their principles, their ideologies and that was all good, but they didn't always have their actions. Nature was all about action. Action, or death. The stagnant did not survive.

She would have thought a woman who could heal anyone and anything (pretty much) would have more of a reckless streak, but if anything Sanna was even more careful. She was down at the doctors the second there was a chance of a flu shot, some hypochondriac for diseases and illnesses that she could never possibly get. She clung to Gabriel and the telepathic peace he gave her like a limpet. Felicity was the same. Gabriel could wash all the bad things away, could protect them, and her sister had wanted that more than anything.

Dahlia had never considered herself much made for peace. The world could have peace once it stopped forcing her to fight; she wasn't going to drug herself on telepathy to make it easier. She wanted to remember the anger. She could draw strength from her spite, and choose kindness, without having everything else removed so kindness was the default.

She wrapped her scarf tighter around herself, and quickened her pace down Sidney street. She kept her head low. It was a chilly morning. The days were quickly growing darker, sleepier without the cheerful effect of Christmas lights yet to brighten the hours.

She hated autumn. Half the plants died. She should have moved somewhere else, already. Somewhere less seasonal. Or possibly somewhere tropical. Felicity loved England, though. Or maybe she simply loved Gabriel too much to leave him. It wasn't that Dahlia didn't understand – Gabriel had given them a home, somewhere Felicity could stop and put down roots, somewhere she felt safe and accepted, where she didn't have to run. Dahlia would always be grateful for that, for what he'd given Fliss. But now...

She felt a sharp prickle of resentment.

Gabriel was distracted. He had larger goals in mind. He had Isaac goddamn Morton on his mind, it was obvious. The fact that he hadn't even noticed her slipping out of the house just proved it! He was completely distracted, where he would have noticed everything before. Did Felicity not matter at all now? She'd thought Gabriel might actually have a plan for when he got hold of his magnifier, but apparently not.

She walked faster, splashing through the puddles. A chill seeped through her eco-friendly trainers. She'd seen five houses looted on her walk already, windows smashed, as its inhabitants slept haplessly, and house alarms screamed for nobody. Bins had been left uncollected on the street. Scrawny cats and half feral dogs loitered, ravenous without their usual schedules of domestic feeding bliss.

She hated cities, for the most part. Even the pretty ones like Cambridge, cobbled and fringed with their green areas and potted plants, felt manicured and tamed compared to the countryside. The wilder a place, the calmer she felt there. Brick, mortar and concrete made her fingers twitch to make the dandelions rise and shatter the pavements.

Gabriel really was going to be furious, wasn't he? The thought of his anger sent a shiver down her spine. But someone had to do something. Better to ask forgiveness than permission, right? She moved past a ransacked grocery store and onto Market Street. She eventually paused on the edge of the market square, unnerved by its eerie emptiness all the same. Whenever she'd been in central Cambridge it had been stuffed with people; they seemed to spring from every corner, spread across every street and spare pavement chattering away, taking photos and moving fast. More than the silence, it was strangely scentless. There was none of the smell of noodles or meat frying for punters to devour, no smoke.

She tried to remember if she'd ever smelled anything in a dream. Mostly, she saw. Over and over again in dreams, she always saw their parents like a fairground ride that kept circling and she couldn't get off no matter how sick she felt with it. Was that where Felicity was now stuck? Crying out in the dark? Praying that the things in the dark didn't find them? No. *No.* Her heart raced.

She edged closer to the centre of the market in its ghostliness and empty stalls, keeping low and pressed to the wood and brush of fabric curtains. She tried to imagine what to expect, to guess what M would be like in person. At least the lack of people meant Dahlia probably wouldn't mistake them...

M sat in the middle of the market square, perched on the edge of a fountain that had long since dried up. She was alone. There were no monsters hulking at her sides, no visible nightmares, not even some strange and unusual dream creatures perched on her shoulder.

Dahlia swallowed. It was really her, wasn't it?

It seemed impossible that she could be where she said she would be, that it could possibly be so easy. Dahlia glanced around at the rooftops but she still couldn't see any monsters waiting to ambush her. Perhaps it wasn't a trap. Perhaps it wasn't the bang and sparkle Gabriel liked and pretended he didn't, or the fairy tale witches with their horns and cloaks, but ordinary people with their bad decisions and greedy natures.

M looked ordinary, at a distance. She had short curly red hair that fell a little above her slim shoulders, pale skin, and she wore dark but ordinary clothes. No witchy gowns. Just black jeans and a thin, cheap black winter coat to ward her against the cold. She looked to be around Felicity and Gabriel's age.

Dahlia stared, perhaps for too long. She searched for some obvious signs that this was the woman who had put the city to sleep, who had killed Ari, who had done such awful things. She looked so *normal*. Pretty, even. Dahlia hated herself for thinking that. The loathing turned to anger, at all this stupidly ordinary–looking woman had done.

She curled her fingers into her pocket, stroking her fingers over her vine seed. Controlling nature was always easier when she had something already, instead of making something out of nothing. She kept her gaze locked on M as she breathed gently on the seed, coaxing it to light despite the chill and the grey. She blew out another breath just to calm herself, before she let the seed drop. It sprung to life on the ground and she hurled the vines out across the square, catching M from the back. She dragged her across the market cobbles until the woman was dangling in front of her, wrapped head to foot in thorns. Take that, Maleficent! Her face was scraped by the stones and it gave Dahlia an undue satisfaction, as did seeing the perfectly coiffed hair in disarray.

Their gazes met as the thorns rotated the dreamweaver. M's stare punched back into hers utterly without light, some black hole of a stare – the exact opposite of Isaac's. Both were bloody creepy. Dahlia blamed that for the uneasy feeling which plunged over her, some ache of tension in the bridge of her nose, some certainty that she should look the other way or flee. Definitely flee. She planted her trainers into the floor and held her ground.

Felicity was superstitious. She checked her horoscope, and wouldn't speed under a ladder. That hadn't stopped the bitch from catching up to her sleeping, had it? Dahlia wasn't going to let anything like a bad feeling stop her from what she wanted.

"What did you do to Isaac?" M asked. "Where is he?" Her tone was silvery; it slipped in and out of Dahlia's ears like little darting fish. So close, she was oddly difficult to look at. The feeling that she had to get away from the dreamweaver, the blooming dread, only weeded itself more firmly between Dahlia's intestines.

Dahlia took a half step back, before catching herself. It was some kind of defence mechanism, it had to be. She gathered what details she could: those bruise black eyes, that blood red hair, that fairy enchantress look that seemed that it must absolutely be a dream. Hadn't she thought that M was only ordinary a few moments before? She had delicate features, a slight frame. The more Dahlia stared, the less it seemed M could be a normal person. The less it felt like Dahlia could possibly win.

Chapped lips.

She focused on the dreamweaver's chapped lips, or tried to – it was some sign of a real person, because only real things were flawed. They were human lips. Infallible lips. The lips of somebody that she could beat.

"Where is he?" M demanded again. "You're one of De Vere's strays. You...ohh. You're plants. You took out my dreams at the border."

Dahlia blinked, startled, not having expected M to know who or what she was. She had to be connected to the nightmares somehow. It was a fine reminder of who she was dealing with at any rate, and Dahlia straightened.

"And you're M," she replied. "I'd say it's nice to meet you, but...well. It's not. Isaac's busy. He sent me instead, if you want to pass on a message? Possibly along the lines of 'this is how I wake everyone up?'"

"Call me Morphina," M flashed a disarming smile. "You lot like your code names." Morphina's head tilted and her stare seemed to bore right through Dahlia. It picked out the pieces and threads of her like she was a tree and Morphina was confident of having her fingers twisted all around the roots. She seemed to regroup herself. "It's Dahlia, isn't it? Dahlia Huang?"

"You've met my sister."

"I assume that's why you're actually here, yes." She studied Dahlia with something like interest. "De Vere doesn't know, does he? He didn't send you. You're acting alone. Negotiating alone."

Dahlia considered her options for a moment. It was already obvious that Morphina really hated Gabriel, so lying that she was there on his orders would hardly help her cause. Even if the lie that people knew, that she had back up, was a comforting one.

"Yeah. I'm here alone. Morton's with De Vere, they didn't notice me leave. He's safe with us. For now."

"For now," Morphina repeated.

"That's right," Dahlia said. Snapped, really. She squared her shoulders and did her best to keep herself calm. "And he'll continue you to be safe if you do exactly what I tell you to and wake the dreamers up. Wake my sister up. Leave them alone."

Another smaller smile curled across Morphina's pale lips, there and gone in an instant. It didn't reach her eyes.

"You cut to the chase, I like that. But I'm not sure you're really in a position to negotiate with me. Sorry."

Dahlia squeezed her vines tighter with a clench of her fingers and relished in the involuntary gasp she got in reply.

"Am I not? You want Isaac, don't you? And you don't want to die. That sounds to me like I've got quite a bit to negotiate with."

"Dahlia, oh Dahlia…you're dealing with someone who raises nightmares. I've seen more frightening things than a girl who just wants to save her sister." Morphina's voice had turned almost kind. "You care about her too much to have any real leverage over me, and you're not going to kill me. You don't know what that would do to your friends. They may stay asleep forever. So, let me down, before you get hurt. My fight isn't with you."

Dahlia wanted to snarl, mostly because it was true. She wanted to squeeze, and keep squeezing, but Morphina was right. How could she? She might make everything worse. Still.

"Your fight was with me the second you put my sister to sleep. And, as for leverage, you still seem to care about Isaac. You invited him here."

Morphina's brow furrowed at that, her head tilting to one side. A beat passed before she spoke.

"Come on, don't be so stupid," she said, instead of responding directly. "You were brave enough to come here on your own, so being stupid now by thinking you can fight me on your own too would just be tragic." Some of the darkness faded oddly from her face, like its own magic, and left her eyes sleet. Gun metal cold, but not that chasm of black. "Let go and we'll grab some lunch. Talk, like civilised people. You must be tired."

Dahlia hesitated, if only for a moment. It seemed a spectacularly bad idea to let Morphina go – currently, at best, she could bring the dreamweaver back to the house and they could decide what to do with her there. Maybe Gabriel could get in her head when he was closer. While they were awake and she was awake there was nothing to be afraid of, was there?

"I don't think so."

"I know that tiredness," Morphina continued. "It will kill you. You can barely think straight. It's already getting difficult for you to focus. You can't afford to drag this out, so don't waste your energy trying to hold me like this. You have one minute."

"I'll manage thanks." Dahlia steeled herself. Morphina was probably only bluffing anyway. What was she going to do, make all of Dahlia's clothes vanish in a public that was all empty or make her teeth fall out? Maybe conjure a killer clown? She could handle all of those. Nightmares didn't have shit on reality. "And if I don't, that's not really your concern. Wake my sister up. I won't ask again. *You* have one minute."

Morphina shook her head.

"Wake her up so she can be a pawn in your leader's army? She is better off as she is."

"Dying?" Dahlia's fury rushed back. The vines tightened again at a flick of her hand, the anger pulsing through every inch of her bones, her guts, her very atoms.

Morphina exhaled a sharp breath.

"She would die for him anyway, if he told her to, and probably even if he didn't," she said. "You...you're not so enamoured."

Was that why she was still awake? Why she hadn't fallen with the others? She suspected Sanna hadn't because of her healing powers. Tiredness and attacks didn't affect her in the same way. As for Gabriel...well, who even knew.

Morphina's eyes turned black again. Had they ever been otherwise?

The vines dropped.

Morphina crumpled in a heap to the cobblestones.

Dahlia stumbled back and grasped for control again, trying to figure out what the hell had just happened. The vines remained slack on the floor, withered into the cobblestones, as sad as the husks of shed skin that snakes left behind. Unresponsive. Concrete-dead.

Morphina straightened and smoothed down her coat. She clicked out her neck, rolled out her shoulders with an unnerving calm.

Dahlia fumbled for a weapon – vines, again, new ones. Or something poisonous. The ground beneath her feet. Anything! None of it came. She could barely feel the flowers around her, barely feel the earth beneath her feet and then – nothing. A choked sound left her throat.

"Besides, everything dies," Morphina sighed. "Shouldn't you know that by now? Isn't that the way of nature?" She stepped closer.

Dahlia skittered back.

"Not at twenty-seven! Wake her *up.*" Her powers weren't working. How the hell weren't her powers working? She wouldn't, couldn't, be helpless. That was the worst thing she could possibly imagine when she was – no. *No.* "What have you done?" She hated the crack in her voice. It was too obvious. She could practically watch Morphina drink it up. She looked taller than she had seemed before, larger than life and Dahlia was five years old and afraid.

"You never did like feeling helpless, did you?" Morphina's head tilted. "That's all dreaming about losing your clothes is. Embarrassment. Vulnerability. Being exposed for what you really are."

"What have you done? I'm not asleep!"

"Once a nightmare is alive, you don't have to be. It's not a dream any more. This is *reality,* at least for a little while. It's easier when you're asleep, but your fears are common and there are so many asleep already, for me to draw from."

"No." No. Morphina couldn't just – do this. It was too much. It was impossible. "No, just stop this. Stop all of this."

The whispering instinct to run turned into a howl. Dahlia stumbled back another step, then she curled her fist and swung.

Morphina didn't seem to expect to be punched in the face. She staggered back and the feeling of unease vanished, before returning full force.

Dahlia didn't wait to see her reaction. She threw herself forward again, because people had survived fights before superpowers, and this was *for Felicity.*

Morphina swiftly raised her hand and Dahlia's vines turned on her. They caught her around her ankles, her throat, hoisting her struggling into the air before her next punch could land. Impossible. They were hers. They were supposed to be hers. Dahlia's adrenaline spiked. The urge to run won out, but she couldn't run any more.

She'd had the dream before. To be helpless, again, in the moments when she most needed to be strong. To feel a horrifying powerlessness, with the plants that she adored revolting against her care and commands. She'd had that stupid dream so many times.

She watched the spray of blood across her parents' faces, once, and did nothing.

Morphina stopped in front of her. Her face was inches from Dahlia's, and twisted. There was blood on her mouth from where Dahlia had hit her.

"Safe." Morphina spat the word back at her like Viper's venom. Whatever veneer of calm rationality she'd presented before had crumpled away. "He's not safe, not around De Vere. None of you are. You really want to come here and bargain? How about this then, messenger. Get Isaac out of there, and then I'll *consider* letting your sister wake up. But you don't get to threaten me. I don't like being threatened."

Dahlia's heart hammered in her ears. "You'll wake all of them up."

"No," she said. "Your sister, for Isaac. Fair is fair, don't you think? You're lucky to get even that. I could tell you to kill De Vere to save her."

"What? I'm not – I'm not going to kill anyone! I'm not you."

"Then I suggest you bring me Isaac, so I can." She gave Dahlia an oddly pitying look, then, seeming to settle. She wiped the blood away from her lips. "I like you, Dahlia. As I said, the rest of you should never have been dragged into this, it's the only reason you're still alive. A courtesy. I don't expect you to be able to fight the telepath. He won't let you. But he cannot control the sleeping and I cannot let you stand with him. If that means killing you, then that is truly unfortunate, but I would consider it a necessary evil."

Dahlia's head swam. She stared at Morphina in disbelief.

"Why do you even want him dead so badly? What's he ever done to you?" It was true that she and Gabriel did not always see eye to eye, but Gabriel wasn't some kind of monster. All he was ever trying to do was stop the people around him from suffering. Dahlia had seen it.

"Do we have a deal or not?" Morphina returned.

Gabriel would be furious if she let the magnifier go, after everything. Those two had history. Siblings had more history. Morton didn't even *want* to be with them, did he? He was only going to be trouble. Sabotaging. Some kind of distraction and a trap.

But if she gave Morton to Morphina, the dreamweaver

would kill Gabriel, wouldn't she? And there was no guarantee that she would keep her word about not killing the rest of them. Everything she could do would be magnified – Dahlia had felt that power, that impossible sheer power when she touched Isaac. The dreamweaver had implied she'd kill Morton too, but who the hell would kill him when they could use him to be that strong? Nobody would. Morphina would be unstoppable, and they wouldn't have Gabriel to fight her like he'd always fought the bad guys before.

Felicity could be saved though. She was more useful than a magnifier anyway, if Gabriel wanted to think like that. She could reach Morphina in a flash the next they tracked her down and snap her neck between blinks, if that was what it took, before Morphina could kill anyone. Felicity, awake, was never helpless. She could always run. *They* could always run, all of them. Morphina wouldn't be able to hurt Gabriel then anyway.

She would have her sister back.

"Isaac for Felicity – *unharmed,* and you don't pull any crap and kill her or put her to sleep again straight after." Dahlia willed the fear out of her tone, she willed herself to sound in control of the situation. "How do I know you'll keep your side of the deal?"

Morphina released the vines.

Dahlia bashed her knees against the street, hand flying out for balance.

"I suppose you'll just have to trust me," Morphina said.

"I don't trust you."

Morphina raised her brows and reached down a hand to help her up. Or, maybe, to shake. Some kind of devil's bargain. It felt like their breaths were the only sounds in the world.

Dahlia exhaled and took her hand.
"Deal."

9 - Isaac

Five Years Ago

Isaac peeled his gloves off and set them down on Gabriel's pillow, in the small indent left by his head that morning. He'd held Gabriel close, so he wouldn't hear, so he couldn't know. He'd kissed him for the last time, half certain that Gabriel would sense his plans in the desperate press of his lips and the bite of his fingers clutching onto him. He half hoped that Gabriel would, but he didn't.

Light had streamed in through the chink in the curtains and dust motes danced golden in the air, swirling around the routines of their life. Gabriel had been reluctant to leave for class. It was chilly outside and chillier still in their draughty student accommodation, but warm beneath the covers tangled up in each other's touches.

The sheets were still unmade from their lazy start to the day, and a mug of half drank tea perched on the bedside table on top of one of Isaac's sketchpads. The sheets were cool as Isaac skimmed his fingers over the ridges and creases, smoothing them out. He liked their sheets. They were a print of Van Gogh's *Starry Night*. Gabriel had got them for him.

Isaac's stomach hurt, thinking about it, thinking about every thoughtful and lovely gesture that Gabriel had ever done.

Mona walked in at exactly the time she said she would. Her jaw clenched with grim determination, and she had her scarlet curls piled in a messy bun atop her head. Dark shadows of sleeplessness sunk beneath her eyes.

Isaac drew his hands back and shoved them into the pockets of his hoodie.

"Are you ready? You could die for real, you know." She came to a stop in front of him, her arms swinging restlessly at her sides. Her voice stayed flat and unchanged. "If the nightmare is too strong—"

"Then I die. Yeah, I got it. Thanks for the reassurance. Are *you* ready?"

She'd said that faking his death was the only way that he would be free, and the only way to save Gabriel. So long as Isaac was around him he was a risk. It was the plan, or die for real. Really, he'd been lucky to get to live life with Gabriel as long as he did. He couldn't have expected it to last forever.

Except, of course, he had. He'd thought they could have happily ever after, right up until Mona showed him a dozen nightmares of what Gabriel could be, *would* be, with Isaac by his side. Right up until he watched Gabriel waltz across campus, adjusting and controlling other people's minds like he had every right to do so. Right up until Mona asked, if Gabriel had done the same thing to him, would Isaac even know? How much could he truly trust his heart when it came to a telepath?

Mona exhaled a breath between her teeth and pivoted. She examined the room and Isaac squashed down the prickling sense of intrusion. It was often like that around her; an uneasy feeling, an omen, a bad dream. Some nagging instinct entirely different to those that engulfed him around Gabriel. Isaac had long since stopped quite trusting his own mind. His own heart.

"Your fear is making this difficult," she said quietly. "If you want to survive, you need to calm down. His mind is very strong. I need yours to be stronger or we're not going to stand a chance. You must stay focused on the dream, and remember that it is *only* a dream."

"Sorry." Isaac tugged a hand through his hair. "Sorry." He laughed and shook his head. "Where's Gabriel to screw with your emotions when you need it?"

"That's not funny."

By his sketchbooks were Gabriel's medical textbooks. Scattered, dog-eared, half forgotten. Gabriel liked the thought of being a doctor – of saving people – more than he enjoyed studying. He'd never been a brilliant student. Sometimes, Isaac wondered just who Gabriel had talked into letting him try out medical school. Yet, despite all that, he could imagine Gabriel as a doctor. He'd be a wonderfully calming presence in a ward.

"It's a little funny," Isaac said softly. "It has to be."

With Gabriel present, he would have felt safe. Maybe that was the problem. It was easy to mistake the muting of fear for safety, and safety for love, and terror for the falling of it. Being seen, all the way to the bones of him, was horrifying and intoxicating all at once. Every thought, every weakness, every scrap of darkness and every secret thing was Gabriel's to know already and Gabriel loved him anyway. Isaac could only make guesses in turn; study Gabriel's face for clues, watch as power unravelled him. As Isaac unravelled him. Or, maybe, as Gabriel unravelled them both. Still, right then, it would have been nice to have Gabriel's abilities to settle his anxieties. It would have been nice to just have *Gabriel*.

Mona chewed on her lip, trailing her finger over the edge of the desk, her gaze fixed on him again.

"I hope you're not having second thoughts," she said. "You won't get another chance. He'll see it in your head, delete the whole idea. You'll have to start from scratch and that's assuming he's not watching out for it after that. If he's watching out for it—"

"I *know*." Isaac wrenched himself away from the textbooks, the crinkle of sheets, the smell of Gabriel's cologne. "I said I'm ready." He closed his eyes and took a few steadying breaths, he counted to ten – all the little tricks he'd used before Gabriel. His pulse settled, but he couldn't fully shake the unease, the mourning for what was to come.

She watched him a moment longer, distantly, like he still wasn't quite there. Her hands fluttered like she twitched invisible strings, or batted at invisible ghosts that neither he nor the rest of the world could see. Then she seemed to slide back with some effort.

"Get on the floor and remember to keep it in your mind that you're not actually dying. It will feel like you are, but the dream is for him. Not for you. You must stay focused."

She'd more or less said that already. She must have been more nervous than she let on.

Gabriel was going to be heartbroken, wasn't he? Nothing, absolutely nothing, was going to make it any easier. This wouldn't work for anything less. If Isaac simply vanished, Gabriel would chase.

Mona glanced at him, expression unreadable, before she

held out a hand for him to take. She didn't grab onto him, but the chance to refuse seemed equally impossible. She was there. Gabriel by day, and Mona by night, and never any rest for Isaac's mind.

Being a ghost to the world would be peaceful, compared to that. Nothing would be his fault, no one would be able to use him. It wouldn't be his responsibility any more; all his wretched power meant nothing if nobody knew to touch him. No one would get hurt because of him again. He'd be *safe.*

He took her hand.

His power flared and hers grew, hungry, draining. He felt a rush of dizziness, a rush of panic. His wrists sliced through with blood and it hurt. It was cold. Thoughts of cold led to thoughts of ice, of Lola and Alec, and then thoughts of death and all that could happen when he made the mistake of letting someone touch him.

But he didn't want to die.

He didn't want to be afraid.

In that moment, scared, however irrationally, all he wanted was Gabriel.

Her eyes widened and turned black, terrified.

"Stay focused!" she hissed.

Something shifted in the corner of Isaac's vision. A shape, a figure. The power in Isaac tugged and swelled, a current to sweep them both up.

He wanted Gabriel to fix everything. He was scared of what that might look like – that was the whole point of all of it! But it hurt. There was so much blood. He'd never seen so much blood in his life. Gabriel always fixed everything, always made him feel better, and maybe Isaac had made a horrible,

horrible mistake because he didn't want to die before he even graduated. He didn't want to lose the man he loved.

"Remember why we're doing this," Mona said, squeezing him tighter. "Isaac, *please.*"

She had never touched him before. They should have practised. He was an idiot.

He wanted Gabriel to fix everything, but what if Gabriel's idea of fixing everything was as bad as she said it was? What if the man he loved was as bad she thought he was, and Isaac was simply too dumb to see it? He thought Gabriel loved him, but what if Gabriel had always just loved the power? What if, beneath that beautiful smile, he was a monster and he'd simply whispered in Isaac's ear that he should be blind? Isaac wouldn't know. Gabriel was a powerful telepath. If Gabriel ever wanted to, he could get away with atrocities. Maybe if Isaac stepped away for long enough he'd know the truth. Gabriel's telepathy didn't last forever.

Isaac's vision fogged. It was difficult to remember that dying was only a dream, when dreams so often swallowed the dreamer whole for their duration. He heard footsteps in the corridor, heard the door open.

Isaac Morton died.

Gabriel's eyes shone black and terrible above him as he passed out.

Now

"I brought you your gloves," Sanna said. She tossed them onto the kitchen table beside Isaac, studying him. "I thought you might want them back."

"Thanks," Isaac replied, surprised.

The last hour or so had been rather intense. According to Gabriel, his friends lay in the upstairs bedroom withering away because of Mona. Isaac had seen the beds. Gabriel's friends all looked shrunken, halfway to corpse-like, and hopelessly stupidly young. He remembered Gabriel's voice cracking around his pleas, that old and familiar desperation to save just one more person. And then another one. Another one.

Isaac couldn't fault him that, he supposed. Gabriel's heart was in the right place. It was everything else that became questionable. He'd kidnapped Isaac, wasn't that proof that Gabriel would go too far? That Mona had been right? That Isaac hadn't made the worst mistake of his life?

It was around that point, looking at Dahlia's sister and the empty chair beside her bed, that Gabriel realised that his earth elemental wasn't where he expected her to be. A look of horror had dawned on his face. It would have been funny if the sick tinge of guilt which joined the horror didn't make Isaac's stomach roll.

Gabriel had promptly marched out of the room, checked on Sanna, and then swore as he registered that Dahlia must have gone to meet 'M' in Isaac's place. He'd been firing up to make a final charge on M when Dahlia had shown up, a bit shaken by Isaac's estimation, but essentially fine. Gabriel had then promptly hauled her into the study to have a chat that was really having an argument. Possibly they thought it was subtle but really it wasn't. Gabriel had told Isaac and Sanna, in no uncertain terms, to stay out of it.

Apparently, Gabriel had a study. And no sense of teamwork. The first was more of a shock. Back in the day, Gabriel had always been more inclined to work when he had company, a white noise of thoughts. He'd liked it best when Isaac was close and focused on drawing something. A study was too quiet, too reflective, too cut off from the world.

Isaac shoved away the memories. He focused on carefully sliding his gloves back onto his hands. Some of the tension eased from his shoulders at their familiar weight.

"Does he often do this?" he asked, jerking his head at the ceiling in the vague direction of the noise. "You guys don't seem like much of a superhero squad. More like a superhero dictatorship."

He shouldn't have doubted that Gabriel would quite literally go down the superhero route after graduation, though it was (Gabriel said) actually a consultancy. They weren't *technically* superheroes. They took on cases to solve crimes with their powers.

Gabriel's base, from Isaac's quick tour of what exactly he was dealing with, had four bedrooms, two bathrooms, a study, living room, kitchen and then a basement training room. The stairs, which in a certain kind of household would have been lined with family photos, were instead decorated with an array of newspaper clippings and printouts of online articles.

Gabriel and company recovering a stolen painting. Gabriel and company uncovering a drug ring. Gabriel and company preventing multiple murders, planned by someone who could extend their own life force by taking in the life force of others. It went on, and on, and on.

Sanna frowned at him, filling the kettle with water.

"He's not a dictator. He's our leader."

"Was he the one who decided that?"

She gave him a long, level look, like she was trying to reduce him down to an essence.

"Look," she said. She placed the kettle down on its stand to boil, and meticulously spooned even amounts of coffee into four mugs. "I get that you have some kind of ex-boyfriend issues with him, and I'm very sorry about that because I can tell you're still hurting a lot, but you should be a little kinder."

Isaac blinked.

"You haven't been around," she continued, her voice staying perfectly placid, almost eerily so. "You hurt him. So I don't think it's very fair for you to stand there and judge him like you know him, because you don't. Not any more. He's a good man. He saved my life."

"He saves a lot of people. He saved me too, once." Isaac knew it sounded bitter when it left his mouth, dismissive even, but – well. It was true. "Your gratitude isn't a reason to let him order you around. You don't owe him."

She turned to face him, slowly, staring at him like he'd said something unbelievably stupid.

"Yes," she said. "I do." She made a gesture at his gloves. "You wear those all the time, don't you? So you must know how hard it is when your power is done through touch like ours are. Now, I have better control than you do, I don't just heal everyone I touch whether I want to or not. But I used to. I was overwhelmed. Can you imagine healing someone who's hurting you when you're trying to push them away?"

Isaac opened his mouth and then closed it. His shoulders tensed all over again. Yes, he could imagine that. He could imagine that only too well.

Sanna watched him. "And…what about having someone stab you with needles all day every day, or having someone slicing you up to see how quickly you'll heal yourself, all so they can figure out to replicate it and turn you into medicine?" She smiled. "And you're lying there, kinda hoping that this time you're going to die because then at least it wouldn't hurt, but you don't. You just keep living. You keep healing. Can you imagine that?"

"I'm sorry," Isaac rasped.

"In case you can't, it's hell," she said, still in the same calm voice. "Gabriel helps make it not hell. He came for me when nobody else heard me and he makes the days *bearable.* He makes being in my head with my memories something that I can do. Just because you don't personally like it, just because you don't want his help, doesn't make him a monster for giving it."

It clicked.

Isaac could see it in her serenity, in the way that she could talk about the things that had hurt her so easily, so bluntly to a stranger, without any hint of pain except the memory that it would have hurt her once. It was like a telepathic bubble of peace, keeping all the bad emotions away. It was Gabriel all over, but Isaac had never seen it quite so absolute before her, quite so refined.

She didn't seem blank like Liam had been, didn't seem vacant, but...his gaze roamed over her, suddenly certain that every inch of her mood was artificial and carefully managed.

Even when Gabriel had been with him, even when he'd changed Isaac's emotions on multiple occasions when he was anxious or upset under the guise of helping or reassuring him, it hadn't been *all the time.* It couldn't be. Kissing was physical contact, and physical contact meant that Gabriel couldn't use his power on Isaac.

Nothing Sanna did, or could do, blocked telepathy for even

a second.

Isaac's fingers flexed uneasily at his sides.

She returned to making coffee for them all, turning her back on him.

"The people who took you," Isaac said carefully, "did so for their perceived notion of a greater good. Gabriel is the same, he works for the greater good. Just because you benefit more from his version of what that looks like, doesn't make him right."

"It doesn't make him wrong either."

No, it didn't. Isaac could concede that point.

"You said I hurt him…" He watched as Sanna arranged all of the coffee mugs on the tray. "Does he…has he talked about it? Me. Is he, I mean…" *Is he okay now?* It felt like such a stupid question. It wilted in his mouth at the look she gave him.

"Come on," she said, brushing past him. "Let's go see what they're talking about. He didn't say how long we should stay out for."

Isaac followed.

***

The study, even in the grand scheme of studies, was so utterly un-Gabriel-like that for a second Isaac genuinely considered it was more likely that he'd walked into another dimension. There was a large mahogany desk which dominated most of the room, and a cabinet filled with golf trophies at amazing odds with anything that the Gabriel he knew had ever cared about. He did remember Gabriel saying, once or twice, that his father was into golf. Or, at the least, Gabriel had said that his father had liked being the *kind* of man who played golf, meaning a man who was rich and of a certain social status.

So did that mean...surely he wasn't in Gabriel's family home? Isaac cast his memory back over the years, but came up blank. He had no idea where Gabriel's parents lived. Gabriel hadn't like to talk about them any more than Isaac had liked to discuss his own roots.

Gabriel turned to face them, brow furrowing. For a second, he seemed to have forgotten that people could walk into a room without his express permission. The dark bags of exhaustion beneath his eyes were enough that airports would probably charge for premium luggage allowance.

"Sorry," Sanna said. "I know you said not to disturb you. I bought coffee?"

Isaac folded his arms across his chest and raised his brows.

"You don't get to beg for my help and then cut me out," he said, before Gabriel could open his mouth. "Didn't you say you wanted me on your side? I can't help if you won't talk to me."

The irony of him saying that flickered noticeably across Gabriel's face, and he just as noticeably clenched his jaw to get it back under control. He glanced between Isaac and Sanna for a moment, before seeming to come to a decision.

"Dahlia went to see the dreamweaver," Gabriel said, with a lethal sort of cheeriness in his tone. "I can't access the memories to see exactly what happened, but *apparently* she wants to trade Felicity for you."

Isaac didn't allow himself to outwardly react, though his heart gave a cold lurch.

"She *what?!*" Sanna rounded on Dahlia, dumped the coffee on the desk, and promptly launched into a lecture on how irresponsible it was for the earth elemental to swan off without telling anyone. "You could have got yourself killed!"

Sanna said. "You're not invulnerable! What happened?"

They listened as Dahlia, with a distinct air of impatience, relayed the details of her meeting with 'Morphina' again.

Isaac could practically feel Gabriel's telepathy honed on him, not quite *prying* for a response, but certainly watching out for one. Isaac turned his face away, taking the added opportunity to observe Dahlia, to try and piece together the fragments of what he'd missed.

Dahlia's shoulders were hunched but, as she finished her story, she jutted her chin up at him in defiance of having done anything wrong. It was more comforting than she likely intended the gesture to be; her clear annoyance proved her mind hadn't been especially altered by Gabriel in the way Sanna's was.

"Somebody," she protested, "had to do *something*. Fliss is, you know, actually dying. So don't get mad at me. If she was awake, we could win—"

"We're not trading Isaac." Gabriel's tone was final, and Isaac was hit by a wave of not wanting to argue. It wasn't so much that he *couldn't* have, he just suddenly didn't want to. "Isaac." Gabriel tried to search out his attention, shifting soothing. "We're not handing you over, alright?"

"You'd pick him over us?" Dahlia spat. "No wonder the dreamweaver thinks you're evil and that we're all pawns in your army."

Gabriel reared in fury at the accusation. "You can't possibly believe—"

"Please don't fight," Sanna said.

Isaac glanced longingly back at the door as they bickered, rising in volume, talking over each other. He imaged walking out, away from all of it, and running until he couldn't breathe.

Then he sighed, because he couldn't do that. Never mind that Gabriel probably wouldn't let him get so far as the front door.

Gabriel was in full righteous flow.

"I understand you may be feeling a little neglected, Dahlia, and I know you're scared, but we do not win by giving into the demands and threats of—"

Isaac stepped forward, between Gabriel and Dahlia, and figured it wasn't cheating to put his gloved hand on Gabriel's arm. It was using his resources.

Gabriel's mouth snapped shut.

"With all due respect," Isaac said. "It's not either of your choice if you hand me over or not. It's mine. I'm not your prisoner after all, am I?" He offered the last question with an innocent head tilt, because there was no way that Gabriel could say 'yes' or outright deny Isaac his agency when he phrased it like that.

Gabriel scowled. "Of course not, but—"

"And *I*," Isaac talked over him, "have no intention of being traded."

The relief that crossed Gabriel's face was palpable.

"Of course you don't," Dahlia said bitterly.

Isaac looked at her, expression hard. "I make other people's powers stronger, trading me would literally make everything worse. I'm not saying that to save myself. If you can guarantee I would be more harmless in her hands than *his*," he jerked his head at Gabriel, "then by all means, hand me over. Can you guarantee that?"

Dahlia looked down, which seemed a good enough admission of 'no, I can't.' Her lip trembled. Just like her sister, she looked abruptly young and Isaac felt another wave of nausea.

What the hell was Gabriel thinking, getting these people to fight for him? To play hero?

"What are the terms of the agreement?" he asked Dahlia, in a gentler tone of voice. "Unless people are really careful in how they phrase things, there's usually a loophole. Something we can use to defend ourselves." He sifted through his options, and through everything that Mona might have told Dahlia about before. She wasn't looking at Gabriel any differently to normal, despite Morphina's continued claims about Gabriel being evil, so perhaps Mona hadn't gone into specifics.

"I literally just told you what happened," Dahlia said.

Isaac gritted his teeth. "Tell me again."

Dahlia glanced at Gabriel, as if for permission, before relating the story of what had happened once more.

As Isaac had thought the first time, it all sounded a bit nebulous, foggy, lacking in concrete arrangements. Mona could be like that. It was full of loopholes, sure, but so full of loopholes that it barely offered any protection as an agreement at all. He sighed. His first instinct was still to run, to abandon all bargains and disappear. If this was the same thing that it had always been with her, his presence would hardly help. Still. If he simply left, he had the nagging suspicion that Mona would be convinced Gabriel had done something to him. Imprisoned him. Isaac's stomach twisted. He'd have to show his face, at the very least.

"We should invite her here," Isaac said. "We can say it's for the exchange."

"We're not trading you—" Gabriel began.

"*Here?*" Dahlia demanded, aghast, in the same breath. "Are you crazy?"

"I know we're not," Isaac said to Gabriel. "And no," he said

106

to Dahlia. "I'm not. I just don't see how you'd reasonably lug your sister's unconscious body somewhere else. I mean, I'm sure you *could*, but given that she's currently hooked to a drip it doesn't seem the best idea."

"You want to bluff," Sanna said. "Pretend to go along with her deal, so that we can get her here. Then we can stop her."

"I want to pretend to go along with the deal and get her here," Isaac said, "so you can all sort this out without a fight. There's this thing called talking; you may have heard of it."

Gabriel looked sceptical. "You didn't make it sound like just talking would fix the problem earlier."

"You wanted my help." Isaac turned away from all of them, with a surge of frustration. "Take it or leave it." He focused his attention on the cabinet of trophies, with a mixture of vague curiosity and a less vague instinct that if he was skulking on the other side of the desk there was less chance of accidentally touching someone.

The awards belonged to a Michael De Vere. So, he was definitely in Gabriel's family home, right? It was surprising that Gabriel would have kept his father's things, but then again, who knew. He'd kept Isaac's. The revelation, either way, was a strange one. He'd never visited Gabriel's childhood home, but he'd met his parents once in passing when they came up to visit. It had been a brief meeting and a briefer conversation. Gabriel had been in a foul mood the rest of the day.

"You said she knew who you were," Sanna said, to Dahlia. "That must mean she can see through the nightmares, or at least that she has some kind of connection or awareness of what happens to her creations. I could use one of them to get in touch with her and put out the invite. If we're agreed, that is. She could also send a bunch of monsters on our location."

You really think this will work, Isaac? Gabriel's voice sounded in his head. Quiet. Not especially happy. Mostly tired.

"Yes," Isaac said. *Trust me. She just needs some reassurance that you're not planning to use me. That this is only temporary. She's not a bad person, she's just scared. Please.*

Gabriel nodded and released a breath.

"Okay."

The plan was set. Plans did tend to be once Gabriel made up his mind.

Sanna invited Morphina over for that evening.

***

The four of them sat with the dreamers in the bedroom, waiting.

It had been easy enough for Sanna to find a living nightmare by the city borders to pass on their message, from what Isaac gathered. She'd returned physically unscathed, though Gabriel had vanished with her for a while after, with a troubled look in his eyes.

Dahlia had deigned to continue talking to Isaac long enough to say that Sanna healed. Fast. But that didn't mean she didn't hurt like the rest of them – it just made her difficult to kill. Isaac had suspected as much from their earlier conversation. He thought it must be disturbing to not having any physical markers or proof to show for the life one had led, for trauma.

He kept by the wall; hands shoved deep into the pockets of his hoodie as if having his skin stuffed into as many layers as possible would somehow delay the inevitable.

Dahlia and Sanna stood at the ready. Sanna's hand rested on Dahlia's shoulder, no doubt ready to heal the younger woman should anything bad happen. They looked so easy, so comfortable with each other and their contact, that Isaac felt a foolish stab of envy.

He didn't reach out to take Gabriel's waiting hand yet, or even peel his gloves off. If it was him and Mona verses Gabriel, it may have been an easy choice. If he knew for sure that Gabriel would honour his promise and that Mona wouldn't hurt him, he could have been selfish. He could have run. Frustration welled in his throat. The urge to run flickered, and snuffed. This plan had been his stupid idea.

You still haven't told me how you know her, Gabriel said.

Isaac's head twitched at Gabriel's telepathic voice. He really couldn't get the hint of 'I don't want you in my head', could he? Worse, Gabriel's voice was gentle in a way that always made something in Isaac cleave. He was asking telepathically to be kind, to give Isaac his privacy from the others, wasn't he? It wasn't an order for answers.

The more time he spent with Gabriel, again, the more the past and what he thought he knew got tangled.

The cracked window was the only reprieve from the stifling room, from the stench of fear. The autumn breeze curled through the trees outside, cold and crisp and full of the longings of the season.

"If she's not willing to pay ball," Gabriel said, aloud. "I'm going to try and stop her, just so you're aware. I can't risk my people further."

His people. Isaac wasn't sure if he wanted to snort or cry.

"Are you sure this is going to work?" Dahlia asked. She chewed on her lips, watching Isaac too. He was sick of them all watching him. "Maybe we should just attack when we have the element of surprise."

"If we attack first, then fail," Sanna replied. "There's never going to be a chance to talk. We don't even know for sure if she'll really come."

The three of them all looked wrecked by exhaustion, even more so than they had when he first saw them. Their tiredness did less to make them seem human, and more to make them seem like cadavers that had been re-animated but still couldn't quite fake life convincingly enough. It was a slackness in their movements perhaps, some empty shine in the eyes.

Gabriel closed his eyes and dragged a hand through his hair.

"Thanks," he replied, to Isaac's less than flattering thoughts, as if Isaac had made the comparison aloud. "Can you focus? I need you to focus, Isaac. I'm not going to kill her, if that's what you're concerned about. I wouldn't. You know that. I don't kill people."

Rather than answer their questions, mental or otherwise, Isaac finally peeled off his gloves and shoved them into the pockets of his hoodie. He steeled himself, in case he was needed, and stepped to Gabriel's side. They watched the door.

They heard footsteps on the stairs.

The dreamweaver had arrived.

10 - Isaac

Mona appeared in the doorway of the bedroom with nightmares flanking her on either side. One was a tall man with a crazed look and a blood-stained axe in his hand, the other one of those children's drawings full of darkness and teeth. The monsters dwarfed her slight frame, yet within moments the sense that she was something tiny and fragile was obliterated.

A familiar urge to run crawled up Isaac's spine.

Her gaze took in the scene, moving briefly over the dreamers on the bed.

"Isaac." She spoke sharply. "I'll cover you. Run."

"I was hoping we could take a moment to talk first," Gabriel said. His fingers closed on Isaac's arm above his hoodie, as if he was worried that Isaac was going to forget the whole plan and go wandering off. He pulled Isaac closer.

"No," Mona said. "Isaac—"

"It's okay," Isaac said. "It's alright. We just want to talk."

Morphina froze, staring at him.

Isaac could hear his own heartbeat all too loudly.

It seemed an age, a lifetime, since he had last seen Mona Sanderson. The last time had been a week after he died. Her hair was shorter than it had been then, but his other

111

memories of her were fogged, like remembering a person through a pane of frosted glass. He only had the blurring after images of death and freedom – her effects.

He remembered dying. His bones ached with it, with the chill of it, and he felt another selfish rush of gratitude for Gabriel's body warmth pressed against his. Alive. He was alive. He would do what he could to stay alive, to stay free.

He'd regained consciousness in her bedroom with no memory of how he got there, three days after he supposedly killed himself. She wouldn't tell him what had happened in those three days. Once he'd regained some strength, she'd told him to run or die for real. Something on her face had haunted him.

He'd ran. He'd hid.

He'd had no doubt she would kill him if he didn't.

The next time he'd heard from her had been an hour before Gabriel walked back in, with her message, too late to be of use.

They watched each other warily.

"He's not in my head," Isaac said. "I can get him to touch my skin if it will make you believe me – you know powers don't work on me when someone's touching me."

Gabriel obeyed the cue. His hand dropped to meet Isaac's bare one, winding their fingers together. He did it as casually, as carefully, as he used to do it when they were first together.

Isaac drew in a breath before he could stop himself and Gabriel's grip tightened. He wasn't sure if Gabriel meant to keep him from jerking away, or if the firm hold was meant to steady him and keep him upright as he adjusted to the contact. Nothing ever quite prepared him for it; everything in Isaac lit up, too sensitive, too much. Isaac could feel the press of Gabriel's fingers seemingly right on his bones like Gabriel was painting his fingerprints there.

A dead body began to form on one of the empty beds, rotten and broken and so realistic that Isaac could smell the stench of it.

Gabriel flinched. He opened his mouth to say something.

"Don't!" Isaac said quickly to Mona. "Don't summon anything – we just want to talk! Please. Don't make him use his gifts on you while touching me."

The last bit gave her pause. The body faded away like it had never been there. Her jaw tightened and she shifted uneasily on her feet, glancing at their hands.

Isaac squeezed Gabriel's fingers hard, willing him not to do anything while they were touching. He debated if it would be better or worse if he let go.

There was a tense, crackling silence.

"Gabriel De Vere," Mona murmured. She didn't look over at Gabriel as she said it, glancing over at Dahlia instead, whose fists clenched under the dreamweaver's stare. "You probably don't remember me."

Isaac released a shaky breath.

"Mona," he said. He ignored the jolt of the room's occupants at the name, because it grabbed her attention back to him at least. "I've got this under control – Gabriel's not going to do anything. You know he's not making me say it, he's touching me. This has all been a huge misunderstanding. You don't need to be scared."

It did not have the effect that he was hoping for.

Mona gave him a look of quelling contempt.

"Says the man who's scared," she replied. "Did you ever have any intention of coming with me? Or was this all a

113

trap?" She must have seen some answer on his face, because she immediately scoffed and turned to leave. "I can't be here with both of you, Isaac, *you know that.*"

Dahlia's vines shot out to block the exit.

Mona stiffened. She turned back to face them once more and the monsters at her side grew taller. The axe murderer shifted his hold on his weapon, ready to swing.

"You want to pick a fight with *me* in the same room as your sister?" Mona's lips twisted, without mirth.

"I want you to wake my sister *up*," Dahlia snapped.

"Drop the plants."

"Wake Felicity."

The two of them glared at each other, before Morphina's attention moved to Isaac and Gabriel's joint hands again. She swallowed. Then her stare landed, finally, on Gabriel himself. There was something awful to her expression when she looked at him. Mona's fingers flexed at her sides, agitated.

"I should have known that deals with any of you meant nothing," she said. "You don't let people go, do you, De Vere? Not when they've hurt one of your own. I've heard the stories."

"If my reputation precedes me so, then you knew that hurting my friends was a poor idea before you did it." Gabriel's tone had a familiar, deadly, protective edge. "So you only have yourself to blame for anything that happens to you."

The knot in Isaac's stomach worsened. He used to love that protective edge. He shot Gabriel a dark look, because it wouldn't help them with her.

"But," Gabriel said. "Nothing bad needs to happen you if you let everyone wake up."

"No one's going to hold you here, alright?" Isaac bit out. "This isn't a trap. We just wanted a chance to talk to you. To get this all straightened out before anyone else gets hurt. No one here wants to hurt you."

"They don't *want* to hurt me," Morphina raised her brows, "but they will. If they have to?"

"No," Isaac said.

"Yes," said Dahlia.

Isaac shot her a look too, but Dahlia either ignored him or didn't notice. Isaac could have snarled. He did his best to press on, as delicately as anyone might when picking through an active minefield.

"One of you has to de-escalate before people get hurt. More hurt," he said, as clearly as he could. "Gabriel will if you do – just let his friends, let everyone, wake up. That's literally all he wants. Then you can go."

"I think we both know that's not *all* he wants, or I wouldn't be here."

"What's that supposed to mean?" Gabriel snapped.

"I can handle him," Isaac promised. "I'll make sure he leaves you alone. There'll be no retaliation. If this was all some accident–"

Mona snorted.

"You have no control over him." Her lip curled. "You never did. He's too in your head, and he has been for too long."

"He's not in my head!" Gabriel couldn't possibly be, right then, Mona knew that. She had to know that. "He's touching me! *Trust me*, I'm not under his control. None of us are. That's a bad dream."

"Sometimes, Isaac," Mona said. "People can be in your head without telepathy or magic powers. Didn't take much, did it?" Her lip curled even further, into a full sneer. "What, did he kiss you and say he really loved you and you caved? We had a deal too, if I remember correctly. Yours was that you stay far away from him. And now you're on his side? *Traitor.*"

Isaac's mouth felt dry. It was true that he'd always been rubbish at saying no to Gabriel before. He didn't know if that was because Gabriel wiped the 'no' from his head like Mona always insisted he did, so it didn't occur to Isaac that perhaps he should refuse, or if he'd simply liked pleasing Gabriel because he'd liked making his boyfriend happy. Mona had pointed out that Gabriel could have made him think he liked it, to mask the telepathy that was truly going on. Isaac didn't know any more. It couldn't be the point right then. He kept as calm as he could.

"He's not in my head, telepathically or otherwise. I haven't changed my mind about…anything. The situation changed, that's all." He held his free hand up in a placating gesture, to forestall any sudden moves from either party. "I'm here to help resolve it. Temporarily. Then I'm gone again, for good."

Mona laughed. It was a shrill, broken, pitying sound. "Even if all that's true, he knows you're alive. Do you really think he won't find some other emergency where he absolutely needs your help even if he lets you go this time? Some other monster? It's not like you shoot fireballs out of your eyes. How are you going to stop him if he wants to use you? All he needs to do is cuff you to a chair—" Mona's eyes flicked to Isaac's chafed wrists— "and it doesn't really matter if he's in your head or not. You're not going anywhere. You know that as well as I do."

"I'm just here as a temporary negotiator." Isaac's voice cracked.

"Oh, please." She shook her head, apparently sick of that line. "You're not a negotiator, you're a walking weapon that's always loaded. Him bringing you to a negotiation isn't peace talks, it's a threat. Like having a nuclear option in the back pocket. If you don't know that, you're an idiot."

Isaac didn't know what to say, to that. He wanted to put his gloves back on.

"He's not a weapon," Sanna said quietly. "That's uncalled for. He's a person."

Isaac glanced at her, surprised again by the defence. It was usually only Gabriel who said things like that, and half the time Gabriel wanted to use his gifts so who knew if he meant it. Isaac found his footing. He steeled himself and tried again. One last time.

"This...this putting people to sleep, it isn't like you."

Mona looked at him, flatly, all laughter gone.

"I didn't invite you here, Isaac. I thought you arranged our first meeting, at the square. You told me that he knew you were alive, that you needed my help hiding from him again. You *begged*. You told me to put everyone to sleep so he didn't have an army to hunt you down with. I did. I came. She," Mona jabbed a finger at Dahlia, "met me instead, to tell me that De Vere had you. Now this."

Isaac's insides jolted, thrown once more.

"No," he said. "No, you're the one who told *me* he knew. I'm only here because you put everyone to sleep. Then you were there, at the marketplace, as agreed. As you said you would be."

They both stared at each other.

Isaac's stomach-ache grew worse. Horror dawned. Because if neither of them had conspired to meet in Cambridge, where

117

Gabriel *lived,* who had?

"As I said." Mona's voice turned dreadfully soft. "You clearly don't know him as well as you think you do."

"You think *I* invited him here?" Gabriel demanded. "Why would I warn him that I was coming for him?"

"To make him believe you were me," Mona shrugged. "To lure him back to where you could control him. I don't presume to know the specifics of how your sick mind works. I imagine you wanted a mutual enemy; someone you could bond over so you can get your boyfriend back."

Gabriel spluttered at the accusation, eyes wide.

"Or you're lying," he said. "And trying to make Isaac think I'm some kind – some kind of villain!"

Isaac's head reeled. It didn't make sense that Gabriel had sent the message either, even if they were both now accusing each other. If Gabriel had sent the message, he would have waited for Isaac at the marketplace, he wouldn't have come running into Isaac's house like he did. Gabriel hadn't been *faking* that. The expression on his face had been too raw. Or maybe Isaac was remembering wrongly. Maybe Gabriel had drilled a different version of events into his head.

No. Gabriel wouldn't have suggested putting the world to sleep. He'd never instigate something that meant people's minds were out of his control, however good a bluff it would be. If Gabriel was going to pick a 'villain' to bond over, it wouldn't be one he had a very real chance of losing against.

"Isaac," Mona said, through gritted teeth. "I came here to help you. The deal can still stand. Let go of the telepath and—"

"You're not having him," Gabriel said. "You can't seriously think I'd let that happen."

118

Morphina and Gabriel stared at each other, for another beat.

"Well," the dreamweaver said, bitterly. "I'm so glad we had this chat. I'll just be going then."

Dahlia's vines didn't stop blocking the exit.

Mona shot Dahlia an icy look.

"Wake my sister up," Dahlia returned. You're not going anywhere until you save her. Until you wake all of them up!"

"The deal was that I would wake her up when you gave me Isaac. Looks like that particular deal is off. *Get out of my way.*"

"Not until you wake my sister up."

"Look—" Isaac began, about to suggest that they let her go, because at the very least it wouldn't make the situation worse.

"—From what I heard," Gabriel said, "you only want Isaac so you can kill us both anyway, so I don't know why you're acting like I'm the villain here. You'll forgive me if I'm not so eager to die. Now. Nice chatting, as you say, but Dahlia is right and I strongly advise you wake my friends up. The next time I ask it won't be a suggestion."

Mona's gaze darted around the room – trapped on every side – but she didn't wake the dreamers up. Of course she didn't. They were the only leverage, in a room full of seeming enemies, that she had left.

Isaac's stomach sank. This was not how everything was supposed to go. He started to disentangle himself.

Gabriel's grip tightened on him again; no doubt scared to face a dreamweaver with only the limits of his own power to rely on, or maybe not thinking at all.

Morphina zeroed in on the movement.

"Fine," she said. "Fine."

Isaac sagged in relief.

119

"You want to threaten me? Fine. I'll make this simple for you," Morphina said. "Give me Isaac and let me go, or I'll kill every dreamer in this room until at least one of you gets the message. It will be your fault."

Isaac stared at her, dumbly. The relief vanished.

"Archangel?" Her mouth twisted around the name, as she looked to Gabriel. "What's it to be? You'd let him go anyway, apparently. Prove it. Your team or power? You're *a good person*, all you want is to save your friends, so it should be an easy choice for you. Sleeping is a lot better than dead, isn't it?"

"You're not having him," Gabriel said. He didn't even pause.

Isaac's stomach bottomed out at the fact that Gabriel didn't even pause, though he'd known he wouldn't.

"Gabriel!" Dahlia protested. She didn't sound surprised, but she did sound furious. "For god's sake. Give her the magnifier."

"My decision is final," Gabriel said, drawing himself to full height. "We have no way of trusting her. She might kill us all anyway. She's scared. Frightened people do awful things and call it justice. Don't they, Mona? It's an excuse. It always is. You know the reason I don't let people go? Why I wouldn't just let you go? It's because your kind don't stop when I do!"

Oh, Isaac really wished he hadn't just said that.

"My *kind?*" Mona laughed that shrill laugh again. The monsters at her side grew taller still, their heads touching the ceiling. A huge wolf formed protectively in front of her, drool dripping from its large yellow teeth. It growled and stalked a step towards them, towards the sleeping beds of the dreamers.

Dahlia lashed out, with her vines.

120

Morphina dodged out of their way.

Pure panic flashed across Gabriel's face.

"No!" Isaac cried. He tried to wrench free before Gabriel could use his telepathy, but Gabriel didn't let go and they staggered forwards. Then, in a split second, the three of them collided. Him. Gabriel. Morphina. They went down in a graceless tangle of limbs. Somewhere the wolf snarled and then whimpered. He felt both of their hands on his skin. He felt both of their powers begin to magnify. He felt their minds connect as Gabriel's telepathy surged towards Morphina like a tidal wave.

The fear rose in Isaac's chest and engulfed him. He couldn't breathe. For a second, just a second, time seemed to stand still.

Isaac's gaze met the dreamweaver's and in hers – a hunger, Gabriel's hunger, Gabriel. That was what it was. What those dark eyes had been, and had always been. They looked the way Gabriel looked at him at odd moments, in the corner of Isaac's vision, when he was lost in thought. All-seeing, propriety, awful. Possessive. It wasn't Mona's look. Isaac had been having nightmares about that look for years.

It was the stare from the night he died. Aside from the cold, it was all he remembered.

Black.

Morphina recoiled away from him, but it was already far too late.

Her monsters had lunged forward to attack, and Dahlia didn't hesitate. She grabbed Isaac's newly freed hand and threw out the other one. Thorns gouged straight through the wolf and snapped the neck of the axe murderer.

Isaac felt the power in him lighting up, up, up like toxic

radiation. Too much. He couldn't control it. He couldn't control any of it. Mona was right – if Gabriel was determined, what the hell could Isaac do against him?

"You will wake my friends up," Gabriel growled. "Now."

Isaac slammed his elbow into Gabriel's ribs and tore himself out of Gabriel's grip.

The dreamers had already began screaming.

Mona fled out the door.

Dahlia dropped Isaac's hand in a heartbeat, and reached her sister first. She fell to Felicity's side with a thunk of knees on hardwood floor.

"Sanna!" Her voice choked. "Do something!"

Felicity's eyes were open, her body rattling as she shrieked and twisted, her eyes smeared that awful bottomless dark. Empty. It spread like ink, like poison, through her veins.

Sanna reached the dreamers a second before Gabriel did, her hands straining to reach them all at once so she could soothe their pain, heal and fix.

Isaac stumbled away, hitting the ground. He scrambled further away still, backed against the wall, as far as he could possibly go where he couldn't touch them, accidentally or not.

Gabriel's hand flailed, useless, in the empty space.

"What happened?" Gabriel rounded on him. "What's happening? What the *fuck* was that?"

The room smelled like winter air, crisp and sharp. The room smelled like rotting flesh.

Alec and Lola flickered into the world like ghosts. Like nightmares. They looked exactly how Isaac remembered them. Alec had been a short, sporty kid still growing into his limbs, with brown hair cropped short to his skull and big blue eyes; Lola a soft, round girl with long blonde hair and lots of freckles.

It shouldn't have been possible, but dreams didn't care about the rules of what was possible.

Isaac could never stop magnifying bad things in his nightmares. He never could stop reliving them, and everything his powers could do.

All of the air tangled up snarling in his lungs, clawing dizzying at his throat. He hadn't even realised he remembered their faces so clearly. Seeing them seemed an unspeakable cruelty – he wasn't even asleep. It was bad enough to see them in his sleep, but awake...

A choked sound escaped him.

Spiders crawled up from beneath one of the beds, huge and hairy things with glittering eyes as black and vacant as the dreamers' eyes were.

Dahlia swore and recoiled.

Isaac froze. Alec and Lola seemed smaller than he remembered them being, and all the more horrifying for it. His knees locked.

"Isaac!" Gabriel strode forwards. "Isaac, is this you? You need to calm down. You're not touching her. You can't do this." He sounded awed and uncertain all at once.

"Stay away from me!"

Gabriel wouldn't be able to feel the nightmare's minds, would he? He couldn't sense, couldn't control, couldn't read any dreams or nightmares bought to life.

Alec raised his small, eight-year-old hand into the air. Power crackled beneath his palms, turning his fingers the same stiff blue as a corpse's.

"Gabriel," Isaac rasped, in warning.

Gabriel jolted out of the way of a bolt of ice just in time.

The corpse from earlier re-appeared on the empty bed, half rotted, screaming like the dreamers were and clawing at its own gaping hole eyes. Blood streamed down her face.

"No," Gabriel whispered. "No, Ari. *Isaac.*"

"Gabriel! They're fading – she's fading!" Sanna yelled. "You need to try and reach their minds, now!"

Gabriel whipped to face Sanna next, barely seeming to know where to put his attention.

Alec Mandel and Lola McGabe had been the only other powered humans in Isaac's home town. Alec had the gift of ice. Lola could animate paper – small origami models and paper dolls sprung to life. Funny, how powers could vary so from the common to the bizarre, the beautiful to the dangerous.

They had been playing.

Sanna kicked a spider out of the way as it skittered towards Dahlia, pincers snapping.

"Cover me," Gabriel growled. "Isaac, grab a bat or something, at least." His gaze locked on his friends.

Isaac grabbed something at least; his gloves. He shoved them on.

Dahlia kicked into action again in a whip of greenery that shot up to contain the scattering creatures as fast as they could climb.

The screams continued, the monitors whirring haywire, so deafening that it was impossible to think.

The urge to run bolted up Isaac's limbs and he lurched to his feet and stepped towards the door.

Blood trickled out of Gabriel's nose.

"Isaac." Gabriel reached for him, distantly, not looking

away from the dreamers on the bed. Desperation cracked across his face. "I can't reach them on my own – I need you – you have to—"

Isaac's back slammed against the wall again and he wasn't even sure when he'd moved away.

Gabriel's head snapped to him when his grasping fingers closed around air.

Isaac. Come—

Alec sent another bolt of ice in Gabriel's direction.

Gabriel crumpled, pale, teeth chattering, as it pierced his shoulder. Distracted by the dreamer's minds. He jerked out of it then. His hand flew to his shoulder. He gasped.

"Isaac – for god's sake!"

Isaac had never been in the habit of touching bare skin even as a child; his parents had always been so very careful about that. With gloves he could, yes, but never without. Never without grasping onto the folds of fabric instead of flesh. Who could know, after all, what it would do if they had powers? Who could know what lay dormant between bones and chemical combinations that he might spark?

He'd wanted to touch. To hold hands. To do those things that kids and the human race always did without thought.

He couldn't stop staring at them. He couldn't move. He couldn't breathe.

More and more spiders churned into the room, a new one re-spawning almost as soon as one of its brethren was dispatched.

Isaac had touched Alec's hand in a moment of carelessness, of some stupid affection perhaps. He couldn't remember any more. He'd just been happy, he just hadn't *thought*.

Lola McGabe froze.

The power had blasted out of Alec's skin, skittering across the floor in a hungry lunge of ice. She'd been standing too close.

Alec had loved making ice sculptures with his powers, beautiful life size horses and tiny crystalline birds. Lola had looked exactly like an ice sculpture instead of a girl. Her breath had snatched up in her throat in shocked fear and then just stopped, dusted with frost like a flower on a winter's morning. It had seemed grotesquely pretty for the crime.

They'd killed her. Isaac had killed her. Everything in her stopped. All because he couldn't control it – magnifying, no matter the consequence, a walking bomb. The nuclear option. Imagine what Gabriel could do with that? Imagine what Gabriel could do to people's minds, even if he wasn't actively looking to control them, merely by the force of grabbing Isaac in an argument. He could tear their minds apart. Telepathic shrapnel. Blast radius. Isaac's fault for getting too close. Mona was right; Isaac was the option that should never have been on the table.

Dahlia roared in frustration, slamming another spider into the wall. It crumpled husked and insubstantial by Isaac's side.

Nightmare Alec raised an icy palm again, cold creeping across the walls, puffing their breaths white in the chill.

The next second the two of them vanished, sputtering out.

Telepathic calm washed over Isaac. Safety. Forgiveness. *Love.*

Gabriel's eyes were squeezed shut, hands clamped over his temples. "Isaac." He spoke through gritted teeth, doubled over in pain, but it was an unmistakable command. *"Help us."*

Isaac blinked and finally took in the rest of the room properly.

Sanna crushed a spider skittering towards him and left it writhing on the floor, immobile in some spider-agony. Her face flushed with exertion.

Dahlia spun through the room, nearly impossible to see through the flickering vines that wrenched apart spider bodies that crumbed to nothingness, only bad dreams.

Sanna caught her hand, healing her in an instant. She stamped down on another hairy spider leg and Dahlia finished it off, thorns ripping through its convulsing body.

Isaac took a step forward and breathed out. He reached for Dahlia's hand, for Gabriel's.

The screaming stopped before he could touch.

The room stood airlessly, lifelessly, still.

The monitors keeping the dreamers alive flat-lined.

"No," Dahlia whispered. She rushed to her sister's side again. She shook her body, lifeless as a rag doll's, eyes still gaping wide and vacant and body entirely too unmoving. "Please, no."

Her sob broke the dead drone of the machines.

Felicity stirred.

"Dahlia – get back!" Gabriel sounded terrified and his hold on Isaac's emotions faltered. *Get back.*

The command forced them all to his side, bodies lurching like puppets on strings to obey.

The dreamers rose, corpse-like.

Isaac stared at them with an awful twist in his gut.

"Fliss." Dahlia struggled against Gabriel's hold, straining to reach her sister's hand. "Fliss, are you there? Felicity? Can you hear me?"

Dahlia's sister didn't even look at her.

Should Isaac attack? Do something to knock them out?

Gabriel said to help but Isaac didn't know how to help. His gaze shot to Gabriel – the ever fixer, and the one who couldn't afford to be a nightmare too.

"Gabriel, let me go!" Dahlia hissed. "I swear to god you will let me go—"

Sanna moved to stand in front of them, hands flung wide like a human shield just as Pyrate's flames tore in their direction.

Isaac hissed a curse word.

A scream of pain ripped out of Sanna's throat, some terrible sound, her skin bubbling and healing in a vicious cycle. The air stank of burning flesh.

"Gabriel." Isaac hesitated a second, noting the other dreamers rising too, before he darted to Sanna's side. He grabbed her hand while the false calm of Gabriel's influence buoyed him again. It made it easier, that calm.

A strangled sound left Sanna, her scream gutting out.

The power buckled Isaac's knees. His head fizzed and black spots popped in his vision. She was hot to touch, and the air around her felt scalding. He buried his face further into his hoodie, bracing himself against the lingering heat. It was the last moment to be calm but he couldn't remember the last time he felt such peace. He could sink into such a peace.

Sanna's skin healed. The fire licked at her without even touching her, or so it seemed. Her clothes continued to singe and smoke, but the fire didn't seem to burn even a scrap of her skin. It was impenetrable. Touching Isaac, she was invulnerable.

Hands took hold of Isaac's hips, above his clothes, steadying him, pulling him further behind Sanna and further away from the possibility of burning.

The nightmare – Dahlia's sister – blurred and vanished. It was too fast for Isaac's eyes. One second, the three of them were standing among Pyrate's smoke and ashes, and the next instant the three dreamers were gone.

The fire remained crackling and hungry. Smoke billowed through the room, the bedroom adrift in grey and gold. The machines sputtered out as the flames spread across wires, duvets, chewing up the wooden frames of the beds.

"Shit," Isaac said again. He felt another wave of dizziness and clamped his sleeve over his mouth. He glanced at them all, numb, frozen, gasping, and then sprinted to get water. "Get back!" he yelled at Gabriel. "Get everyone out the room!"

The smoke alarm began to wail.

Isaac lurched into the bathroom, stubbing his toe on the door frame. Pain throbbed up his foot. A bottle of hand soap smacked against the floor. A mug – nothing big enough –

There's a bucket in the cleaning cupboard, Gabriel said in his head. *I'll get it.*

Their hands knocked into each other in the haste to fill the bucket, before Sanna seized the overflowing vessel off them and vanished into the bedroom in a blaze or orange and black.

Gabriel watched her, grimly.

Isaac threw up.

The fire doused, hissing and spitting.

Dahlia crumpled in the corridor, dead-eyed, staring at the black char where her sister had been.

11 - Gabriel

"I'm so sorry about your friends."

Dahlia's screams, her grief, her accusations, echoed in Gabriel's head. Ari's body, reappeared rotting and broken on the bed, echoed in Gabriel's head. The look on Morphina's face, dark as a shadow caught in the corner of his vision, echoed through his head.

It had been half an hour since Felicity, Jack and Lucy had died and vanished. Half a-bloody-hour. All in all he really wasn't in the mood to deal with Isaac right then.

Leave me alone. He shot the order at Isaac's brain.

Isaac walked back in five minutes later.

Gabriel tightened his fingers in his hair; head bowed in his hands. A headache slammed between his temples. He wanted to lie in a dark room and sleep. He couldn't do that.

"I told you to leave me alone," he said. "Shouldn't you, of all people, take the hint? It's your trademark, isn't it?"

"Dahlia's wrong." Isaac's voice was tender, unbearably so because it was probably out of guilt or pity. "She's just upset. It's not your fault."

Gabriel had watched Sanna crumple, deflate, some husk of herself. Her self-loathing seeped down the stairs like smog; that she should be forever fine while one by one the people she cared about were picked off by some pain or other. That she would always remain flawlessly healthy even if she tried, and there had been times when she'd tried. That she couldn't help.

Dahlia's mind howled in the room above, so loud that Gabriel was amazed it didn't shatter her and him with it. Grief always felt like it should break the world and the cruellest thing seemed to be that it always kept turning despite that, limping along and dragging the rest of them with it to keep bearing it. Worse, there wasn't even a body. Felicity was gone. They were all gone. They had all gone to Morphina and, what next? What horror? He dreaded the thought of facing their corpses on the battlefield. Surely she couldn't do that? Not without Isaac? How powerful was she?

The thought prevented him from ordering Isaac to leave again, because he still couldn't win without his magnifier. He swallowed bile.

He had to win. He'd already failed so awfully.

Isaac's footsteps padded across the cool wood floors of the living room, before the rug softened them and he collapsed into the velvet armchair opposite.

Gabriel felt the silence of Isaac's mind – that damn silence – swallow the room. He flinched away from the death-silence, that came every time Isaac thought about Morphina. He feverishly smoothed the rough edges of Dahlia's mind instead; the ragged cuts, the raw grief catching too much to bear. He did everything he could to make it more bearable for her. Grief was always a tricky mental state though, with each edge he soothed another jutted out and another wound split open with another memory. He couldn't help. He couldn't keep up.

What was the point of him if he couldn't help? It wasn't about him. Except it was. He'd told the dreamweaver that she couldn't have Isaac, and he hadn't stopped her. It was his fault. He should have done something more. At the same time, he didn't know what he could possibly have done differently. In all the battles before, he had always been able to turn up and tell his enemies to stop. It had been peaceful. There had been no need for bloodshed, for such grotesque violence. He hated violence.

The living room walls, its heavy oil paintings, seemed to be closing in on him.

In his head, in Dahlia's memories, Dahlia and Felicity crowded together in their small joint bedroom long before he knew them. For once, then, Felicity had been still. She'd gathered Dahlia in her arms so tight, so tight. Then she took her sister, and they ran, ran, didn't stop running as if in running fast enough they could teleport into different skins entirely.

Felicity brought back shot glasses with each far-flung trip she took, and Dahlia had been too young to drink, so each time her sister would fill them to the brim with fruit juice as she whispered about all of the places she had been and all the places they would still go together, even if Dahlia had stopped believing she meant it. But, still, it had been a promise.

He could feel Isaac's mental weight on the top of his head as he dithered, before the armchair opposite squeaked as Isaac leaned forward, gloved hands clasped over his knees in Gabriel's eye line.

Should he have handed Isaac over? Even with everything that had happened, he couldn't, wouldn't. If Morphina could do all she had done without permanent use of a magnifier, what would she do to the world if she had Isaac in her grasp for more than a few terrible seconds? No. She'd probably have killed them all the second she could. Besides, it was Isaac. Beneath all the justifications, all the logic, there was that. It was Isaac, and the words had left his mouth before his brain had even finished processing.

It didn't make it better. It probably made it worse.

Gabriel needed to stop thinking, start doing, as the action heroes did! As he usually did. All he wanted was to rest. To sleep like sleep was oblivion, without thought or responsibility. They weren't nearly done enough, safe enough, for sleep.

He needed to send the others away before they got hurt; somewhere far enough away from Morphina's reach that they could rest at least. He would tell Dahlia and Sanna to get themselves out of the city, to get themselves safe. He should have done that so much sooner. He'd been arrogant.

Isaac cleared his throat, drawing Gabriel's attention back.

"It's not your fault," he said, again, more firmly. "You know that, right? Because you've got that look on your face like you don't. You don't control what other people do. Not like that, telepath or not. No human can."

"Ironic coming through you."

"Your power doesn't directly magnify other people," Isaac spat right back, prickling immediately, predictably. "It's literally not your fault if she killed them. You didn't tell her to. And you didn't give her the power to kill them."

But I didn't stop her. Gabriel couldn't say it aloud, so he sent the thought to Isaac instead, helplessly. *She even told me the consequences.*

He'd told Morphina to wake the dreamers up, he'd driven

133

the command into her brain. She'd certainly woke them up. She'd woke them up all the way from the dead.

He should have been more specific.

Isaac's anger deflated as quickly as it had come at the reply, and Gabriel glanced up at him. Without the anger, Isaac's face was left gaunt, crumpled with tiredness and they'd barely started, worn. Had they been young once? They were still young now, he knew. It didn't feel like it.

"I'm sorry," Isaac said. "I – I didn't come to fight you. What do you need? What can I do to help you? I want to…" Isaac trailed off. He shifted off the armchair, so he was on his knees in front of Gabriel, trying to hold his gaze. He placed his hand on Gabriel's knee, a comforting weight, testing if that was okay.

Gabriel didn't much feel like he deserved comfort. Maybe he hadn't directly given Morphina the power to kill his friends, he wasn't the magnifier, but he'd still helped bring her to the house, still insisted. Anything so that Sanna and Dahlia would look at him like he was doing something, and doing it right, that he was saving all of them and Ari hadn't died for nothing and he was right to have spent time chasing Isaac down. Isaac, with all of his mixed signals.

Could Morphina have done anything if he hadn't taken the risk of talking? He should have struck immediately, the second he took Isaac's hand. Wiped her mind. Commanded her to let the dreamers wake with specific orders not to harm them. He should never have let his friends persuade him otherwise, never have let Isaac persuade him to soften his natural instincts. He should have gone with his gut instead of compromising. Look where compromising had got them! Other people's opinions were clearly useless.

Isaac peered up at him, earnest and worried. His thumb stroked soothing circles through Gabriel's jeans.

Gabriel's throat locked tight. Funny, whenever he'd imagined Isaac alive again, he'd never imagined it would get his friends killed. He'd forgotten the trouble Isaac always attracted.

"You know," he said. "I'm surprised you haven't taken the opportunity to flee considering how obviously that's all you want. Do you think I don't hear it?"

Isaac flinched. His hand stopped moving.

Gabriel pulled his legs up onto his own chair, away from Isaac, away from the foolish temptation to lean into him and pretend that the years had never happened. "I don't know what I did to you," he said instead. "That you think me such a monster." He wasn't sure if he meant it as a question, an accusation or a broken sort of confession. The thought of having done something terrible to Isaac, without ever realising it, appalled him.

When they made their deal, Isaac had said Gabriel forced Isaac to trust him. To feel safe around him. Did Isaac truly think that? Yet, if he thought that, then Gabriel must surely have done something right for Isaac to trust him? To feel so safe with him? It felt an impossible, double edged sword.

Isaac curled his hand into a fist in his lap. He didn't say anything. His mind went silent again, thinking of the dreamweaver.

Gabriel looked away first.

He didn't remember being a bad boyfriend. He remembered encouraging Isaac out of his room and into living his life, he remembered protecting him from anyone who might want to take advantage of him. He remembered being on his knees, Isaac's blood on his hands, desperately trying to put him together again and wondering then, too, how he could have failed the man he loved so badly. How he could have missed the signs of Isaac's obvious unhappiness before he committed suicide. But Isaac had never seemed unhappy with him. How could he not have saved him?

Except Isaac hadn't died after all.

Isaac spoke after a long moment. "She deals in dreams, in nightmares," he said. "She makes nightmares come to life, that's literally what she does. What's your biggest fear, Gabriel?"

Losing you. Again. Losing them.

Powerlessness.

Not being able to save anyone, no matter how hard he tried.

Gabriel had never considered that love might be a weakness before.

He'd never considered that his feelings for Isaac might be more of a liability than a triumph. Yet, if he hadn't been so wrapped up in Isaac, he could have stopped Dahlia from going to meet Morphina in the first place. None of it would happened.

"I magnify you, when you touch me," Isaac said. "Your power is in your mind. So is hers. You may be more powerful than her when you have me, but that doesn't mean she can't use your powers against you when you're terrified. The greater your fear, the stronger she gets, right? I – I couldn't stop magnifying." *I know I made it worse for you, I'm sorry.*

Gabriel looked at Isaac again properly, if only out of surprise at the targeted thought tossed in his direction. At the flare of sound, so familiar-unfamiliar. He blinked. It was impossible not to react. He felt worn too, thin around the edges, a patchwork-telepath. He didn't know how to begin absolving Isaac of his guilt, of comforting him, even if it felt he should.

Isaac swallowed, before peeling off one glove.

Gabriel's gaze flicked to Isaac's pale hands. They were unmarked from a life of being hidden behind cover, even if someone could just as easily grab Isaac's chin, or his cheek, or any other patch of bare skin less easily covered by layers of clothing. His heartbeat quickened.

Isaac, before, had always been something steadying to him. If Gabriel wanted the world to shut up he could hold him close, kiss him, and everything other than Isaac would vanish because he couldn't read Isaac's mind when their bare skin touched. It would be just him, just them, together and happy. He could lose his mind in Isaac's magnified silence if he wanted to, then.

"I don't think you're a monster," Isaac offered. "And running isn't *all* I want. I just – it's never been—" He didn't finish. He took Gabriel's head in his hands like it might just be something precious, fingers resting warm against Gabriel's temple.

The power flared. Isaac's body quivered, and he drew a rough breath, but his hand stayed resolute. He did his best to help, in what way he could think of, and Gabriel *ached*, not knowing what to do with that alongside everything else that Isaac had done and said. It was as if Isaac couldn't decide what they were, or what he wanted them to be, any more.

The power tore through him, turning up the volume of Dahlia's grief to deafening. Gabriel's headache swelled.

"Focus on me," Isaac said, like he used to. "On the quiet of not being able to hear me like this. Can you do that?"

137

Gabriel tugged his head away.

Isaac's hand faltered a second time, before he tucked into himself. He moved back, off his knees, onto the armchair.

They weren't what they were before.

Before, Isaac's mind hadn't had those strange silences, those death silences caused by Morphina, when Gabriel wasn't touching him at all. Before, he hadn't thought Isaac hated being around his telepathy – as if that didn't just mean Isaac hated being around *him*. He was a telepath. He didn't get to turn it off any more than Isaac could stop magnifying. Didn't Isaac get that?

Either way, he couldn't bear the silence any more, even if Isaac was trying to help. Especially then. It just brought him back to that day, and the blood on the floor, and then he recoiled from that hurt right into Dahlia's hurt so crushing above him. There was nowhere for his brain to go any more.

The silence stretched between them, crowded by the years spent together and apart.

"I can't stop my worst fears being my worst fears," Gabriel said, finally. He could protect Isaac from his sorrows, his terrors, his waking bad dreams. There was nothing he could do for his own, no matter how much he might want to.

Isaac closed his eyes. "I wasn't suggesting—"

"—so there's no point dwelling on that particular failure." Gabriel kept his voice brisk, cold, all the better to stop Isaac from trying to help him again. If Isaac did that, then Gabriel was going to crumple or cry or scream and he couldn't do any of those things.

"Gabriel—" Isaac began.

"I don't suppose you've come to me with a plan to stop her? Because otherwise I don't want to hear it. Not from you. Not now."

When Morphina attacked, Isaac had just *frozen*. He'd just stood there! Gabriel had needed him. He knew he was supposed to be the one who didn't need anyone, but he'd needed Isaac and Isaac hadn't been there. Isaac had left him to fight alone. Again. What was the point in Isaac offering to help, after everything was said and done, when he could never seem to be there when Gabriel needed him most? He let the fury of that steady him instead. It was better than the pain.

Isaac chewed up his lip, like he always did, gnawing on the bits of himself like his life was a piece of meat too tough for him to digest. He put his glove back on.

"I wanted to see if you were alright. That's all."

"As you can see," Gabriel smiled tightly, "I'm fine."

"You're not *fine*." Isaac eyes were abruptly ablaze. "Lie to them all you want, tell them you're fine, but don't you *dare* try that act on me. I know you better than that."

Gabriel wanted to snarl. Because Isaac didn't get to do that, he didn't get to act like Gabriel was something worth dying to get away from, and then go on to act like he still had any right to the knowing of him. Isaac hadn't wanted to know him, had he? Gabriel had let him, and Isaac's response had been to *die.* Isaac's response had been to find monsters and nightmares instead of saying a word to him, hadn't it? And now Gabriel himself was the *bad guy* in the relationship? Now he was the one they were all scared of? No.

He couldn't breathe.

"You're very comforting, Isaac," he managed blandly.

Gabriel could smell the blood and the smoke all over again, and all he could hear was the animal-cry of Dahlia's despair in his head over and over and over. He watched them vanish in front of him again. And, as always, like one of those sickening fun-house rides that it was all too late to get off from – Isaac's body on the bedroom floor. Red wrists and blank eyes and always silence.

When Isaac's present mind wasn't silence, it was frustration, anger, fear, and the most desperate longing. A thorny sort of love. It wasn't the happiness Gabriel had once worked so hard to foster. He didn't know when or where that had gone. All he'd wanted was for everyone to be happy.

"I just meant..." Isaac rubbed a hand over his face, getting himself under control. "I just meant, it's okay if you're not... okay. You don't have to pretend with me. I know you."

"Do you?" Gabriel snorted. "You know I'm an evil monster and a tyrant, right? You and the dreamweaver. She wanted to save you. From *me*. Why would she think she needed to do that?"

Isaac's brain filled with frustration again, and his jaw clenched. He gave Gabriel a look, as if Gabriel was being somehow deliberately obtuse.

Gabriel stood. He couldn't command Isaac not to leave, but he couldn't be there. Not with him. He headed for the door before he did something he regretted.

Isaac shot to his feet too, blocking Gabriel's way and snatching hold of his wrist.

"I met her before I died," Isaac blurted. "Mona. I mean – Morphina. Whatever you call her. You wanted to know how I knew her. She's the one who faked my death."

Gabriel froze. He'd suspected, but...

It seemed a bloody cheap shot to say it when Gabriel was the one walking away for once. His feet stayed planted on the spot all the same. Despite everything, despite his resolutions, he focused on the feeling of faux leather circling his skin. The warm impression of Isaac's fingers.

"How?" he asked.

Isaac let go. He crossed the room, came back after shakily pouring them both a measure of Gabriel's father's whiskey from a decanter. His father hadn't even liked whiskey, he'd just liked the thought of being the kind of man who drank whiskey from a crystal decanter, just like he loved being the sort of man who played golf, or lived in a house like this, and then was angry when his dreams came true but still felt empty. Isaac offered the glass like an olive branch. When Gabriel took it, Isaac immediately gulped a mouthful of his own drink. He grimaced at the taste – ever the sweet tooth – and didn't sit down again, restless.

They stood facing each other instead across the living room, a breath out of touching distance. Gabriel had never once brought Isaac to his family home, before. He never imagined that he would. It was a stifling place in its sleek grandeur, in what it took to get it. A flick of his telepathy and his parents had always got everything they wanted before it occurred to him that, perhaps, he could say no.

"You didn't see her in my head then, either." Isaac twisted the glass in his hands, looking down. "She's...dreamy, dream-like, I mean. It's like how Dahlia couldn't decide if she was an enchantress or not. It's why you can't always read my mind, though you guessed that already I think. It's why you can't control her if you're not touching me. She – she came to me. In the nights when we were – back then. In my dreams. And in life. She showed me things."

"She *showed* you things? You realise that just because she

141

shows you a nightmare, that doesn't mean it's true?" Gabriel's headache needled at him, and his eyes narrowed. He tried to remind himself to be forgiving. Isaac was scared. He was scared, and blind, and he couldn't be held accountable for being only human, fallible and foolish and frightened. Gabriel didn't feel so forgiving. Abruptly, all of the emotions he'd been desperately struggling to squash burned through his lungs like the whiskey sinking to the pit of his stomach.

"She makes them true," Isaac said. "That's what she does! And I magnify. I would have ruined you – me – everything! I couldn't stay. I don't think you're a monster but I – I would have turned you into one, into something worse, into something you deserved better than being. Providing she didn't kill us first. I already was changing you. It was…it was better that I left."

Morphina could have left instead. Had Isaac even considered that option, then? Of course he hadn't! It was all Isaac and his magnifying, all the time, as if he was the sole thing capable of making people dangerous and not just a tool as much as any other power. If he wasn't furious, Gabriel would have felt so damn sad.

"And when you say she faked your death, just to clarify," Gabriel kept his voice as pleasant as he could. "You mean she saw how much I feared losing you, how it replayed in my head when I went to bed, and you both decided to use it against me. My *saving people hobby*." Okay, pleasant was going well. He gulped hard. "And she just did the same thing again by killing everyone I swore to protect. Except, you know, she actually killed them this time! I mean, I see them dying all the time. I see me failing them all the time. It must have been so *easy* for her."

Isaac didn't meet his stare.

His blood boiled that Isaac wouldn't even meet his eyes. Didn't he deserve that much?

Look at me.

Isaac's head snapped up at the command; his breathing ragged.

"You never talked to me," Gabriel said, and his voice cracked despite his worthless best efforts. "You never even thought to try, did you? You bitch that I always do what I think is best without regard for anyone else, but isn't that what you did?"

If I talked to you, it would have been impossible to leave. I couldn't risk it.

Gabriel stared, even if he was pretty sure Isaac's thought hadn't been deliberately directed at him. He wondered if Isaac even knew the reasons, himself, why it would be impossible.

"You asked me to trust you," he said. "You told me all we had to do was reassure her. I trusted you." And look what had happened.

"I didn't mean for this to happen." Isaac held up his hands. "You're a telepath, you know I didn't. I didn't do any of it to hurt you—"

Gabriel's glass shattered in his hand. Whiskey stained into the rug.

"Oh, you never *mean* to, and yet here we are. How could you not mention this before?" Gabriel took a step closer too. "I don't care what you intended. If you thought for a *second* that this might happen, how could you keep your mouth shut? Again!" His mind snarled and Isaac winced and for once he didn't care at all. He took another step closer and Isaac, even towering over him in height, skittered back like the coward that he was. "You used my worst fears against me to fake

143

your death," Gabriel's voice broke again. "You let my friends die, you tried to *stab* me, and now you tell me that you didn't mean to *hurt* me? I'm sorry. I didn't realise there was a non-hurtful way to stab someone. Stupid me. Well, thank you for coming down to educate me. I feel so much better now."

"Gabriel…"

Gabriel dug his nails into his palms. "You did hurt me. Worse, you hurt them! Do you get that? You think I'm so stupid, so terrible, but do you *get that*?"

"Gabriel—" Isaac's hand pressed to his head, face twisting with pain. His other hand fumbled to set the whiskey glass down.

It didn't help. Gabriel's calm, his control, his everything, was crumbling.

"You made me watch you *die*." Tears sprang to his eyes, despite everything he'd done to hold them back. "You made me spend the last five years of my life thinking that I failed you, failed to save you, all because you couldn't even have a conversation with me!" He laughed, had to. Raspy, breathless, like he'd been punched. "You literally faked your death rather than break up with your boyfriend in person."

How could Gabriel possibly win if his very fears of losing made it certain? How could he possibly be good enough when he was only human? He clearly hadn't been good enough for Isaac. He dashed a livid hand at the tears.

"What exactly did you think I was going to do to you?" Gabriel asked, as he took yet another step closer. The world swayed, exhausted and sickeningly close and hopelessly distant and all tangled up and too quiet. "You say you want to break up and I tell you that you love me, that you don't really mean that? Is that truly what you think of me? It was

144

never impossible for you to leave. *I* was never the monster. Arsehole."

"Says the man who literally *kidnapped* me!"

Fear, still – always that fear and desperation, seeping through the cracks. Isaac's worst fear was what someone would do with his gifts, he knew that. He feared what Gabriel could do with his powers magnified – omniscient, omnipotent, god-like. A flame could only ever be a flame but minds, oh, minds were powerful even before he took the steering wheel.

But it wasn't like Gabriel would ever do anything morally wrong.

Isaac should have known that. Isaac should have known him.

Isaac's eyes screwed half shut, and blood began to trickle from his nose. "Gabriel – stop." *You're hurting me.*

Good!

Isaac shoved his gloves off, ready to lunge. Ready to send them down into the carpet in a desperate grapple of limbs and power and silence.

Stop, Gabriel ordered. *Don't move.*

Isaac's hands froze in place, his body trembling. He glared at Gabriel.

"Good," Gabriel spat again, as an alternative to a punch. It didn't land – at least not on Isaac. Because it wasn't good, nothing about this was good, nothing about this felt good.

"Yeah, fine! Maybe I did think that!" Isaac's voice rose, loud enough that the whole house could probably hear them. "I did think you'd do something like that, and you know what the worst part is?" He smiled that vicious smile again. "I don't think you'd even be aware of doing it because you are

145

so goddamn used to getting your way all the goddamn time! You would have probably put it down to reassuring me and making me feel better."

Gabriel dropped his hold on Isaac's mind, shoving him away almost. Isaac could have talked to him. He could have fought for him, with him. But Isaac had chosen to run. Maybe he would always choose to run, given a choice. And Gabriel would always still fight for him, like an idiot, because loving someone meant fighting for them.

"Not everyone is as pathetic at controlling when they use their powers as you, Isaac. Maybe you'd be better at it if you grew a spine."

Isaac's mouth snapped shut. His expression snapped shut. His mind did anything but; the wave of world-ending terror hit Gabriel like a blow.

"And you want to use me to play god," Isaac managed, coldly. "It's what you've always wanted, enough that she picked it up in your dreams like a siren call. Why the hell do you think we were so scared of you? Why do you think we did what we did? *Archangel.*"

Gabriel's eyes widened.

Isaac walked out.

12 - Gabriel

I t had been five years since Gabriel allowed himself to seriously think about The Archangel Project.

He cleared up the whiskey on the rug, poured himself another glass and swept away any memory of the loud argument from Sanna and Dahlia's heads. They didn't need the added stress. They needed to be a team now, a united front.

Alone, he wasn't enough, he knew that. He was just Gabriel, he was never enough. He could influence someone's mind but only within the proximity of his powers. When he was gone, inevitably, whatever telepathic commands he gave them would fade within a few days or less. He couldn't change anything. Not in any permanent way. Not without being there, all the time.

He followed after Isaac eventually, once he was calmer. Because, maybe, if Isaac knew about The Archangel Project then they could have a proper conversation about it. Maybe he could explain. Maybe Isaac had just misunderstood everything, because Morphina had messed with him all of those years ago. That must be it. It wasn't that Isaac didn't know him, he'd merely been manipulated by an evil villain who used Isaac's worst fears against him. He had to believe that.

All of the superheroes in the stories he and Isaac had bonded over once, adored as children, had their monsters of the week. There was always a new threat to be faced. There was always more evil in the world when evil, so unlike good, seemed to require so little effort.

His hand shook and he abandoned the second whiskey glass on one side, before he headed up the winding dark wood stairs. The alcohol numbed Dahlia's hurts, Sanna's terrors, Isaac's absences. It made the world fuzz and softened the silences. It made the world and his thoughts so clear. Isaac had never been a drinker, he hated anything that made him lose control over himself, but it had always been quite traditional in the De Vere household.

The bedroom, hideous and charred, was full of sunflowers. Sunflowers, daffodils, roses. Anything with a flash of colour to it, anything alive, anything beautiful as if that could somehow replace the ugliness of what had happened. It looked like it could have been abandoned for years, the site of some old ruin.

Dahlia's bedroom door was slammed shut, but he could feel her and Sanna in there still. They were huddled together with a bottle of his mother's fanciest red wine. He hesitated outside, for a moment, his mind reaching out again. He worked subtly so they wouldn't feel his touch smoothing them out, nudging them, shaping them. Someone had to hold it together. He plucked away Dahlia's urge to chase after the dreamweaver, not about to risk that again.

If they drank too much they would sleep, let their guard down. He couldn't allow that either, so he took that urge too. The best he could offer them was a few hours to grieve before they regrouped.

Work done, he headed for his bedroom instead, to the ever-siren call of Isaac's brain that still churned silence, and stared at him. He must have been thinking about that night. By all the silence, Isaac must have spent as much time thinking about that night as Gabriel did. The moonlight caught Isaac just so from the chink in the curtains, and made him seem more like an apparition than ever before. It drew the colour out of him.

Isaac's eyes shone in the darkness, so astonishingly lovely that it almost hurt. He was sitting on the window ledge with Gabriel's headphones slapped over his ears. His old sketchbook was laid open on his lap, his fingers tracing the curve of the comics he'd once drawn. It had started as a joke between them, and it would have been Isaac's final year project if he'd been alive to finish it. It was a story about a telepathic superhero called Archangel, and his friends, some fantastical version of life in bright bold colours and sweeping dark shadows, some update of a superhero comic for a world where people actually had powers.

The university had let him keep the one larger work that Isaac had started, or rather Gabriel had ordered them to hand it over. It was tucked up in the attic because Gabriel couldn't bear to look at it and couldn't bear to hand everything of Isaac away either. That final image, unfinished, had been darker than the rest. Archangel stood in the light of a stained-glass window, haloed by red-gold sunlight, triumphant and powerful beyond measure. The rest of his body, and what Isaac had intended, was lost to history.

Gabriel stared a moment more.

People had such a ceremonial idea of morality. It was

something that they polished off every so often, stuck on their chest like a badge for special occasions, and otherwise ignored once the majority of the world was content to call them a 'good person.' They would make the right noises when something was outrageous, they would share an inclusive video, but they wouldn't take direct action. They wouldn't vote, they wouldn't march in the streets. Politics veered between a dull and controversial conversation starter, more than something that people felt they could change.

Evil never gathered dust. It spread, it festered, and it consistently put in the work. Bad people kept doing bad things, long after the good people called the state of affairs good enough.

Then the 'good' people whined about how evil always won and how the world was going to hell as if they weren't part of it. As if they couldn't fight. As if they weren't allowing it when they saw something awful happen and figured that it wasn't really their problem or that they couldn't do anything about it, so why bother? But hey, they were good people. So it wasn't their fault if evil won. There were simply too many bad people.

Isaac was worse than that. He knew exactly what he could do, he knew he wasn't helpless, but he was so scared of doing something that he preferred to do nothing. Be nothing. Be dead. Just in case he made the wrong choice or backed the wrong person. People like Isaac shouldn't be allowed to just do nothing.

Gabriel took a step forward, reaching his telepathy out.

Isaac.

Isaac jumped, wrenching the headphones off. His head whipped around. The sketchbook clattered to the floor.

150

Gabriel walked over, picking it up and glancing at the page. Isaac had been looking at the strip of Archangel and his sidekick sitting together on a rooftop above the city. Most of the page was two hands, fingers tentatively entwined. He closed the sketchbook gently and set it down on the other end of the windowsill.

"What solution to evil would you propose?" he asked Isaac, seriously. "You never give me alternatives, when you don't like my ideas. You always just say no."

"I don't need to have an idea to know yours is going to go badly."

"No, you having an idea would, I suppose, mean you having an opinion on the future of the world beyond 'everyone gets an opinion.' I should have known better than to expect some commitment on the matter."

Isaac's spine stiffened like an angry cat, even at the obvious bait, before he released a breath.

"We're not doing this now," he said. "You're drunk. You're upset. Are you saying it's true, what she showed me?"

Was Isaac saying he'd done what he did, not being 100% sure?

"Okay." Gabriel held his hands up, in mock surrender, and nodded. "You're right. Asking you to solve all evil in the world is a bit of a tough question. Let's start smaller. Prisons. Any thoughts?"

"What do you mean?"

"Prisons." Gabriel pressed on ruthlessly. "Who are they serving? How much do they really do to lessen the evil and crime in the world?"

Isaac stared at him.

Gabriel continued. "With my telepathy, I could reform in a

second what prisons claim to try and spend a lifetime doing, only to toss their charges back out and straight into a prison pipeline loop that they can't escape from." He snapped his fingers – that was how quick he could do it! "I could be that escape. *We* could be that escape. Why is that so bad?"

"As if," Isaac said, with a twist of fear, "you would stop at that."

"So this is what it's all about? What you and Morphina are both so scared of?"

Gabriel supposed he could understand that people would be scared of the radical changes that The Archangel Project proposed. People were always scared of progress, of what was new. It was both a relief and an agony to find that Isaac had faked his death over something that wasn't bad at all.

There were six days to go before Gabriel lost for good, but mostly likely less because they weren't world record holders of sleeplessness and it felt like the world could glitch from one hour to the next like a bad simulation. Three nights, three days, without sleep. He felt like he might be dreaming, like if Isaac wasn't in his line of sight that he might have been some sleepless, hopeless hallucination that Gabriel had conjured up by sheer force of longing.

"What else could it possibly be?" Isaac asked softly, studying his face. "Us? We weren't the problem. Sometimes I think we were the only thing that wasn't the problem. I told you I'd ruin you. I – if I magnify what my nightmares make you – you must see this has the potential to go badly. Power corrupts. I couldn't do that to you. Look at everything you've accomplished here, without me."

Gabriel swallowed. His heart did something stupid.

The point was...the point was that evil spread. What was

the point of stopping Morphina, of stopping any bad person, if there was simply another bad person the following week? Even rats seemed to learn better than humans in that regard.

The Archangel Project would stop all of that. With Isaac's power, with his own, couldn't he change the world for good? Watch over everyone? And – should they falter, should they turn to cruelty or ill intent, he could stop them. Wipe the very possibility away.

Simple.

At least in theory.

In practice, if Isaac wasn't in his line of sight he might have been some sleepless, hopeless hallucination that Gabriel had conjured up by sheer force of longing. In practice, Isaac died, and the focus required to micromanage a planet was more fitting of his religious namesake than any living creature alive, telepath or not. Even with Isaac, he used to have doubts. The task had seemed enormous, impossible, always missing some puzzle piece that might make it work. He'd tested it out with the campus and even that had been a strain.

And yet, and yet...

Isaac had done it.

When he died, and combined his powers with Morphina's, Isaac had shaped a reality. It hadn't *lasted,* perhaps because Isaac and Morphina had gone separate ways and broke contact. What if they hadn't?

Isaac said Gabriel wanted to play god with him. He'd said that Morphina had showed him something. He had to have seen The Archangel Project which meant that it could *work.* It was everything Isaac feared, it was everything he feared so strongly that he'd died for fearing it. It must be the type of thing that Isaac had nightmares about. And...if it was the type of thing that Isaac had nightmares about...

Well then the dreamweaver could bring nightmares, dreams, to life.

She could make it real. She was the missing piece.

Evil would never get to win again.

"Gabriel." Isaac set the headphones aside, shoulders still tensed. "What you're talking about," he said slowly. "Is mind control, not morality. You're talking about world domination and mind control. Don't commit crime mind control, I'll give you that, but still mind control. It really does make you sound like a comic book villain."

That *was* what it was about. What it was all about. It was what Ari had seen before the nightmares tore her eyes out of her skull and killed her in fear of seeing the possibility of it actually happening. It was what Isaac had run from.

Everything began to slide into place.

"Mind guidance," Gabriel said, before he could stop himself. It would be easier if Isaac was scared, Gabriel could use that. But that would also be unspeakably cruel. If he could just get Isaac on his side, properly on his side, get him to choose to *stay*...well, it wouldn't be as effective as his fear, but it would certainly be better for both parties involved.

"Anyone you don't think good enough gets blanked and changed to fit what you think is the proper way to live," Isaac snapped. "That's what Mona showed me. Some guidance. You know, there are people out there who say love should only be between a man and a woman too and that anything else is just wrong. That people like us need *guidance*. Imagine if some shitty telepath got hold of that."

"That's completely different." Gabriel waved a dismissive hand. He darted forwards, mind aglow, because if Isaac could

154

just *see.* "You literally can't be a telepath and be like that, people like that are blind and bigoted and see the truth of nothing. With you, Isaac…" Gabriel's voice softened with hope. "With you, I can see everything."

No one would ever have to get hurt again. Tonight would never happen again. It wasn't just his opinions, it was good. But he needed Morphina. He needed Isaac, despite his promises. He most certainly couldn't let him go.

"Omniscience. Omnipotence," Isaac said.

"If you like."

"Bloody hell, De Vere." Isaac looked at him as if he was suggesting drowning puppies, rather than salvation, redemption. A slight green tinge spread across his cheeks. "Listen to yourself."

"You would prefer the days of capital punishment?" Gabriel kept his voice gentle, patient. He reminded himself again, painstakingly, that Isaac's ignorance and his stubbornness was not his fault even if it was sometimes very hard to remember that fact. He didn't do it to be bad. As Isaac himself had said, he didn't *mean* to. "You would prefer perhaps, like Morphina, to kill those you disagree with instead of reforming them? Rehabilitating? Or maybe we should leave the rapists and the murderers to it to express their free will. They're only doing what they think is right, you know."

"Don't twist my words!" Isaac drew in a calming breath, curling more and more into himself. His shoulders hunched like a crumbling fortress wall. "I disagree," he continued in a steadier voice, "with prescribing personal views and beliefs universally. You have bias as much as anyone else. We have no way of knowing what is truly right—"

"—I mean, when it comes to murderers and rapists we can

155

probably make pretty good guess—"

"—You're not actually divine!"

"I know, unlike divinity I actually do stuff to try and help. Also unlike you." He said it mostly to flush Isaac's cheeks with anger instead of that pale nausea. To see Isaac's passion flare. Predictably enough, Isaac glared at him. It was the exact proof that Isaac cared more than he allowed himself to, more than he pretended. Still, Gabriel's chest ached. It would have been wonderful to have Isaac on his side. But Isaac, for all of his power and breath-taking possibility, was no telepath. That seemed so clear now! He didn't see the world like Gabriel did. "Don't you think, as humans," Gabriel continued, "we have a moral obligation to help as many we can? To save as many people as we can?"

"I don't think your solution is saving people. I think you'll get a taste of power, and then start micromanaging everything, and then get drunk on power. You obsess."

"I don't do that."

"You did that with me! You couldn't let me be upset about anything. You always had to fix it."

"You say that like it's a bad thing."

"It is a bad thing!" Isaac snapped. "Grief is human. Pain is human. People have a right to feel those things. People have a right to make their own decisions and not just do your version of the greater good. Where would you stop?"

"It's stupid to let the people you love be in pain when you can help them! It's stupid to let murderers exist when you could obliterate them and make them better! You don't know what I'm going to do. She showed you a nightmare of me. I'm your – I *was* your boyfriend, you should know me better than a nightmare."

156

They stared at each other, for a beat.

You're drunk, Gabriel. Isaac's thoughts were pointed, but more pleading than unkind. *Stop it. Please stop talking like this.*

"Just because you don't want hear it, doesn't mean it's not true."

"I know what she showed me was a nightmare," Isaac said. "I know you're more complicated than my worst fears. I told you I don't think you're a monster. But the risk..." Isaac squared his shoulders. "You would take all of the world's pain onto yourself if you thought it would help, I know you would, and it would *break* you." He had the look of a man with a gun to his head. "*I* would break you. You can't be responsible for everything. No one can. No one should be, that's how we get corruption and unchecked bastards in power."

For a second, Gabriel paused. Isaac was being sincere. He wasn't saying it out of cowardice, he genuinely believed that, didn't he? If Isaac Morton had ever taken a stance on anything, it was this.

Isaac continued. "You know I can't go along with this, won't go along with this." His jaw set in a hard line. "And you promised to let me go, so there's no point talking about it. We get rid of Morphina. We're done. That was our deal. Or are you going to prove yourself to be everything that she thinks you are?"

For a second, Gabriel paused, but it was only a second.

The fear radiated off Isaac, stronger than before. It sunk all the way down to his atoms. It was utterly maddening. Wouldn't Isaac be so much better without it? What evolutionary purpose did that kind of modern anxiety serve?

Gabriel could churn up the fear more if he needed to

strengthen the nightmare for Morphina, soothe as he pleased...how different was that to Isaac's normal mental panic anyway? The man was a walking anxiety attack. Maybe it failed before because the dream was confused. He hadn't known what was going on. He knew now.

Gabriel touched Isaac's cheek, just once, and felt him shiver. "I promised, didn't I?"

Promises could be broken. But they did need to get a handle on Morphina, first. With her powers, she might turn his beautiful vision into a terrible one. Wasn't that what nightmares did? Distorted dreams into something awful? But if he could just figure out a way to control her too...he could handle the rest. He'd always handled Isaac's power fine before, hadn't he?

Isaac squeezed his eyes shut. He trembled for a half a moment, teetering like a glass about to tip and shatter. He twisted his hands in his lap.

"And even if you succeeded, even if it all worked perfectly, what happens when you die anyway?" He sounded like he was desperately trying to convince himself. "Everything crumbles. You can't just – you can't just bluntly force morality. It would just be worse when you were gone."

"Perhaps humans wouldn't feel the need to commit crime when society is better."

Isaac snorted, as if the idea was so ridiculous.

"You have a very low opinion of the world," Gabriel said reprovingly.

"And you have a very high opinion for a telepath. The powerful made society for their own ends, and they always will. That's how power works. For someone to be powerful someone else has to be powerless. You know—" Isaac froze, as something occurred to him. "No."

"No?"

"Sanna," Isaac said. "You have a healer. If your healer was magnified..."

Well, there was that, yes. He could likely extend his own life-force significantly, making at least one of Isaac's counterpoints null and void.

Isaac's fear exploded again, rabid and distressed.

"You can't stop planning this. You and your follower *cult!*"

Cult. Ugh. As if Gabriel had been nefariously planning this all along or something! And now Isaac was panicking, practically hyperventilating, questioning everything all over again. That was no good when they had to work together.

Gabriel reached his powers out to Isaac, taking away the memories of the last ten minutes. It was all so easy. It had always been easy.

Isaac blinked at him, dazed.

"What?"

"You nearly fell asleep," Gabriel said. "Are you okay?"

"I—when did you get in here?"

"I came to get my headphones," he lied. "You were half asleep." He batted the concern away idly; it wouldn't do Isaac any good. Their conversation had obviously distressed him, and they obviously weren't going to reach an accord, and he needed Isaac *focused.* He wasn't going to be focused if his mind was making ludicrous and more than a little hurtful jumps about Gabriel being some kind of supervillain just like Morphina said. Gabriel couldn't fight if he was expending too much energy on keeping Isaac from fleeing, again.

"You told me not to sleep," Isaac said.

"I'm tired. Things are shit. Look," Gabriel plucked up the

headphones he'd supposedly come for. "I'm sorry I yelled at you, earlier. It's shit. Today is shit. I thought you were dead for five years, mourned you, now you're alive and…it's a bit much."

"I know," Isaac said. He deflated. "It's all a bit of a mess, this. I – I really didn't think she would hurt them. I *swear* I didn't. I don't want anyone hurt."

"I know, I know." Gabriel sat down on the edge of the bed. "I know you don't. And I suppose I did, you know, kidnap you. It must have been frightening for you."

Isaac snorted, a thin humourless smile twitching a corner of his lips. It was still a smile. He shifted so he was sat on the bed too, so their shoulders brushed, but he didn't quite lean into Gabriel. He wanted to, though, Gabriel could feel it. Before, he would have tugged Isaac closer because of it. He left it alone. Let Isaac see how much harder everything was without a telepath in his head taking care of his every need! Isaac had no idea how lucky he'd been.

Gabriel tugged a hand through his hair and forced himself to focus. *Focus.* His own smile vanished.

"Isaac, I need you tell me everything you can about the night you died, and what she showed you. If she didn't send you the message, and I didn't, we need to find out who did."

"Yeah." Isaac gusted out a breath. "I suppose we do. Deal, right?"

"Deal."

13 - Dahlia

"We should never have stopped here," Dahlia said. She clutched a glass of red wine tight in her hand, and wasn't sure if red or white was better. In red, she saw the blood, the flames, the sacrifice. In white she imagined nothingness, paleness; her sister was not white and yet somehow for all the blackness of mourning clothes it was white that most seemed the colour of death. Endless, leeching, white. "We should have kept running. Far from here. She could have ran forever, she should have…"

"This isn't Gabriel's fault."

"I know it's not. It's *hers*. God, I can't believe for a second I thought she was ordinary. There is something very wrong with her."

Sanna looked troubled. "She's hurting."

Dahlia rolled her eyes. "She can join the damn club."

What right did Morphina's hurting give her to hurt others? Yet, Dahlia could understand it only too well. She could feel the urge planted deep into her bones; not for pain, but for justice. The world didn't want to listen to peace. Peace was easy to ignore, and easier to break. She could see exactly why a woman like that would wrathfully put the world to sleep and it made Dahlia wanted to slap her. Slap Morphina, and

161

smack her own reflection too for the failure, for matching her too close to monsters and for understanding them too well. She'd taken comfort in the thought that Morphina, that Mona as Morton called her, was merely an ordinary woman who had gone astray. But maybe that wasn't comfortable at all. Ordinary made *it all* ordinary; this fearful hatred, this violence, simply another everyday occurrence.

She wiped angrily at the tears on her face. A headache pounded in her skull.

The memory of Felicity's screams dug deeper into her brain. She could smell smoke from the next room, could feel it clinging to her clothing, to every crevice of her. She felt sick. Smoke and ash were all she had left now. There wasn't even a body, merely the memory of one.

Would it have happened if she hadn't tried to make that stupid deal? She didn't know if killing Morphina would have murdered the dreamers too, but there seemed little point to any of it now. They were still dead. She shouldn't have hesitated.

Killing Morphina might have saved them.

"Do you believe her?" Sanna asked. "When she says that she didn't send the message?"

Dahlia wasn't sure she cared right then. She cared that, whether Morphina had started it or not, she could have finished it and saved Felicity and she had chosen not to. She didn't care about why the dreamweaver did what she did, she didn't want to think about it. She just wanted it to stop. She wanted everything to go back to the way that it was before and that was never going to happen.

Sanna continued to look at her, kind, but currently maddeningly removed by the little bubble of peace that Gabriel

162

maintained for her. She should have been howling with rage, crying, she shouldn't have been wanting to talk logically! The last thing Dahlia wanted was logic. She wanted someone to listen and agree when she said that Morphina was a murderous bitch who deserved to die for what she had done. She didn't want solutions, or a placid philosophical discussion.

Dahlia's fists clenched.

"It doesn't matter," she said. "Her reaction wasn't to stop, was it?"

"Somebody could be using her."

"Sanna. I *don't care.*"

"Yes, you do," Sanna said. "If you didn't, you wouldn't be so mad about it."

Dahlia spluttered. "Felicity is *dead.*"

Sanna's frown deepened. She still wanted to fix the world, didn't she? To heal all of its hurts as if the world deserved that. Her and Gabriel both and yet what could they do? Felicity was still dead and it still hurt. It was all that Dahlia could think about. Maybe there were moments when Dahlia wanted to fix the world too, but right then she didn't want to fix anything. She wanted to bring the world crashing to its knees for what it had taken from her.

The silence stretched between them, gaping without understanding.

Dahlia wanted to scream again, but her throat was raw. She wanted to do something more than scream. She wanted…she wanted to get up and hunt down Morphina…she didn't know what she wanted. Every time she thought about it too closely she felt what she wanted grow jumbled and slip away. It was probably Gabriel all over, or maybe the wine.

She wanted to hunt down Morphina. She got to her feet, then stood there, blinking, not entirely sure why she had stood up in the first place.

Sanna head tilted to one side, her expression blank. Without her usual makeup her face seemed oddly stark, more vulnerable than Dahlia was accustomed to. Sanna's standard combination of dark blacks and bruise colours dared anyone to try and harm her for real.

"I don't think it was her who sent the message," Sanna said. "And I know it wasn't Gabriel. That means whoever did set this up is our real enemy. I know you don't want to understand right now, but we don't have time to grieve. I'm sorry."

Dahlia's eyes narrowed.

"We need to understand who did this and why, so that we can stop them. Otherwise more people are going to get hurt." Sanna said it like it was a numbers game, like she hadn't known Felicity or Jack or Lucy. Like them dying wasn't *worse* than somebody else dying.

"You can't understand everyone," Dahlia bit out. "Sometimes they're just psychos, who deserve to be forgotten. Next you're going to tell me to forgive her. That she just needs help."

"Helping someone and forgiving them don't have to be the same thing," Sanna replied quietly. "What she did was unforgivable. But acts are unforgivable, not people. Just like actions are good or bad, not people. Dahlia, I know you're upset, but this isn't like you—"

"Oh, spare me."

"You can hit me if you like," Sanna said, in response to her expression. "If it will make you feel better. I'll heal anyway."

164

"I don't want to hit you," Dahlia snapped. It was mostly true. It was true, at least, that the fact Sanna offered that so simply made something nauseous coil in Dahlia's gut. She looked away and drank more; only to not feel for a moment, or perhaps in the hope that in the next glass the not feeling would finally come. There would be oblivion without thought.

She glanced at Sanna again, and her calm. Gabriel could give her that, perhaps, if she asked. Not feeling might be better.

No. She wasn't going to be tempted by that. She wasn't going to do that to Fliss. Felicity deserved to be grieved; Dahlia wasn't going to lessen her.

There was ash stuck beneath her fingernails. She picked at it.

Dahlia closed her eyes. She finished her glass. She forced herself to concentrate - what use, what time, for grieving. That was what Fliss would say, so however much she hated Sanna for saying it, she wasn't wrong. Her sister wouldn't have sat there drinking in self-indulgent pity when there was work to do. Plants may need time to grow, but life went fast; faster than anyone could expect. The clock was still ticking. Someone else was still due to lose their sister too, if they didn't fix it.

"Gabriel can't track her down because too many people are asleep," Dahlia said. "There are too many silences. Her mind is too much like a dreamer's mind, for him. But there are other ways of finding people. Old ways. She's got to be staying somewhere."

"She could be staying anywhere," Sanna said.

Dahlia jutted her chin up. "Then I'll look anywhere. Everywhere."

Sanna's careful expression hadn't shifted. It was too careful. "And then what?" she asked.

Dahlia knew. She didn't know. Her head *hurt*. Things half remembered, half heard, flittered away from her in fragments. She abandoned the bottle and walked out, into the hallway, down the stairs. She heard Sanna stumble to her feet and follow after her, catching hold of her arm.

"Dahlia."

"I can't just sit here."

"You'll get yourself killed."

Dahlia shrugged, one shouldered. She could hear Gabriel and Isaac's raised voices up the stairs, in the bedroom. She was going to go insane staying in the house with them. She couldn't breathe. Everyone was too busy debating the morals of what they should do instead of doing anything.

"Don't shrug at that," Sanna hissed, some of her placidity crumbling. "You think Fliss would want you getting yourself killed?"

Anger pressed Dahlia's lips thin.

"I think." She wrenched her grip free of Sanna's hand. "That Fliss would have liked to still be alive."

Sanna followed her out of the house and onto the street all the same, pausing only to pluck up their coats. Dahlia didn't know how she could possibly think so calmly about details like coats and gloves and keys to the house, except she knew exactly why.

"You don't have to come with me."

"I'm not leaving you alone," Sanna said. "Besides, even if you don't want to find out what's actually behind this, I do. I'm not letting anyone else get hurt."

Dahlia could imagine Sanna didn't want Gabriel to be killed

166

either; she'd lose her telepathy medicine if that happened. It was an unkind thought, but she didn't think she was wrong.

Dahlia's limbs itched to run. She'd never been much of a runner. She tried to think; it was clearer as she walked away from the house. Her brain felt much more settled, much less like the rug was constantly being yanked away. It was a horrible house, full of false grandeur, like those tacky frames painted to look golden and antique so people could pretend to be more important than they truly were. There was nothing natural about it. There was little natural about the home that she and Felicity had grown up in either. It was a small flat in the city, with a rubbery potted plant that struggled to bring enough oxygen into a place that felt airless on every level. Slammed doors, more raised voices, nowhere to go. Her and Felicity had sat together in their bedroom listening, praying they wouldn't hear footsteps on the stairs. Praying wasn't worth anything except false hope – just like telepathy!

Running. Summoning nature. None of it had been enough to change human nature and there were only so many places in the world that two kids could run.

Sometimes, in her worst moments, Dahlia remembered the spray of blood on her parent's living room wall and thought the end of it was almost a relief. At least it had meant that they were free to go, to move forward, to grow.

If she was Morphina, where would she go? She'd tried to think it before, without success, but she'd never met Morphina then. She knew a little more now, but the exact thought needed time. She started with the first house on the right.

"Hey." Sanna looked ready to reach for her again.

"Go back to the house if you don't like it. I didn't ask you to come."

"Gabriel wouldn't like you breaking into people's houses."

"And his good opinion is all that matters, right?" She stormed through that first building without success. It had lasted longer than some of the others – Gabriel had tried commanding the world to stay awake – but in the end the family next door had fallen too. They all cuddled together in the master bedroom. The baby had fallen first. Babies, despite the popular opinion of young mother's kept awake by screaming, didn't know they weren't allowed to sleep. Dahlia felt another fresh flash of fury, of grief. For Fliss, for all of them.

Sanna didn't go anywhere. Dahlia didn't know what to do with that. Felicity always used to bolt when she was being particularly prickly; her sister hated any reminder of anger. She'd always come back. She'd always go again, but still, she'd always come back. Except she wasn't coming back any more. Dahlia just wished, just longed, just ached, for her sister to come back.

She strode through empty houses for hours, kicking in the windows when she had to, methodically. Nothing. There was only concrete, the occasional stinking corpse, yet more markers of how epically they had failed to save anything. What the hell had they all been playing at thinking that they could be heroes? Why did it have to be them? Felicity should never have been in the line of fire. It should have been someone else's job. Someone trained.

Gabriel would say that thinking someone else should fix the problem was an excuse to do nothing. He'd told them they could change the world. Dahlia didn't want the world to change if it meant Felicity wasn't in it.

The ground rumbled as she walked, splintering in tiny world-shattering earthquakes for one.

Sanna yelped and dodged one, stumbling back to keep her distance. She kept following though, stubbornly. Loyally. Almost like people didn't leave.

Dahlia wanted forests. She wanted trees, and mountains, and sweeping fields. Something big, so she could feel small enough that maybe the hurting turned small too. Something big, so she could feel powerful as it bent to her wishes all the same.

She wanted her sister back.

Forests began to grow out of the pavement.

14 - Isaac

"They're not here," Gabriel said. "Isaac—"

Isaac yanked out of the general sphere of Gabriel's reach before he could touch, drawing his hoodie tighter around himself.

Gabriel frowned at him.

"Dahlia and Sanna aren't here. I can't hear them! Something must have happened! Isaac—"

"You didn't hear them leave?"

Gabriel's frown deepened, tinged with that same sick guilt.

"I was focused on you," he said.

Isaac remembered, again, those eyes like Gabriel's eyes. What had happened after he died, in those three days he couldn't remember? He had asked Gabriel if anything odd had happened but Gabriel had little to say on the topic. He'd been consumed by grief. If anything odd had happened, it seemed just as likely to be caused by a telepath falling to pieces. And he had, Gabriel admitted softly, fallen to pieces.

Gabriel had a not dissimilar look in his eyes now. Isaac knew that look.

"You better not be thinking about ordering me over," Isaac said.

"They could be hurt!"

"Or they could be buying cereal. You need to get better at not knowing everything."

"I'll consider it when my friends haven't *just been murdered.*"

Isaac winced, and had to reluctantly admit that Gabriel might have a point.

Gabriel took the opportunity to grab hold of his wrist.

It was an ungodly hour of morning. Isaac had a murderous headache, growing only more murderous, and the bitter scent of coffee in front of him was starting to make him nauseous, never mind the porridge that Gabriel had shoved in front of him before Isaac even committed to feeling hungry. Cinnamon porridge. It had been his favourite at uni. The world fizzed in and out of focus. He struggled to concentrate.

"You need to save your strength," he said. "This isn't over yet."

"They're wrecking houses." Gabriel sounded appalled. "They're looking for her. How could they be so stupid! They're—" Gabriel faltered. Pain crossed his face, predictably.

Isaac gently took his hand away, steadying Gabriel with gloved hands on his clothed waist instead.

"Easy," he murmured. The kitchen around them was chilly, the first rays of sunshine picking in through the grubby window. He guided Gabriel to sit around the large wooden oak table that was designed to make the place look traditional and homey, but mostly looked out of place among the straight lines and gleaming white counter tops.

Gabriel sagged, closing his eyes for a breath. His free hand massaged at his temple as if he could banish exhaustion by force of will alone.

"We need sleep, or we're not going to win this," Isaac said. He let go of Gabriel once he seemed less likely to crumple to the ground, and rubbed his own bleary eyes. The world still seemed somehow foggy with his tiredness. "Reckon we can fight our way out of the city long enough to catch a nap?"

Gabriel's attention swung back to him.

"I'm not going anywhere until I have my friends back."

"They'll come back here because they're not stupid, and then we get some sleep." Isaac kept his voice measured, because frustration wouldn't help. It would just be another emotion ramming into Gabriel's brain. "I know you feel like that's giving up. But we can get some sleep, regroup, and then go at her on full battery. Come on." He met Gabriel's eyes. "We're a wreck like this, you know it."

Gabriel looked at him for a long moment. Then he nodded.

"I was thinking we should get out too," he admitted, very quietly. He said it like he thought his own body's need for rest was something of a failure, like he should have just been able to keep going based on the mere fact that he was needed. Isaac wouldn't have been surprised if he actually thought that.

He'd never seen Gabriel quite like he was, but he'd seen him burnt-out a few times at university, when he simply kept going and going and pushing himself. The memory of that, of Gabriel's generosity and his obvious concerns for his friends, warred with the other versions of him that Isaac could both imagine and recall. His mind flashed back to those eyes again, to Gabriel's nightmarish face, and he bit his lip.

"There's something I didn't mention," Isaac began, "about the night I died. I told you about the eyes, but what I didn't tell you was—"

A window shattered.

A branch grew into the kitchen with an impossible swiftness, soon scraping the ceiling, curling and trying to break through as the two of them stared.

They both rushed to the front door.

As they watched, in what felt like a matter of minutes, Cambridge didn't look normal any more. It didn't look like the world Isaac knew, at least. Trees sprung impossibly tall and enormous from the ground, making a forest out of a city. Moonlight, barely, twinkled through the canopy and dappled the ground silver. Shadows slicked and shifted in every corner. The air smelled of pine and oak and petrichor.

Isaac felt like he must be dreaming. He didn't know the world could change so fast.

"We should go find them," Gabriel said. He was already reaching for his boots, and for Isaac's skin. "We can't wait here. This is – weird. Dahlia's not strong enough to do this, not when she's not touching you."

Which meant that Mona was the most likely culprit, except this was hardly the death and destruction implied.

With Gabriel's telepathy, magnified, it was easy enough to find Sanna and Dahlia again.

"Holy shit," Sanna breathed, running up to them. "Is she – can she really do that? Just from touching you?" She stared at Isaac. "This is because she touched you, right? You don't know any other dreamweavers?"

Isaac shrugged, uncomfortably, wrapping his arms around himself, unsure. He fiddled with the tips of his gloves and wondered if he should invest in a balaclava. Or possibly a ski mask. He didn't know if it was him or not but he wouldn't have been surprised.

Dahlia's eyes were wide with wonder, face lit like a child's as she feasted on the sight of nature sprawling untamed across the concrete.

"She's got stronger again," Gabriel said. "Maybe all the dreamers are powering her up or something. They must be."

For all of the beauty, it wasn't a comforting thought. But it *was* beautiful. It was fantastic. It was honestly fantastic. If a little eerie, in the darkness and the moonshine. The trees grew gnarled and twisted and old, wild trees, like the type of trees that most English forests had long since forgotten existed, remembered only in fairy tale illustrations.

It should have been dawn. It should have been a new day. It wasn't.

Isaac took a tentative step forward, then another when his soft tread through the undergrowth didn't lead to anything springing out at him like a nightmare Jack-in-a-box.

"Be careful." Gabriel caught his arm. "It's still too quiet. Where there's dreams—"

"—There's nightmares." Yeah, Isaac had figured that out. "I'm trying to focus on the dream part, considering imagining a big, scary monster might make one pop up and I'm pretty sure she's settled on wanting us dead."

Before, Mona had held off out of mercy, or courtesy. Now the lines seemed drawn clear. She wouldn't waste time talking to him a second time. It still nagged at him who had sent that message, if not her. He glanced at Gabriel, wondering if Morphina was lying or if he was. Or if…

That suspicion, that memory, nagged at him. Of a Gabriel with a nightmare's eyes.

Dahlia moved to bend over the nearest tree, examining the red-gold leaves crusting the ground. She stroked her fingers over them, seeming to concentrate for a moment, before she darted forward and pressed her hand to the trunk of the tree. Her face dropped.

174

"They're not real."

"A dream is a dream, brought to life or not," Gabriel said.

"Dreams are manifestations of the mind," Sanna mused. "It's as real as anything else you might want to think up. We're not dreaming." Her brow furrowed. "And we're still going to be dead all the same if a nightmare gets us. According to statistics of common nightmares, at least it probably won't be wolves, or bears. Not in the UK anyway. Apparently snakes or—"

"—Don't say spiders," Dahlia muttered.

"I honestly don't know why you hate spiders so much. You're like the goddess of nature."

"*Plants.* Spiders aren't plants."

"They're important parts of the ecosystem," Sanna began.

"This is your dream isn't it?" Isaac's voice was quiet.

Dahlia's gaze shot to him. She was barely visible in the gloom, even her flower tattoos seeming duller. Scrubbed away by everything that had happened. She looked back to the tree beneath her hands, head bowed, her expression hidden beneath the black waterfall of her hair.

"I...I always hated cities. For what they were. Smoke and concrete. Dead. She's made the trees *dead*." Dahlia's jaw clenched. "She's taunting us. Me."

But they weren't dead trees, just dream trees. Illusions more than dead things. It may have been an apology, for Felicity, but he suspected Dahlia wouldn't want to hear that. An apology, a forest, wouldn't bring her sister back.

Gabriel squeezed his shoulder at the thought.

"We'll help her," he promised, his voice low velvet by Isaac's ear.

Isaac managed a queasy, guilty smile.

Surely a nightmare Gabriel couldn't be behind everything? Why would any version of Gabriel ever want to put the world to sleep or get people killed? It didn't make sense. He was missing something. That nightmare, if his memory was even accurate, had been five years ago. Why now, even if that was the case?

"For now," Gabriel said, "let's get out of here." He looked to Dahlia and Sanna. "I think we all agree we need sleep. Which means we need to get far away from her."

Sanna and Isaac murmured their agreements. Dahlia rounded on Gabriel, bristling.

"I'm not just leaving Fliss with her. We need to get their bodies back. Give them a proper burial before we do anything else." She searched out Gabriel's eyes. "You agree, don't you?"

Isaac watched Gabriel waver, wobble. Dahlia's emotions were strong, and Gabriel's defences were weak. He'd seen it happen before, when Gabriel could get caught up in what other people wanted too closely. Gabriel's own guilt wouldn't help.

Isaac stepped between them, even if that wouldn't help. It at least made Gabriel look away, to look at him instead. He seemed dazed.

"We're getting some sleep," Isaac said. "We'll find the bodies after. They wouldn't want you to get hurt trying."

"Nobody put you in charge," Dahlia snapped at him. "You don't even know them. I'm not going anywhere without my sister."

"You can't save your sister half dead."

Dahlia's eyes flashed. "Clearly none of you could save her anyway!"

Gabriel winced at that, and Isaac knew he'd lost.

"We'll get the bodies first, then go," Gabriel said. "Give them a proper funeral. All three of them."

Isaac stared at Gabriel all the same, given that Gabriel had already agreed earlier that sleep was clearly the best plan, though perhaps he should not have been surprised.

"I'm so tired," Isaac said flatly, "I can barely see straight. You have been awake longer than me. If she has them, then they are pretty obviously bait. We cannot afford to bite at bait right now. There is more at stake than them, they're already dead. We're not."

Dahlia made a furious noise at his words.

Gabriel looked at him, lost again. He was swaying on the spot. Barely able to stand. Couldn't Dahlia see that?

They would have to go past the nightmares which bordered the city to escape. If they were too exhausted to win that fight...well, it wouldn't much matter if they had bodies with them or not.

Isaac sighed and peered through the treeline instead of arguing further, trying to get a sense of the streets through the labyrinth of woods twisting them in every direction. At least he could still see the roads, the pavement, the buildings beneath the growing moss and ivy. He suspected that may not last, as the shadows stirred and the trees grew and grew.

He exchanged a look with Sanna, desperately. He couldn't exactly force any of them into a car after all. He wasn't the telepath.

Sanna moved to take Gabriel's hand, leading him back towards the house. They needed the car regardless.

"It's so quiet here," Gabriel said, peering around himself.

"Gabriel," Dahlia insisted. "You still agree with me, don't you?"

"Sure he does," Sanna said cheerily. "We're just picking up the car. It will make it faster to find them. I can drive."

"Right." Dahlia melted with relief.

Isaac felt a rush of gratitude as Sanna met his gaze, mouthing something along the lines of 'I've got this'.

"Is everyone asleep now?" Sanna asked Gabriel.

"The dream is everywhere. It's like being blinded," Gabriel replied. "The world feels more like a dream than it normally does, all foggy. There are - there are people." He frowned. "They're muffled."

The sooner all of it ended, the better. If the nightmares got too strong…Isaac glanced at Gabriel. Mona would probably try and flee from them. She wouldn't want to get too close. It would be easier for her to kill them from a distance, less risky. She could simply send nightmares to overwhelm them.

They headed back through the woods, the bickering puttering out as the disquiet grew and they turned off Station Road. They weren't supposed to be at Station Road. The woods made it difficult to navigate.

"Dahlia," Gabriel said. "Can you do something about these trees?"

"That would give away our position," Isaac pointed out. Another confrontation with Mona wouldn't go well right then. "We don't want that."

"No, we want to waste more time, don't we?" Dahlia muttered.

"Getting some sleep is not wasting time!"

As they moved the air grew close and claustrophobic, the trees wedging tighter and tighter together. Less light managed to find its way through the leaves. Isaac knew there should still be street signs, shop fronts, but they were

178

increasingly difficult to discern among the dark murky greens that swallowed Cambridge up.

"The shadows are moving," Sanna said to him, so quiet that Isaac almost didn't hear her. Her voice had grown tight. "Do you think…"

One second, Dahlia was there, the next she was gone.

Sanna yelped. They drew tight together into a clump in an instant, back to back, hearts hammering. They scoured the trees for any sign of her.

She couldn't have disappeared. Even a nightmare couldn't make someone actually disappear, right? Isaac honestly didn't know what the extent of Mona's abilities was. Even Gabriel, in all of his power, could only work with a mind that was already there. He didn't summon into the world creatures that had only existed in thought. Reality had limits which dreaming did not.

Sanna vanished next, into the darkness, in a blur of movement.

It clicked, then, what might be able to move that fast. *Who.*

He and Gabriel circled, back to back. He was amazed that they hadn't had their necks snapped already.

Ice crept up along the branches and adorned the under-growth with frost. Somewhere else, in the other direction, Isaac could smell smoke.

"Isaac." Gabriel's voice was rough with fear. "Now would be a great time to take your gloves off."

Against a nightmare, without Dahlia, without Sanna, they were going to need all of the help they could get.

15 - Dahlia

Dahlia sped through the trees. The cool sting of the wind whipped her face and she buried her head instinctively into a familiar neck, reaching bewildered for the feeling of pine trees beyond the scent of them. But it was just the scent. Gone.

She looked up to see her sister's face. Doll-like, lacking animation, empty. Gone.

She could smell smoke in her nostrils.

The memory smacked her, crippled her.

Gone.

The speed was familiar and nauseating; it greyed her vision it was so fast. She may have passed out. She must have passed out. She fell into the scent of pine and rotting flesh.

When she came to, it was in a cathedral. Or, maybe, a particularly grand church. She always imagined that should the world end, it would do so in a pub, or a petrol station, or maybe an airport. One of those places that felt temporary and strangely unchanging. One of those places without nature, except perhaps the occasional wilting potted plant that deserved so much better. A cathedral seemed similarly endless, if somewhat more ostentatious and pretentious a choice.

The floor was cool and slightly dusty beneath her cheek, worn by years of feet. She closed her eyes against the flickering light to let her head settle.

"Well," she muttered, "this is overly dramatic."

She was hit, first, with unease. With powerlessness.

Morphina.

Felicity.

Dahlia abruptly twisted onto her knees and vomited coffee inches away from Morphina's boots, head not settled at all. She wished she'd had the presence of mind to make sure it hit the dreamweaver, because that was about as much defiance as she could manage in that particular second. She could still remember the feeling of ice cold – *dead, dead, dead* – arms around her. Her sister's dead arms around her.

"Hey, hey, you're alright." Sanna rubbed her back. She was warm, grounding, and Dahlia turned to her like a flower towards sunlight. "Breathe." Sanna kissed the top of her head. "You're okay, breathe. I've got you."

Dahlia gasped choked breaths. She wiped her eyes furiously.

"I wasn't actually going to kill her," Morphina said. Her voice sounded distant, absent. "She was already sleeping; she wouldn't have hurt anyone there." Her tone shifted wistful. "She has such magnificent dreams."

It was like getting kicked in the stomach.

"Yeah, well, *funny thing*," Dahlia spat, "you did actually kill her." Intention changed nothing. Felicity would never dream anything again. Dahlia recoiled, limbs trembling, and struggled to her feet. She snatched for thorns that once again refused to come and could have howled for it. It was like having a limb ripped away. Her jaw clenched and she glared

181

at the woman sprawled on a pew a few metres away from them. "And you best hope I don't get my powers back around you, or I'll actually kill you."

"Lia," Sanna hissed in her ear. Her grip tightened, hauling Dahlia back. "Don't antagonise her."

Morphina sighed heavily, as if a sigh could mean 'again with the pointless threats?' Any pity, any grief, vanished from her face.

"He shouldn't have promised he could protect you," she said. "He shouldn't have made you fight for him – you were never supposed to be a part of this."

"For him?" Dahlia's voice broke. "This was never for *Gabriel.*"

Felicity slouched on another pew, eyes vacant, limbs stiff and useless like a marionette which had its strings cut and now spooled broken where it lay.

This was because it was wrong. Because she was wrong. This was, always, for Felicity.

"You wouldn't know," Morphina said. "He could have planted any number of telepathic commands in your head and you would be none the wiser if he told you not to be."

"I would know," Dahlia snapped. "Because if Gabriel was controlling me he wouldn't let me feel like *this.*"

Any remaining coffee threatened to climb out of her throat again. Her attention flicked around the cathedral. There were dreamers all over, or she assumed they must be dreamers. She hoped they were sleeping and not dead. They drooped across most of the surfaces, sitting or standing blankly, like people dropped somewhere with no hope and only waiting to do. Listless. Waiting to be sprung to life like the puppets they'd become. Just like her sister.

Morphina followed her gaze, arms folded across her chest. "They're not dead. They're dreams."

Dahlia absolutely refused to ask questions. She didn't want to listen to Morphina justify it, she didn't want to indulge whatever mad fantasies she had with an ear. She turned her head away, not wanting to get caught in so much as curiosity, but her gaze inevitably snagged on her sister again. Her throat crumpled. Because she wasn't a dream, she was a nightmare, and she wasn't her sister any more. She was gone. In all the ways that mattered, she was gone.

And it was Morphina's fault.

The grief was sharp, daggered, ready to fly out of her control.

"I-" Morphina rose and took an uncertain step forward, before stopping. She cleared her throat. "I don't want to put the world to sleep, I want to put the world out of his reach. Whatever telepathy he has used on you will wear off in around three days. Once you are clear of mind—"

"I don't want to be clear of mind!" Sanna's voice whipped out with an edge of panic. "And him being a telepath does *not* mean that we cannot make our own decisions." Her fist clenched before she released a calming breath, flexing her fingers. "Look." Her voice was still wobbly. "I know you're hurting, I know you're scared. I can still feel it despite – despite everything." She pressed a hand on Dahlia's shoulder as she stood up too, stepping forward in turn, standing between them. "But you said it yourself, you didn't write the letter to get the magnifier here. And Gabriel – he would never have put the world to sleep. As you implied, putting the world to sleep means putting it out of his reach. He would never do that."

183

Morphina stared between them.

"We need to work together," Sanna said. "If you weren't all so emotional you would see that. Can you think of anyone else who would benefit from all this?"

A shard of unmistakable fear sliced Morphina's face, but she said nothing. Not for a long moment.

"It doesn't matter," the dreamweaver said. "They will be dead soon enough. Problem solved."

It hit Dahlia like a bucket of ice water. How had she not even thought of it before? Gabriel wasn't there. Nor was Morton. Which meant...no. No.

"No," Sanna said it aloud. "No, you can't."

What could a telepath, even magnified, do against a nightmare? They didn't have minds to manipulate, and Gabriel would never raise a hand against his own. Even if his own were dead dreams. He was probably rotting on the forest floor already, dying of some slow and impossible poison.And Isaac...what could he do? He was a coward. He froze in a fight. He hated Gabriel. He'd probably abandon him first chance!

Dahlia's brain buzzed. Her world bottomed out beneath her, nothing left. She stared at Morphina, unable to speak for the rage clouding her lungs, her throat, beneath her tongue. If she opened her mouth to speak she would scream or cry and never stop doing either, she was sure of it.

Sanna marched forwards, her face resolving into something steely. She looked ready to tear Morphina limb to limb, anything to keep a hold of her cocktail of telepathy, or maybe just to save him.

"Dahlia," she yelled. "Go!"

Dahlia bolted as Sanna threw herself forward at Morphina,

all six foot of muscle and studded clothing. Invulnerable, as ever, except for the fact that she really wasn't.

Dahlia sprinted straight into Felicity's chest.

Her heart rocketed and she reached again for thorns, for vines, and wished right then that she could spit poison and wished she didn't have to do any of those things. Could she, even, against Fliss? She didn't know how people did this. All she wanted was to crumble, to pretend that Felicity's eyes were cold because of winter, not because of this, never because of this.

She shoved Felicity's chest and dodged for the door again. She was blocked, again, before she'd even taken a step. Her vines wouldn't come, her thorns wouldn't come, nothing would come and all she could look at was dark, empty eyes like ink that were nothing like her sister's had been. The seeds felt dead in her fingers.

A scream ripped through the room.

Dahlia struggled against the unrelenting hold on her shoulder, forced to face Morphina again.

Sanna lay on the floor, her body twitching. Her powers worked frantically to keep up with the chair leg impaled in her chest. Her breath came awful, spasming, before sounds ceased to form as she only gasped and scrabbled at the wood.

Morphina placed her hand on top to prevent Sanna from ripping the wood out.

Dahlia had already puked up everything in her stomach.

"An age-old trick for things that just won't die." The chill around Morphina, the shadows in her eyes, slicking through her clothes, creeping along the floor, were more prominent than ever. "Shouldn't be so reckless, sometimes death is kindness. You should know that. You know life. Don't you

just wish—" she twisted the makeshift-stake as Sanna heaved
– "you could just *die*? I know in dreaming you count the ways.
I've heard them. Do you want me to make it true?"

Dahlia's knees dissolved beneath her.

"Stop it." It barely came out at first. "Stop it! You said you
didn't want to hurt us!"

Morphina glanced over at her, her dark gaze distant and
assessing, like she didn't even consider Dahlia a real thing
right then. Her stare was the same ink black now as Felicity's
was, hollow and filled with possibility all at once.

"Please." The word tasted like bile in Dahlia's mouth. "Stop
it. I – I won't try and run."

"Dahlia, don't," Sanna spat. "We can't just leave him to die.
After everything—"

"Please," Dahlia said, staying focused on Morphina as best
as she could. "You already killed my sister. I won't run, you
don't need to kill her too."

Sanna's chest kept healing and breaking again, trying
to form even around the chair leg gutted in her rib cage.
Suspended in life, unable to move past it, barely able to pass
out when each second was a cycle of breaking and getting
better all over again.

She couldn't bear it. She didn't know how Sanna did. She
tugged again at Felicity's unyielding hold on her.

"She's not going to stop trying to help him," Morphina said.
"I thought maybe—" the dreamweaver shook her head. "Tell
me your friend won't attack me the second she can."

Dahlia didn't know how to promise that. She could try, but
Morphina wasn't wrong – if Gabriel's life was on the line,
Sanna would defend it for so long as she had breath. Panic
clouded her vision, tunnelling, because she couldn't watch

186

Morphina *murder* another of her friends, she couldn't. She had to do *something*.

"You know," an icy voice came. "This is a prime example of free will being overrated. People make such monstrously wrong choices when left to their own devices. I suspect if you were the one being tortured you'd agree it was better the person doing it didn't get the choice to hurt you."

For a second, the whole world stopped. Dahlia sagged in relief. Her heart felt ready to give. Her knees threatened to buckle.

Gabriel.

She had never been so happy to see anyone in her entire life. This must be why people believed in superheroes – for a second, it felt like everything was going to be okay.

He stood in the doorway, attention fixed on Morphina, His magnifier was nowhere in sight but, god, he seemed radiant. Sure, powerful, as ready as ever to make everything right in the world. *Good.* Not perfect, no, but there. Ready to fight her corner.

All of the colour drained from Morphina's face.

"No," she whispered. "Not again. Not you."

Morphina stumbled back away from Sanna and Dahlia rushed over, wrenching the chair leg away with shaking hands. She sent it clattering left, coming to a stop at Felicity's feet.

She didn't know the precise moment her sister had let go, but she knew for sure that the Felicity she knew would never have stood and watched someone in pain. She may not have fought always, as much as Dahlia sometimes wished she'd stand and fight, but she would never have just watched. She would have got them out of there. Her sister would have

187

helped.

Gone.

This was not life.

The anger in Dahlia's chest grew some more, sparking up like a forest fire might.

Sanna gasped in pain, curling in on herself even as her body began to heal. The colour flooded back to her face, and despite the protective hedgehog armour of spikes and studs that she surrounded herself, despite the life that clung to her so steadily, she seemed smaller than ever. Crumpled. Tears streaked black down her cheeks.

Morphina had done this.

Dahlia pressed her lips into Sanna's hair, breathing in the scent of apple shampoo and life. It chased away false pines and rotting death, the powdery aftertaste of ash. She rubbed circles in Sanna's back, small and insubstantial.

"She's okay," she told Gabriel, half trying to convince herself. Sanna was always okay. She had to be okay.

Gabriel moved to stand protectively in front of them. Tall, absolute.

For a moment, Morphina remained frozen where she'd staggered. There was a stark horror on her face, a kind of world ending dread. Then she dashed for the door.

All of the dreamers surged to attack.

16 - Gabriel

S moke and frost coiled through the air, sweet among the pine.

Isaac was warm against his back, fingers squeezing warm against his own too. The power wasn't enough. Even with Isaac on his side, Gabriel wasn't going to win.

His heart jumped into his throat, sick and thudding.

There were minds glinting in the city like drops of light, but they were far away and felt half buried in silt like shiny pearls discarded on the bottom of an ocean. He soothed over their minds either way, couldn't help it; anything for some semblance more than the uncanny silence of the dreams, anything to help. When he saw Jack's and Lucy's faces, there were no thoughts behind them. There was nothing for him to grab.

He raced through his options. He couldn't command a mind that wasn't there and the minds of the waking would not reach them in time, they huddled away in wonder and fear and Gabriel smudged away the fear and thought it might be dangerous to leave only the wonder.

He was powerless.

He remembered the last time he'd been powerless. He remembered Isaac's blood on the floor. He *never* wanted to be powerless again.

"Isaac." He kept his voice low. "I'll cover you – go."

Isaac laughed. It wasn't a particularly amused laugh, flat and panicked.

"Yeah. Right," he replied. "I'm not leaving you to die. How much of a coward do you actually think I am?"

Gabriel swallowed, at that. It was nice. It was so nice to hear that, arguments aside, they weren't so broken from what they used to be…but it also wasn't the time. This would be the one time he'd beg Isaac not to be brave.

He squeezed Isaac's hand and then slipped free.

Isaac's mind was there instantly, close and frightened. Grim. Overcrowded. The most beautiful thing he'd ever heard, so steadying in the pit of silence that threatened to swallow him whole.

Gabriel's chest ached.

Lucy's head tilted, her young face seeming older in the half shadow of Jack's flickering flames. She stared at Gabriel mournfully, accusingly. He hadn't saved them.

Get out of here, Isaac. Gabriel ordered. *Now. Run.*

He should have saved them. But maybe he could still save Isaac.

The first bolt of fire erupted from Jack's hands. The flames spread quickly along the trees. One strike, two, three - the world lit up in red.

Isaac seized his hand tight and ran.

"You bastard," he snarled.

Gabriel didn't have the room to reply. He narrowly dodged a bolt of ice slicing through the air like a blade. A spit of poison blackened the bark of a tree near his head. He scrambled to put himself behind Isaac, at least, or in front of

190

him – in some way between Isaac and danger. There was no way to do that when they were surrounded on every side.

He should have watched his loopholes; he should have explicitly commanded Isaac to leave him. Isaac had got rather good at doing what he wanted despite telepathy, hadn't he?

The undergrowth crashed behind them. He pushed his legs harder to keep up with Isaac's rabbit-quick tearing through the trees.

As awful dreams did, being chased made it abruptly difficult to run. The air had turned into something soupy and impenetrable. The roots of the trees snatched and grabbed and twisted and clawed at their feet and limbs like hungry hands. One root snaked around his ankle.

Gabriel stumbled and hit the ground hard. The air knocked out of his lungs.

Isaac yelped and went down too, stubbornly refusing to release his hand.

Gabriel rolled on instinct, drawing Isaac to his chest to cover him. He wasn't sure if the air around him was too blisteringly hot in the smoke or simply too blisteringly cold. Isaac's breath was quick and panting against his throat, matching the roar of his own pulse.

The power in him lit up and up and up until he felt he could hear the world and –

Sanna screamed in agony and Dahlia pleaded fearhorrorguilth elplessness

Jack raised a hand their direction, the flames around him rising in a great hiss of heat and—

A knife hurtled straight into Jack's chest.

Even in a dream state, even dead, Jack seemed to look oddly surprised, oddly wounded, before he crumpled.

Gabriel's stomach dropped out. His gaze snapped down to Isaac as he drew another knife from a sheath and –

He dropped Isaac as if he'd been scalded, scrambling back. *No.*

Isaac's hand froze, quivering as it struggled against Gabriel's mental grip. *Are you serious?*

Don't kill them.

They're already dead! Isaac shot him a look, as venomous as Viper's tricks, before grabbing his hand with the one Gabriel hadn't mentally pinned.

For a terrible second, Gabriel expected another knife to hurtle through the air and embed into his friends' bodies with a sickening squelch.

Ice sliced through the air and caught Isaac's side instead.

Isaac's other knife clattered to the floor. His hand flew stunned to his abdomen. His pain exploded in Gabriel's head strong enough to make Gabriel cry out and cringe in turn, his own hands reaching to assess some phantom hurt before he caught himself. Focus.

Gabriel looked between Isaac and Jack – Jack, stumbling up again, all guts and gore and silence. Impossible. Obscene.

The roots of the trees moved to bind Isaac's knife-throwing wrist.

Gabriel seized the scruff of Isaac's neck, hauling him up from the ground. He stamped on the vine. He wrenched hold of the stinging cold of Isaac's shock and tossed it away.

The ground beneath them turned into something slippery and icier than ever.

It was Gabriel's turn to drag them forward, stumbling and graceless. They found the road. The concrete smacked beneath their feet, under the mass of undergrowth – tree roots, broken glass, fallen leaves the colour of rust. Heat burned close to his face and ice close to his hip. He lost track of it.

There had to be some way to get rid of the nightmares, to stop them. A dreamer could wake up, but this wasn't dreaming any more. This was a dream come to life; an impossible thing, bound only by its own internal logic.

He grasped for minds that wouldn't come. The fear left him dizzy. He couldn't breathe.

The trees, mercifully, also blocked a clear shot as they twisted and ran, hands soon untangling again to go faster, to make less of a target.

Terror lashed through Isaac's mind, trailing after him like a ribbon of blood.

The dreamers chased.

In the corners of Gabriel's vision, his friends looked the same as when they'd been alive. They had the same mannerisms, the same expressions, everything the same as if they'd been chasing down a villain on the job. Except for the fact that Gabriel was their villain. Except for the fact that there were no minds there. Which meant...which meant...there had to be a way to turn that to his advantage, somehow. Something that wasn't a knife in Jack's chest. Which meant they may be predictable? They would do as they did when they were alive, or what Morphina expected them to do, or what *he* expected them to do? They were still dream-creatures, insubstantial, stuck in their paths like ghosts.

Fire buried into the tree in front of them, cracking it like dry kindling. They both sprang back, stumbling, lurching into different directions, flinching from the heat.

Isaac reached for a knife, twisted—

No!

Isaac's mind thrashed against the sudden cup of Gabriel's telepathy. Viper crashed into him a moment later in the shock of sudden stillness.

Isaac slammed his knee up into her, shoving her away.

"They're already dead!" he roared. "Your friends are dead!"

It was true. Gabriel knew it was true. It didn't make it easier. The silence of their minds didn't make it easier. His mind recoiled from chopping them up.

Viper spat, a glob of poison searing through Isaac's jeans.

Isaac kicked at her, feet colliding with Viper's ribs with an ugly snap.

Isaac was going to die again.

He didn't know how to help.

Isaac was going to die again.

He dropped his mental grip on Isaac's knife-hand and the next second it slashed silver and deadly through the air.

Gabriel didn't shut his eyes. It seemed an insult. It hurt to watch.

Isaac didn't pause before pouncing into Jack next, stifling a bolt of fire with his hand. His eyes glinted with ferocity in the forest light and the ball of flame died as he pressed against it.

Powers didn't work on Isaac while he was magnifying.

Of course, powers didn't work on Isaac while he was magnifying them.

The knife slashed across Jack's throat. Violent, awful, without hesitation. Isaac moved with a lithe and lethal grace.

Neither of the dreams made a sound, dying. They were dead already. They crumpled like someone had cut their strings, shrunken somehow as they fell to the forest floor.

Even in a dream, Gabriel supposed, one expected a zombie to die when he was decapitated.

The fire flickered out like nothing, leaving behind only blackened roots and dead things and the pain in Gabriel's side. The frost stayed.

Isaac had just driven a blade into two people with an expert and horrifying precision.

Gabriel's stomach heaved.

They're dead. Isaac thought. *I can't hurt them.*

Understanding, sick and unwanted, rushed through Gabriel. He couldn't stop it when Isaac's mind was so close and already so entwined with his own. He couldn't pull back fast enough even if he didn't want to see.

Isaac knelt to wipe his blade on a leaf, eyes fixed on the smaller figure slower to chase their longer legs.

Alec Mandel.

Just a nightmare. Isaac's mind repeated the mantra, so resolute that it felt more like panic. Clinging for hope. *It's just a bad dream.*

The young boy looked hopelessly small and fragile, especially compared to Isaac in all of his height. Frost trailed him, thickening in the air around them.

Isaac's hand shook; he was Goliath before David, knowing the end to come.

Gabriel's legs carried him forward, leaden.

"You were a kid," he said. "Just a kid. It wasn't your fault. It was a tragedy, and it wasn't your fault."

He made Isaac believe it. He forced him to believe it, drove it into his psyche, for that moment at least. For once, he didn't hold back. He didn't try and be subtle.

Isaac's mind caved beneath his power. Gabriel could have

195

told him anything and he would have believed it, hammered a thought in like a nail into a coffin. He could have told Isaac all the ways to fall in love with him again – part of him wanted to. He wanted to ask for all the truths, and all the co-ordinates for all of the ways that they'd somehow ended up going wrong.

It's not your fault.

Isaac's shoulders relaxed and the nightmare of Alec Mandel, shivering and vicious, vanished in drips.

"You're in my head," Isaac said, still staring at the spot where Mandel had been.

"I'm going to bury my friends," Gabriel replied softly. "You should bury your ghosts too."

Their breathing sounded heavy and ragged in the silence of the forest. Gabriel's shoes squelched and sucked into the mud and mulch.

Gabriel's mind wavered back to a small bedroom, and screeching machines, and tears and the most dreadful quiet. He took a step towards Viper's body, the guilt stuck in every particle of him. Could he even bury his friends in this fake, dream forest? There was no real soil. No proper burial. When Morphina was gone the forest would be concrete pavement, and his friends just bodies left on the road like garbage. Could he use fire, perhaps? A burial for kings? Jack would want a fire.

Viper twitched.

"Oh shit," Isaac whispered. He seized Gabriel's arm and hauled him back.

Gabriel's tired mental hold on Isaac's mind wobbled as he watched Viper and Pyrate stagger to their feet, congealing and hideous and empty. Relentless.

His stomach went cold. Was there no stopping them? No rest for them? No peace?

He shoved Isaac behind him, backing up. He couldn't watch him die again, he couldn't. Blood on the bedroom floor, cold skin, and terror rising like puke when he wouldn't wake however much Gabriel reached for his mind. His mind spun back to it, always, always, always.

"Run," he rasped. "Go. Please."

"*You* run," Isaac returned, "for once in your goddamn life. I've got a better chance at holding them off then you do."

Gabriel's mind stretched far and far and farther still, past blurry exhaustion, until their minds were like city lights from an aeroplane.

Fire swelled between Pyrate's hands.

At least Dahlia wasn't frightened any more.

Gabriel wouldn't close his eyes, he promised himself that. He wrenched his thoughts away from the world, from the sky, from the crying in the dark and turned his face so that Isaac would at least be the last thing he saw. Stupid, stubborn, wonderful Isaac.

"I'm glad I got to see you again, no matter what." Foolish blurting; foolish goodbyes. "I love you."

"Gabriel."

The fire never came. The poison never came.

"They're gone," Isaac said.

17 - Gabriel

They walked out of the forest and away from Morphina's immediate sphere of influence in silence, crumpling to sit just outside of it. Central Cambridge had been swallowed.

It didn't make sense that Morphina would let them go when she could have killed him.

Gabriel didn't release his vice grip, his own mantra, until he was certain Alec wouldn't appear to life the second that Isaac's guilt did. Even if the other dreams had gone, why tempt fate? Still, it was something to think about.

Isaac's nightmare had vanished when Isaac's fear did. Hadn't that happened before?

Gabriel didn't know how to stop being scared on his own. He thought he might be too tired for it, or maybe the fear was too big. He lay back on the concrete, the sky spinning grey and endless above him. His head throbbed. He closed his eyes.

Isaac swore quietly under his breath.

Gabriel drew his eyes open again and rolled painfully on his side. His limbs felt like tar.

Isaac sat on the curb, with his head buried in trembling hands.

Let me see your side, you're hurt.

Isaac shot him a look, but peeled up his shirt with only a grimace rather than a protest.

Gabriel stared. Beneath the dozen protective layers of clothing that Isaac wore each day, he'd only glimpsed the smallest slithers of bare skin since their re-acquaintance. Even when they had been together, skin had been a rare luxury at first. Isaac's face. Occasionally the curve of his wrist. A tantalising stretch of hip or stomach. They'd worked up to more over the years. Gabriel hadn't seen the mess of healed and healing scars beneath Isaac's shirt before, of battles fought, but they hadn't been there the last time he'd seen Isaac without any clothes.

He wondered if Isaac had killed anyone else, anyone who wasn't a dream. Even if they hadn't actually died, Isaac's intentions had been more than clear. His capabilities. The practice. Where had he learned to fight like that? He didn't think the Isaac he first met could have hurled a knife at anyone, even a nightmare. He didn't think the Isaac he first met could have smashed his knee into someone's ribs.

But hadn't he tried to run at the cottage?

Isaac always tried to run first. Always.

Except the one time that Gabriel told him to go. To abandon him.

Isaac was hurting and Gabriel wiped his mind clean of the pain again. He nudged at Isaac's head with a sick curiosity but he wasn't even thinking about the scars, just the livid patch of skin red from cold and scraped raw by the ice rushing past him. Sanna would be able to fix it in a heartbeat. It was lucky. It wasn't as bad as it could have been. They had to find Sanna. Sanna could always fix everything. Except Sanna couldn't touch Isaac and heal him at the same time. Gabriel's stomach twisted.

"It's okay," Isaac told him. "I'm okay. Save your strength." He sounded more gentle with Gabriel's telepathy than he had been in a while.

"I'm sorry." It still felt, to Gabriel, like he couldn't do enough to help. He sank his fingers into his hair, struggling to shove the pain away. He could keep going. He had to. Isaac was hurt, Sanna was hurting. Dahlia was scared and not scared. There were worlds to save. Gabriel didn't get to stop.

Morphina would not have just let them go; something had happened.

"Gabriel." Isaac's voice turned firm. "It's okay, you can stop. I'm telling you to stop. Just – give yourself a second, for god's sake. You look like you're about to keel over. I promise you I'm okay. *Trust me.*"

Gabriel released a breath, letting the telepathy unspool without intent.

"Sorry," he found himself saying, again. He hesitated, then held out his hand, in offering. Where Isaac's mind often comforted him in its closeness, in its aliveness, he knew Isaac found it less reassuring to have Gabriel's telepathy unfettered, however much he didn't want to magnify either. His mind was raw with the ghost of Alec Mandel – he wouldn't want Gabriel seeing that. He would want to know that his thoughts were private.

Isaac didn't take his hand. He practically hurtled into Gabriel's arms, arms wrapping around him in the same vice grip that Gabriel had held his mind in before. He buried his face in Gabriel's neck.

Gabriel froze in shock.

It was, unmistakeably, a hug. Isaac was hugging him.

It was the most, closest, contact he'd had with Isaac in years. It was the first time Isaac had properly initiated it since his return from the seeming dead, genuinely, without any intent except simply to touch. He was definitely cold - horribly, viscerally cold. But he was Isaac.

Gabriel's breath got stuck somewhere in his throat and his mind derailed blank beyond the details. The unfamiliarity of Isaac's lean body pressed against him, more muscled than it had been. The familiarity of it too; the essential Isaac-ness of him. The scent of him was the same. So was the power that flooded every crevice of Gabriel's body in response to the touch.

He wrapped his arms tighter around Isaac, holding him close in turn.

He found Dahlia and Sanna – alive, thank god –

The exhaustion tugged at him and his hold on their minds slipped away. He bit back a groan of frustration and closed his eyes, counting his breaths, counting Isaac's too. Everything felt rather far away aside from the two of them, sitting on this roadside. He ended up soaking up the feel of minds without taking any command of them. It was a sweet sound after the silence of the nightmares.

They needed to move. They didn't have time.

Gabriel didn't move. He tried again, and felt his telepathy slipping again, as if minds could turn over one ankle and stumble.

He was so tired. Would it be so bad to fall asleep with Isaac in his arms? He felt safe.

"I know I hurt you," Isaac muttered. "I can only imagine how much. I'm sorry about that too."

"You're sorry." Without the warning of Isaac's thoughts beforehand, the conversation ambushed him entirely. Or maybe that was sleep-deprivation.

"I also know that doesn't make it better."

Gabriel didn't dare so much as twitch in case it frightened this version of Isaac away. This closer-to-what-he-used-to-be Isaac.

"I got…" Isaac faltered. He released a shaky breath. "Sorry – I know you'd prefer to read my thoughts."

"No, it's okay." Isaac wasn't in the habit of talking to him, especially not any more when it sometimes seemed all he had for Gabriel was snark or accusation. But, even before, they'd struggled. Or, rather, he'd struggled to find words for things that came so much easier in thoughts and feelings without words at all. He'd never thought Isaac minded, he'd thought Isaac understood that they just spoke different natural languages. The impression he'd always got was that Isaac got some guilty pleasure out of hearing his own thoughts narrated back to him, as if hearing them from an external source gave him clarity. Or maybe Gabriel had been projecting. Maybe that was him. The doubt came as sharp as the flash of a scalpel. "I'm listening," he said.

"I—" Isaac's grip tightened. "I convinced myself that everything I felt for you was what you told me to feel, but…"

Gabriel bit down hard on his tongue. He'd promised to listen, however much he wanted to yell that wasn't true. How could Isaac think that was true?

"I got scared," Isaac started again. "Alec – everything. I hate what I can do, you know I do. And you make it feel like it's okay, like it's safe, but it's *not.* You make me forget that. You're right. I was a coward. I'm sorry. It wasn't – it scares me. All of it. I got scared that you were messing with my head just because I knew that you could, if you wanted to. I got scared of me. Me. And what I might make you. I let it overwhelm me. You were my boyfriend...I should have trusted you enough to at least talk to you. Maybe everything would have been different then."

Isaac was babbling. Gabriel couldn't find the strength to pull back and sift through his thoughts.

God, he could have killed Isaac's parents, wherever they were. Who made a kid that scared of their own gifts? Gloves for as long as he'd known, skittish of being touched as if humans weren't a species made for contact. Of course Isaac was scared. He'd only ever been taught fear.

"I know it wasn't a lie now," Isaac said softly. "At least, not everything. Not the way we feel about each other. I mean, if it was, it wouldn't still hurt so much." He laughed a little, and then he was silent for a beat. "I really fucked up, didn't I?"

Gabriel barely knew where to start, he only knew that he had never wanted his love to be a hurting thing. He'd wanted Isaac to be happy, comfortable. He'd wanted for Isaac to not have to be scared any more. He'd wanted him to never have to ask for what he wanted, only to know that it would be given. He pulled himself back with what felt like godly effort, only to let his forehead rest against Isaac's. Sitting upright was too big of a chore. Even for telepaths.

"Isaac—" He wished he had the right words, something that could make it better in a quick and easy flash. He would have taken *it* away a long time ago if he could. But those fears were too large a thing, too complex and old, for him to be able to wipe them away even if Isaac let go of him long enough for him to try. That fear was Isaac to the bone. But

Gabriel would try. He'd always try. "Isaac, look at me." He forced himself to focus. "What you are – what you can *do* – is okay. I know you think power corrupts but you could never – you're not that. You've never been that." Isaac did the wrong thing, mostly out of his fear to do anything wrong at all, but he was hardly some corrupt and awful monster. Even now. Even ever, no matter how frustrated Gabriel sometimes got with him. He couldn't possibly be. "What we do with power is what defines us, not what we have the possibility to do. The actions other people take because of you are not on you, you are not a telepath. You can only be responsible for your own kindness and your own cruelty."

Doing nothing allowed for neither.

"You may be slightly biased. But thanks."

One day, when he said it, Isaac might actually believe him.

"Only slightly," Gabriel drawled instead. "Ex-boyfriend's prerogative."

Isaac startled into laughter, not so hollow and flat this time. It was beautiful. He'd missed that laugh.

"Mm," Isaac said, flashing a grin; not vicious that time, the cute and slightly nervous one that Gabriel hadn't seen in so very long. "We never did technically break up. And I haven't seen anyone. You're probably technically still my boyfriend, you know."

Gabriel's heart went off like crazy, like it might race right out of his chest because the human body really was too small a container to hold everything he thought about Isaac Morton. He remembered his own, foolish last-not-last words. He wished he could have heard Isaac's thoughts when he said them. He wasn't sure he dared to. He definitely didn't dare to ask, though, so maybe he should not judge Isaac's not asking either so harshly. He didn't want to say 'I love you' again though, not if there was even a chance that Isaac thought he was trying to force him to believe it.

The human propensity to do awful things out of fear always amazed and appalled him. There seemed to be so many things in the world for people to be afraid of. The fear of everything different and unknown, the fear of not fitting in and the fear of not being unique enough. Fears of too much and too little. Of being seen, of being ignored. Of being too powerful, of being too powerless. There never seemed to be any winning in most people's heads.

Perhaps he should force Isaac to believe he was okay. People were the worst judges of themselves.

Isaac's grip tightened on him again as he pulled his head back to meet Isaac's eyes.

"I'm sorry," Isaac said. "I shouldn't have said that. It was unfair, after – after what I did."

"Don't be sorry, not for that." Gabriel shook his head, not ever about to regret that laugh, or Isaac *joking* with such lightness. He wasn't going to let himself read more into it than joking, the giddiness of surviving against the odds, however much he wanted to. Still, he considered Isaac. "Isaac," he tried again instead, focusing a little better without the echo chamber of Isaac's nausea. "It's your power. Not mine, not Morphina's, not anybody else's. It shouldn't be something that someone else can use just by touching you. I mean – look at Sanna, she heals with touch, but she doesn't just heal everyone she touches. She doesn't live her life in gloves."

"No, she lives her life with you in her head. I don't want that. I mean, I know you're trying to help her, I know you're her gloves, but—"

"— I'm not sitting in her head telling her not to heal things every time she touches something. That's her. That's not me."

Isaac's brow furrowed as if he'd never even considered that. "…What are you saying?"

The concrete road had never seemed so comfortable.

"Gabriel!"

A sharp slap stung his cheek.

Gabriel blinked.

Isaac had moved – when had he moved? They were lying on the concrete floor and his vision was swimming.

"Don't fall asleep," Isaac said, his face white with fear. "Come on. We need to stay awake. Are you okay? You look like crap."

"Thanks, babe."

Isaac shot him a look.

Gabriel smirked, because it would make Isaac feel better.

Isaac rolled his eyes, but a smile did twitch his lips. He pulled Gabriel up to sit once more.

Still, Gabriel didn't want to stay awake. A traitorous part of him only wanted to sleep, to dream of better times. He took Isaac's hand and rubbed his eyes blearily with the other, vision foggy. 'Crap' seemed too nice a word for how he was feeling right then. He shoved it away – he didn't matter. Sanna had been screaming. There was work to do. Worlds to save. He didn't get to be crap right now, he couldn't forget that.

Don't fall asleep. He tried ordering himself, but he wasn't sure how well it worked.

Isaac watched him. "There's no chance I'm going to be able to persuade you to take a break before doing this, is there?" he asked. "You know this is a trap."

"I can't leave them there," Gabriel replied, a little helplessly.

"I'm not suggesting abandoning them. But they're not who Mona wants to hurt, they'll be okay—"

"—You can't feel it, you don't understand." Gabriel's voice shifted agitated. "They're *hurt*."

Isaac nodded. He didn't look surprised, only sad. He seemed to try again all the same.

"Your friends may not want you to walk into a trap for them. Mona is trying to *kill* you, and you cannot simply tell her not to. Do you understand that? You could die. Actually die."

"Don't talk to me like I'm stupid. I know the risks. I've been this doing this for a long time."

"I'm just saying, you don't have to do this." Isaac ducked to lock their gazes when Gabriel avoided his eyes. "Nobody expects you to be more than human except you. Least of all me. I know what you look like when you're at the end of your limit, and Gabriel…" Isaac's worry was plain on his face. "You're way past that."

Gabriel scowled. He pulled his hand away, not wanting the pity, not wanting Isaac to see him as something weak. He'd never done that before.

"It's okay not to be able to fix everything," Isaac said. "Nobody can do that."

Gabriel wanted to snap 'when was the last time you saw a superhero call a sick day?' He didn't say it though. Isaac was trying to care for him, in his way - tugging back, in contrast to Gabriel's perpetual need to tug forward. It had balanced them out well once upon a time.

'Once upon a time' felt like an impossibly long time ago.

"As you said, there's no chance you're going to persuade

me not to do this."

Isaac swallowed hard. His shoulders slumped small.

"I won't force you to die for me, if that's your concern," Gabriel said. "I'd never do that." He steeled himself. "You can go if you want. It's your choice."

"Our deal."

"Isaac."

Isaac stared at him, wide-eyed. He chewed on his lip, his hands twitching to his pockets, to his gloves.

"You don't expect to survive without me by your side, do you?" Isaac studied his face. "You begged me for my help. You need me."

Gabriel said nothing. What could he possibly say to that? It was true. He didn't stand a chance without Isaac, now more than ever before. Reasonably, he should order Isaac to stay by his side, to fight for the greater good. But he would never ask someone, least of all Isaac, to die for him. Not when it came down to it. Did Isaac truly not know that?

Isaac shuffled back, putting space between them, and stood. His thoughts, his desperate desire to run, flooded Gabriel. For a beat, Gabriel was certain he would.

Then, Isaac gave an almighty 'I cannot believe I'm doing this' groan.

"Let's finish this."

18 - Dahlia

Gabriel was alive.

She felt the familiar brush of his mind against hers, steady and reassuring, surrounded by city air. Some of her fear leached out of her. For a split second, Sanna's shoulders relaxed too.

Gabriel was also standing right in front of them.

The dreamers rushed forwards.

The Gabriel in her head vanished; a bad, sputtering connection.

Her fear sparked, and she reached for her vines – that time, they came.

"Stop," Gabriel said.

The rest of the dreamers froze. They froze in the way that people always froze under a telepath's command, quivering slightly as if something in them was straining against the hold.

Morphina froze too, before turning and walking back away from the door to stand in front of Gabriel. Her eyes bulged with fear, some wild caged thing. As Dahlia watched, the fear vanished, spiralling away from her face like water down a sink, leaving the dreamweaver disturbingly blissful in countenance. Tranquillized.

Dahlia's breath quickened as she looked around the room with its frightened statue monsters.

Sanna squeezed her hand. She'd felt it too – two Gabriels, she must have! So which one were they in a room with? Not their Gabriel. Dreamers didn't stop when their Gabriel told them to; he had no power over them. However nice that would have been.

Dahlia's stomach sank.

Sanna tugged at her hand, drawing Dahlia to her side, away from the Gabriel who wasn't Gabriel at all. She stepped slightly in front of Dahlia once more, despite the fact the blood on her clothes hadn't even finished drying yet. It was sweet. It wouldn't do much against a telepath if this Gabriel could hear their every thought like their Gabriel could, but it was sweet. It felt like more protection than she'd had before.

For all of her faults with him, Dahlia had never considered that she might need protection from any version of Gabriel. He would never have hurt them.

The Gabriel in the room didn't glance over. He didn't react to the shift at all. His eyes were still resting on Morphina, intent, focused on some telepathic communication perhaps that they were not privy to.

"…since when can you control the dreaming," Dahlia said. Her mouth had gone unbearably dry, desert-scorched with unease. Her palms felt entirely too clammy by comparison, clenched around Sanna's hand. Any relief she'd felt had well and truly vanished. She had to talk, just to hear it, to reassure herself with the sound and the doing of it.

Because Gabriel didn't control dreaming.

They were all tired. Maybe she was reading too much into it. Maybe she'd imagined that other Gabriel in her head. The tight, frightened squeeze of Sanna's hand told her she really wasn't reading too much into it.

"Gabriel," she said, louder, when he didn't reply.

"That's not my name." He turned his head towards them, the dreamers still quivering under his control. "Archangel," he said, after a moment. He flashed them an entirely familiar and reassuring smile. "You can call me Archangel. I'm not Gabriel."

His smile may have been familiar, but his eyes were black. They were black like Morphina's eyes were, like Felicity's eyes had become. They were the eyes of a dream brought to life.

Dahlia's spine straightened.

Archangel. That silly nickname. She'd found it on a little comic strip under Gabriel's bed; a story about a telepathic super-hero who made a thing of being everyone's guardian angel. The pages of the art book had been worn with age, but much loved. It explained nothing. She'd teased Gabriel with it, told him Archangel should be his code name, his superhero name in the field. She remembered the scraps of artwork they'd found in Morton's hideaway cottage and wondered if that was why Gabriel had such worn and well-loved scraps of drawings.

Another prickle of fear dripped cold down the back of her neck. Her free hand closed around the seeds left in her pocket, humming with a life different to the empty dream forest beyond the door. Empty. Was he some empty thing too? Like Felicity? No, not like that. Felicity was dead.

Was Gabriel dead? No. She'd felt him. She was so sure she'd felt him.

"You're a nightmare," Sanna said, speaking what Dahlia

211

hadn't wanted to say. To say it aloud made it far too real.

"Nightmares are frightening things," Archangel replied. "I'm so much more than that. I don't want to hurt you, don't worry." His gaze darted between them. "Put the vines away."

"Whose nightmare are you?" Dahlia pressed. There were two of them. One of him. And he couldn't get in their heads, could he? Gabriel would have already done so. Gabriel would have siphoned away the fear and the hurt because he couldn't bear to leave them.

Annoyance flashed across Archangel's face.

"Put the vines away. I'll explain everything."

"Explain it first!" Dahlia pulled the seeds out, a bold threat, and grew more vines. They curled between them and Archangel in a protective barrier. She told herself that if it came to attacking him, she wouldn't hesitate. Even if he looked like Gabriel.

His eyes narrowed.

Felicity's arm closed around Dahlia's throat.

Dahlia startled again, jolting against the hold. It did no good. Her sister's grip was like iron, clamping her against her cold chest and – and she didn't want to attack. It was stupid.

Sanna jolted forward, one hand ready-to-heal on Dahlia's arm the second after.

"Don't!" she cried. "Don't hurt her. It's all a lot to take in. She's putting them away. We didn't mean—"

"She meant it," Archangel said. "But I appreciate you trying to protect your friend." He looked to Dahlia, not releasing her from his stare even as he spoke to Sanna. "But, next time, you should know I can have her neck snapped. I would rather not, but I will not be threatened. Do you understand?"

Dahlia glared, dizzy with panic.

"She understands," Sanna said quickly. "Don't you? Lia?"

The fear in Sanna's voice tugged at her like Sanna's hand did. Whatever calm Gabriel had given her once, was fading. At least that proved, however bitterly, that he didn't have any lasting commands on them like Morphina had so insisted that he did.

"I want to hear it from her." Archangel tucked his hands into the pockets of her jeans, for all the world casual.

Felicity's grip tightened.

Dahlia grew dizzier. She itched to tug at the arm around her throat. She itched to spit in his face that he would turn her own sister against her like this. She reluctantly let her vines shrink back into her pockets. Her hands trembled, though she jutted her chin up. Her own fear sank its roots and curled deep. She wanted to accuse Sanna of being a coward. She wanted to snarl asking how someone invulnerable could be so very scared.

She wished she wasn't scared. She wished she was invulnerable too.

I understand.

He didn't react. He couldn't hear their thoughts, could he? That confirmed it.

"I understand," she said aloud.

"Very good." He offered up that warm smile again. "Thank you."

He didn't command Felicity away from her though. It would only take a second, less than that, for her sister to snap her throat in their current position. No, not her sister. Felicity wouldn't. Felicity was dead. Felicity's mind, whatever it was now as a dreaming thing, less than, was entirely under his control. It wasn't her. She was exactly the puppet that

Morphina had dreamed Dahlia might be.

It was hard not to feel like it was her sister; fast as light, too cold and not quite right any more. It was hard, exhaustion-dazed, not to forget. She couldn't forget the screaming.

Dahlia's eyes burned with something suspiciously like tears, and she wanted to blame it on the tiredness. She wanted Gabriel. Gabriel wouldn't do this. Her head spun.

"Isaac and Gabriel are in trouble," Sanna said. "We need to go and help them. You don't want them dead, do you?"

"They're fine, I called the dreamers off. They'll get here soon enough on their own accord. He wouldn't leave you here with her." His head tilted, as if he was listening out for something that they couldn't hear.

The thought of Gabriel arriving, which had seemed so comforting only minutes before, chilled Dahlia. She had the sneaking and irritation suspicion that she'd been relegated to the position of bait. Of damsel in distress. It seemed absurd. She refused to be a bloody damsel.

"You asked me whose nightmare I was." He spoke as if he hadn't threatened them. "I'm hers." He gestured at Morphina, still frozen, still with that unnervingly blissful expression on her face. "And Isaac's. I'm a little bit of Gabriel's dreaming too, perhaps. But mostly I'm hers. She's been cooking me up for years."

"At the house," Sanna rasped. "When they died - she lost control. She didn't mean to do it."

"Isaac magnified them both," he agreed. "With Gabriel there, trying to control her, it connected their brains enough that he magnified her for the first time in five years. Dreaming already has so few limits and he's so very strong." He seemed to smile thinking of Isaac; not quite fond, but

214

something darker and more possessive. "I knew I had to get them together again. It was just what I needed to give myself a form once more, rather than merely influencing people's thoughts."

He spoke too as if he was a thinking thing, a scheming creature, more than just some empty dream mimicking at life. But then again, a dreamweaver's dream may just feel more real to her than life itself, certainly more real than anyone else's horrors.

"You...you knew you had to get them together," Sanna echoed. "You're behind this, all of this. You sent the messages."

"Well, not *personally*. I was somewhat lacking in hands at the time." Archangel waved his own. "But I commanded the people I needed to make sure it was done. The second I learned that he was still alive."

"My sister is dead," Dahlia growled. Her fists clenched, though she didn't dare summon her plants again. She focused on the quiet comfort of the seedlings in her pocket, and the scraps of weeds and grass in the vicinity at least. She focused on anything but her dead sister's hands. It was his fault. Morphina's fault. Gabriel's fault. Isaac's fault.

Felicity shouldn't have died for *this*.

"It's unfortunate," Archangel said. "I'm sorry about that."

"You're sorry. I don't care if you're sorry! I care that she's dead!"

"You are tired, grieving. I understand. You need rest. Sleep deprivation really does have some horrible health defects. Close your eyes."

Dahlia's eyes felt heavy, but they didn't close. Not quite. She swayed on the spot and braced herself with a fresh surge of spite.

"I bet," she whispered, because she knew it would sting, "that it just *kills* you that you can't get in our heads. Not properly. The waking are a bad connection to you, like the dreamers are to Gabriel. Aren't they?"

Felicity's grip tightened on her throat again, but even gasping she felt an absurd satisfaction.

The warmth, the smile, the pretence had slipped from Archangel as if it had never been there. He had the same look that Gabriel did when he was confronted by a rather frustrating problem. With something he couldn't fix.

"I'm trying to help you," he replied. "You will feel better if you rest."

"I'd feel better if my sister wasn't dead because of you." Like hell was she going to let him just brush that aside.

"I'm not him," Archangel returned, "do not try and guilt me." He gentled his tone, exhaling a breath. "I hope it brings you comfort that this is all for the greater good. She will be the last to die so unjustly, I promise you that." He turned away, focusing on Morphina once more. "Mona will never hurt anyone again, I'll make sure of it."

"Yeah?" Dahlia glared at him. "And how are you going to do that?"

Perhaps the words should have comforted her. They didn't. Her eyes darted to Sanna again, and then to the broad expanse of the nightmare's back. He couldn't hear her thoughts, so she could attack, right? Well, she could, if Felicity wasn't holding onto her.

"It's simple, really," Archangel shrugged. "I'll tell her not to."

"Isaac won't help you," Morphina managed. The speech

seemed to be a struggle. Her shoulders tensed. "He'd die before he helped *you* rule the world. He did."

The doubt niggled; it crept in like a winter's draught, pieces winding together.

"Yes," Archangel said. "And do you really believe Gabriel is going to let him die a second time? You know he won't, otherwise you wouldn't have tried so hard to keep them apart. To stop me."

"You can't force him to help you," Dahlia began, "Gabriel said—"

"Gabriel's unwillingness to force him is not the same as his incapability. He'll see the way forward."

"Gabriel won't help you," Dahlia said. "Not if you're behind all of this." She laughed, wildly. "Our friends are *dead* because of this. If you're him in any form, you must know that's not looking great for you. He doesn't forgive the people who hurt his friends."

"We'll see soon enough." Archangel did not seem concerned.

The door opened. Jack and Lucy entered, appearing rather worse for wear.

Sanna gasped, taking an aborted step towards them. Her hands rose instinctively to help, before she jerked to a halt. Something like a whimper snagged in her throat, horrified and helpless, like an animal with its leg caught mangled in a trap.

Dahlia's fury rose up in its hackles like a protective bear. If Morphina had just let them rest, let them *die,* this would never have happened. Their bodies wouldn't be disrespected, used up, bruised and sliced like they'd both been on the losing end of a fatal knife fight. Her stomach rolled and she pressed a hand to her mouth, as if that might hold away the nausea.

They looked and smelled like death. Death would have been kinder.

Her eyes darted to Morphina. If she brought the nightmare to life, shouldn't she stop it? Shouldn't stopping her stop all of them? The nightmares would lose strength, die without her power. She sustained them. It would all end.

Felicity's hold tightened warning on her throat. The rest of the dreamers took up positions around the room in silent coordination, puppets and monsters twitched on strings. Waiting.

Stay away. Dahlia thought it as loud as she could, screaming it. *Gabriel, if you can hear me. Stay away. Please.*

Gabriel couldn't fight a dreaming army, and she abruptly wasn't sure how well he'd fight a nightmare version of himself either.

The second they were distracted, she'd make damn sure he didn't have to.

19 - Isaac

I saac couldn't believe he'd had the opportunity to walk away, and that he hadn't taken it. The doubting part of him whispered that Gabriel had planted a silent command to stay, despite his outward words, but he didn't think that was actually true.

Gabriel was too tired.

Gabriel had always had a problem with setting boundaries, Isaac knew that. He had seen it plenty of times at university; somebody asked Gabriel for help, and he couldn't seem to say no. Isaac could remember one time it got so bad that he'd faked a crisis, begging that he was burnt out and needed to get away. He'd known Gabriel would come with him if he thought Isaac needed saving.

The two of them had rented a cheap cottage on the coast, wrapping up warm against the blustering sea air and the frigid rain. It was hardly seaside weather, but it had been a perfect long weekend all the same. They had spent most of it cuddled up, away from people and all of their needs. Gabriel had actually slept peacefully for once. They'd taken long baths and long walks together. Laughed, cooked. Isaac could have built his life around weekends like that.

Isaac really wished he could use the same card again. The

words 'let's run away, you and me, together,' perched on the edge of his tongue. He didn't say it though. He didn't say 'I love you, please'. Even if it was true, he wasn't sure it wouldn't be manipulation, if he did, when he remembered too well the box of his belongings under Gabriel's bed and hadn't said it earlier. He wasn't sure if any kind of running, when Isaac was the one who suggested it, wouldn't feel like an attack.

If Gabriel had been burnt out all those years ago, and in need of rest, then the Gabriel next to him was a smouldering lump of ash and char. He looked like he hadn't taken a break in years, like he didn't understand the concept any more, even when Isaac offered it. His eyes tracked things that weren't there, his steps were unsteady, and he had the pinched look of a man with a migraine who would do better with pain meds and a dark room than a battle.

He'd used Sanna and Dahlia's minds to pinpoint their location again, leading Isaac deep into the dream territory. Even amongst all of the trees, the church stood out on the crossroads. The lights were on inside.

"Something's wrong," Gabriel said, staring up at the building.

That's because we both know this is a trap. Isaac glanced over at him, stomach knotted, and had the grace to at least not say it aloud. It wouldn't make a difference to Gabriel. Not when he had someone to save, not any more.

"You said they were hurt, your friends. Are they…"

"They're frightened," Gabriel said. He grimaced. "I can't—" He touched a hand to his forehead. His muscles quivered. He looked ready to pitch to the ground again. "It's her, it must be. She's blocking me. I can't get a proper hold."

"You need rest. Sleep," Isaac said, before he could stop

himself. "You can't win a fight like this."

"I can win any fight with you on my side."

Isaac sighed. He eyed the front of the church too. It was a deceptively grand building that's insides frequently failed to live up to the architecture. A hollow shell of a pretty thing. What use of gods and prayers?

Maybe we shouldn't go in.

Gabriel shot him a look – so obviously outraged, so accusing.

"At least I didn't actually say it!" Isaac shot him a look back. "I can't control my thoughts, and she did just try and kill us. I'm not saying I won't come with you." Still. He didn't want to. He still wanted to run. Everything in him screamed to run, then keep running and maybe move to America because there was more open land to hide in there than in England. It wasn't *cowardice,* to not want to go in. Or maybe it was. That didn't mean it wasn't common sense if something bad was waiting for them. "I'll go for her when we get in," he said. "You get your friends. We get out and we get a proper plan, alright?"

Gabriel nodded. "Thank you," he said, quieter. "I know you don't like fighting."

I didn't fight for you back then. I can fight for you now, even if just once. He didn't say it. He didn't know how to begin actually saying something like that outside his head. Still, he knew Gabriel heard it.

They exchanged another look, and for a moment the clocks had turned back, and the whole world was ahead of them. They were Isaac Morton and Gabriel De Vere, the dream team instead of the nightmare one.

Isaac offered his bare hand once more.

Gabriel took his hand, hesitated, and then pressed a small kiss atop Isaac's knuckles. Then he marched them forward like a warrior to battle, resolute and unfaltering. What would it be to be that unfaltering? That sure of one's own mind? Isaac envied him. He was glad Gabriel was holding his hand because he wasn't entirely sure his own nerve wouldn't have given out if Gabriel wasn't pulling him along.

But he also knew the second they walked in that he was right.

They shouldn't have come in.

"What is this?" Gabriel asked.

Isaac barely heard him, he was too busy staring as his eyes adjusted to the light. Gabriel stood beside him and Gabriel stood in the centre of the church. He turned his eyes to Isaac and they were monstrous, an old memory, everything that he had been scared of. Isaac knew those eyes. He stumbled back on instinct, forgetting that Gabriel was still holding onto his hand.

"You…" His voice came out cracked. "Not you."

Dahlia and Sanna were huddled in one corner. Felicity stood behind Dahlia; one arm hooked painfully tight around her throat. There was blood splattered dried and stinking on Sanna's clothes.

Mona quivered on the floor, her limbs held with the peculiar stillness of a paralytic. Unwilling. Inescapable. Her expression was happy, or at least not frightened.

"Isaac." The other Gabriel's voice came out breathless, reverent. He strode across the room, hands rising as if to touch.

Isaac recoiled, tearing free of Gabriel's hand.

Gabriel stepped between the two of them.

The other Gabriel stopped.

"It's good to see you again, Isaac," the other Gabriel said. "Though I have to say, I'm not sure what I think about the haircut. Or the fact that you let me believe you were dead. That was cruel."

The two Gabriels looked almost exactly the same as each other, they even wore the same dark blue jeans, the same t-shirt.

"Who are you?" Gabriel demanded. His shoulders squared.

The other Gabriel's head tilted, eyeing Gabriel's protective posture, before he smiled.

"Call me Archangel."

"Archangel," Gabriel repeated. "Why is Isaac scared of you? What have you done?"

The two of their gazes met, and something seemed to pass between them. Isaac could imagine Gabriel pressing his mind forward, tentatively, like he was poking at a painful tooth in the roof of his mouth or prising at a splinter. Something tiny and wrong and utterly beneath his skin. Surely, he must feel how wrong Archangel was?

The dreamers stood loosely around them all, vacant jailers waiting for a catalyst to action them.

Dahlia's eyes were red with tears. Sanna's shoulders had a horribly defensive set, like a hedgehog curled to make itself as small and spiky a target as possible. Her hand trembled on Dahlia's wrist, holding on for dear life.

Isaac felt like the ground was going to open up beneath his feet.

"I didn't hurt her." Archangel inclined his head towards Sanna. "That was the dreamweaver. She was going to kill your friends when I arrived. I saved them."

Gabriel's attention darted to Dahlia and Sanna as if to confirm the truth of it, and then back to Isaac. He reached his hand back out towards him. Isaac wasn't sure if it was because he wanted more power, or because he was hoping to in some way to shield Isaac's mind from the copycat in front of them.

All of their plans of going straight for Morphina had derailed.

Their fingers brushed, power flared.

Felicity rammed a candle into Sanna's throat.

Isaac stumbled back from Gabriel like he'd been scalded.

Gabriel wheezed like he'd received an electric shock, no doubt from an echo of his healer's pain. He snapped his hands above his head in a placating gesture, in surrender.

"Stay back from the magnifier for now," Archangel said. "I don't want this to be a fight. We're on the same side, you and me. He is not on that side. He would ruin everything we could achieve with a half a chance. Get on separate sides of the room."

Isaac stumbled back. He willed himself to think of nothing, to feel *nothing*. It was more impossible than it had ever been. All he could think about was dying, and the cold, and the weakness of it. Old memories, buried so deep, began to bubble. It felt like the walls were closing in. It that moment, the last five years were nothing. All of his training, every fight, every tactic he'd ever tried to study against telepaths was worth *nothing*. He was twenty years old, he was on the floor, and he was dying.

He put himself as far away from everyone else as he could and yanked his gloves back on.

Felicity stepped back.

Sanna's throat began to knit and heal as she gargled and choked, some awful wet sound.

Dahlia flinched.

"This was you," Isaac said. "All along, this was you. The nightmares-"

"The nightmares were all her," Archangel said, gesturing at Mona. "Technically. I didn't know if you remembered me." His expression was hungry. "I don't think you do, not properly. We met the night you died. It takes a lot of energy to bring something like me to life and a lot to kill someone like you. But you...you're all energy, aren't you? We had three days together, before she got us under control."

"*You sent the messages.*" Isaac felt sick, and sicker still as Archangel explained yes.

"You've been alive this whole time?" Gabriel looked aghast.

Archangel made a 'so-so' gesture wobbling with his hand, grimacing, pivoting towards his counterpart.

"Minds are...complicated. I have existed and lived in a way. I have had no physical presence in the world beyond the dreams. She killed me. Or tried to."

Isaac could imagine what having Gabriel nestled in his head might feel like, and that was bad enough. He couldn't imagine what Morphina had gone through. Mona didn't look like he had just swept away the dust of the bad things.

"That's not what's important," Archangel said, waving a dismissive hand. "The Archangel Project is. That's what I was made for. I want to see it done...I think we can see it done."

The look on Gabriel's face had transformed to something terribly like wonder, with a hunger to match his nightmare double's. He should have been looking at the scene around him, but Gabriel wasn't, was he? Gabriel was tired, and hurting, and Archangel stood in front of him like the possibility of all of his dreams come true.

"No." Isaac meant it to come out strong, but it came out closer to a whisper. A strangled sound. He turned to Gabriel, but Gabriel's attention was fixed on Archangel and Archangel's was fixed on Gabriel like nothing else mattered. "Gabriel," Isaac said, louder. "Listen to me—"

But Gabriel was not listening, at least not to Isaac.

"You hurt my friends," he murmured. "You must know that's not a good place to be in."

"There is a difference," Archangel returned, softly. "Between being a hero and being a good person. I know that. I think part of you knows it too, you're always struggling with that line. End goals have sacrifices that make them up. Saving the world has a price. Sometimes it's not a price that you can pay and still be good by the time you're done. Gabriel…" He took a step closer, then another. "The world needs someone like me to hold it accountable. Someone like *us*. You know it does. Or are you willing to have let your friends die for nothing?"

Isaac forced himself to focus.

He was not twenty years old any more, he was not dead, he was not dying. He pitched his voice loud and clear. "And who," he spat, "holds *you* accountable?"

"Me," Gabriel said, equally soft and breathless, before Isaac could continue.

Isaac's heart jolted.

"You can control the dreamers," Gabriel said. "I can control the waking. Between the two of us, we have the world covered. We can hold each other accountable. We are

226

balanced."

"My thoughts exactly." Archangel smiled at him, and a look of perfect understanding passed between them. "All our lives, there has been something missing. No more. We are each other's destiny."

"It's not destiny," Dahlia protested, "it's bullshit."

Her voice seemed like it was coming from a very long way away. Isaac's ears were ringing.

It was that look that did it. It was that look which brought everything crashing down. When he'd walked in with Gabriel, he and Gabriel had been a team, of sorts. He could still feel Gabriel's kiss on his hand. He'd thought that maybe they were starting to understand each other, that maybe he had been wrong, that maybe if they only survived that everything would be okay.

He was not wrong. He had never been wrong. Mona had never been wrong.

He was such an idiot.

Both of their stares turned on him.

Isaac swallowed, and he started to edge back towards the door.

"Well," he tried for a smile. "Looks like you two stopped Morphina. Great job! That's our deal done, then."

Dahlia made a betrayed noise in her throat.

Don't run, Gabriel ordered.

Felicity appeared behind Isaac, blocking his way in the same second.

Isaac froze. His panic throbbed and swelled and Gabriel snuffed it. He tilted his head to track the two of them, uneasily, putting as much of the room as possible into his periphery vision. They'd said not to run, but he could still walk out, or hop, or skip. All of the little tricks and loopholes that were not technically running. All of that would mean nothing when he couldn't block Gabriel's powers, though.

He suddenly felt very, very stupid for not running earlier when he'd had the chance. Mona was right. Sometimes people didn't have to be in your head to control you, sometimes being dumb enough to love them was enough.

"You promised," Isaac said. "Gabriel, we had a deal, you promised. You said I could go. You said you would never force me to die by your side."

"You're not going to die," Gabriel said. "It's alright. You don't need to be scared." He bit his lip, but the tic of nerves seemed less charming now. His voice came out commanding. "Don't be afraid, Isaac."

The tension eased out of Isaac's fists, his shoulders. No, it was pulled away. Gabriel stroked over his mind like he was wiping away blood beading from a wound, and Isaac wasn't afraid but he knew he should be. Somehow that was its own kind of terrifying.

"This won't work without you," Gabriel was saying. "We're not strong enough, *I'm* not strong enough...but with you." He gave Isaac a slow smile, eager and bright and hopeful. "You know me. You said it yourself, it was only ever your fears..."

"I'm never going to be on your side with this." It burst out. "I died because I didn't want this to happen." He expected Gabriel to flinch, but he didn't. Isaac swallowed. "If you do this...it's not going to be kind. It won't be good. If you are touching me you cannot control my mind, you know that. You will not be able to take it away when I feel scared. You will not be able to protect me. You will not be able to make me happy."

Whatever else Gabriel had always wanted, Gabriel had always wanted him to be happy. He'd wanted Isaac to feel safe and loved and taken care of.

The words seemed to give Gabriel pause.

"You're in my head." Isaac focused on the memories, the good memories. He thought about that weekend away, and their first kiss, and their first meeting and the moments in between. Gabriel posing, trying not to laugh, as Isaac sketched him on a sunny picnic blanket. The two of them dancing together in Isaac's first year bedroom after Isaac confessed that going to crowded parties always made him nervous. Isaac going to great lengths to ensure that Gabriel got a surprise for his birthday for once. "I love you. I *know* that you love me. Now…" Isaac strengthened his resolve, and thought about everything he was scared of, everything that had once made him think it was better to die than be in a relationship with the man he loved. He slipped his hand towards the knife in his pocket. "You're the telepath. Read my mind, and tell me that forcing me to do this with you isn't going to be torture."

"He is one man," Archangel said sharply, tugging Gabriel back the other way. "And whether he loves you or not, he's saying it now because he wants something from you. Are you really going to be so selfish as to pick love over the entire world? Because he didn't pick you. He *abandoned* you."

Gabriel's expression was wrecked, torn, entirely overwhelmed.

Isaac's hand closed on his knife.

Dahlia's vines lashed out and plunged straight into Morphina's chest.

For a second, Isaac was too stunned to fully register what

was happening. Then, "No!" He took an aborted step towards her before Felicity seized hold of him. He threw his weight back viciously.

"Stop!" Gabriel commanded, but it wasn't directed at Isaac.

Mona's eyes widened, faltering from black to blue, to pain. She didn't even get the opportunity to run.

Dahlia's vines crumpled under the order.

The dreamweaver crumpled with her.

20 - Gabriel

"You killed her."

Gabriel's mind washed numb, so stupidly surprised.

Morphina – Mona – sprawled on the floor of the church, seeming so very small. He'd wanted her defeated, stopped, of course he had, but –

But never like that. He'd never wanted her dead.

All of the nightmares crumpled to the floor before vanishing too, barring the dead who remained, just that. Bodies stiff and mangled on the floor.

Archangel was gone as if he had never been there, with her. He may have been alive without her, and that may have been her power, but she was still life support to them, wasn't she?

Dahlia stared at him, trying to order her thoughts, to force her limbs to move. Her breathing came hard.

Gabriel's anger began to prickle, then sting, then *burn*. It seared through everything.

Isaac rushed to Mona's side, dropping to his knees beside her. His hands flew to her pulse before recoiling, still afraid to touch. "Oh god."

The force of the vines had shoved grotesque into her chest, other impossible thorns gouging at her throat.

"She deserved it," Dahlia spat. "After everything she did – after Felicity – she didn't even regret it! Not properly! She only regretted losing. She hurt Sanna. That copy of you hurt Sanna. What the hell, Gabriel? You weren't actually listening to that crap, were you?" Tears sprung to her eyes.

"She was still a person." Gabriel could feel his temperature rising. "She was still a person, that was murder. It doesn't matter what a person does, that doesn't give you a right to kill them! I could have – I could have—" He tried to get himself under control, but he was *so tired*. He could feel himself babbling but it was pouring out of him and he couldn't stop. "I could have saved her. I was going to make her better!"

He wanted to cry too.

"What, with that *nightmare?*" Dahlia looked at him with something like cool pity then. for all of her fury. "Not everyone deserves to be saved. Not everyone deserves a second chance! Sometimes, it's not about rehabilitation. It's about justice."

"That was murder, that wasn't justice!" He could barely breathe for how much it wasn't justice, how much it wasn't the way to deal with any it.

"I saved us!"

"*You?*" He couldn't believe what he was hearing.

It was easy to get a proper sense of Mona with her flickering dreams and illusions wiped clean away. Without her illusions her scarlet curls were lacklustre and limp against her scalp. She didn't look powerful. She didn't look like some fairy-tale enchantress who could raze worlds and summon monsters. She looked like a young woman who may have been in his class, once. Like she could be anyone on the street, tired of life and expecting everything to have worked out differently than it had. Like anyone who had grown up scared of their own mind.

He hadn't even remembered her.

He should have remembered her.

"Bad people deserve to be punished." Dahlia's voice shook a little. "She would have killed us; she wasn't going to stop. So I stopped her and him. I *saved* us."

"Seriously?"

"Guys, please," Sanna began.

"That's not the point!" His blood roared his head. "Bad people don't just do bad things for no reason."

"That doesn't mean we forgive them for their trespasses. I don't owe anyone forgiveness. Look. It's over, alright?!" Dahlia strained again against his command to be still. "Isn't that what matters? That it's over? The world is safe."

"Safe." Gabriel repeated it hollowly and found himself laughing. She actually believed that. "Safe?" How the hell was the world safe and good and moral with another murderer in it? In a world where any crime or sin could be justified by virtue of who won and wrote the history textbook? Humans could bend over backwards to justify their own monstrosity, they couldn't see it! None of them could ever see it.

"Yes! Safe! She can't hurt anyone ever again." Dahlia's mouth wobbled. "She can't hurt me."

Archangel had seen it. He was right.

And Isaac was edging towards the fucking door already; couldn't even wait for the body to cool. Love? Isaac's love must be a joke. What could it possibly mean when he wouldn't stand and fight for it? Not when it truly came down to it.

"You're not leaving right now," Gabriel snarled at him. "Do

you even care that she's dead?" It was like getting slapped. How could Isaac already be leaving as if it was okay? As if any of it was okay? As if he hadn't said he loved Gabriel five seconds ago.

"Of course I care," Isaac said. "But it's not like this is somehow surprising. Isn't this the way a fight always goes? With causalities?"

"Oh, don't start with me right now." How could Isaac say that?

"We're all tired." Sanna took a step closer, reaching for him. Carefully. It was a maddening carefulness, as if Gabriel was some kind of bomb wired up to blow. As if he was the one to be wary of! He'd never deliberately hurt anyone! And yet Isaac still thought him some kind of monster, didn't he? Even now, he was something to frantically be escaped, something crazy. Archangel was so right. "None of us are at our best," Sanna continued. She settled her hand on Gabriel's arm.

"Well, she's definitely not!"

"Oh, shut the hell up," Isaac snapped. "She was my friend. You're not even mourning *her,* you never even knew her name."

"Your friend?" Gabriel plucked up the word. "Yeah? You have an interesting definition of the word. How many times did she ask you for help only for you to stay hidden away in your goddamn cottage, Isaac?"

Isaac flinched.

"It's not—" his fingers flexed. "It's not like that."

"Then what is it?"

"Are you actually saying this is my fault now?" Isaac's eyes brimmed with hurt. "I came here, for you, and you would have…"

"No." Gabriel deflated, a little. No, it was his fault. Of course it was his own fault. *He* was a telepath, he should have been paying attention, he should have seen it coming. He should have known. He should have stopped Dahlia. He should have saved her from the worst of herself. He should have saved all of them.

How could he do it, with the world, if he couldn't do it with Dahlia? How goddamn powerless was he on his own? But…if he'd been holding onto Isaac when she'd had that thought…

"Ah, crap," Isaac said. "Gabriel, no. You did everything you could, you always do. This is not on you. This isn't your fault. It's not like you killed her."

"But you're still running from *me*."

There was nothing to keep him any more, was there? Certainly not Gabriel. Isaac might love him but that was never going to be stronger than the fear, was it? Any moments they'd had, any possibility for more, for what they had been – gone.

Isaac closed his eyes, pained.

"No – I— I mean, you were on his side. You told me not to run! Even when you promised. What the hell am I supposed to do with that? I can't trust you."

What good is loving you when I can't trust you?

"Let's all just go home," Sanna said. She squeezed his arm once more. "Please. We're all tired. Everything will be better in the morning. And you guys need to talk. Keep your deals."

He would blank Isaac from everyone's memory, let him live a quiet and wholly insignificant life in a mountainous log cabin somewhere. He would never see him again. He would never be able to change anything, not really, not properly. The world would just keep being shit and red haired twenty something women would still end up dead on the floor because someone was frightened and angry.

His insides clenched all over again. His vision swam.

"Gabriel, come on." Sanna had the same damning sort of concern on her face as Isaac did. He wanted to insist he was fine, because he was always fine. It was simply that nothing about the current situation was fine. "Let go of Dahlia, yeah? She's not going to do anything or hurt anyone. Not any more."

Sanna.

Sanna was there.

The idea sparked.

"You can save her." He whipped to face her. She had to be able to save the dreamweaver; this had to be worth something. All of this had to be worth more. There had to be ways of saving the world that didn't come to blood and violence as if that could be right. And if Sanna could save Morphina, now…well, it didn't have to be nothing. This never had to happen again.

Everything he'd hoped for could still happen.

"Gabriel…she's gone," Isaac said. "I'm sorry. You said it yourself, she's dead. Look – Sanna's right. Let's just go home, I'm sorry. We'll get some sleep. We'll talk."

But the thought flickered through Sanna's head. The confirmation. And the thought flickered through Isaac's head that he was placating a dragon.

Gabriel straightened.

"Save her."

It wasn't a question or a suggestion.

Sanna seized Isaac's arm, her eyes flaring the colour of moonlight.

"Gabriel—" she began.

Obey me.

"No," Isaac said. He wrenched his arm back. "Wait – no – what are you doing?"

Be still.

Isaac froze before he could reach for skin, flee, do anything. His panic exploded. "Gabriel. Please—"

Shut up. I am done listening to you.

"This is insane!" Dahlia strained against his control, next. "You can't be serious. You want to give her a second shot at killing us?"

Save her.

Gabriel had nothing to say to Dahlia any more. Not after what she'd done – she knew how he felt about murder! He clamped his control down on all three of them and it was *easy.* It was stupidly easy when someone was in the room with him. If anything, it took more effort not to than it did to seize their minds. It was only ever the half-control that took effort, care.

Around them, across Cambridge, he could feel minds stirring woozily back to consciousness. Maybe he couldn't save the world, maybe he'd never be powerful enough for that, but he could do home. Wasn't that what happened in the stories? Superman saved the world when he could, but, mostly, he saved his city from threat. Or maybe Archangel had been right, and good people simply couldn't save everyone.

But Gabriel could save her, at least. Hadn't enough people died for this already, without her joining them?

He flicked the switches. Their fear vanished, resistance squashed – no point having terror around the dreamweaver. No more point having terror at all, really, when a person

237

could be spared its agonies and it clearly caused nothing but misery and trouble to all involved.

"Dahlia," he said. "Bind her."

Nobody could save the world alone, but together…

It was stupid, too, to be disappointed in them. He was stupid to ever think that they were or could be better than any other human on their god-forsaken planet. Like everyone else, they would never escape their own self-absorbed heads long enough, as if it was all so relative and their individual selves mattered most.

Dahlia wanted to save her sister.

Isaac didn't want to be responsible.

Sanna wanted her telepathic fix more than anything else.

He could do that too. He could help with that.

Someone had to.

He was so *tired.*

Sanna touched a hand to Morphina's chest. The skin knotted healed, weaving back together from the wicked sharpness of Dahlia's thorns. Colour spread through her, softened her, beneath the ugly stain of blood.

The silence stretched. Stretched. What if it wasn't enough? What if, even with Isaac, it wasn't enough?

More.

Isaac shuddered and hit his knees. He looked like he wanted to talk, but couldn't.

More.

Gabriel searched her face for any signs of life.

C'mon. C'mon. Come back.

Blood dripped from Isaac's nose.

Morphina shuddered and gasped, panting as if she'd been jerked conscious from some deep slumbering dream. Her eyes flicked wild around the room. That black had drained away, streaking down her cheeks like smudges of mascara.

Dahlia's vines pinned her to the floor, but the dreamweaver didn't even try and attack. Disorientated, dazed, reeling. Her mind was as silent as it had ever been – no, quieter.

He'd never given much thought to souls, or to afterlives. Believing everything would magically be better after death seemed like a shoddy excuse not to do everything a person could do in their current existence. But…but was it possible to bring back just a body? Some vital spark erased? Could she still control dreams and bring nightmares to life?

Gabriel's head tilted curiously. Excitement shot through him. Because imagine, just imagine, what could be done if such a skill was harnessed? Pain, chronic illness, all those unpleasant ailments could be wiped away in an instant. If they could resurrect a person, what couldn't they do?

He took a step closer to get a better look and sent a command at Dahlia to bind Isaac next, just in case.

"Gabriel," Isaac said, because Gabriel hadn't told him how long to shut up for. "Not to be a cliché, but you *really* don't have to do this. We stopped her, and now you saved her. It's over. You said – you said you loved me."

He had said that. It was true and it was enough that Gabriel turned to face him, examining Isaac's stricken expression. He remembered Isaac's words. *Torture.* The selfishness rose and he squashed it down. He stepped closer, heart hammering, but only to pluck Isaac's knives from their holsters and toss them across the room. Nasty, violent things. Each time, he felt Isaac's mind buck against his holdings.

He settled his hand on the back of Isaac's neck.

Some part of him relished the shiver – the reaction,

the change from Isaac's ever useless efforts to control his responses and expressions. The man was an emotional wreck. Didn't he need someone like Gabriel? Where was he without him? Living in a cottage touch-starved and isolated, in terror of the world. Running. Always running. Was that not torture too? He soothed his thumb over the sudden knot of tension above Isaac's spine.

"Fuck you." Isaac's mind wasn't snarling now, it was *roaring*. As if anything about Isaac had ever been as listless and passive as he tried to pretend. He swayed dizzily on the spot.

"Only if you ask nicely, dear," Gabriel replied, idly.

He focused on Morphina's mind. He lunged for it, pouring all of his powers into the crevices and creases. He had to see if it would work. A mind was a mind, and dreaming was still that. He understood that now. Subconscious, but not some magical thing devoid of sense or influence, just harder to control. He dragged her consciousness into the spotlight, like a moth to a cork board, thinking of what Archangel's mind had felt like and wondering what a woman who spent her life engulfed in dreaming felt like. It would drive anyone mad, wouldn't it? It wasn't her fault.

It wasn't any of their fault.

But Gabriel was sick of making excuses for them, when he could be better.

This couldn't happen again and – unless he did something – it would always happen again. Humanity was fucking like that.

"Gabriel, don't." Isaac thrashed against the vines. "No. I'm saying no, what does morality say about people saying no?"

The power washed through him. He was strong on his own, but with Isaac in his hands it felt he could be invincible, or at least something like it. Temporarily changing someone's mind had always been easy for him, a matter of will, but he'd never had much luck actually *changing* them. People were stubborn and his sway over them faded with time and absence. There was always time and absence, in the normal range of his gifts.

But with Isaac, with her there now, he *focused.* The world narrowed down.

Isaac's power washed over him so easily that it could only be a gift; it didn't feel like something wrenched and stolen unwillingly.

He changed her. Rewrote the codes and buried them deep, deeper than he'd ever dared go before. Blood trickled out of his nose too and he swayed along with Isaac. His head throbbed. His chest ached. Every inch of him ached with the need to sleep. Soon he could taste blood in his mouth too, a flood of copper like he'd bitten down on his tongue. Everything washed hazy around the edges.

"You're going to kill me," Isaac gasped. "Stop, please. I can't—"

"Shh. You've always been stronger than you give yourself credit for. We're nearly done."

Mona Sanderson groaned on the floor, twitching against the vines. Her muscles tensed. Her mind fought him, it darted away from him like mist – but dreams were dreams and it was time to wake the hell up.

He pushed deeper.

She shuddered and went still. Her mind settled.

Gabriel grinned at Isaac, triumphant. Just look at what they could do together!

And then his world went black with exhaustion.

21 - Isaac

Gabriel crumpled and Isaac dropped with him.

The spell on the room broke and he crawled away from the reach of Gabriel's slack hands. He only stopped moving when his back hit the wall. The wall, safely devoid of ability, was a cold and solid welcome. His vision swam. He struggled not to let himself pass out too, though the possibility of oblivion whispered to him like a lover's sweet nothings. He couldn't stop shaking.

"Oh my god," Dahlia said. Her vines coiled back from Mona like she'd been scalded and curled protectively around her. She folded her arms across her chest, stumbling back without the force of Gabriel's telepathy to bind her will and her limbs into his chosen place. Tears spilled down her cheeks.

Mona slumped to the ground, unconscious, but alive. Was Gabriel right? Could he have helped her more if he'd done something earlier? Could he have stopped all it from happening? Was it his fault?

None of them spoke further, perhaps all wrestling with trying to find the right words to say. What were they supposed to say? Praise be the bloody miracle?

Isaac turned onto his side, retching. His stomach heaved. He spat coffee grounds onto the floor and it still felt like there

242

was something poison inside him.

Somehow, he hadn't expected it. He should have expected it. He'd thought they were making progress. He'd thought – his mind stumbled over Gabriel telling him to run, Gabriel close. It had been like it used to be, or at least closer to that. He'd hoped – what had he hoped? He shouldn't have. Gabriel had a single-minded compulsion to do what he thought was right, especially when he was pissed off.

But, back in the day, Gabriel had always listened when he said no. It was an unbreakable rule. It was *the unbreakable rule.*

Would he be so desperate to save people if Isaac hadn't died in his arms?

He wiped the blood from his nose, but it kept coming. Black spots danced in his vision. He couldn't get warm. He felt like an empty battery.

"Is he dead?" Sanna asked. "He's not – he's not dead?" She sounded panicked.

Run. Run. Run. Isaac wasn't convinced he could even stand up, let alone run. What if standing up and stumbling drew their attention to him? He wished they would just forget. Let them forget he'd ever been there.

Of course they wouldn't.

Nobody ever did.

Isaac dropped his head against his knees and squeezed his eyes shut. Gloves. Where were his gloves? He tucked his hands protectively against his chest, as if holding them close would somehow keep them from touching anything else. He didn't know where his gloves had gone.

He heard footsteps crossing the room, but it wasn't towards him so he didn't lift his head. He couldn't think. Couldn't feel.

Or maybe he simply felt too much for any of it to register as anything other than raw. His breathing quickened.

He tried to count to ten. Ten didn't work. Twenty didn't work.

He couldn't breathe. Oh god, he couldn't breathe.

Gabriel would have been able to calm him with a smile and it made him sick.

"Don't touch—" Dahlia began.

Someone coughed. Gasped.

Isaac's head shot up.

Gabriel pushed himself up on the floor, one arm shaking – but not dead. Of course he wasn't.

Sanna let her hand fall, uncertainly, from his shoulder.

"Are you alright?" she asked. "What were you *thinking?*"

Gabriel was definitely not dead. He took one look at Morphina and a smile spread across his lips; that delighted smile that Isaac had once cherished above all other sights in the world. Nauseous relief and air-stealing terror flooded Isaac's already airless lungs. It was impossible to retreat back further. He stumbled to his feet, staggered, making a grab for the wall to stay upright. He hit his knees all the same.

Don't run.

Isaac grabbed at the adrenaline, the urge, the failing strength in his limbs with a vicious hope. Not again. It couldn't be happening again.

Didn't Gabriel say that Isaac's power was his own? Why didn't it feel like that? Why didn't it *ever* feel like that?

"I'm alright," Gabriel said, to Sanna. "Thank you."

"You're overusing your powers," Sanna said. "You need to stop now, okay? You can stop now. We're safe. Nobody's dead." She looked at him with such a fierce protectiveness.

"Gabriel – I did as you asked." Isaac gulped. "You *promised.*"
He had to believe that promise still meant something because
he didn't know what else he had. Gabriel, for what it was
worth, had always been a man of his word before. Even if
those words could be silvered and distracting. "You promised
you'd let me go." He had to believe, but he just felt like a
stupid child gabbling about promises over and over. A broken
record.

Gabriel frowned, rubbing the back of his head. He glanced
at Mona's unconscious form too, before propping himself up
against a nearby pew.

"It's alright, Isaac. You should get some rest."

It wasn't alright. Nothing was alright. The rough telepathic
hold on him hadn't loosened.

He wondered if Sanna and Dahlia understood his caution
now. Gabriel De Vere could be a kind man, a great friend,
many good things. But that was the Gabriel De Vere who
had his limits, who was only a man and couldn't taste the
possibility of being something more.

Isaac didn't have the cover of touches to hide his thoughts.

Gabriel stayed still, the silence broken only by all of their
ragged breathing. None of them moved either. Then, he
exhaled a breath.

*Isaac, go over to Morphina now and hold your hand against her
skin.*

"Gabriel." Isaac pushed, slowly, to his feet. "Please, this is
madness. We stopped Mona, we stopped the dreamers. Isn't
that enough? You've done enough."

"It's not morality," Gabriel murmured. "It's mind control, I
know. I did listen to you. I always listen to you, Isaac."

Isaac didn't dare hope, but hope was cruel enough not to

245

listen to dares or reason. Hope did whatever the hell hope pleased and so, for an instant, hope still rose in Isaac's chest and softened the frantic racing of his heart.

"But do you know what I've realised?" Gabriel met his eyes. "I don't care. Not if it means this doesn't happen again."

"Gabriel—you need sleep—"

Shut up and do it, now, no hesitation. Why do you always have to fight me? You hate fighting anyway.

Isaac winced.

Before, Gabriel's power had been a hand on the back of his neck. It was unsettling, controlling, calming; but not inherently damaging. A hand on the back of one's neck was frighteningly close to the jugular, but it wasn't that. Now, it was as if Gabriel's telepathy had seized him by the throat, locked around his windpipe to hold him hostage, like tightening a leash around a misbehaving dog.

How had he been so stupid as to hope? And how could he be so stupid that he still wanted to? Gabriel wasn't good for him.

It was everything that Isaac had spent the last five years running from, his every nightmare come to life – quite literally, soon.

Part of him, the smallest and most awful part, had been relieved when Dahlia gouged thorns straight through Mona's heart. There were enough monsters in the world already without, in fear, literally summoning more to make every-thing worse. Especially when Archangel could control the nightmares. Killing her had been the easy fix to the problem, the one Isaac hadn't dared to take.

Of course, Gabriel would never think himself capable of losing control. Or, perhaps, Gabriel was just no longer thinking. Angry, hurting, frightened. Everything that he accused them of being.

Isaac walked over and touched his hand to Mona's cheek. He prayed nothing would happen, he prayed he'd exhausted himself, he prayed he'd pass out. Maybe, maybe that time, he'd run out of power to give. It couldn't be endless, nothing was endless. Maybe he'd just die for real.

He searched out Sanna's gaze, because she must realise Gabriel's greater good was as bad as the one she had been faced with, but she wouldn't look at him.

Morphina's eyes flickered open, sluggish and pale blue once more.

Nothing happened.

Then the power flowed out of him and he was drowning. Of course it would. He didn't want it to.

She lost control. Just like Alec Mandel had.

Archangel flickered to life. He was even more handsome than Gabriel was, compared to the version they had seen earlier. He was more exaggerated. Gabriel ten times over. Gabriel squared, with all those little human bits smoothed away. The new Gabriel looked like the form a god might take if he decided to wander around earth with the mortals. There was nothing tired about him. But the last time had been an accident. The creature in front of him was Isaac's worst nightmare, deliberately done.

Isaac closed his eyes briefly. He heard Sanna and Dahlia's voices like distant things; everything seemed so very distant. It was the same feeling as it had been before, hungry and draining and yet the power kept coming and *coming*. It poured out of him. It scraped him hollow, and yet just when he thought there was nothing left it was like another bit inside him was wrenched away.

"I really don't care about the ethics of telepathy when it makes people happier, safer, better. If they can't be decent on their own—" Gabriel's voice rose, as if he was trying to justify Isaac's very thoughts to him, and god he probably was, "—then I'll make them decent. Look at her, Isaac. All of you. She's alive, and she's never going to hurt anyone again. Is that not better than murdering her?"

She's hurting me right now, Isaac thought, pointedly.

Gabriel's shoulders tensed.

Could Gabriel really know that Morphina wouldn't cause more harm? Or was he insane on some chemical cocktail of power and lack of sleep?

"Oh, this is good. We should do Dahlia next," Archangel murmured to his counterpart. "Before she tries to kill someone else."

"I'm not going to kill anyone!" Dahlia snapped. "What do you mean 'do me'? You stay the hell away from me."

"For god's sake!" Sanna's voice cracked. "Look at them both, they're exhausted. Even if it was right, it's not right now." She took a step between them. "Gabriel, it's enough. You know this is enough. Look at Isaac. This is about making the world stop hurting and that's good. But he's *hurting.*"

Archangel's gaze moved pitilessly over Isaac next, as if assessing the truth of the comment.

There was a beat, then.

"She's right – he's exhausted." Gabriel scrubbed a hand over his face. "We all need rest. We haven't slept in days. We have time. It…it doesn't have to be like this."

"I don't need him to be awake." Archangel moved closer to Isaac, reaching out a hand to touch, to brush Isaac's sweat-damp hair back from his forehead. "He can magnify in his sleep, too. It's his default setting."

"What? No, don't." Gabriel started forwards too, stumbling. "You'll hurt him, look at him. It's enough for one day. There is a way to do this and it is not going to be torture." Gabriel swallowed. "We're telepaths, we're smarter than that. Better than that."

Archangel's head tilted and he gave Gabriel that cool assessing look next. After a moment, however, he did drop his hand.

Isaac's heart hammered in his chest. At least Gabriel defended him on that, he supposed. At least. Could he escape, with a little more time?

"We need to put him somewhere secure. He'll run the second we give him the chance, even if it literally kills him," Archangel said.

Gabriel nodded, as if he wasn't agreeing to a prison cell.

Sanna bit her lip, her hands twisting anxiously in front of her, but she said nothing.

"Everyone up," Gabriel commanded. "We're going home. The city will be waking up soon."

"Come on," Dahlia said. "Just let go, alright? We're your friends. Don't listen to him. You're upset, I know you're upset, but—"

"Exactly. You're my friends." Gabriel looked between them. "Which is why I need to do this, for your own good. I see everything you could be, everything you feel…and it's not this. You're better than this. We're all better than this. Up. *Now.*"

Everyone staggered to their feet, even as their limbs trembled with the effort of it. Telepathy didn't allow for refusal.

Rage streaked through to the terror, a match to flint. Because really? Gabriel was *really* going there? Isaac felt like a puppet on strings.

"Odd sort of better when you can't even keep your word," he spat. "You said, if I helped you stop Morphina, that you would let me go. She's stopped. You haven't! We had a *deal.*"

"You could make him forget that." Archangel spoke to Gabriel lightly, almost musingly, as if his suggestion was nothing but an interesting thought experiment he hadn't had the opportunity to try before. "It wouldn't hurt him so much then. He might even be happy, with some work."

Gabriel shot Archangel an uncertain look back.

Archangel raised a brow. "You want him to be happy in this scenario, don't you? As much as possible?"

Isaac's stomach dropped.

"You can't do that. Not if you want to use my abilities." He clung to that fact. "Your lies, your power over me, ends the second you touch me, whatever you do to them. You don't get away with doing that to me."

Archangel shook his head, a small smile flittering across his lips. "Now, now. We both know that's not quite true or you wouldn't be looking at him like that."

Archangel's black stare bore into him, swallowed him whole. Maybe Gabriel was too used to relying on telepathy and could no longer read a person's face, but Isaac could see the malice glimmering clearly in the nightmare's eyes.

"Telepath, Isaac," Archangel continued. "You can't lie to us. If that had ever been true you wouldn't have felt the need to play dead for five years. You would have just told me to piss off right then."

He looked so smug that Isaac couldn't help but flare. "Maybe I'll die properly this time."

No.

The thought vanished from his head. Isaac groped at the absence, uneasily, trying to figure it out by the shape and feel of what was missing.

The smile vanished from Archangel's mouth.

"Stop fighting me. Stop fighting us." There was no snarl in Archangel's voice, it had been replaced by something quiet and infinitely more dangerous. "How many times do we have to tell you?"

Isaac's head throbbed. His jaw clenched.

Maybe this was something he could wake up from like a bad dream.

Wake up.

Wake up wake up wake up.

Gabriel moved over to him, clutching the pews for balance, so very earnest and concerned. "It's alright," he said. "You're safe, I've got you, okay? I won't let anything bad happen to you. I know you don't trust me right now, and that's fair, but you must know that. I meant what I said. I listen. I – I love you."

The safety flooded into Isaac's brain, as warm and familiar as a hot bath on aching muscles. Isaac knew it wasn't true, but oh he wanted it to be true. It would have been easy to let it be true. It was nice if it was true.

"You're better than this," Dahlia whispered. "This isn't you. What the hell are you doing to him?"

"He's okay," Gabriel said. He wiped the tears from Isaac's cheek with the hem of his sleeve.

"Look, Gabriel – I'm sorry," Dahlia said. "You're scaring

me. I'm sorry. I just did what I thought was best."

"Then the world deserves better than your best."

"This isn't better." Dahlia's shoulders shook. "The world doesn't deserve this. This isn't justice, this is some kind of sick joke. Let the *nightmare* go."

Gabriel turned to face her next, his face softening with concern as he watched the tears fall from her eyes too. He looked like it was a kind of agony and it probably was – the pain on Dahlia's face vanished. Her expression evened out with the drugged up sort of elation that came from having the bad forcibly stolen away.

"You don't need to be scared. You don't need to be scared of anything any more." Gabriel offered her a gentle smile, even as he swayed on his feet. Sweat beaded his forehead without Isaac's powers to bolster his exhausted reserves. He looked waxy.

Isaac knew Gabriel would kill himself to suck the pain out of the world and, even then, it hurt. It hurt to know that. To watch that. To watch the way that Archangel watched Gabriel, with an eager hunger, like he was going to suck the marrow out of him. Like he was going to gobble up all the good and grow fat on it.

So, Isaac didn't think. He punched. He lunged for Gabriel to stop that power, feeling his mind clear. They hit the cold ground, scrambling and grappling, and then another set of arms had wrapped around Isaac's waist.

Archangel dragged him back, still kicking. His grip felt impossibly, inhumanly strong.

Isaac slammed his elbow back into the nightmare's ribs, feral, but it did nothing.

Gabriel cupped a hand to his bleeding nose. "Everything,"

he said. "Is going to be okay."

"Okay," Dahlia said, placidly.

No, no, no. Not okay. Definitely not okay.

"Okay," Sanna said. She sounded relieved, as the telepathy infiltrated her too.

Gabriel turned on him again.

"Okay, Isaac?" he demanded.

The not okays swept away, as if they'd never even been there. It was okay. Everything was going to be okay. Isaac wouldn't make it worse, would he, by staying? He didn't want to make it worse. Everything was going to be okay. He was so very tired of running. He was so very tired of fighting. He had always hated both of those things. He sagged limp in Archangel's arms, a small smile on his face.

Peace washed over him.

"Okay," Isaac whispered.

II

Part 2: The Dreamers

22 - Gabriel

Gabriel remembered very little about the journey back to the house – only the joy of people stirring awake around him. It was a spring of human life and consciousness. The lights of their minds were sparking back on, so comforting in their familiarity. Not always good, not always perfect, but they could be. He soothed what he could of their panic and grief as he passed, even if only for a little while, clutching hold of Isaac. It was the only way he could keep going. He had to keep going. They were so scared. He could help them not be.

Happily ever after.

Time skipped and fuzzed around him. His limbs felt weak. The second he got back to the house he crashed on the bed, snapped his headphones on, and slept. He couldn't check on anyone, couldn't think, he was officially done. The world was saved and he finally got to be *done*. He woke up for a glass of water. Slept again in a vaguely more comfortable position where he didn't get a headphone imprint pressed into his cheek. Pissed. Slept.

He woke up feeling better than he had all week. His head didn't feel like some raw minced thing any more, just…tender. His body, too, seemed less like an animated sack of bones all

257

jumbled up in the wrong order. He stretched out, his back giving a pleasing click. It was a new day and he felt new. Rain pattered softly outside the window, filling the room with its gentle music and fresh scent.

The world, as he heard it, was calm. He couldn't remember the last time his mind had been able to soak up the world and not find any sharp edges to cut himself on. For a few minutes, he didn't even think to move, luxuriating in the wave of happy emotions without pressing closer to pick out any of the details.

Then he remembered.

Gabriel sat up so fast he nearly fell out of bed, flailing to balance himself, mattress springs giving an offended squeak at his gracelessness. His telepathy lunged for the closest minds – for Sanna, Dahlia for – the look on Isaac's face came back to him. The horror. Oh, god. What had he done? What the hell had he done?

Archangel everything's changed so many dead reform rehabilitation

no more billionaires harvest program did you see the news? Archangel Does anyone else think we should feel a little more freaked out about this?

He winced, his head giving a warning throb. He'd overtaxed himself, hadn't he? Even so, in the details, it was overwhelming. Gabriel was used to skimming the thoughts around him, but the familiarity of the world had grown to make it more like ambient white noise for the most part. He, typically, had always known what to expect. The house would be filled with the patterns of Ari and Dahlia and Felicity and Sanna and Lucy and Jack all clattering around normal life, and next door might be thinking about money and the baby. What he heard was new. Of course it was new. New didn't mean bad.

Through this world now was a common thread, something unfamiliar. Something separate to the minds that it touched, that entwined around them, so to speak. He couldn't quite put his finger on it.

Gabriel exhaled a breath and tried to find something he could anchor on, something that would give him answers instead of more questions. Even if he had to do it the old-fashioned way and talk.

Sanna was outside.

He got up, leaving his headphones discarded on the mattress, and hurried out of the bedroom. Dahlia's room next door was empty, the burnt dorm after that was empty too and the flowers were wilting. It still smelled like char. His stride turned to full on running, slamming open doors and thundering down the stairs and out of the front and –

Sanna stood by an orderly line of people, as radiant as a benevolent saint as she healed each one of their ailments in turn. Her brow pinched with concentration, but she seemed calm too. Purposeful. She didn't notice him until his mind brushed against hers, at which point she turned and smiled.

"You're awake!" Her brow furrowed. "You should shower."

Gabriel looked down at himself, still dressed in clothes rumpled by the battles that had come before, and back up. His head spun. Sanna didn't look hurt but with Sanna that didn't necessarily mean anything. If Sanna's appearance actually reflected the reality of the hurts she had carried she would be more zombie than woman. Or simply dead.

The line of people waited for relief from their ills – an old woman with arthritis, a young boy with a cold, aching joints, broken bone, cold –

259

Sanna's hand on his arm jerked him out of it before he could spiral further into their thoughts.

He'd normally done a better job, in the past, of hiding when he'd overdone it on using his telepathy. He did his best to compose his expression.

"Breathe," she said, studying him closely. "You're okay. How are you feeling?"

He wasn't sure he could stomach the concern in her voice. He cleared his throat.

Normally, faced with an array of pain, Sanna would have been happy to help, but worn. She would have wanted to unwind after. She barely seemed to register that the illnesses must cause suffering to others, she only felt her joy in being able to heal them. There was no guilt that she was healthy and they weren't. That was good. It wasn't entirely like her, but it was good.

"How long was I out?"

There were whispers from the crowd of people of "it's him! It's actually him! Archangel!"

"Couple days, you were completely wiped."

"Where's–" Gabriel barely knew where to start.

Sanna glanced back at the people, then to whatever she saw on Gabriel's face. Whatever it was made pity bloom in her mind. He really must have looked terrible.

"Go back in the house," she suggested. "Change. Have something to eat. He'll be on his way back soon – he'll be able to explain everything to you."

She said 'he' like something reverent.

"Wait," said the the old woman with her arthritis. "If you're him—" They were edging closer. Their questions rose and vanished, rose and vanished, in an endless cycle.

Gabriel backed away before he could stop himself, uncertainly, and he didn't even have to form the command for them to turn away from him as if they'd forgotten he was there, and go back to what they were doing. Even Sanna staggered back, before he caught her arm again.

"Gabriel." She beamed at him. "You're awake." Her brow furrowed. "You should—"

"Get back in the house, shower, and you'll come find me when you're done here?"

Her head tilted, but she nodded.

Gabriel retreated back into the house, his heart hammering. He grabbed some painkillers, swallowed them with water, and put the kettle on for tea. He should grab his headphones again. As the water boiled, he went into the living room and turned on the TV instead. His face – *no*, Archangel's face – was on every channel. Gabriel forgot about the kettle as he stared, absorbing the flood of new information. It did help a bit. The TV wasn't a mind, after all, to focus on.

Nobody seemed too concerned by the sudden changes that had overcome the world. Nobody even seemed to truly question it, they simply reported on the new initiatives in a factual way.

The Harvest Project would make sure that food was not wasted, and many a stately manor had been requisitioned to support the new plans for housing for all. Crime rates had dropped to nothing almost overnight.

On first glance it was absolutely everything that Gabriel had ever hoped for. It was change, *real* change. A small part of him couldn't believe that it all actually worked. He'd spent so long imagining it…

"He's on his way." Sanna's voice sounded from behind him.

"You really should shower and make yourself presentable. I've got your tea."

He accepted the drink on automatic.

"Dahlia," he began.

"She's working on setting up greenhouses for the new compound," Sanna said. "You know Dahlia, always happy when she's surrounded by plants. She's fine."

"I need to talk to her." Gabriel didn't necessarily *regret* entirely what he'd done, but certainly his method of doing it had not been his moment of greatest kindness. He'd been much too harsh on her – she was barely more than a kid, and she'd just lost Felicity. His mind flashed back to the looks on their faces, the tears rolling down her cheeks, Isaac's pleas. The guilt thickened in his throat and made it impossible to swallow. He focused on the warmth of the mug seeping through the cradle of his palms and realised he was shivering.

"It's all taken care of." Sanna switched the TV off. "You can stop worrying. I know that's difficult for you, but, really. Listen." She took his elbow, steering him towards the stairs. "Everything is okay now. The Archangel Project worked."

He remembered drilling that thought in – *everything is okay.* Funny, how he suddenly couldn't quite trust her opinion on the basis of his own powers. Still. The world did *sound* happy, in so far as he could hear it, didn't it? Maybe he was simply too used to there being a problem, waiting for the proverbial rug to be yanked from beneath his feet.

"Isaac." It came out raspy.

"He's fine, too," Sanna said. "He's with Archangel."

How do you know he's fine? Gabriel bit back the question. It was a useless question to ask right then, when he would need to see Isaac himself to know for sure anyway.

"You said he was coming here." They came to a pointed stop outside the bathroom, with him still clutching a steaming mug of tea. "Isaac too?"

"Isaac too." She poked his shoulder. "He told me you've got about fifteen minutes...so."

"Shower." He took the hint. "Right. He told you? He's...in your head?"

He focused his powers on her, but it sent another lance of pain through his skull along with a wave of nausea. He caught the wall for balance. Right. No powers. He wasn't going to start feeling better until he stopped for a bit, he knew that from experience. What he probably needed was food, a dark room, and some quiet. He couldn't shake the nagging feeling that he had time for precisely none of those things.

Sanna gave him a 'well, duh' look.

"He's in all of our heads," she said. "Shower. He'd rather not waste telepathy on unnecessary PR because you look like a warmed-up corpse that's not going to impress anyone."

Gabriel blinked and wondered if he should be offended. Probably.

"You'll feel better," she added, more kindly.

Gabriel relented. If he was seeing Isaac and Archangel again he wanted to feel like he had bit more of a mental defence than he currently did, and he probably didn't want to smell like smoke and blood for his own sake as much as public relations. It was true, too, that he felt a fraction more human when he emerged from the bathroom. He found clean clothes and by the time the car pulled up in the driveway outside he was at least somewhat ready.

He headed out to meet them, with a vague sense that he must be dreaming. The crowds from earlier were gone. He still sucked in a breath as Archangel stepped out of the car first.

He was...well. It was weird looking at someone who looked like him, wasn't it? Except for the eyes. Archangel's eyes were as black as any of the nightmares before him had been. He'd changed into fresh clothes too – white t-shirt and dark jeans. He looked *real*. More real than a dream felt like it could be. The colour scheme was the same as the Archangel from Isaac's comics, so long ago.

Gabriel ground to a halt.

Isaac followed Archangel out the car. His hands were cuffed behind his back, and his god-awful haircut was gone. It was closer now to the style from their last year at university. He looked content. Gabriel wasn't dumb enough to think he was content without help...but at least Isaac didn't seem hurt.

Gabriel took a step closer, pausing as two nightmares appeared to flank Isaac on either side like prison guards. He released a steadying breath and watched them approach.

The look on Isaac's face made something in him prickle. Given their last meeting, he expected to be hit by Isaac's overwhelming sense of betrayal, but there was no trace of it. No distress. There wasn't even a flicker of concern.

"You're in his head," Gabriel said.

"Hello to you too," Archangel replied, coming to a stop in front of him. He gestured at the house. "Shall we? We have work to do."

"He doesn't like us in his head."

"He doesn't like a lot of things. He's happier like this. You wanted him happy."

Yes, Gabriel had obviously wanted Isaac to be happy, but – well. He hadn't thought it would be so unnerving. The

Isaac he knew would very much not be happy in his current situation, he would be glaring at Gabriel, trying to think of loopholes to whatever telepathic commands he'd been given. Infuriating, prone to running and being a general disaster of a human being, but so alive. Isaac looked like a prisoner surrounded by monsters.

(He looks like that because, the nagging voice in Gabriel's head sniped, he is a prisoner surrounded by monsters.)

Archangel raised his brows.

Gabriel didn't know what to say. Once upon a time, he would have been advocating exactly what Archangel was doing, so there was no *rational* reason for it to disturb him. If Isaac was to be a prisoner surely it was better that he didn't suffer for it? He stepped out of the way to let Archangel pass, only for the dream to guide Gabriel to walk in front of him.

Archangel was keeping him away from Isaac still, wasn't he?

"Will he answer if I talk to him?

"It's telepathy," Isaac said. "Not invasion of the body snatchers. Shouldn't you know that?"

Gabriel felt like he should know the rules of this new world...but he didn't. Archangel wasn't touching Isaac, so he couldn't be magnified, and yet everything that Gabriel could hear seemed utopic.

"Has he..." there was no good way to ask it. They entered the kitchen. Sanna was nowhere in sight. "Have you touched him yet? Does he – has he processed what's going on?"

"He knows," Archangel said. "He is less happy when I touch him, as you may imagine. Lots of screaming and cursing. You know, he actually tried to *bite* me yesterday." He gave Isaac a look, somewhere between annoyed and indulgent, and something icy slid down Gabriel's spine.

Had he ever looked at Isaac like that? Like he was more tool than man? The answer came immediately. Yes. Yes, he had. He'd done that the last time he saw Isaac, hadn't he? He'd done it whenever he'd considered the use more important than the act of using. He hadn't expected it to look so startling on somebody else's face.

No, not someone else. On his face. That was his face.

"Oh, god." Gabriel caught the edge of the table to steady himself, feeling shaky for an entirely different reason as the enormity of what he'd done struck him.

"You should eat something." Archangel's head tilted as he observed Gabriel's reaction. "You'll feel better then. The pizza place down the road will bring us a bite...sit down and stop looking so horrified in the meanwhile. You know we can't treat him like everyone else, not with how his powers work. Isaac." Archangel flicked his fingers in the direction of one of chairs.

Isaac sat down. Gabriel didn't know if it was reluctant compliance, genuine compliance, or telepathy.

He steeled himself, drawing on his own powers. Something slammed him into the table, shoving the air out of his lungs. A groan rose unbidden to his lips. Something sharp pressed against the back of his neck.

Archangel sighed.

"Stop or I'll have you knocked out."

Gabriel stopped. His eyes met Archangel's.

"Isaac's mind is a delicate ecosystem," Archangel said. "Do you want to scramble it? I mean, I don't personally want him to be comatose, though he would be easier to handle that way I suppose." Archangel smiled faintly, in response to whatever

266

appalled expression had crossed Gabriel's face. "No, I didn't think that would be to your liking. Stay out of his head. One telepath is quite a lot to be getting on with, don't you think? Let alone one telepath and you with your brain half fried clattering around with all the grace of a rhino attempting ballet."

Gabriel managed a small nod.

The pressure on his back eased, allowing him to straighten once more. He glanced behind him to see a nightmare step back. It looked like a mad scientist, impossibly strong, complete with a syringe of some no doubt nefarious substance that could be used to knock out telepaths. Gabriel rubbed an uneasy hand over his neck.

"Good. Now, are we quite done with the dramatics?" Archangel asked, in an oh so polite and reasonable tone. Gabriel recognised the tone. He was the one who used that tone on the villains he'd once fought, when they still thought they could win long past when it should be obvious that they had already lost.

Heat rushed to his face.

Archangel gestured at a chair.

Gabriel sat down. His dug his nails into his palms.

What was he even exactly dealing with here? Weren't they supposed to be on the same side? Weren't they supposed to be good, the two of them? It didn't feel good. Well, okay, there were bits that were good. There were bits that were everything that Gabriel had only dreamed could be possible – and then, there was Archangel. Then, there was Isaac, sitting across the kitchen table from him with a blank expression on his face as if the two of them had ever been so emotionless towards each other. There was Isaac, saying nothing, doing nothing, as if the two of them weren't discussing his fate. All that came from Isaac was the same, placid, happiness that filled everything Gabriel could hear in the background.

"You have questions, I'm sure," Archangel said.

"Is Isaac…can I talk to him? *Properly* talk to him, for a moment. I know we want him happy but he's not going to be happy with this, and I…"

"Next question. Perhaps you would like to know what the casualties are? Or focus on how we are going to proceed with maintaining order?"

"Right." Gabriel tried to focus. His attention slid back to Isaac. "Sorry. Just – are you alright?" he asked. He glanced at Archangel. "You've let him sleep, right? Since everything?" He looked back at Isaac. "Has he let you rest?"

Archangel's tongue clicked with irritation, but Isaac spoke.

"Yes," he said. "He's let me sleep. People who do not sleep die and I am more useful alive."

The colour drained from Gabriel's face at that response. It wasn't – well, it was true. He hadn't expected Isaac to say it so bluntly.

Archangel's eyes narrowed in Isaac's direction, so presumably he'd loopholed some command. Certainly, despite the fact that Isaac's voice was measured and steady, the comment itself had an edge of accusation for all that it may have been factual.

Right. That was it. Gabriel's eyes darted around the kitchen, searching for anything that he could use to get a better grip on the situation. Telepathy, judging from what little he had seen of Archangel's powers so far, was out of the question. It would be like a kitten walking up to a panther and picking a fight.

"You try so hard to be a good person," Archangel said, soft and pitying. It snapped Gabriel's attention back to him. "I know you can't help it – you can't bear to see anyone in pain. You can barely stand to think that he *might* be in pain, even when you can hear all evidence to the contrary."

Gabriel kept his voice as light as he could. "You make that sound like an insult considering being good people is what this is all about. I know you said heroes aren't necessarily good, they do what has to be done, but…well." Gabriel didn't see why one couldn't be a hero and also try to be kind.

Archangel had yet to take a seat. He prowled around the kitchen table, heading in Isaac's direction.

Gabriel stiffened. The mad scientist nightmare placed a warning hand on his shoulder, keeping him from standing too.

"I say it like that because you are not a good person, Gabriel De Vere," Archangel said. "You are a sanctimonious control freak who likes to pretend he's good and has a god complex larger than god himself. So we're going to need to fix you too."

"Fix me?" It came out hoarse. "I don't need fixing. I'm not the one here who needs fixing!" His gaze landed on a knife. He hated knives. He couldn't simply sit there and pretend that Isaac sitting there like that was okay. Gabriel knew what he looked like when he was actually happy, and this was…not that. What had he been *thinking*?

Archangel stopped behind Isaac, and his expression was not unkind as he placed his hand on Isaac's shoulder above his shirt.

"I can't have my double walking around being a bad person, having bad thoughts like how best to stab a telepath without

269

them noticing. What sort of impression does that give? We must stick by our principles. Don't be a hypocrite."

"I'm not—" Gabriel floundered, anger catching in his chest. "I'm not a bad person." He'd thought Archangel, out of all of the people in the world, would understand that. Sure, he had kidnapped Isaac and stuffed him in a boot. He had forced Sanna and Dahlia to his will. It wasn't, technically speaking, a pure slate. He'd ignored some boundaries here and there, some consent, but it was all for the greater good. Archangel *knew* that, he had to know that. The bastard wouldn't even be alive if it wasn't for that! He was doing the exact same thing right now with Isaac!

That couldn't be the point. Didn't he just think Archangel was bad for doing that?

"I'm supposed to be the counterbalance to you," Gabriel said instead, carefully. "I'm supposed to be holding you accountable. If those are my flaws, then they are yours too."

"Yes." Archangel seemed unbothered.

Gabriel once again didn't know how to respond. He knew he often didn't do enough to save the world, he knew he didn't always get it entirely perfect, but he tried. Didn't the trying count for anything? To be judged and found so utterly lacking by his *own face...*

"But I do not try to be good," Archangel continued, with a shrug. "I do not pretend that I'm good, like you do, because I'm not here to be good. I'm here to make the world good."

"That's what I'm here for too. That's our destiny." Whatever Gabriel had done, hadn't it been for that? For the peace in the back of his mind? For everybody's happiness?

"Your reaction to Isaac says differently." Archangel looked down at the magnifier beneath his hands and his grip tightened – possessive, controlling.

Gabriel jolted against the mad scientist's grip on his shoulder on instinct. The nightmare pinned him more firmly to his seat.

"I come here," Archangel murmured, "and you do not talk about how we can help the world. You do not want to progress. You want to talk about Isaac Morton like one man is more important than the entire planet. Because you love him. And loves makes someone the most important thing in the world, doesn't it? Love is irrational. Beyond good, beyond evil."

Gabriel forced himself to release a breath, he forced himself not to struggle.

"A temporary adjustment period," he said. It tasted like ash in his mouth. "Humans needs those. In my defence," he tried for his best smile in return. "You know mornings are not my best time of day. I'm sure I'll get over the topic eventually! We only have the rest of our lives."

Archangel laughed; he even sounded fond, for all of his condemnation.

Gabriel knew that laugh too, because of course he did. He was going to be sick.

"You're not going to stop loving him of your own accord, Gabriel. We both know that."

Tentatively, oh so tentatively, Gabriel reached out to Archangel's mind.

Archangel's mind didn't feel like a living creature's mind, from Gabriel's experience. If a mind was normally a pinprick of light then Archangel was shadow, opaque and shifting. Easy to get lost in. He didn't know where to begin grabbing, or taking control. It wasn't a dreamer's mind, and it wasn't

271

the mind of something awake as he knew it. Yet, it was undoubtedly a mind.

Archangel moved his hand from Isaac's shoulder to cover his mouth, muffling the venom that escaped Isaac's lips the second the telepathic link between them broke.

Archangel's eyes turned white.

Isaac's eyes turned terrifiedfuriousbetrayed and Gabriel buckled against the table like he'd been sucker punched by the blow of emotion sent in his direction. He might have hit the floor if not for the mad scientist.

"I thought you were ready to set him aside for the sake of the world," Archangel said. "But clearly I was wrong."

Archangel's power must have been something enormous before, so big it was almost unnoticeable because it was everywhere – part of the new world's atmosphere. It felt like it all lashed directly at Gabriel. It drowned him.

Isaac tried to say something, but Gabriel couldn't hear it.

He wrestled with Archangel's presence in his mind, grappled for control, for air, for life.

"You're a coward, Gabriel De Vere." Archangel's voice turned icy. "You are selfish. You can dish it out, but you can't take it. Does that not make it an abuse of your gifts? Does that not make you evil? You cannot treat others in a way that you wouldn't want to be treated, and you're too weak to do what needs to be done. You do not deserve the power you have."

Gabriel stared at Archangel – the dream was grotesque in the waking light. Some mixed up tangle of half formed desires and rampaging terrors, nothing like him. It clicked. It *finally* truly clicked.

He should have listened to Isaac. No, he'd listened, he'd

always listened. He just hadn't bothered to understand. He'd been so sure that he had it right. That, between the two of them, the world would be perfect. But Archangel wasn't him with power over dreamers, just like Isaac had tried to tell him so many times. Archangel was the nightmare version of him that lived in Isaac's deepest fears. He was everything that Gabriel ever wanted, twisted. He was the worst-case scenario.

"He will learn his lesson, with time," Archangel said. "And now so will you."

Archangel's mind drove into his with an iron force of will, enough to leave Gabriel gasping and dizzied all over again. Gabriel jerked in the hold, or tried to, but a dream was an impossible thing. It did not obey the same laws as everything else. In dreams, the dead could rise, and telepaths could be omnipotent. Especially when they held a magnifier. There was no limit to Archangel's power, no possible counterbalance.

Gabriel's stomach bottomed out.

Even when he imagined his perfect world, even when he had imagined The Archangel Project, he had always factored in a limit. He had never imagined Archangel. Isaac had. Isaac knew what it was to be without limit, Isaac knew power better than anyone.

"Don't," he said. He held his hands up. "Please don't. Whatever you want—"

Archangel didn't let him finish before he took control of Gabriel's brain.

Gabriel had never thought, truly, what it was like to have your emotions taken from you. He'd never thought that it was a *conscious* thing. Or, maybe, maybe Archangel just

273

did it slowly, enjoying the power too greatly because didn't Gabriel enjoy that power in his darkest moments too? Gabriel fumbled for the spaces, like phantom limbs when he knew something should have been there, but there was nothing.

He clung to his memories of Isaac, desperately, even without the emotion. His counterbalance. His *real* counterbalance. Because wasn't that what Isaac was? He knew what he looked like in love with Isaac. He knew what Archangel was taking from him.

He remembered the way that Isaac had sat on the bed when they first met, all wide-eyed and vulnerable in a way that made Gabriel ache to protect him. Made him vow, silently, there and then that he would. He remembered the first feelings of Isaac's interest, so breathtakingly shy like Isaac's attraction was as fragile as a butterfly's wing. He remembered, during one of Isaac's final year projects, he'd presented a wall of charcoal comics strips – based on Gabriel, based on a superhero called Archangel. Isaac had spent the whole night thinking filthy thoughts at Gabriel to wind him up, to distract himself from his own nerves. He remembered him on the floor, blood on his wrists, so pale and so quiet and so world-ending because how could there possibly be a world that went on turning when Isaac Morton wasn't in it?

It all frittered away like grains of sand in the water.

He tried not thinking about it, tried to tuck the memories away like secrets, hide them from where Archangel plucked them. It did nothing. He'd never had to defend his own mind before.

The name was the last thing in his brain, clutched close like a treasure.

Isaac Oliver Morton.

Then that, too, was gone.

23 - Isaac

"I can make it stop hurting," Archangel said, when they were back in the car. "All you have to do is ask."

"I will kill you."

"You're the one who made a deal that the world should forget about you." Archangel smoothed down his shirt and flashed him Gabriel's smile. "Remember?"

"I was also promised freedom once Morphina was defeated."

"Maybe now." Archangel waved at the driver to go. "It will be easier for you both. You will stop fighting, free of the hope that your fairy tale prince of old will magically come and save you" - Isaac flinched - "and he will finally get some peace." Archangel's voice softened in some dreadful imitation of compassion; at least, Isaac hoped it was imitation because the alternative was worse. "Not having memories is an opportunity for him. A reset. You have thought yourself that you are a contagion, that you could only ever ruin him. Now he's free, now he won't think he might have a chance against me to cause him guilt. He's going to take the break you always wanted for him."

"Do not," Isaac could barely get the words out, "use my worst thoughts against me."

276

"I thought the knowledge might comfort you."

Isaac snorted. He would have wrapped his arms tight and defensive around himself if he could.

"Sure," he said. "Is that why you haven't put your mind control back on me yet? To comfort me?"

"Is that you asking me for comfort?"

Isaac eyes flashed with fury.

The last few days had been an exhausting whirlwind. Upon return to the house, when Gabriel had finally collapsed into a deep and immediate sleep, Archangel had solidified his control. His telepathy had been turned first to all the newly awakened in the city, before being directed outward across the UK. Not being a telepath, Isaac did not know the exact process. One would think that world domination was more dramatic to watch but Archangel simply sat there with an intent look on his face most of the time and the dominoes around him fell.

Renovations for a new main base of operations began. Mona was dragged, screaming, to be locked up somewhere in its foundations. Everything was okay. Everything was great.

For a while, Isaac had floated along in a bubble of perfect pliant happiness, even going so far as to curl up to finally sleep with his head resting on Archangel's lap.

Okay shattered when Archangel turned his gaze further outwards still, to the world at large, and touched Isaac's skin to make it happen. The bubble popped. All of the gnawing worry, all of the terror, that had been kept forcibly at bay slammed into him at once. Isaac saw past the cloud of 'this is fine' to a world on fire.

Not-okay looked like everyone who passed them having tranquil expressions, despite the fact that they may have lost

277

people they loved to the sleeping curse which had swept over their homes. Not-okay looked like anyone who questioned Archangel as he moved around the city barely getting the first accusation, or even question, out before their eyes went blank. Not-okay was the nightmares which didn't vanish, but became the new overseers of Archangel's society as the hours advanced.

Not-okay was the fact that, beneath Archangel's all-seeing gaze, it didn't matter if you were a murderer or if you had stolen baby formula to feed your children – you were flattened all the same. No nuance. No consideration of circumstances. To Archangel, it was black and white in a way that Isaac could acknowledge it had never been to Gabriel. You were bad or you weren't and, to Archangel, everyone in the world had some sin to be judged by. No one was good enough. No one was perfect. The possibility of doing anything that Archangel personally considered wrong was stripped away, inch by inch.

And Isaac gave, and gave, and gave until his skin felt raw. Until he couldn't breathe. Telling Archangel not to touch him did nothing, fighting back had done nothing but leave him even more restrained.

"Isaac." When he wasn't looking at Archangel, he sounded so much like Gabriel that it only hurt more. "I am serious - all you have to do is ask." He placed a hand on Isaac's knee, in a gesture that was clearly intended to be reassuring. Isaac tensed. "This life does not have to be uncomfortable for you. You will not be hurt, you will not have to fight people who might want to take advantage of you, because they will never have the chance with me around. You can do your artwork. I'll take care of everything. I'll take care of you."

Isaac clenched his jaw and said nothing. He wasn't sure he trusted himself to speak. He wanted to throw something. He jerked his leg to knock Archangel's hand away, even if it wouldn't stop the creature from touching him when he was determined.

"I know how lonely you have been," Archangel said, even softer. The words echoed in Isaac's head. "I have lived in the corners of dreams, no more than a whisper. Humans are made for more than cottages in the woods without anyone to share them with. You can have company now."

"Company? What, you?" Poison dripped from Isaac's tongue. "I'd rather die alone."

"You know you can be happy with me – you were happy with him, once. I know how to behave like him, and I can make it so you forget the bad. Turn off all your fears."

Ah, so that was why Isaac had his brain back. It was so Archangel could dangle the carrot of how much better life would be if he surrendered to it completely. If he stopped trying to fight. After all, Archangel could certainly use telepathy on him most of the time. But not all of the time. And that left him with at least one person who had a chance of fighting him, and Archangel couldn't stand that, could he? Archangel made Gabriel's controlling tendencies look mild.

"Aren't you a little busy ruling the world to play house?"

"I am powerful," Archangel said. "More powerful than he ever was. More powerful than I ever used to be. You made me that, you dreamed me up. I do not need to touch you all of the time for my commands to hold on the world, perhaps only every three days or so. I could wear gloves, so the spell need not break in the meanwhile. I could..." he wet his lips, considering, "maintain you."

279

Maintain him. How romantic. Like he was a bloody piece of machinery. Isaac swore under his breath and would have hurled himself out the car if not for the fact the child-lock was on.

"I didn't realise you cared about my opinion in the matter. You certainly don't seem to have cared about anyone else's. Why not just go ahead and do what you will anyway?"

Archangel didn't say anything and the silence stretched between them.

"You want me to break, is that it?" Isaac demanded. "You want to console yourself with the fact that I asked for this? You said it yourself, you are not a good person."

"No," Archangel said, eventually. "But we never forced you to love us. That was the one thing that we never did."

Isaac's whole body turned hot, then cold, and he needed to get out of the car and he couldn't get out of the car.

Love. That thing beyond good, beyond evil. It went against everything that Archangel was, when forcing him to love would by Archangel's standards make him happy.

But not by Gabriel's.

By Gabriel's standards that was a horrific thing to do, wasn't it? It was tantamount to rape. There was no consent under mind control after all.

It felt much too late to know for sure that their relationship had always been real – though he supposed Archangel could have been lying. Isaac didn't think so. Gabriel's, and so presumably Archangel's, lies tended to leave one feeling better and not worse.

Isaac wanted to say it then, he wanted to beg. Make it stop hurting. Take the memories of him away from me too, please.

He didn't.

Cambridge disappeared in the back window of the car and Isaac didn't know when he would see it again. He didn't know what would happen to him. He didn't know what the future would hold. What he did know, despite everything he might in uncertainty or insecurity convince himself, was Gabriel Hugo De Vere.

And Gabriel loved him. Not necessarily well, certainly not always sweetly or simply, but that love was buried right down to the core of him.

So, of course, nothing that Gabriel had any hand in was without it. Archangel would never put Isaac's happiness over the fate of the world, but the feeling was still there in some terrible way. Morphina and Isaac might think of power without limit, without humanity, but that wasn't Gabriel. Gabriel was, and always had been, so very human in his power. If there was a limit to Archangel, even the smallest fragment of humanity, then there was something, some small hope, that he could be defeated. Isaac had to find it. Use it. Love was the best most awful weapon he had.

He breathed through the pain and did his best to make it small, make it manageable, to crush it into a ball in his chest.

"I bet," he said, "you wish you could forget what you've done to me too."

He let the pain go, let it explode through his mind like telepathic shrapnel.

Archangel swore. The car swerved on the road as the telepath clutched his head and –

Everything was okay.

It was okay.

Nothing hurt any more.

***

As the days slipped by, Isaac got a distant sense of how the world was shaping up because Archangel rarely liked him to be too far out of reach. The only exception was the hours in which Archangel would vanish on some errand that he didn't want Isaac present for. Thus, they soon fell into routine.

Most of the task of running the world was still in the hands of whatever people normally looked after such affairs, only with Archangel's new parameters in place. All Archangel was doing was removing malice. Exploitation. Or, at least, that was what Archangel said and the reporters reported. In his lucid moments, Isaac didn't consider either source entirely trustworthy given the circumstances.

Isaac, for his part, spent most of his days painting in a telepathic bubble of peace as Archangel had promised. Archangel tried to talk to him, sometimes, but he'd always get a look of frustration on his face like Isaac was being somehow disappointing.

He was never allowed too close to any weaponry, even under telepathy. Weaponry, in general, meant kitchen knives. Any actual weaponry likes guns or grenades were being systematically disposed of across the globe apparently. Isaac had asked Archangel, in one of the times when Archangel was using him to magnify for a global sweep, if he planned to mind control any bears or wild dangerous animals too in light of this ban. Archangel's response had been that murder, even in self-defence, was wrong and no defence for possessing weapons. He refused to be debated on the matter again.

It was only ever in the moments that Archangel touched him that Isaac's mind was his own, but those moments were lasting longer and longer. Each time, Archangel would try and talk before putting Isaac under again.

They were sat on the sofa, in Archangel's new centre of operations. It was less grand a place than one might expect – a tiny flat that could be easily secured against the outside world, some distance from Cambridge city centre. The door was locked. Isaac was firmly secured so he couldn't do anything of consequence. Archangel's hands were closed around his wrists because it was the least intimate way to do touch, and Archangel liked to pretend he was a gentleman.

Archangel's eyes were open, but unseeing. At least, they didn't see Isaac. They looked through him, focused on the world, renewing the rules in place and checking if there had been any issues.

Archangel's eyes were open, unseeing, and full of tears. It made something uncomfortable twist in Isaac's gut, made him falter against lobbing more heartfuls of betrayal in Archangel's direction.

So, for the most part he didn't look at Archangel's eyes because he didn't really want to spend even more time contemplating the psychological toll of filtering through every dark impulse in the world. Of feeling all that buried pain, nightmare or not.

He remembered when he learned that Gabriel was a telepath.

It came up the first time Isaac agreed to go clubbing with Gabriel, because wasn't that what people did at university? At least in first year, at least a bit.

"You'll regret hiding in your room your whole life," Gabriel had said. "People can't live like that. We can come back if you don't like it."

283

"I know I don't like it," Isaac had replied, sitting at his desk with folded arms. "I didn't like it last time. Got punched in the face, didn't I?" He shook his head. "Look, if you want to go, go. You don't need to stay here with me." The thought that Gabriel might pity him *twisted* deep in his gut.

Gabriel simply hummed. "Valid points, but you're missing one. You see, last time, you didn't go with me." Gabriel flashed him that smile. "Trust me. It will be fun."

Isaac found he did – trust him, that was.

"Besides," Gabriel had said, offering him a hand. "I can't dance with you if you don't come. What's the worst that can happen?"

(Ice. Death. Accidentally touching someone's bare skin.)

Still, Isaac had wanted – despite knowing how bad an idea it was, he'd wanted. Gabriel had looked so earnest. So, they had gone, and it didn't matter that Isaac thought he probably looked ridiculous trying to do clubbing in gloves and a turtle-neck. It was hardly standard attire, was it, for such a thing? Much too hot. But Gabriel hadn't looked at him like he was ridiculous. He'd lit up beaming and led Isaac through the crowds that had parted when they walked through.

That was a strong hint.

Isaac could have well believed that Gabriel was the kind of man who could part the red seas, let alone a crowd of people responding instinctively to his stride – but the small space around Isaac had been carefully maintained throughout the night. Whenever Isaac began to feel panicked, like it was all going to be a bit too much and he needed air, the crowds would shift back from him. Nobody approached him who knew him from home to ask what the hell he was playing at, trying to be normal after what happened with Alec and Lola.

Clubbing, in the long term, may not actually have been for him, but it hadn't been impossible. It had felt like he was just like everyone else.

But Isaac also knew, from the first time he'd gone clubbing, that people didn't tend to react like that. It was something he'd noticed a few times around Gabriel before. The world bent around him, orbiting him like he was the sun.

Isaac had ended up fleeing.

Gabriel had followed.

They'd got chips from a stall and sat on a quiet curb, the cool autumn air ruffling Gabriel's curls. Gabriel's shoulders had slumped, hunched in defensively. He'd looked vulnerable during his confession of telepathy, not just awkward; indeed Gabriel had been tensed in a way that Isaac could only recognise as terrified. He'd spent enough time scared to know it when he saw it.

He remembered his own uneasy thought that Gabriel could have used his powers on him, and saw the way that Gabriel had flinched. The way it had been his turn to look ready to bolt.

"I'm sorry I kept it from you," Gabriel had said in a rush. "I just – I wanted to not be a telepath. With someone. Just for a little while."

And Isaac had understood that so fiercely that it ached inside him, because wasn't that him too? Just wanting to be normal, even if they weren't normal. He'd wanted someone he could spend time with that wouldn't constantly be thinking about his powers, someone who could accept him as a human. All of the fear in him, all of the anger, had cleaved in an instant.

Because, really, he hadn't told Gabriel about his power

either, so it wasn't like he'd done anything different. How then could he possibly judge Gabriel for not bringing up the conversation first? Isaac had hesitated for a beat, before taking Gabriel's hand in his gloved own and squeezing. Even through the layer of material it had felt daring, intimate, to actually initiate touch of any sort.

The tension left Gabriel, though. He'd met Isaac's eyes and the understanding was on his face too. Connection.

Isaac found himself asking if it hurt.

Gabriel had seemed surprised by the question, or rather that Isaac asked that over everything else. He'd looked down, picking at his chips with his free hand, as if unsure whether he should say anything at all.

"Sometimes," he'd replied, eventually. "I suppose you'd find out anyway, if we're—" He stopped. "I don't know. It can be overwhelming. There's a lot of good in the world, don't get me wrong, and I love – I love that I can makes things easier, better, for people. Like you. Tonight. That makes me…" he'd cleared his throat, colour on his cheeks, but Isaac remembered how *happy* Gabriel had looked when Isaac slowly relaxed and they danced together. "But sometimes it's…hard," Gabriel continued. "You see the best of people but the worst of them too. You feel…I've never lost anyone, but I remember the first time someone at school grieved around me. I was, what, six? I thought I was dying." Gabriel laughed, but it hadn't been like any of it was funny. He'd glanced over at Isaac. "It's nothing I can't handle. Don't worry."

"Is it…" Maybe it was a self-centred question, but Isaac hated the thought that he might make it worse. It seemed likely. He knew enough to know his head was not the most calm place in the world. He wouldn't wish it on anyone else, if Gabriel felt and heard that.

Gabriel shook his head. His expression grew warm, then tentative, then a little mischievous.

"You're always happy to see me, Isaac. It's nice."

Isaac's heart slammed as it clicked, then, what other thoughts and feelings Gabriel might have overhead in his head. Yet, Gabriel hadn't run away screaming, had he? He was sitting next to Isaac on the curb, rather than anyone else. He was *choosing* to spend time with Isaac still. Did that mean that Gabriel felt, perhaps, some of the same things that Isaac did?

Gabriel had winked at him, perhaps a bit tipsy, but charming. He'd used Isaac's hold on his hand to pull them both to their feet.

They'd only been better friends after that.

It was one of the many reasons that Isaac had been so against The Archangel Project once. He was not the telepath, but surely no one person could possibly hear everything in the world and not be a little broken by it. It was hard enough sometimes being one human, let alone having an entire planet in the back of your head. Archangel was powerful, more than powerful enough to do what he was doing without any limit on his telepathy. But Gabriel wouldn't have thought to think if he could bear the weight of everyone and everything – in Gabriel's mind, if you had the ability to help then you were obligated to do so. He never did remember to factor emotional capacity as part of ability.

It was difficult to watch Archangel, for all of his awfulness, crumple beneath the weight of trying to single-handedly make the world better and do nothing.

Isaac had spent so long doing nothing, trying to be nothing.

He'd thought it was the safest option for all concerned. Part of him still did – Archangel wouldn't be able to achieve world domination if Isaac wasn't sitting opposite him, after all. Still, nothing no longer seemed like a viable option. All of the arguments he'd once given himself were falling to pieces.

There was no justifying that someone else was going to fix the problem or that it would simply go away on its own this time, because Archangel had Gabriel's 'chosen one' insistence that he could handle everything on his own, so he wouldn't let anyone else get involved anyway. There was no fearing that Isaac would make it worse. The worst Isaac had once imagined had already happened, despite his efforts to do nothing. He couldn't help but wonder if it would have still happened if he'd been less insistent on *nothing.*

What if he had stayed, all of those years ago? What if he had tried to actually tackle the problem? What if he had let himself believe that he could affect positive change if he tried? That he had a voice, and that Gabriel should bloody well listen to it. Maybe Gabriel wouldn't have felt he had to do everything on his own, carry all of it when it came down to it, if Isaac had stayed.

He hadn't allowed himself to ever think that before. It had never seemed his place to speak up when he might be wrong. When he might do as Archangel did, and with the terrible surety of righteousness stop listening entirely. He had given all of his power away instead. Over and over, he had shoved the power away, because he was scared what he would do with it, because he'd seen so many times in history what men with power could do and he didn't want to be that.

Other people had done what they wanted with his power instead. Archangel had.

So, as the days turned into weeks, every three days Isaac had a day where Archangel could not hear him. It was in those hours that Isaac tried to think of a way forward, a plan. The plan, when it came through the hurt, came slowly.

He remembered Gabriel sitting next to him on another curb, the world rising in trees around them.

It's your power. Not mine, not Morphina's, not anybody else's. It shouldn't be something that someone else can use just by touching you.

Archangel's hands dropped from his wrists. He curled into himself, burnt out in the way that Gabriel always used to get when it was too much and he would finally have to succumb to headphones. It was a worse reaction than it had been the last time, but in a few seconds the telepath's expression was composed once more.

Okay plunged over Isaac again.

But the next time, when Archangel touched him, Isaac didn't just assume he was a magnifier and so he would magnify. The power was his. He could clutch it tight, he could make choices, he could say 'yes' and 'no' for himself without saying yes or no for somebody else by virtue of the word. He wasn't the telepath. He didn't get to pick what they did. He just needed to practice.

He wasn't going to let the world, nor even a monster, break for his own inaction. Not any more.

Truly learning that would be the first step.

24 - Gabriel

"I really think this would be a good idea," Gabriel said. "For the people!" He hurried to block Archangel's path out of the room, shoulders set with determination.

Archangel looked exasperated, strained, but he did stop.

"You want to throw a *ball* for the *people?*"

"People need outlets, ways to let loose. With books – I mean." He stopped himself.

Archangel shot him a sour look at the mention of novels all the same.

As a telepath, Gabriel liked to believe he understood more of the difficulties Archangel faced than most. Maybe that was why Archangel came to visit him so often. One of those problems was how much the world still had reminders of grief, of pain, of hurt. People read books, they watched films, they listened to music and went to the theatre and all of those spoke of pain. Pain that the world no longer felt. Each time they thought about it, it caused questions; not necessarily a longing to return to tragedy and violence, but questions. Unease which had to be tempered and wiped away, because even if people didn't want those things they registered the sudden change upon the world.

Some felt it wrong to remember how much something

had hurt them once only for it not to hurt any more. They thought they deserved to feel it, as punishment. Some said there was no true happiness without sorrow. Others argued, coolly, that it was a part of the human experience and so it should not be taken from them. That, above everything else, was freedom. It was unfocused, but persistent, and only growing more persistent with time. Gabriel gathered it made Archangel's telepathic web buck. It was hard work, trying to wrestle with all of that.

"I should burn books," Archangel muttered.

"Don't burn books." Gabriel recoiled. "Nobody good ever burns books."

"You know," Archangel dragged a tired hand through his hair. "This isn't your problem. You have done enough. You can – stop." There was an odd expression on his face. "You're allowed to stop."

"And when do you stop?"

"You're not me."

No, he wasn't, but it was impossible to miss that the two of them could have been twins even if Gabriel didn't know the exact circumstances of how the new world came to be.

Gabriel had come to himself on the floor of his new residence, with his head pounding, and Archangel watching him quietly. The last thing he remembered was applying to university, unpacking his boxes in his new room. He'd remembered feeling hopeful, on the cusp of something better, on the cusp of everything. Nobody at the university knew he was a telepath after all – they could get to know him as he was, couldn't want him for power, and they wouldn't think to ask him for favours. He'd hoped that maybe, with a fresh start, he wouldn't shape himself into what they would like.

291

Maybe he would just see if they liked him. Maybe he would know what he looked like without them there, like a tree that still made sound when no one was around to hear it.

After that, it all swam blank.

Archangel had explained that he'd removed Gabriel's memories, as part of The Project. It was a chance for peace. Gabriel was a telepath – but it didn't have to be hard! He could live a good life. He could be a hero and help people. All he had to do was follow Archangel's orders. Then he wouldn't go wrong again, like he apparently had. Everything would be okay.

That night, Gabriel had stared into the mirror and tried to judge by the face staring back at him how much time had passed since his last real memory and what those years had been like. Mostly, he looked tired.

As far as Gabriel was aware, Archangel did not erase people who saved lives. So, what kind of person had he been? What had happened? What had he done that was so terrible? He'd never wanted to be a bad person. If he could make up for what he had done, in any way, he had to.

"Everybody needs a bit of help," he smiled. "Even you. And I want to help. I think I can." Maybe he had done enough, maybe he hadn't, but he didn't quite know how to stop.

Archangel seemed to relent, at least a little. "Why a ball?"

"A ball is in so many of the stories," Gabriel said. "A recurring thread, so I was thinking it could make this world more palatable, if they think it is too much like a dream at the moment. Too uncanny. They need something that they understand, something that can be a little out of this world, like a fairy-tale, to normalise. It provides structure. Motivation. Something different."

"I suppose it will be good," Archangel said, almost to himself, "for you to have a project. Something to keep your mind occupied."

"Yes. Exactly. An idle mind is the devil's playground!"

And Gabriel's mind, well, he didn't exactly know how he was supposed to be filling his days. Archangel had suggested he try writing a novel without pain, or playing solitaire, but Gabriel couldn't imagine an entire life spent like that. He had to have been made for something more than that. He *wanted* more than that, though maybe that was selfish of him. He still remembered when people had suffered, still remembered how it had felt; compared to inescapable poverty he really couldn't complain about being locked in his childhood house forever more, playing cards with himself.

Okay. 'Locked in' was maybe harsh, Archangel was trying to help him, encourage him towards better self-care. It did feel a bit like being imprisoned though. And Gabriel hated his childhood house. His father hadn't even liked golf, for god's sake! And it was so weirdly bare, like half of the building had been swiftly transformed and stripped on short notice. There were places on the wall, like on the staircase, where the paint was lighter than the rest of the house because something that used to hang there that wasn't there any more. It reminded him too much of the empty spaces in his head. He felt like he was in a mausoleum.

Still. He understood Archangel's reasoning – he looked too much like Archangel, after all, to simply go wandering around like he was anyone else. It was better that he stayed where he was. He could hear the world, and he could rest which was all that Archangel wanted for him. He could learn to untangle himself as a separate identity from society, or some such yogic bullshit. It was just so – well. He had worked hard to put the needs of the greater good over his own. Now he was supposed to be selfish and think about what he wanted? Now he was supposed to not carry the weight of what other people might need?

"Fine," Archangel said finally. "You can run your plans by with me when I come and see you. I'll send someone who can help you plan in the meanwhile."

"Thank you! You won't regret this."

Archangel stared at him for a moment more, his expression unreadable.

"I need to go now. Don't disappoint me."

Gabriel was left on his own again – but at least he had a purpose this time.

***

In the nights alone, Gabriel dreamed distorted flashes of memory, like something in his brain was trying to piece itself back together.

He had spent many hours of his life contemplating the full force of his telepathy, its potential, and all the many ways that his gifts could be used. For good, always, but what was good exactly?

His mother was crying, makeup smeared down her cheeks. He was seven. She knelt before him and told him to be good, to make her happy for the party. He could do that, couldn't he? He could make her happy? He was such a good kid. He was her little angel.

He learned what happy was supposed to look like from her. Everyone in the world felt happy like that now.

He was four, and his parents' thoughts were like a hornet's nest in their cramped apartment with the mould in the wall and they wanted a nicer house and a bigger car and then they wanted the lottery numbers and then they wanted to be the most popular family in the new neighbourhood and most of all they wanted a child who didn't stare quite so much. Who wasn't so unnerving.

As he grew older, as his powers grew stronger, he gave them all of those things at first. They loved him a little, then, at least for that. They told him he was *good,* he was such a *good kid.* When he was a kid, he'd thought being loved was the same thing as being good, because wasn't it only possible to love something good? People didn't fall in love with monsters in the stories that his parents had told him. If you were a bad person, you were ugly and undesirable and it was obvious to everyone around you.

He was sixteen and his father was furious. Boys are not supposed to like boys you need to marry a nice girl what is wrong with you and why would you embarrass us like this? What would people say? The Flynns are a respectable family, their son would never—

Of course, his father never outright accused him of using his powers on Charlie Flynn. That would be too much. That would be an ugly scene. But Gabriel heard the thought, the accusation, all the same. He didn't think he had used his powers, but it made him wonder if he could have done it by accident, and Charlie wouldn't meet his eyes after that. Mr and Mrs Flynn thought it was all Gabriel's fault at any rate, because *their* son would never do something like that. Gabriel started training his gifts after. Practising, really, properly, practising. He couldn't stop being what he was, so he was going to damn well be in charge of the story, to never have to question if he'd done something awful without knowing it.

He was eighteen and there was a young man with white eyes, shrinking from a punch – and he was beautiful – and Gabriel –

295

Gabriel woke up. He heaved air into his lungs, and his head hurt like nothing else as he sat hunched up in bed. The room was dark around him. The world was, mostly, peaceful. A few doors down someone felt more ragged than usual but as Gabriel got his powers under control, any reflected distress they felt was wiped away. He was a telepath though, and so for the most part the emotion did not swirl away from him like it might do everyone else. It stuck beneath his skin like a splinter. Some days it did go. Gabriel didn't know what was different about those days.

His whole body trembled, and he didn't know why. He wiped his hands furiously over his face and his fingers came back wet with tears he didn't even remember crying. The memories, the dreams, slipped away from him. He tried to fumble for something out of his reach, but he couldn't get at it, and it hurt less to let whatever *it* was go as the minutes passed. As the winter sunlight streamed in through his childhood window…it was gone.

He could have woken up in every morning of his life, ever, and nothing would ever change. He was stuck.

The house stood as silent as the grave. He exhaled a final shuddering breath and forced himself out of bed. He wandered barefoot around the dawn, feeling like a ghost. Something in him ached like an old wound.

The world kept turning.

Gabriel focused on the ball.

***

As the days wore on, plans for ball came along well. He wanted it to be extravagant, magical, the kind of affair that couldn't be ignored. Something around Christmas, because for better or worse everyone always had a lot of memories associated around that time of year anyway. He wanted suits and princess gowns. It would be a celebration of the new world, of everything that had been accomplished. They could broadcast the event and –

Well, he was hoping he could convince Archangel to take the night off. One night. Whatever Archangel said about being able to handle being the oversight of the whole world, Gabriel knew telepathy. He knew it must be taxing, even without the actual migraine of overusing one's powers. Besides, one night wasn't going to break everything, was it? The Archangel Project wasn't that fragile. People were, in their hearts, good. They wanted to be good. They just needed a little help towards that end because life could make being good difficult sometimes.

Also, there was no better way to celebrate all that they had accomplished then by contrasting it with how everything had felt before. It would be one night for people to process and feel in full capacity, for them to realise and remember how much *better* life was now.

One night a year. Ritualised. It would make everything easier to swallow.

"No."

"What do you mean *'no'*?" Gabriel demanded. "It's a great idea! Sanna agrees with me. Don't you, Sanna?"

Sanna Nieminen had been Archangel's answer to both Gabriel needing company and help setting up the ball. She was healer and spent most of her time working in a special clinic. But, with her at his side, he was allowed out into the world – she could heal him if something happened. Gabriel had tried asking what exactly Archangel thought would happen, they weren't in the old world, but Archangel hadn't given him an answer. He'd simply said that it was better to be safe than sorry.

It did make Gabriel wonder, again, what exactly the relationship between him and Archangel was.

"If you don't like it," Sanna said earnestly. "We can just not do it that way next time. Or you can, you know, start doing your telepathy thing whenever you like. But I think it's important for you to know that the world isn't going to break if you're not constantly plugged into it." She smiled at Archangel, adoring. "People might surprise you."

Sanna was, from what Gabriel had learned of her, the kind of person who focused on everyone else so she didn't have to focus on herself. She thought it was great that Gabriel had no memories of the last decade or so of his life. She'd been adamant that if she could forget things, she would. In a heartbeat. She only forgot details when she visited Gabriel. Archangel explained it was so she didn't trigger any of his memories because Gabriel couldn't be trusted to keep his telepathy to himself.

"That's not what I'm here for," Archangel said. "You can enjoy the party. I will not be there, and I will certainly not be ruining a celebration with people feeling miserable. That doesn't even make sense!"

Once upon a time, Gabriel would have agreed. But once upon a time a party would have been a space to break away from all of the stressors in the world, to forget pain. That was no longer an issue. Their responses to the world had to evolve and adapt, surely? Archangel's expression offered no such flexibility, no desire to compromise or change or ease the rules he had set in even the smallest way.

The words came out before Gabriel could stop them.

"People can't redeem themselves or move on from something that they can't remember. Something that they can't feel. It's – I don't like people suffering any more than you do, but you're not – blocking the pain doesn't heal the wound. And I know some wounds don't heal so pain management is all that's left, but for most things—"

"I said no."

Gabriel's nails dug into his palms. He wished his telepathy was stronger so he could *make* Archangel bend to what he knew was the right way forward. Archangel thought he was doing the right thing already though, didn't he? And he was not bending, and so they were stuck. Again. Always, always stuck.

"I'm a telepath," Gabriel said. "I think I know what I'm talking about as much as you do. I know how people think."

No.

Gabriel winced at the smack of Archangel's power, sucking in a sharp breath. He let it drop. Soon enough, Archangel left back to his world, and Gabriel stayed exactly where he would always be. Archangel didn't use telepathy on him to the same extent as he did on everyone else, but Gabriel also suspected how swiftly that could change if he stepped outside of the guidelines which had been set for him.

The sense of being caught, not in a safety net but some crueller and more restrictive thing, grew. He just didn't know why.

"He needs time off," Gabriel said, because that was what Sanna cared about. "It's going to drive him crazy."

Sanna nodded in agreement, concern pinching her brow.

"We need to make it happen."

299

But how could they stop a telepath for one night and one night only?

25 - Isaac

"What," Archangel demanded, "do you think you're doing?"

His touch, at first gentle enough, turned fierce. His hand moved from its customary position on Isaac's wrist to both hands seizing his face, examining him like he was trying to figure out the malfunction in the machine.

Archangel looked furious to have power denied from him, even for a moment.

They were sitting on the sofa once more, and though the window had been opened to let in the fresh air, Isaac hadn't been outside in a long time. People came to the door to deliver the groceries he needed but beyond that…there was Archangel. It was almost as lonely as it had been in the cottage, except worse. There was no real chance of forgetting the loneliness or pretending to play along with a telepath in order to escape. There was no chance of fake surrendering and taking it back. Archangel heard the schemes that crossed his head…but he couldn't stop him.

Isaac squeezed his eyes shut, breathing ragged, but he held the power back.

Archangel's grip tightened further.

"Stop it," he said. "How are you blocking me? You can't do

301

that."

Cold sweat sprang up on the back of Isaac's neck; he felt a rush of exhaustion like he was working a muscle he'd never fully worked before. It wasn't too far from the truth. The weight of Archangel's power upon him was enormous, a leviathan greater than any he had ever known. But the one thing that Isaac's nightmares had never counted on was his own strength, that was the thing about nightmares.

He had been told all of his life that he magnified, that he shouldn't touch anyone because he magnified and when someone touched him, and he began to magnify, it had always felt like something beyond him. It wasn't something he did, it was something that happened to him. The tunnel opened up between him and whoever was touching him and he lost control. It rushed out. It magnified. Doors opened could be locked, though, he was finding that more and more when he dared to slam them shut with enough force.

He just needed to concentrate. Concentrating was difficult.

His gifts meant that anyone he magnified couldn't use their powers on him. Why the hell should they be allowed to use his powers on themselves, whether he wanted to give them power or not?

"Isaac," Archangel growled.

A triumphant smile curled the corners of Isaac's mouth, vicious and pleased, despite the exhaustion. He opened his eyes again and stared up at Archangel's face, so similar to Gabriel's, relishing in the sight of those black eyes. Black, not white. Archangel's power stayed as it always was, without Isaac's magnifying to add to it. Isaac exhaled a shaky breath.

"I can out-wait you," Archangel said. "We both know you can't keep this up forever."

"Yeah? And we both know I'll keep getting better at it. It will get easier. I don't need to keep it up forever. Just long enough to really screw with you."

This...this proved that Isaac could do it. He could stop magnifying if he wanted to. It was *his* power. A rush of guilt followed, for all the things that might not have happened if he'd learned that earlier.

His concentration broke. He began to magnify.

Archangel's attention stayed fixed on him for a moment, before once again moving past him. Focusing on the world. When he finally let go, Isaac's head pounded. It wasn't as overwhelming as it had been the night in the church with Morphina, but...

Archangel rose, pacing the flat like a trapped tiger. In the last month, the flat they 'shared' had begun to look more and more like a twisted mimicry of the life that he and Gabriel had once imagined. Or rather, perhaps, the life that Gabriel had imagined. When Isaac's mind was his own it felt more like a set, or a life-sized doll house, than anything real.

One room was a studio for Isaac to work in; complete with empty canvases waiting to be filled, tubes of different coloured paints and sketchbooks and charcoal. The other room was the bedroom, complete with Van Gogh bedsheets as if they could revert time and pretend none of it ever happened.

"There is a ball that will soon take place." Archangel rounded on him, and Isaac had a moment to be completely bewildered by the change in topic, before the nightmare continued. "One night in which the world has its emotions back. You will attend, and if you can honestly say after that the world is better suffering then it is in my hands, I will not punish you for fighting me."

Isaac swallowed, doing his best to keep his expression composed. His heart still thundered because – well, he wasn't a complete idiot. He was well aware that Archangel could throw him in a literal dungeon, or use his telepathy to make Isaac's life a torment. Those were not very Gabriel things to do but he was not dealing with Gabriel. Had he said this couldn't get worse? That had been such a dumb thing to say. If Isaac believed in anything, it was that it could always get worse.

"But if you find you doubt your convictions…" Archangel's gaze seared into him. "You will stop fighting. You will cooperate. You *will* surrender to me."

"And if I refuse to take the deal?" Isaac's mouth felt dry. "Because this doesn't sound like a great deal to me, you know. It kind of sounds like I lose either way. And right now…" Isaac squared his shoulders. "Right now you can't make me do anything, and you know it. You're scared because I'm winning."

Archangel smiled; it was not a nice smile. It was not a smile Isaac recognised.

"I consider refusal to be forfeit." Archangel stepped closer. "I have been lenient with you, Isaac. I have allowed you your paints, your comforts, the gilded cage which you so despise. It does make me wonder if you have ever experienced real torture. A dark room, nothing to do, no one to talk to. Pain. Hallucinations…those are all in the mind."

The visions swarmed Isaac.

He looked down as bugs broke out of his chest, crawling white and fluttering out of the cavity they had made in his ribs. Nausea gagged up his throat.

He looked left at a cry and Gabriel was on the floor, and he was the one with blood coming out of his wrists. His eyes were growing blank. Isaac jolted to his feet.

He looked right and squeezed his eyes shut, but closing his eyes didn't stop the feeling of rancid breath on the back of his neck. It didn't stop the feeling of creatures crawling over him, into his ears and – it was so cold. If he opened his eyes, he knew he would see Alec and Lola.

The visions vanished as quickly as they had arrived. There were no bugs, no Gabriel, only him and Archangel in the flat. Isaac shuddered, trying to acclimatise, to shove the memories away. It didn't work. It had felt so *real.*

A gloved hand caught hold of his chin, gently tipping his head up.

Isaac glared, fists clenched at his sides.

"I am sure you are aware that the thought of breaking you gives me no joy, because you have banked on my feelings for you to keep you safe no matter how you fight me," Archangel said. "Just like you banked on his feelings to achieve your scheme five years ago."

"That's not—" Okay, that was true. Isaac had done that. His throat tightened. If Gabriel had ever been as monstrous as Isaac feared, his whole plan with Morphina would likely not have worked. He wouldn't have had enough freedom to even meet her in the first place. He wished he'd seen through the fear of what might be enough to know that at the time.

Archangel watched the acceptance slide onto his face, he waited for it before he spoke again.

"If breaking you is for the greater good I will do it. And I *can* break you. Do you believe me?"

Isaac did. It might take a while, but Archangel would be

able to. He knew Archangel saw it in his head too, however much Isaac tried not to tense. He tore his gaze away, because – well, Archangel did play Gabriel well when he wanted to, but the look on his face was so un-Gabriel that it was terrible. It was the look that had haunted Isaac throughout the years. He was sure Archangel could feel his pulse skittering.

Archangel let go.

"Or, of course," the nightmare said, in a reasonable tone of voice. "You could surrender now, and we could forget this ever happened. We could go back to how we were. You do not have my telepathy to stop you from making mistakes, so it is only understandable that you would err without my assistance. I cannot hold it against you if you truly repent."

Isaac snapped his head around again to glare at Archangel again for that, a wave of hate rushing over him matched only by terror. He wanted to smack that oh so magnanimous tone aside so hard it left Archangel's teeth bloody. He wanted to go quiet, and hide, and be safe and okay and not have the full weight of a telepath trying to crush him into submission.

Who was he kidding? He didn't want to be punished for fighting. He wasn't *brave.* He wasn't a hero. If he could stall that agony he wanted to, however selfish that was. Taking the deal would let him leave the apartment, it might even give him a chance to escape, to *run...*

Isaac hesitated. He was still going to fight, regardless though, wasn't he? He wasn't going to run. Taking the deal would only delay the inevitable, and Archangel must see that too. He was trying to spook Isaac into being powerless again, into promising anything, giving everything. If he could stop Archangel from magnifying, he had to.

"You need me," Isaac said, though his voice shook. "More

306

than I need you. I will never stop fighting you. I was willing to risk *dying* to stop you once before. Do you believe me?"

Archangel's expression soured. His fingers twitched with the seeming urge to deftly bat all such defiance aside, to tighten all possible loopholes. But even if he could fix it temporarily he would still have to touch Isaac again. He couldn't simply wipe it all away.

Nothing in their current deal, even if Isaac accepted it, said that Isaac had to magnify for him before the ball. People would have a chance to fight. Yet, if Archangel truly believed the world could be better, he wouldn't need to keep such a strict control would he? Emboldened, Isaac stepped closer.

"If you want to make deals, Archangel, let's make a proper one." He didn't allow himself to hesitate before he pressed his lips to Archangel's ear. Let him feel the possibility of power, and let Isaac be hidden as he spoke. "We go to your ball. No telepathy. If you can prove to me that the world is truly better in your care then I will stop fighting you. I'll surrender."

Gabriel, at least, had always wanted Isaac by his side. Too badly, maybe, if Archangel was anything to go by.

Archangel's breath hitched at the closeness, so convincingly human.

"And if you do not doubt?" The telepath's voice remained steady. "I'm not going to let you go."

"No." Archangel would never let him go; Isaac knew that. The nightmare wasn't wired that way. "But if I don't doubt, you don't punish me for fighting you, as you said. You will *never* try and punish me for fighting you. And you will let Gabriel keep his memories."

"Excuse me?"

"You heard me. You stop using telepathy on him, too, at

that ball."

"What makes you think he's coming?"

"Because if he's not, I'm not." Isaac said it with more confidence than he felt. "You didn't take his memories for his sake; you took them because me and him together can match you, maybe even stop you, and if he truly is the man I loved—" No. It wasn't past tense, that feeling, however much Isaac might have wished it so. "If he is truly the man I love, he might just try that." He pulled back, to meet Archangel's eyes. "You took his memories because you wanted to control him, but you can't afford to break your own creator. You might need him."

"If that's true, why would I ever give him his memories back?" Even as Archangel asked the question, Isaac could see his mind whirring over what Isaac had said. "Do you think me stupid?"

"You think love is a weakness," Isaac said. "Beyond good. Beyond evil. Beyond any moral arguments I might make. I love him. You can't afford to take too long to break me when you need my powers…and which of you do you think I'm more likely to break for? Hint, it's not you. It's a gamble, sure…" Isaac raised his brows, and smiled. "But we're only human. You're not stupid, but are you so insecure of your power that you truly think we can stop you?"

Archangel's mouth clicked shut. He stared at Isaac for a long moment. His arrogance warred with caution, with that Gabriel cleverness. He would see Isaac's thoughts and think that meant he understood everything better than anyone else possibly could. He'd think Isaac the arrogant one, for thinking he could hope to overcome a telepath.

"So, do we have a deal?" Isaac asked, even as he knew the

answer.

Archangel snarled, and turned away.

"I'll save you a dance."

26 - Dahlia

L ife under the control of an omnipotent telepath hell-
bent on the greater good was about what one would
expect. There were many hours when she did not
think about it. There were some hours when she found
herself considering only spaces, tracing the silhouettes of
defiance and freedom. Then, there were the nights.

She suspected she wasn't the only person in the new
world plagued by nightmares, particularly given the literal
nightmares that patrolled the streets ready to carry out their
new overlord's bidding. She never remembered exactly what
she dreamed about any more, but she would wake up in the
morning with a pounding heart and the memory of a woman
with hair like fire who might just set the whole stale trickery
of it all ablaze.

Morphina seemed to dance on the corner of all of Dahlia's
thoughts, like a glitch in the system.

Archangel had swiftly allocated Dahlia to work on his
'Harvest Program' once she woke up from sleep. Sanna had
been no doubt sent to work as a healer wherever Archangel
pleased. She wasn't sure, she hadn't seen Sanna since the
night in the church, but Archangel had been gathering all
powered people and re-allocating them where he thought

them most helpful, so it seemed likely. She hadn't seen Gabriel either. Sometimes, late in the night, she thought it odd that Gabriel had vanished. It wasn't like him. The thought always slipped away.

That night, Dahlia was awake long past everyone else, staring at the invitation she had received earlier in the day. It was a full-on fancy invitation, printed on thick black card with silver writing.

Dahlia Huang
You are cordially invited to the first Annual Remembrance Ball.

Something uneasy, something that was the antithesis of everything Gabriel and Archangel stood for, had crept over her as she read the words. It kept her from sleep. Could she be nervous? She used to be kept up with a stomach-ache when she was nervous. Before. She didn't *feel* nervous though, even if she should have been. Yet, there was that something. Something that didn't fit the head-space she had been floating in for weeks, something nagging.

It whispered to her, pointing out that not everyone had been invited, so why had she? What criteria set who got to attend? How could she know it was good? The other part of her mind whispered that of course it was good. Everything was good. Everything was okay. Archangel would never use her as leverage.

The Remembrance Ball is an opportunity to let loose and reflect upon the past that brought us to our present. The dress code is formal. Food will be provided.

Her brow furrowed, as she traced her fingers over the swirling lettering. Was she allowed to simply not go? It must be an option if she could consider it. She couldn't be entirely certain. It might be like those things you were technically allowed to not attend but were subtly punished and judged for avoiding - like parties thrown by work.

Felicity had always wanted to attend one of those proper old-fashioned balls. She'd longed to sweep down winding stairs in a beautiful gown, looking like something out of a movie. Cinderella had been her sister's favourite…always running, until she was caught by the right person.

Would it be wrong to go, when Felicity never would? Or should she go for Felicity's sake? The memories of her sister no longer wounded her, but they weren't gone. Sometimes, it would be a whole day before she remembered Felicity was dead. She always remembered though, especially after the sun went down.

The dorms the harvesters slept in, at least on the main compound, were comfortable enough but plain. There were three rows of bunk beds, and an en-suite bathroom with a line of separate toilet and shower cubicles. Dahlia had the bottom bunk by the corner nearest the door. Like *hell* was she going to be on a top bed so far from the soothing hum of the earth, even if she did spend all day in the fields or in the labs working with scientists on how to produce better harvests to dole out to people. As for the door…well.

The ball will start at 7pm sharp. We look forward to seeing you then.

Memories flickered through her mind, of another dorm, of

fire and char and the screech of life support machines failing. She sucked in a startled breath at the smack of emotion that came with the association. Normally, it just played through her head like something that had happened to someone else.

"Dahlia."

The figure appeared in front of her and stole all of the air in her lungs so she couldn't even scream. For a second, she only stared.

"Fliss." She didn't so much *say* her sister's name as form her lips soundlessly around the shape of it.

Felicity Huang looked the same as she always did when she was alive – it was as if she had simply sped in from outside, so fast that it was like teleporting from mid-air. If there had been a fuzz before, in Dahlia's thoughts, a knowledge of what had happened and a general placidity about everything that had come to pass to match it, all placidity vanished then as she continued to stare. The hurt, the *wound*, burned through everything, through any telepath's commands.

Dahlia didn't think she was dreaming.

The room around her was heavy with sleep, restful breathing. Looking at her sister, Dahlia didn't think she would ever rest again. She shoved a fist in her mouth and realised she was choking on a sob. She didn't dare even blink, in case her sister vanished, even if she couldn't possibly be real. Felicity was dead. The grief of that had been softened, forcibly muted, but now it was back, and it was *roaring.*

Every moment when she had quietly done her new job, when she had stayed where she was told and done what she was told regardless of the fact it had never been what she wanted in life, swept over her with a bitter taste. It was like waking up from sleepwalking. The world was real, and it had been stolen from her. Her will, her dreams, her pain...all of those things had been taken because some telepath thought they knew her life purpose better than she did. Her sister had been killed, and the reason for that was still parading around like a benevolent bloody dictator, talking about *the greater good.* Throwing *parties.* Fury chased the heels of grief and Dahlia shot to her feet.

"I'm not your sister," Felicity said. "I'm sorry for choosing this form, but it's the one you have enough of a powerful emotional connection with for this to work. I need to talk to you – this is Mona. Morphina, as you call me. I've been trying to get through to you for a while."

Dahlia had known it couldn't really be Felicity, but she still stiffened. She clamped down on the earth around her, kept it from rumbling, from exploding. Her jaw clenched with the effort of not lashing out. Yet, it was her sister, or at least looked exactly like her. She couldn't attack, even when it wasn't really her. No doubt that was the whole damn point. She was the only person Dahlia wouldn't, couldn't, have attacked right then however much her powers threatened to jerk out of her control.

The dreamweaver successfully had Dahlia's full attention, whether she wanted to give it or not.

Morphina's gaze – Felicity's black eyes – roamed over her, before landing on the invitation clenched in Dahlia's hand.

"Oh, good," Morphina said. "You got one. Do you get a plus one?" She leaned in to try and peer at the card. "A plus one will make this so much easier. We don't have much time to prepare, but—"

"What the hell are you doing here?" Dahlia managed. She shoved the invitation under her pillow, more because

Morphina seemed interested than out of any real urge to hide it. Her lip twisted in a sneer. "If this is you asking me to a dance, the answer's no. I don't like you."

"Somehow, De Vere has convinced Archangel not to use his telepathy for one night," Morphina replied flatly. "During the Remembrance Ball. It is not a large window for us to act but it is nonetheless a window when we will be able to act freely, perhaps the only one we'll get. That's why I ask about your invitation." The flatness vanished and Morphina prowled a step closer, offering an entirely too sweet smile. "So yeah, I am asking you to go to a dance with me, flower girl. To stop Archangel. You still want that, yes?"

Dahlia's mouth clicked shut. She took a second to try and wrestle down the tumult of new emotions smacking into her, drawing a few deep breaths.

"Yes," she said slowly. "Obviously I still want that." Even if this was some kind of trick of Archangel's, the notion of her rebellion could hardly surprise the bastard. "How do I know it's really you?" She'd seen Archangel control dreamers, control *Felicity*, before. "How are you even *here?*"

"Obviously it's me because you're capable of asking that question." Morphina rolled her eyes. "He doesn't allow room for doubt. He could just make you believe and do everything he wanted and wouldn't be wasting time having a chat."

That...okay. That was a fair point. That didn't mean she had to be so patronising!

"As for how I'm here..." Morphina sighed. "That is a long story we'll probably get to...the more prudent point, before you ask, is that he can't listen to you when you're with me. My nature – my mind – is too dreamlike. It's what protected Isaac from De Vere's telepathy once. You're talking to me,

315

talking to a *dream,* so I am in some way in your thoughts. Corrupting the file, so to speak, if he tries to read it. He would still be able to control you when you're close by – but he—" She stopped, a hint of awkwardness crossing her face. "I'm sure you don't care about how in that much detail, but anyway, you're safe talking to me. So long as you don't tell anyone about this. Am I missing any of your questions?"

Dahlia remembered, what felt like a lifetime ago, Gabriel dragging her to the study to talk because he couldn't simply use telepathy to see her meeting with the dreamweaver. Still.

She felt Morphina watching her, like she was awaiting another inevitable deluge of queries and accusations.

Dahlia released another breath and set her shoulders. Screw it all.

"I take it you have a plan. Hopefully a better plan than last time. Because, you know, your plan last time really sucked."

Morphina blinked.

Dahlia had some vicious glee in seeing her surprised.

Morphina seemed to recover though, raising her brows.

"Do you...you should be feeling your emotions. Do you need a moment?"

"No."

"You're remarkably calm. I thought my presence would disrupt his influence on you, but—"

"Oh, please," Dahlia said. "Like I'd cry in front of *you*. And I don't typically stab my allies. No promises, though. Given it's you."

Morphina paused, as if to consider that. She seemed to reach the same conclusion of 'well, fair enough' and nodded too. She almost seemed amused – at least for a moment.

"Let's walk," she said. "I don't get the chance to get out very often, even like this, and I doubt I'll have long. I want to feel the air. Make the most of it while we plan."

It was Dahlia's turn to blink, surprised, but she collected her trainers without hesitation. She told herself it wasn't for Morphina, and it wasn't sympathy because she could imagine how hellish it would be to not be able to go outside and could just imagine where Morphina might be locked up…and okay. Perhaps it was a little bit of sympathy. The tiniest amount. She did better outside, anyway.

Besides, Dahlia had killed her, so she couldn't call Morphina a murderous bitch without some degree of hypocrisy, and seeing Archangel she could maybe see why Morphina might have been scared enough to put the world to sleep to try and prevent him from coming to a proper existence. She'd made the same call when she killed the dreamweaver, hadn't she?

They were the same.

The thought, which had horrified her beyond all measure once, reassured her in some strange way. Because, despite everything, the two of them were still there. Fighting. Whatever Gabriel had done to Morphina hadn't lasted forever, hadn't completely changed her, and so maybe what Archangel had done to the world wouldn't last forever either. Maybe he wasn't as all-powerful as he appeared.

"So I'm guessing our plan is to kill him during this ball," Dahlia said, keeping her voice low as they trudged towards the shadows of the greenhouses. There were no nightmares in sight, probably because the dreamweaver was there, but it was still better to avoid being spotted. "He'll see me coming a mile off if you want me to gut him with a thorn like I did you." Though that did raise the question of why Morphina was asking for her help over anyone else's. "I assume he checks for poison?" She bit her lip. "We'll have to take out his magnifier too. We won't stand a chance if he's in arm's reach of Morton."

Morphina paused as they slowed, tilting Felicity's head back so she could peer up at the sky. Stars glinted above them; half hidden by cloud. A brisk wind ghosted through her dark hair. She looked so much like Fliss, because of course she bloody did, that Dahlia had to look away.

"Yes," Morphina said. "But Morton…" a smile crossed her face. "You asked why I was here, now. I'm here because Isaac's suppressing Archangel's powers. He doesn't just magnify, after all. That's never been entirely how his gift works. He just never considers that in his worst imaginings because his nightmares have always been about the power people can take from him."

"Suppressing…?" Dahlia tried to wrap her head around it. "But he only suppresses people when he's touching them. And only against using their powers on him. Great that we're not fighting a magnified telepath, but—"

Morphina speared Dahlia with a look.

"Do you really think if he actually has the power to suppress someone's power against him, that he can't stop someone from using their powers on someone else? Given how powerful his ability to magnify is?" She shook her head. "Of course he can. He's just never actually learnt how to use what he can do properly. Never let himself learn."

Dahlia considered that. It was true that Sanna, who also used her powers through touch, could heal other people as well as herself. It wasn't some passive thing when someone touched her. Not any more, certainly. She tried not to think, too, how horrifically powerful that made Isaac. The man was a walking monster.

"If Archangel's suppressed…why the hell aren't you attacking him with nightmares right now?"

Morphina deflated.

"I can't," she admitted. "I'm in a prison cell with strict orders not to fight him. Which is why," she seemed to do her best to regroup, "I also need *you* to break me out before the ball. He's got me stashed somewhere, likely near him, but I don't know exactly where. It's dark and quiet. I think it's underground. Or a basement. Something like that."

Dahlia met her eyes again, before she could stop herself, as Morphina turned towards her. Even a month ago, the very thought of freeing the woman they had fought so hard to stop would have been insane.

Morphina smiled, thinly, like she was the mind-reader.

"I can distract him," she said. "All of Archangel's minions are my creatures. My power. Once I'm free, I can dispel them properly, so then we just have to deal with him instead of an entire army."

Well, okay, that was one reason why it would possibly be useful to free her. The other reason was probably kindness. Dahlia wasn't sure she was quite ready to pick kindness yet, but…

She had thought she'd fixed everything before, when she killed the dreamweaver, and then everything had been so much worse instead, hadn't it? This was worse. She'd never considered her anger to be a weakness, but that day…

Would Gabriel have so completely flipped his shit if no one died? Probably not. But that couldn't be what she focused on. That had been his choice.

"He's not going to be distracted for long," she said.

"He doesn't need to be distracted for long, just long enough for you to go stabby stabby."

It was Dahlia's turn to give Morphina a *look.* She knew they were both in the murderer club (though hers was resurrected and being the most annoying ally ever, so did that even count?) but there was really no need for Morphina to be quite so flippant.

Morphina's expression, however, was nowhere near so flippant. There was something haunted to the edge of her features, something that sent a chill down Dahlia's spine.

Dahlia swallowed.

"Isn't this fighting him?" she asked, softer. "If you're not allowed to fight him."

"I'm not, technically, fighting him. He didn't order me not to contact you. I don't imagine the idea occurred to him. He does have limits, you know."

Dahlia was not surprised. She had never imagined Morphina might try or want to contact her, of all people, for help. She was even more surprised that Morphina seemed at least somewhat sure that Dahlia *was* going to free her – she certainly wasn't pleading and sobbing her regret in an effort to persuade Dahlia to launch a rescue. She showed no signs of nervous gratitude to be listened to, or any of those cliché markers of redemption best served with humility.

Dahlia admired that, just a little, despite everything. Gabriel, no doubt, would think that they should both be ashamed of what they had done, but, quite frankly, Dahlia wasn't. She could draw strength from her spite, and choose kindness. She could choose kindness as a rule, and not apologise for what she had done to survive, thinking it the right course of action at the time. Maybe, sure, she'd been angry. Maybe she was angry still, maybe she was utterly *furious.* Perhaps her and Mona were the same in that – furious at the world. They were not, always, their best selves, but perhaps best was a suffocating expectation anyway. Some days were just shit. Some days you could only do your best for that day.

She stole another glance at the dreamweaver.

"Is that why you're contacting me? Instead of anyone else?"

"I'm contacting you because I have first-hand experience that you can do what needs to be done."

She meant the killing, didn't she? Somehow, Dahlia had never thought that would be the reputation she got.

"I understand why you did it." Morphina's voice turned softer too. "The stories tell you that the only way to defeat a monster is to kill it, so of course that's what you would do when you're scared. Besides," she shrugged with an air of almost helplessness. "You only did what I couldn't. I should have killed Morton or De Vere when I first met them, a long time ago. I didn't. I—" Morphina faltered. "I wanted to be kind, and they hadn't done anything wrong yet. It didn't seem fair to kill them for what they might do or be. I mean, I thought about it. But I would have had to kill myself too if potential alone was a death sentence. What I can do…what I have done…"

She looked away from Dahlia, across the fields.

In the distance, a giant – a nightmare – lumbered past. It was shaped like a stag, great horned antlers piercing up into the stars.

"This would never have happened if I wasn't so weak," Morphina finished.

"Kindness is not weakness." The words blurted out, before Dahlia could stop herself. "You start thinking like that, you sound like Archangel. That's what he's doing right now. That's what he thinks!" Dahlia realised she was making the ground tremble a little, and caught herself. She closed her eyes. "It's bullshit. We don't get to decide who lives or dies based on what they might do in the future. That's not something we know. That's not something anyone knows."

"Sometimes you can make a pretty good guess."

"And sometimes making that guess is what changes a person. It's a slippery damn slope. One person thinking they know everything is what got us into this mess in the first place."

Morphina huffed, but some tension in her shoulders had eased when Dahlia opened her eyes once more.

"It's just as well," the dreamweaver said. "If it occurs to us that this night could be an opportunity to fight him, that's going to occur to Archangel too. He's not stupid. But he is...arrogant. He thinks he knows everything. That's how he was dreamed up. We can use that."

Dahlia let the topic go – what good would debating the past do anyway? Everyone could always have done something more perfectly than they had at the time.

"I don't think I'm willing to bet my life on his arrogance." The enormity of their task still seemed overwhelming. "Ideally, we need a way of immobilising both him and his telepathy at the same time. Even if he doesn't see me coming, he won't be alone. Gabriel is..." Dahlia's mind flashed through the memories, and she found herself flinching. She never thought he'd make her flinch for all of their arguments. "I don't know what's happening, but it's odd that he's vanished.

It's not like him. He has, like, a compulsive need to get involved. To help."

Morphina snorted.

Binding both telepaths with vines would hold them still so that they couldn't pull away from Isaac, if Isaac truly was capable of suppressing as well as magnifying, providing that he even managed to do that. Would Archangel even risk bringing him out of wherever he'd stashed the magnifier? One problem at a time.

"We'll figure out the details," Morphina said. "Dahlia." She reached out, with a touch like ice as her fingers curled around Dahlia's wrist and squeezed. "Find me."

Then, she was gone as quickly as she had arrived.

Dahlia was left standing alone in a field, the winter air blasting across her skin. She shivered but didn't head back inside, not yet. Her head buzzed too much for sleep to be a possibility.

She began to plan.

27 - Gabriel

"Have you thought that maybe we shouldn't go?"

Sanna's comment didn't surprise Gabriel; the thought had been flicking through her brain with some variations for the last week. He'd been wondering if he should comment on it or if that would be intrusive. People could get snippy when he commented on their innermost thoughts, what with their notions of privacy and all that jazz. In the end he stayed quiet. Still. He was a little surprised that she waited right up until the night of the ball to bring it up aloud. Maybe he shouldn't have been surprised – lots of people put things off until the last possible moment.

She sat on the edge of his bed, twisting her fingers into the frothy tulle skirt of her black ball gown.

"I mean," she continued. "If he's agreed to drop all telepathy, that's on us too, right? On you. You'd…remember."

That was exactly the reason that Gabriel wanted to go. The dreams which had been haunting him had only grown more prevalent. Every night he dreamed and every night he forgot what exactly it was that his brain had been trying so hard to remember.

It had occurred to him to try and break out of the house, to disappear across the country in search of the spaces in his memory. He could start at the university; see if it jogged anything. That must be where it all began after all, if that was where his memories ended. He was also pretty certain that if he did that Archangel would know and stop him. The man had eyes everywhere. Gabriel thought Archangel reminded him of that on purpose. He'd make little comments about what Gabriel had been up to when he wasn't around.

He finished fixing his tie into place before turning to face Sanna, studying her. Her emotions buzzed across the room towards him.

"I'm not going to force you to attend," he said. "The whole point is that people have the choice on whether they want to confront all parts of themselves or not." That was the other reason for the ball. If he wanted his freedom then surely there were other people who did too?

"I thought the point was giving Archangel a night off."

"That as well," Gabriel said carefully. "Spending all your time in other people's heads gives you very little time to spend in your own." He was starting to learn that better than most – maybe that was what Archangel had intended with the isolation? He couldn't read Archangel's mind, so he couldn't be sure. It was maddening not to be sure if someone was a monster or merely a man.

Sanna looked down at her lap again. She wasn't, exactly, frightened either. The new world didn't allow for such a negative response. Yet, something as close to unease as could possibly be eddied in her brain, tugging at him before vanishing, then tugging at him again a moment later. Her thoughts raced. It left him twitchy, anxious.

Gabriel considered his options, before taking a seat opposite her. He waited for her to be ready to talk. What did it matter if they didn't arrive at 7pm on the dot? It wasn't like Archangel was letting him host.

Sanna bit her lip.

"I...I remember what it was like. Feeling everything. Feeling what I *felt.* I don't want that, I – I don't think I can do that." She swallowed hard. "Does that make me weak?"

"I think it makes you human." Gabriel tried for a small smile, but she didn't smile back. He resisted the urge to send another wave of calm at her, some placating thing. It wouldn't help. If she ended up going, it would just make the contrast between her head spaces even greater when all the barriers in place were taken away. "I know we haven't known each other very long," he said, after a moment, though sometimes he felt he knew her better than that. "But I've seen, sorry, but I've seen flashes in your head of what you'd been through. You're the kind of person this level of telepathy was always intended to protect." Gabriel hesitated, wondering if he should continue, if it was even his place. "When people have...trauma. Or more ongoing severe mental health concerns, if that's the right term..." He didn't know if that was the right word for it. "Anyway. People shouldn't be shamed for needing a crutch, any more than someone who needs glasses should be shamed for not having perfect sight. That's not weakness. You've already survived so much, more than most people would literally and physically be capable of living through – it's harder for you than it is for other people. So maybe with you getting through the day in any way you can, still finding a way to help people despite *everything*, is strength enough. You don't have anything to prove to me on top of that, certainly."

She pushed to her feet, restless and agitated. He watched her pace.

"Why do I feel like that's your 'but' voice," Sanna said. There was no bite to her tone, but...well, she was right.

The memories still clustered in her head, devoid of emotion attached to them like they were distant underwater moments, but even without the emotion Gabriel knew what the likely emotions attached to being strapped to a table against your will and repeatedly cut open and experimented on were.

It was Gabriel's turn to bite his lip, telepathy tentatively reaching out, but he couldn't get any real sense of if what he had to say would upset her. The emotion wasn't there. She was a scrambling void, not happy, not *anything* because the bad was gone. It reminded him, again, of his mother.

"Avoidance isn't always the best option." That sounded far too harsh. Gabriel winced. He adjusted on his seat and resisted the urge to loosen his tie once more, pretty sure he wasn't qualified to give any advice on anything ever. "What I mean is...using telepathy to get through the day is one thing, it's actually the obvious choice to me if you have that option."

Before his own broken memories he would have said that it was the only reasonable option – why confront pain if a person could feel happy instead? Why allow anything bad to happen ever? To a certain extent, he still agreed. If Sanna had never suffered what she suffered the whole conversation wouldn't be happening. The best possible option would have been to make sure the people who hurt her never got the chance to hurt her or anyone else. Still, it had happened, and there was no pretending otherwise.

"Look," he said. "If you never touch base with what you're actually feeling, never work through anything, you are never going to heal from it."

Who was Archangel to say that Gabriel shouldn't face the

consequences of what he'd done? How was he supposed to take responsibility, make amends, move on if he had no idea of any of it? It reminded him, yet again with another flash, of his mother. Squeezing his hand. Calling him angel. Begging to be happy, while his father looked on as if wife's heart and mind was none of his business.

"And if something can't be healed?" Sanna's shoulders squared with something like challenge – more challenge than she normally gave him.

He'd definitely said the wrong thing, judging by the look on his face. He itched to wipe the conversation from her mind, start over and get it right, but that would be hypocritical.

"Sanna, it's your choice if you go or not. I already said I'm not going to force you."

"But you think I should go."

"If you want to go, I'll be right there next to you and I can help if the whole 'no telepathy' thing gets to be too much. If you don't want to go, if you want to save everything for another day, that's fine too. You're not going to be letting me down or anything."

She folded her arms. "You're dodging the question."

"It's not my job to decide if you go or not," Gabriel snapped, before he could stop himself. "I'm not answering the question because whatever I answer is what you're going to do. If you go and it goes wrong it's my fault for telling you to go, if I tell you not to go and you sort of wish you had gone then it's my fault too."

Sanna stared at him in silence for a long moment, shocked and wide-eyed by the outburst.

"I'm sorry." Gabriel dragged a hand through his hair and sighed. "Look, I'll help you in anyway I can, I always will, but you can't expect someone else to take responsibility for your decisions. I can't...I can't do that for you." It took everything in him to say that, to admit that. Sure, theoretically, he absolutely could tell her what to do. He just didn't...maybe, he no longer thought that he should or wanted to.

It was one thing for him to step in if someone was going to commit a murder, and another thing entirely when the issue in question was whether or not to attend a potentially psychologically painful dance. He'd always thought that the fix might be black and white, but it wasn't. The more he thought about all of it, the more he ended up in endless grey, and what good was that? Grey wouldn't get anything done because everyone would be too busy debating what was right. Yet...

Her mind continued to whirl, should I and could I, before she deflated. She steeled herself up to it, faltered, ramped herself up and faltered again.

"I'm sorry," she said, quietly. "I can't. I just – I remember how I felt, and I don't want to feel that way again. Not *ever* again. I can't do it."

Gabriel nodded and rose to his feet. He strained up on his toes to press a kiss atop her head.

"I'll tell you how it goes."

Hopefully, the night, one way or another, would be the night for truth.

***

The ball, when he arrived, was everything he had planned and hoped for. It felt a little *magic* even when he knew all the strings behind the scenes.

He wound his way through the crowds of people who had already arrived, heart pounding with – was it nerves? Nerves

329

for his memories, perhaps, or maybe simply to be around people after so long. He'd forgotten how loud it could be to get close.

The whole affair had been decorated lavishly with flowers. That had been Sanna's idea – she'd wanted as much of the wild as possible, so it would be like stepping into a fairy land. People still wanted flowers in the world, after all, along with wheat and grains and vegetables. A world without flowers, Sanna said firmly, would be utterly miserable and for the ball it would be fitting. Roses were as quintessentially fairy tale as one could get, and blooms signified new life and change. Who wouldn't want to see the colours of flowers in the cold dead of winter?

The chandeliers shimmered, glinting like specks of starlight across the wall.

If he said so himself, they'd done a pretty damn good job. No matter what else happened, there was that. He hovered atop the staircase so that he could get a good look at the room below, trying to pick Archangel out in the crowd. The other telepath would obviously be in attendance, because he'd said he'd come, and without Sanna there Gabriel didn't know anyone else. It was an oddly, horribly, vulnerable feeling. He knew he'd had a whole life, gone to university, done far more than live with his parents in a big empty house, but…

It didn't feel like it and there was nothing to reach for, only Archangel's sorrowful assurances that he had done something monstrous. He swallowed. He could feel panic beginning to rise and…he felt the brush of a familiar mind and turned.

Sanna came to a stop behind him. There was a placid expression on her face, as if all of her uncertainty, and all of her conviction had been wiped away.

Gabriel blinked in surprise, but offered her his arm like he'd seen gentlemen do in old movies on something like automatic. "You came." He regretted the words when they came out – dumb as they were, stating the obvious.

"Yes. I had to."

"Had to...?"

"I mean, I thought about what you said, after you were gone, and you were right," she said.

She couldn't have been thinking about it for very long; she'd arrived only minutes after he had. While it was possible she'd had a pretty immediate change of heart once he'd turned the corner, something about the look on her face, the feeling of her mind as he reached his telepathy out...

The conviction that she had to be at the party, that she couldn't simply show her face, that everything was okay had Gabriel straightening his spine stiffly. In the last few months, he'd grown rather good at recognising Archangel's hand at work. He felt a sharp stab of anger and scoured the crowd below him in search of the other telepath again, skimming through minds like a deck of cards, looking for the one that didn't fit and—

He spotted Archangel standing next to a blond man, a blond man whose head turned at the brush of Gabriel's telepathy as if he could sense it like a skipped pebble rippling the surfaces of water.

Gabriel's breath caught.

Archangel's companion had white eyes, as cool and lovely as the silvery chandelier sparkling across the proceedings. There was something about those eyes, about that face...

He found himself staring, unable to quite tear his gaze away. The stranger was dressed in black, compared to Archangel's

331

white, and the effect was startling. He wouldn't necessarily have called the man handsome, but – he was lovely. Quite lovely. Tall and lean. Why the hell was he with Archangel?

Gabriel's heart pounded in his chest and he didn't know why.

"Shall we dance?" Sanna asked, brightly. "Lots of other people are." She tugged his arm gently. "Gabriel?"

His attention snapped back to her.

She wanted to dance. She'd hated the pressure of the summer formal at her school, and then hated herself a little for not going because she didn't even care about that stuff but what if? And she thought she looked pretty badass if she said so herself and she was here with him and she'd always wondered—

"I'd love to," Gabriel said. "You look like a gothic queen."

She beamed.

He let her lead him, head reeling, onto the dance floor.

28 - Isaac

There were rules, Archangel had said haughtily, if Isaac was to attend the ball.

Honestly, the prick had spoken as if it had been Isaac's own idea, rather than his. The rules were 'simple' – don't wander too far off, and don't 'try' anything, because the room was full of plenty of people under a telepath's sway if Isaac thought escape or rebellion was a clever idea.

Isaac had asked him if he had to be home by midnight too, lest he turn into a pumpkin, but Archangel didn't seem to find it funny.

As Isaac stood in a gleaming ballroom, he was torn between the thought that it was nice to be out of Archangel's creepy hologram of domestic bliss, and the old unease at being in a room surrounded by so many people. Even when he knew he was getting stronger, getting better at controlling his powers and not magnifying everyone he touched, the ancient panic of being crushed by a crowd didn't want to go away so easily. He kept his hands in his pockets, lurking against the corner of the room as Archangel greeted and charmed every person who came through the door. Watching that ached. It was Gabriel's hosting face, made large scale, from all of the times they'd had people over.

Gabriel.

The thought that Isaac would see him was both obvious and one he found difficult to prepare for. The last time he'd seen Gabriel, Gabriel had seemed – well. It had seemed like Gabriel was going to fight for him. That he was much closer to the man that Isaac always dreamed he might be, rather than the man he feared he was. Then, the time Isaac had seen him before that, Gabriel had walked over every rule they'd ever had and done everything that Isaac had once thought that, despite his own worst fears, Gabriel would *never* do. So who knew.

Which version was he going to get? Archangel? The confident adult so certain of his own righteousness that no one else's opinion mattered? The broken adult so desperate to not let anyone else die? Or, given Gabriel likely didn't remember him at all, perhaps he'd see the uncertain teenager who'd once sat next to him on a curb and allowed himself to wish, just for a moment, that he'd never been born a telepath at all.

Isaac's throat thickened. He concentrated on keeping his breathing steady, uncomfortably aware that the only reason he could think freely at all was because Archangel wanted to see his reaction when the telepathy dropped. He wanted to prove, once and for all, that Isaac had always been wrong, and he had always been right. Isaac was banking on arrogance, he knew that, but sometimes Archangel seemed so confident that Isaac did think maybe he was the one that was wrong. No. He couldn't allow himself to think that. Confidence didn't make someone right any more than eloquence did.

Everyone at the party looked picturesquely happy, like something out of a movie scene. They swirled and blurred around the room in a swish of colour and fine fabrics, laughing and chatting excitedly about their novelty of a night. None of them came too close to him, leaving a small bubble of space at all points, and so to Isaac it felt more like moving through a dream than ever before. Hazy. There was golden champagne and tables plated high with exquisite cakes and cheeses and canapés and...

"Isaac? Isaac Morton?"

Isaac turned his head, brow furrowed, not especially expecting to be addressed and certainly not by a voice he didn't recognise.

The man talking to him was shorter than Isaac by at least a foot, athletic, with a messy mop of brown hair and bright blue eyes and...no. All of the words Isaac might have said closed up in his throat. It wasn't possible. It couldn't be him. There were lots of people in the world with brown hair and blue eyes, it was hardly an uncommon trait, but it still felt like he'd been punched because Archangel *couldn't,* surely he *wouldn't.*

"It's Alec," Alec said. "Alec Mandel. Remember me?" He waved his hand and a small ice sculpture of a butterfly perched atop of his palm, before melting back into his beer. "We were at school together."

Apparently, Archangel *would.*

Isaac felt like the ground was falling away beneath his feet. For a second, he thought that Alec had to be a nightmare all grown-up. He almost hoped that he was. He wasn't, though. He was very much real. He was very much standing in front of Isaac for the first time since they were both kids.

"Alec." Isaac's voice was raspy. "I—what are you doing here? You shouldn't be here. It's not safe."

The Mandel family had swiftly moved away in the wake of Lola's death. He hadn't spoken to Alec since.

Alec stepped closer, reaching out as if to go in for a handshake or one of those awkward back-slapping hugs. Isaac took a half step back on instinct.

Archangel appeared at his side, slinging an arm around Isaac's waist. It would have been steadying but there was nothing *steadying* or kind about inviting Alec Mandel to be in that room. Archangel's grip tightened, perhaps expecting Isaac to run. Part of Isaac wanted to.

Isaac saw past the momentarily distracting shiny lights, the music, the rich scent of food, to the nightmares still lurking in the corners of the room like cobwebs. It was all a show. Of course it was, he'd known that, even as he'd nearly fallen for it.

Alec's arm fell back to his side.

"It's so good to see you," he still said, smiling, like everything was just fine and their last solid memory together hadn't been ice and coldness and Isaac's powers spinning out of control, and oh *god* Isaac couldn't breathe. He looked at Archangel. "Thank you for inviting me."

"I'm so glad you could come," Archangel returned. "Isaac has been so monumental to all of this, that it seemed only right to have you as a special guest. I know he's thought of you often over the years."

Alec didn't seem to find anything weird about that statement, which only seemed more proof that Archangel must be crawling about in his brain, controlling him.

"Archangel." Isaac felt sick. "What…"

Alec didn't seem bothered by the sight of him, but there was absolutely no way that would hold when the telepathy was no longer there, right? Why else would Archangel have invited him except to make Isaac doubt? To make him lose their bet, and his freedom with it.

"Tell us," Archangel said to Alec, like their meeting was a happy coincidence and the conversation casual small talk between old friends. "Did you enjoy life after you murdered your best friend? Because you couldn't control yourself?"

Alec didn't flinch, but something flickered in his eyes.

"Don't," Isaac hissed, at that. He twisted to try and face Archangel. "Look, if you're angry with me—"

Alec was already talking. Telling.

Apparently, Alec had ended up moving to New Mexico to work as a fire look-out at Gila National Park as soon as he could. The forest fires there could get quickly out of control, and it was a job that didn't require him to get close to very many people. Ice could be handy when it came to fire. He hadn't married. Though he'd been a popular child, in adult life most of his friends were online.

"It's safer that way," Alec said. "But you know that. I've come to terms with my part of what happened, it would never have happened if you hadn't…" He looked at Isaac. "You should have kept your hands to yourself if you couldn't control yourself. I didn't have that problem before you."

It was not the same, but reminiscent, to what Alec had yelled at him right after it had happened. He'd backed away from Isaac with wild eyes, looking at him like Isaac was leaking radiation. He'd started screaming. The adults had come running and – Isaac remembered the way they had all looked at him.

"He can control himself now," Archangel said cheerfully. "He's come such a long way, haven't you, Isaac? Do you want

337

to see?"

Alec held out a hand again, impossibly polite, and most definitely a perfect puppet on a string.

Isaac didn't have his gloves. Archangel had taken them before the whole night started. He froze.

The work he'd done fighting Archangel, that was – it felt different. He looked at Alec's hand and all he could remember was Lola. That day. That moment. The coldness of dying. He realised, distantly like he was watching himself from a very long way away, that he was hyperventilating.

"Go on," Archangel said. "Don't be rude – shake his hand. You can control yourself now, can't you? Certainly enough to think you stand a chance against me, so he should be no problem!"

Isaac could do it, he knew he could do it. His hand simply couldn't, wouldn't, move to take Alec's outstretched palm.

Would telepathy make this easier for you, Isaac?

The question echoed in Isaac's head, smugly, and he flinched before he could stop himself. He tried to remind himself more firmly that he could do this, he'd proven that he could do this, he was supposed to have buried the ghost of Alec Mandel long ago and they were not eight years old any more, but…

A body stepped between him and Alec, and for a moment even Archangel seemed startled by it.

"What," Gabriel snarled at Archangel. "The hell?" Gabriel seemed to catch himself, whirling on Alec with a familiar smile. "Have you tried the mini bruschetta bites? You should. They're great." His gaze bore into Alec's and Alec's hand dropped. He turned towards the buffet table and – was that *Sanna?*

The sense of a trap closing around Isaac grew, because he couldn't believe that Archangel had invited her for moral support. No. Sanna was someone else who had memories that hurt more than most. Someone who might just shatter when her support was taken away for the first time in what – since it all happened? Gabriel had been the one to rescue her, after all, from what Isaac had gathered. He'd been using his telepathy on her for years.

He watched as Sanna made bright small talk with Alec as she escorted him to the buffet, looking spectacular in her corset. His ears rang. Gabriel was hissing something to Archangel, and the walls, the horror, was still closing in and then –

They'd stepped outside onto a balcony which emptied within seconds. The cool air was a blessing on Isaac's flushed face, and he gulped the night down greedily, leaning down over his knees. It took him far too long to realise that Gabriel's hand was still on his arm, lightly, above the material of his suit. That Gabriel had been the one to tow him out.

Isaac's gaze snapped to him. Their eyes met.

Isaac straightened sharply, still feeling a little dizzy.

Gabriel didn't look at him with recognition, but his eyes were warm and fiercely protective, and his posture...it wasn't the posture that Isaac had grown used to, more like the Gabriel of eighteen years old. Confident for his age but still faking it most of the time. He must surely see the memories going frantic in Isaac's head, right? What did that do to someone who had been ordered to forget their whole life? And Isaac couldn't believe, after everything, that he'd taken one look at Alec Mandel and just frozen up!

"Breathe," Gabriel said. He gave Isaac's arm a friendly

squeeze. "Just, can I get you a glass of water, or something? That was—" Gabriel suddenly looked incredibly awkward. "Sorry. I'm Gabriel. Gabriel De Vere. I didn't mean to kidnap you, you seemed like you really needed to get out of that situation. You looked like you were about to pass out. And he wasn't – you know Archangel?"

"Uh, yeah." Isaac swallowed. "Thanks. Yeah. I…I know who you are too."

There was no point pretending otherwise when Gabriel would remember everything before the end of the night, even if he wasn't in Isaac's head in that instant.

"Oh," Gabriel said. "Sorry."

Isaac blinked, surprised.

"I don't have my memories," Gabriel explained, as if Isaac hadn't been right there when it happened. As if it hadn't been his power, and the losing control of it again, that had allowed Archangel to telepath even another telepath when he didn't seem to be able to do it all of the time. "But – I mean, I gathered I wasn't that great a person. So, sorry."

"Archangel told you that?"

It was Gabriel's turn to blink. His head tilted.

Even through the fading panic, Isaac realised abruptly how uncomfortable and weird the conversation had the chance of being. Maybe he should simply have said thanks and let Gabriel be until his memories came back. The only reason Archangel would allow it was because he didn't think it would make any difference to Isaac losing or because he would think it made Isaac more likely to doubt. Maybe it would.

Isaac hesitated a bit, and there were a thousand things he should have said, a thousand manipulations to turn the situation to his advantage if Gabriel wasn't in his head but…

He looked at Gabriel, so not knowing anything about Isaac, so eager to try and fight Archangel to save him despite that, and he didn't want to get into the past. He was sick of their past. He didn't want to think about the tangled snarl of betrayal lodged in his chest, and the fear, and how much everything between them had gone so very wrong. He didn't even want to think about the good bits.

Isaac was done hiding, done bucking off responsibility and power like that meant he couldn't possibly hurt anyone, done *running*. But, just for a moment...

"Isaac Morton." Isaac offered a hand, and that time the gesture was sure. "You should get your friend out of here. It's not going to be pretty."

Gabriel took his hand and shook.

"I don't think Archangel's going to let that happen. She wasn't planning to be here."

Isaac swallowed. Right. Archangel would want his room full of leverage, no matter what else happened.

"Can you read my thoughts?" It would be the quickest way to communicate.

"No. I – there's a block. I've never seen anything like it."

Archangel. Of course.

Isaac released a breath and considered his options once more. He'd wasted time panicking already, which had no doubt been Archangel's plan to leave him on edge.

He considered asking what Gabriel thought of the Archangel Project and...

"Do you want to dance?" he asked, instead.

The dance floor was easier to not be overheard on, if he wanted to justify it, but mostly he maybe wanted to say goodbye. However the night worked out, if it worked out at all, Isaac couldn't afford to keep clinging to the old version of Gabriel. Archangel had been right about that. Gabriel was *not* his saviour, not his hero, not his knight in shining armour from first year to magically transform Isaac's life. Isaac couldn't count on Gabriel to help stop Archangel when he had his memories back, because Gabriel had chosen to bring Archangel to power in the first place. But Gabriel wasn't Archangel either, he wasn't a villain, and if he was a monster then he was a monster in the way that all humans could be, always caught between definitions in a world that wanted simple binaries.

Which meant Isaac had to say goodbye to this version of Gabriel, this dream of him, this start of him as much as everything else. Anything else simply wasn't fair to either of them. It wouldn't give them a future.

Isaac would need strength, and no regrets, for what was to come.

"I would love," Gabriel said, "to dance with you, Isaac Morton."

***

They didn't talk through the dance – the music was too loud, and Isaac was grateful for that. They'd said plenty of words to each other in their life so far that he didn't think he had room for more right then.

If Isaac ignored the looming hope-horror of all telepathy in the room soon dropping, and the figure of Alec Mandel, he could almost even convince himself again that it was a nice party. Almost. Enough to settle him, at least. They'd barely got through two songs before Archangel was calling for silence.

The music cut.

Everyone watched the nightmare, expectantly.

Isaac's heart hammered in his chest, and he considered snatching Gabriel's power then, and letting his own power fly, but – no. Telepathic shrapnel. He had no idea where Gabriel's control was at, not like he used to. He didn't know this Gabriel. He didn't get to be careless.

They exchanged glances, as Archangel smiled out above the crowd. He thanked everyone for coming.

Sanna weaved through people to join them, standing at Gabriel's side. Gabriel leaned up to whisper something in her ear, flashing a reassuring smile. His eyes were worried again.

Archangel held up a glass, as if he were making a toast.

"We have come a long way from what the world was," he said. "Past meaningless suffering and squabbling among ourselves, past being at the mercy of those who would seek to use power only for their own ends, past screaming out in the dark for someone to save us. We have reached a new age of prosperity, of purpose, and goodness."

There were cheers from the crowd, and Isaac didn't know if they were genuine or some canned laughter equivalent prompted by Archangel's telepathy.

"But…" Archangel sighed. "There are still those would doubt, who would choose some fool's notion of freedom over our safety, our happiness. There are those who would fight."

His eyes met Isaac's, Gabriel's, Sanna's.

"They will learn."

The room erupted into screaming.

343

29 - Gabriel

For a moment, it all tingled in Gabriel's mind; something sublime, something forgotten that still lived in his muscles like a collective memory that couldn't quite be destroyed.

He felt, distantly, as the ballroom around him collapsed into chaos. People burst into tears or simply stopped dead, smacked by guilt or fear or some other strong feeling that had been muffled for months. The force of the emotions, after so long kept at bay, sent him crashing down to his knees.

Maybe Sanna had been right to avoid the party.

He couldn't get enough air. Someone called his name, but he couldn't focus on the words after that, couldn't focus on anything except the memories. He closed his eyes, biting back a groan, curling in on himself as if he could somehow brace himself, somehow shove it out.

It hurt. It hurt it hurtithurtihurt.

The memories followed after that.

Five years ago

It was an ordinary day.

It was supposed to be an ordinary day.

He woke up beside Isaac, relishing the way that his boyfriend held him close, kissing him eagerly. A pale chilly sunlight spilled through the crack in the window, and he'd braved the cold of the morning long enough to make tea and bring back mugs that they huddled together with over breakfast in bed. Isaac nestled close to him, sweet and affectionate in a way that Gabriel rarely got to see, but which made his heart ache with pride and pleasure. Isaac had come in leaps, in bounds, when it came to the touch; not in the least in the face of Isaac never touching at all before.

"Okay?" Gabriel asked.

"I love you," replied Isaac.

Gabriel had smiled, and had looked forward to returning to him in the evening, to kissing him again, to maybe going further if Isaac was willing.

He bounded up the narrow stairway that night, up the threadbare carpet and back to their small, shared room. It had been silent, so Isaac couldn't have been home yet from the studio. He'd opened the door and stopped.

"...Isaac."

Isaac lay crumpled on the floor, his blood seeping into the floorboards. His gloves were off. It was a stupid thing to notice, that Isaac's gloves were off, but rare enough that it merely added to the sense of something being horribly wrong.

"No," he whispered. "No, no no no. Isaac?" He fell to his knees and reached for a pulse. He couldn't find a pulse. He couldn't breathe.

Someone was making a sound, a horrible inhuman sound. He realised far too late that the sound was his own. It jolted him out of dazed horror. He lunged to put pressure on Isaac's cuts rather than fumbling at bare wrists, as if he could press the life back into him. He strained for Isaac's mind – for sound, for soul. He pressed with every inch of power that he had.

Stay with me, please stay with me. Breathe. Be okay. Help me. Somebody, anyone, help me!

He caught a glimpse of scarlet curls, of startled blue eyes turning black as pitch sitting on the other side of Isaac's body. Dead. Not dead. The world glitched. His head spun. The vision wavered. The shadow behind the girl grew until it towered above them all.

He couldn't feel Isaac's mind. He didn't think he could feel any heartbeat but his own, lashing too loud and too alone.

No.

He had to save him.

Isaac, I'm ordering you to stay alive.

The ball

"Gabriel." Isaac reeled back from him as if he'd been tugged by an invisible marionette string. His hands flailed, like he wanted to help Gabriel to his feet, protect him somehow.

Gabriel met his gaze, wide-eyed, raw. Half of his brain was still on the fresh remembrance of kneeling over Isaac's body with bloodied hands, willing to do anything and everything if it only meant that Isaac would come back to him. If only he would be okay. Then, he remembered standing in front of Isaac, ignoring his no, breaking the single most important rule they'd ever had. Breaking the single most important rule he'd ever had himself, since he was old enough to understand 'consent' and 'telepathy' and begin to grasp the crossover between the two.

"I'm so sorry." It came out raspy, broken.

He looked around for Sanna – he'd promised to help her, to not leave her alone with the onslaught of emotions. He could barely see her through the flurry of colours and pain. Was it being heightened by Archangel? Or was it simply that repressing it had built the agony up more? Lowered his tolerance?

Gabriel doubled over, pain lancing through his head as years of memories continued to race through his head. He felt like he might be sick across the polished ballroom floor, bile burning in his throat. All of the other memories, everyone else's, all the hurts of the world, stabbed through him.

"Is this better?" Archangel sounded so terribly smug, both in his head and out of it. "Look at him – look at *all* of them. Tell me honestly that this is better, Isaac. They're *breaking.*"

Gabriel had loved broken things when they first met. He loved to put them back together.

Isaac Morton had been a stained-glass window of a boy. Startling colours, beauty, torment, and absolutely shattered into a million pieces.

What arrogance, what ego! The existence of a broken thing required someone or something to do the breaking in the first place. It required someone to be hurt, hurt so badly that they felt like they would never be whole, just so that he could sweep in and play the hero.

With his eyes feverish as they darted between Gabriel and everyone else in the room, shoulders crumpled in on themselves, face pale and stark…Isaac Morton looked…

"Your heart is breaking too, Isaac." Archangel singsonged the words like anything about the situation was whimsical or entertaining. "Do you want me to turn it off? You know I will. Just ask. I won't even make you say please."

Gabriel caught sight of Sanna on her knees and he crawled towards her. She wasn't crying. She looked shell-shocked, fingers buried in her hair, rocking back and forth as her lips moved around words he couldn't hear as the memories flooded her too.

Their eyes met. He strained to reach out to her, to help, but he couldn't find good. He couldn't find any calm within himself to offer her.

Hers eyes filled with tears then. With absolute, desolate resignation as if the bad things would always come and there would never be an end to the tunnel.

Gabriel didn't think he'd ever like broken things again.

Eight years ago

Gabriel loved broken things – he loved to put them back together.

Isaac Morton was a stained-glass window of a boy. Startling colours, beauty, torment and absolutely shattered into a million pieces. Gabriel didn't love him immediately, but he felt a fierce rush of protectiveness at the sound of his brain.

Isaac Morton, getting punched in the face, didn't get angry that somebody had dared to harm him. The sound of his mind was resigned. The sound of his mind was 'well, what did you expect?' and 'I probably deserved that.'

So when Gabriel stepped into that fight on his first night at university, when he dragged Isaac bleeding and more tired than any eighteen-year-old had the right to be up to his room, and told him "you have a goddamn lovely face," and "it's a crime to punch it" there was so much more he wanted to say.

Thoughts were always so much easier than words. Word carried weight, finality.

Gabriel knelt on the floor of a grotty student bedroom, eyes darting over posters picked for a young man trying to be the right kind of artist, and he *ached.* He wanted to tell him:

- You don't deserve to be hurt
- You deserve so much better than this
- Somebody should have protected you
- Somebody should have protected *us*

But he didn't say those things. Those things were too intense to say on a first meeting with someone, and Gabriel had learned his lesson well. He told Isaac his name was Gabriel instead and he didn't tell him 'I think you're just like me.'

Gabriel's bedroom, in first year, was filled with everything that his parents wanted in a son. He would be a doctor, with excellent grades. He would date a pretty girl. He would be charming to everybody, because everybody who met a telepath wanted to be charmed and didn't want to be reminded that he knew all of their secrets. What was the point, after all, of a telepath who didn't anticipate all of your needs and provide for them before you even had to ask?

Isaac was so scared of everything that he made Gabriel brave. One of them had to be.

Isaac was so scared of everything, and yet he was still trying so he was probably the bravest man Gabriel had ever met. All Gabriel could really do was buckle to his knees before him and want to kiss his goddamn lovely face so hard that the rest of the world shut up in awe of a kiss like that.

Maybe, one day, Gabriel figured if he put enough broken things together he'd learn to fix himself too.

He had to see him again.

The ball

"No." Isaac shook his head, frantic. "You deliberately invited people who were hurt – you knew – this isn't fair."

"Oh give it up and surrender, Isaac," Archangel said. "This is starting to be more annoying than cute. I can feel your doubt. We had a *deal*."

"No."

That word, that refusal, wasn't frantic at all. In an instant something in Isaac had hardened, no longer fragile. It was an implacable, unshakeable steel of resolve.

The amusement faded from Archangel's face as if it had never been there. He took a step closer to Isaac, bodies parting out of his way, his expression dark and dangerous. Everything about him, the way he moved, the look in his eyes, made Gabriel itch to throw himself forward and intervene.

He'd never thought that Isaac would need protecting from him.

Even when he'd imagined The Archangel Project it was never supposed to be yet another empire built on a rotten core, on exploitation. But it was. What was the point of the greater good when at its heart was someone scared and alone and imprisoned?

"No." Isaac drew in several unsteady breaths, bracing himself like a ship in a storm but – he didn't run, he didn't backtrack from the telepath advancing on him. He looked ready to *fight*. "This is…this is better. They're free. I may have doubts but I do not doubt that you are wrong. You use people. You've used everyone in this room."

Archangel stopped, staring at him, aghast and bewildered as if that argument was worth nothing, nothing at all.

It was not a version of Isaac Morton either of them had seen before. Not like this.

Seven years ago

"You know I want to kiss you, don't you?" The words blurted out of Isaac's mouth.

Gabriel stilled at the comment, though he should have been expecting it. It was late in the evening. Quiet. There was one person in one of the other rooms, but the campus art studio he and Isaac sat in was otherwise empty. Gabriel had come to fish Isaac out before he starved to death.

He hadn't been expecting Isaac to actually bring it up. Isaac didn't really do talking about his feelings.

Gabriel's heart raced in his chest.

"Yes." There was no point pretending that he hadn't seen the desire spark in Isaac's head before, hadn't seen him imagine it on the odd occasion, hadn't seen the way that his gaze dropped to Gabriel's mouth sometimes when Gabriel smiled at him.

351

He knows, but he doesn't want to. Otherwise he would have brought it up himself.

Isaac's thoughts, his mile-a-minute insecurities, layered thick on the air between them on top of the smell of drying paint and chalk dust. Gabriel exhaled a breath, shifting on his chair. He rubbed his fingers over his temples, trying to focus. He wanted to be present for this, he didn't want to be half tracking Kelly Spellman's thoughts down the hall wondering if she was going to get that internship.

"I do," he said, to Isaac's thoughts. "I just didn't – people can think about stuff and not actually want to do them. Fantasy versus reality and all that…jazz." He couldn't believe he just said all that jazz. He wanted to thunk his head on the table hard enough to forget that ever happened. His cheeks coloured. "I can…it's all emotion. I wasn't sure if it was you, or…me. I didn't want to get it wrong," he admitted, quieter.

Isaac was not, exactly, the most comfortable when it came to physical touch. What Gabriel wanted definitely required touching. Lots of touching, ideally. In the months that they had known each other, Isaac didn't do touch. At least not touch without barriers. He found excuses, otherwise, like he couldn't help himself. Isaac would stand close in his thick jumpers and gloves and let their shoulders brush, or one time he had reached out with a gloved hand to swipe Gabriel's hair from his face. Every time he did it, Gabriel would be hit by a wave of immense want, of something like hunger.

He didn't know if it was because he wanted Isaac, because Isaac wanted him, or because Isaac was so touch starved that anyone would have done for him if he dared.

To date in the months that they had known each other, Gabriel had never once touched Isaac's skin. He knew what might happen if he did, of course, from Isaac's thoughts but that wasn't the same.

Isaac set his paint brush down and stood up.

Gabriel half wanted to ask what was bringing this on *now,* what he had missed to make the tipping point occur, and he half didn't dare say anything at all in case he frightened Isaac off.

Isaac moved around his easel to stand in front of him, his breathing oh so careful like he was measuring each gasp for air, trying to seem casual. He wasn't casual at all. Gabriel could feel his emotions, could feel his thoughts whipping up a tempest of longings. He bit down on his lip, his gaze roaming over Gabriel where he sat perched on one of the other tables.

Isaac hesitated, then. He froze up, desperation and fear all tangling up, all too much, all tugging him in a dozen different directions until it felt like Isaac's brain would leave him hung drawn and quartered. He regretted ever bringing it up – it had taken all of his courage to do so. He'd hoped it would be like hurling himself off a cliff, that saying it was the only step he had to take. He met Gabriel's eyes, all nerves and hope, and Gabriel was helpless.

Gabriel's stomach twisted up into knots, all want and uncertainty and fear and hope too, and they could have stood there forever, dancing around it. He didn't want to wait forever. He reached up a hand, brushing the backs of his knuckles along Isaac's cheek in the gentlest of caresses.

He didn't expect the power rush.

He'd known there would be one, but touching Isaac was like expecting to catch a wave on the beach and then surfing a tsunami. The whole world exploded into brightness, a cacophony of sound. He could hear everyone on campus.

353

wish she'd kiss me what's for dinner am I enough am I broken what if I'm just doing it for attention will I look greedy if I take the last pizza slice sorry should I say something internship money sex grades parents

Gabriel sucked in a sharp breath and couldn't remember how to release it again.

Isaac jerked back so hard that his back hit the other table, knocking off a paint pot. It hit the floor with a loud clatter, spilling a pool of murky water.

"Sorry," Isaac said. "Shit. Sorry. This was a terrible idea. I don't know why I thought this was a good idea."

"Isaac, calm down. Breathe."

Isaac sagged against the table, the tension flooding out of his shoulders. He blinked at Gabriel, lips still slightly parted.

Gabriel pushed himself up to stand, feeling electrified. He'd never felt anything like it. Yet, in the centre of it all, had been Isaac – as quiet as the eye of the storm.

"You don't need to apologise," Gabriel said, and offered a smile. "I think we both know this is going to take a bit of getting used to. It's okay. We have time." He moved closer, slowly enough that Isaac could track his movements.

"Are you alright?" Isaac asked, hoarsely. His mind flashed through ice, through guilt, through an eight-year-old boy and an eight-year old girl.

"I'm alright." Gabriel reached out to soothe before he could stop himself, wishing he could cradle Isaac's brain and spare him the worst of it. He stopped, standing in front of Isaac, where Isaac still leaned dazedly back against the table. "Can we try again?"

The want, the longing, pounded.

Isaac swallowed hard. He nodded.

354

Gabriel leaned in to kiss him, then.

The ball

"It doesn't matter." Archangel composed himself, barely sparing a glance for the world around him. "As you so aptly pointed out…there are other ways I can make you do what needs to be done if you insist on being so blind, so ignorant."

Sanna squeezed Gabriel's hand, rage starting to creep over the resignation on her face, and with her touch came healing. Waves upon waves of strength to provide him a shield when he didn't have the fortitude to make one for himself.

Gabriel pushed to his feet. As the years of memories began to settle, as love and fury and horror burned up in his chest, he could feel his own resolve locking into place too.

Archangel had taken his memories, *stolen* his memories, and then had the nerve to try and manipulate Gabriel with the spaces left behind. To take advantage. How many other people had he done that to? Because he could, and he thought he knew best.

Archangel was a monster and Gabriel had refused to see it until it was too late. Enough, now.

Because, it mattered. It had always mattered what people wanted for themselves, and Gabriel didn't know when along the road he'd ever forgotten that.

The resolve on Isaac's face flickered, his eyes darting to Gabriel with a growing dread and—

"I suggest you do as I ask, Isaac." Archangel's voice carried across the ballroom. "You may not care about yourself, but I

355

know you care about him."

There was no time to react. For the second time that night, Gabriel hit the polished floor in a writhe of telepathic agony.

30 - Dahlia

I t had been easier said than done for Dahlia to discover where Morphina was being held. To *find* her. She could, technically, have been anywhere in the world. But, during Morphina's nightly appearances, they had both agreed that Archangel was controlling enough to want to keep the dreamweaver close. He hadn't sent Dahlia across the world either.

That had still left a hundred places to search.

If she was Gabriel, Dahlia could have merely pinpointed some pocket of telepathic silence to locate the right cell. As it was, she hadn't been about to ask for Gabriel's help even if she could find him, so she'd had to try her investigations the long way around instead.

Morphina had sent her dreams every night, tiny conjurings of dragons or fantastical harmless creatures, to help throw Archangel's telepathy off. The two of them had talked. About the past. About Archangel. Every time Mona spoke about him, about the feeling of having the nightmare in her head, the same haunted edge had crept onto her features.

"I can't," she'd whispered. "I can't do it again."

It had made Dahlia think of Sanna.

Sanna was not a telepath, but she knew when people were

in pain. It had given her a headache. She'd said, so long ago, that Morphina had been hurting which meant, for better or worse, she'd likely have some sense of a woman who was hurting in a world where most people were mind-controlled to feel nothing but good feelings. It would stand out. At least, if Morphina was anywhere close to them, Sanna would be able to sense her.

The problem was that Archangel had commanded them against trying to find each other. But what if they weren't, specifically, trying to do that? Sanna was a healer. If someone got injured in Archangel's employment, she would heal them. Of course, another healer could turn up, but…but powered humans weren't *that* common. Besides, her and Sanna had been through enough together that she'd thought surely Sanna would want to see her too?

It was a gamble, but she hadn't had a better plan, so that morning she'd 'tripped' and ended up in the medical bay with a broken arm. She'd been proven right.

Sanna appeared shortly, stopping dead in the doorway when she saw that it was Dahlia who was her next patient. She looked much the same as she always had – better, even. She had always affected an air of general calm, but she seemed genuinely peaceful. Happy. Dahlia didn't know if it was real or not. Possibly, it was. Sanna had always liked the reassurance a telepathic command could give to her.

"I need your help," Dahlia said. "Finding Morphina. You know where she's being kept, don't you?"

Sanna's gaze dropped to Dahlia's broken arm, clearly putting two and two together. Her shoulders tensed.

"Why do you want to find her?"

Perhaps she thought Dahlia intended to kill Morphina a

second time.

"Because she's hurting," Dahlia said. She let Sanna gingerly smooth her fingers over her arm. It healed with a miraculous swiftness that, after all of their time together, Dahlia still couldn't get used to. Her bones felt all warm and relaxed. "And once upon a time you wanted to help people who were hurting, so tell me."

"You said you didn't care that she was hurting."

"In all fairness, my sister had just died and I hadn't slept. It was…I was just done. We all were."

Sanna's eyes narrowed as she considered.

"You're dodging my question."

"You know why I'd be looking for her," Dahlia said. "She's the dreamweaver. She can fix this."

"This doesn't need to be fixed."

"Then why would I, of all people, be trying to work with *her* to fix it?"

Sanna faltered at that. She let her hand fall from Dahlia's arm, chewing on her lip. She curled in on herself instead, fingers tracing along the crook of her forearm.

Dahlia's gaze fell in turn. It looked like someone had taken blood from Sanna recently. Sanna hated giving blood. She hated needles. All of it. It steeled Dahlia more. Morphina was…nightmarish, she had done terrible things, but at least she'd never pretended otherwise. She'd never claimed to be the hero.

"I get that you like him," Dahlia pressed, softly. "I can even see that he has done some good, in his way. I'm not stupid. But since when," she asked, "have you ever ignored other people's pain for the sake of your own happiness? He's got a woman locked up in a basement somewhere, in pain, being used for her gifts and you're just going to let that happen?" She reached up with her healed hand, twining her fingers around Sanna's and giving a squeeze. "I know you know what that's like. Please. Help us."

For a second, Dahlia could see the fear written across Sanna's face, the despair that the world would go back to normal and nothing would change, and that it wouldn't just be one woman locked in a basement and scared. It would be everyone who had ever been hurt. Everyone that Sanna hadn't been able to help. It would be her, one day, healing from even the worst of torments, without the escape of death if the wrong person took her. In Archangel's world no one could do that to her again. To let Morphina burn for that was selfish, but Dahlia could understand selfish.

"Archangel can make her pain go away," Sanna whispered. "I'm sure he—"

"Do you really think," Dahlia returned, "that he's somehow not aware of it? Gabriel doesn't forgive the people who have hurt his own. He just won't kill them because murder is bad. She's going to live the rest of her life in the darkness, with her nightmares, and it's not going to make her a better person and it's not going to bring anyone back to life and if it makes her sorry, she's going to be sorry that she didn't stay dead. She's going to be sorry that *you* didn't let her stay dead."

"Stop it. *Please.*"

"The Sanna I know," Dahlia said, "the one who was my friend, would never have left even one person to suffer. If she could stop it. If she saw pain, she didn't just ignore it. I was part of your little superhero club because Fliss was, and I wasn't gonna leave her, but you...even after everything, you wanted to help. Has that changed?

"You're lucky," Sanna said. "That I'm on shift. Don't tell me anything else about your plans."

But Sanna had told her everything she needed to know.

Dahlia had waited until later in the evening, when the broadcast of Archangel's ball would take place and everyone would be too busy tuned in to that to miss her. It was seven o clock. The ball would have just started. She was wearing a forest green tux ready to infiltrate.

She stood outside the door of Morphina's cell, unmoving, wondering if she really wanted to free her out into the world again. It went against everything she would have fought for, once.

Without Morphina, without Gabriel, without Isaac, Archangel would never have gained the spark he needed to bring him to life. For so long as all three of them were alive, Archangel would never truly be gone.

Yet.

Dahlia squared her shoulders, exhaled a breath, and let vines the same shade as her outfit creep through the crack at the bottom of the door. Then she wrenched it open with hard, loud bang.

Mona's head snapped up, staring back at Dahlia from the other side of a small room. The dreamweaver looked younger in the gloom; some substance of bad dreams and wisps instead of a woman, but she was a woman. Her face was stiff and blotchy with tears. Without Felicity's form or some nightmares to mask her true appearance she simply seemed tired. She didn't look powerless, though. It would be wrong to describe her, even then, even after everything, as weakened or childlike. Dahlia could admit, privately, that she admired that too.

361

"You came," Morphina said, something in her voice that made Dahlia's heart do…something unwise. "You found me."

"Don't worry." Dahlia swallowed. "I'm regretting it already."

Morphina looked down.

Dahlia cleared her throat, when the dreamweaver didn't move from the narrow bed she was sitting on. "Well," she said. "Are you coming or not? Or do I have to do everything around here?"

Morphina's fingers curled on the edge of the mattress.

"It goes wrong so easily," she murmured. "The nightmares, the monsters. They're always waiting for me. If we do this…" Morphina looked up again, squaring her shoulders. "If we do this, you have to promise me I won't end up back in here again. We can't just stop Archangel and pretend that's fine. Nightmares come back even when people don't. You can't kill them, not really. I've *tried*."

Dahlia's chest gave another dull pang that she didn't want to admit to, at that. She didn't want to imagine what it was like living in a world where the frightening things were always there at a touch, always ready to be summoned the moment that you lost control. She had never lived like that. She had never had such control over her monsters. When she was scared, she could hit what scared her with a branch. It was always someone else. Never her. She'd never had to be scared of her own mind.

"Yeah." She let her arms unfold and crossed the room, clenching her jaw before sticking out a hand for Morphina to take. "It's hard. I lost, and here I am again, like an idiot, helping you. But anything else…giving up…just means the monsters win, and that's just *annoying*. So no second thoughts, okay? Have your existential crisis once we've killed the fucker."

Morphina seemed to make an effort to focus.

"He's commanded me not to leave the room."

It was a terrible idea, an impatient one, one that was bound to draw the wrong types of attention for infiltration, but Dahlia summoned up her strength and tore the whole horrible building down. Let nature take over. She ruptured the earth beneath her feet, until they were surrounded only by dust and debris and so many wildflowers. She panted for breath.

It felt good.

It was stupid, but it felt *so* good.

Morphina stared at her again, like Dahlia was the weirdest thing she had ever seen, and just a little bit brilliant.

"There we go," Dahlia said and cleared her throat once more. "Now it's not a room any more. Let's go. You're not going to tell me you have nothing to wear now, are you?"

Morphina stood up. She looked down at herself, at her ragged clothing.

The illusion swam before Dahlia's eyes, transforming Morphina's outfit into – it was a dress, technically, but it made her look more like a silver butterfly curled ready to take flight. If butterflies came with wings that looked closer to elven armour. Flowers wove through the dreamweaver's scarlet curls, which suddenly appeared long and lustrous.

They were on a tight schedule.

Dahlia continued to stare at her for a moment.

"You look like a murderous forest sprite," she said. "Or a pixie knight. You should pick a genre."

"Thank you," Morphina said. "I knew you'd love it."

Dahlia's glared at her.

"Just get rid the Nightmares."

***

By the time they reached the ballroom, it was clear that Archangel had dropped his telepathy already. The sounds of screaming echoed down the street and made Dahlia's insides twist.

Her gaze landed on the large screens that hung outside the building, broadcasting the events from inside. On the way they had caught glimpses of the evening's entertainment through more large screens that had been set up outside in Cambridge market square – it had looked like a dream, like the kind of event that only rich people ever attended. Something unattainable that prom tried to be and failed miserably at. It didn't look like a dream any more. The broadcast hadn't stopped.

Gabriel was on his knees, screaming. He clutched his head, clawing at his hair like he wanted to rip his own brain out. There was no immediate obvious thing to cause his pain. Around him, people were scattering, fleeing towards the doors.

They didn't appear out in the streets that Dahlia and Morphina were standing on. She watched as the front doors of the hall shook but didn't break, as if people were trying to batter it down, but couldn't.

Would Sanna be in there? The thought made Dahlia's insides go cold. Dahlia hadn't been around when Gabriel first found Sanna, none of them had. She had been the first to join his team, when the idea of a place where powered people could meet and find ways to help was just an idea. She wasn't entirely convinced she'd ever seen Sanna without some crutch of telepathy to cling to, even at the church. It had annoyed her, sometimes, but...

Well. Maybe it was Sanna's choice. She wanted to think that, but nothing Dahlia could see of Archangel's new world looked like a choice.

Off the edge of the screen, Isaac's voice echoed.

"Stop it," he cried. "Just – stop it. You've made your point."

"Do you surrender?" Archangel replied, evenly. "Because I can do this forever. Break his mind, fix it again, break it again. Ah—" he sounded like he was smiling. "You don't like that, do you? You're both so much better at playing the self-sacrifice card. That's easy. You don't have to live with the consequences."

Morphina had an odd expression on her face, and for an instant she seemed frozen too, staring up at her bad dreams. Then she looked at Dahlia.

"Break the door down, he's distracted by them. This is our chance. Before Isaac surrenders, before he gets too close. We don't have long." She sounded – calm, far calmer than Dahlia felt, as if even now with the stakes so high this was a simulation rather than anything real.

"*You* break the door down," Dahlia mumbled. Really, couldn't Morphina just dream the door out of existence or something? Still. She focused. She did it. She nearly got crushed by desperate people fleeing the building who Archangel obviously didn't care about any more because they'd served their purpose, but she did it. At least that was a few less people he could use inside the building. And now there was no door to keep her away from Archangel. Peachy. Was this panic?

She glanced at Morphina, but the dreamweaver was already

moving forward with steeled shoulders. Dahlia hurried after her, dodging suits and weaving around flouncy dresses. She narrowly avoiding getting smacked with a face full of ice and staggered to a halt.

A young man stood in the hallway between them and the ballroom; he had frost pooling from his fingertips, and *nothing* in his eyes.

"Um," Dahlia said. "I thought you got rid of the nightmares."

"I did," Morphina said faintly. "And I think nightmare number one just noticed that."

"So he's not-?"

"He's not a nightmare. He's under mind control."

"Right. Cool, cool." Ice and plants didn't go together so well. Ice *killed* plants. It made it too cold for her seedlings to grow. Already, the cold spread out across the walls around them, creeping along the floor. Her breath turned to dragon's smoke in the chill. "Can you, er, summon something to help us?"

"No." Morphina's voice was flat.

An ice wall began to grow to build a fresh barricade, forcing the two of them to back away in the direction they had come.

"Any – are you going to give birth to any—"

Morphina gritted her teeth. "Anything I make, *he* can use. You want me to make a monster he can command? I can keep them away, or I can summon them. I can't do both at once. I don't have that level of power or concentration on my own."

The ice towered above their heads, about a metre thick, and still growing.

"Thanks for mentioning that earlier!" Should Dahlia smash the barricade before it blocked the entire corridor? She stumbled back another step. The ice man didn't seem to be trying to *kill* them, just keep them out. Keep them from interfering. Of course. All of their plans would be for nothing if they couldn't get close to Archangel – he knew that. He didn't need to kill them.

"You might not have freed me if you thought I was less useful," Morphina snapped back.

Okay, it was not the time to get into that argument, but Dahlia would also rather have bloody liked the last word on the topic if she thought they were going to die. Her mind whirled.

Was it just ice man who was Archangel's minion, or were there others?

"He only let the non-powered humans go," Morphina murmured. "He kept the ones he needed. He must have known we were coming."

How lovely a thought. Dahlia didn't miss the tinge of despair in Morphina's tone, the way that her shoulders sagged like the world was slowly about to finish crushing her. No. This wasn't how it ended, not after *everything*. Not after Felicity.

Dahlia's expression hardened and she took a step closer. There were still mosses and plants in Antarctica, even if they weren't exactly useful in combat. Nature had a way of surprising, of coming out on top, and she liked to follow that example. Unfortunately, trying to punch her way through the ice didn't work as well as she hoped. It hurt. A lot. And it didn't dent the stupid ice.

The ice stopped when it covered the whole corridor. They stood on one side, the man on the other.

The screams echoing through the building quietened, and she couldn't take it as a reprieve or a good sign, only one that

367

they were losing.

"If we made Archangel out of the worst of us," Dahlia said. "Can we dream up something to beat him with the best of us?

Morphina looked at her, surprised.

The moment after that, the ice shattered.

31 - Isaac

"Fine," Isaac said. He swallowed hard. "Fine."

Archangel smiled. It was Gabriel's happy smile and it felt like being stabbed in the solar plexus to look at it – Isaac was tempted to close his eyes again.

Instead, he concentrated on every trick against telepathy he'd ever known and practiced, and forced himself to remember one more time. First kisses and conversations with chips, the way he'd felt when Gabriel turned up at his house again, the way he'd felt leaving the first time. All of it. It wasn't hard. It wasn't difficult to think of Gabriel when he lay broken on the floor, gasping for air that didn't want to come, because Isaac loved him, and this *bastard* thought love was best used as a weapon, and maybe it could be. Maybe love could tie you to a person, but Isaac was going to be damned if it couldn't also set you free.

He remembered Gabriel sitting opposite him in his dorm one winter night, clutching a mug of cocoa. He was dressed in a cosy jumper and looked deflated from medical lectures he was poorly suited to, but he was sitting there, teaching Isaac all of the tricks he could think of to make sure that Isaac would never get taken in by a telepath unknowingly. So Gabriel could know that Isaac would say no, if he wanted to.

So they could trust each other. Because it wasn't just Isaac who wanted to know it was real, was it? It never had been. They'd just kissed for the third time.

Telepathy was snapshots, emotions, it wasn't so simple as an open book. If Isaac's head was overwhelmed by the emotions fuelling him that was the slam of what Archangel would get. At least for all of the three seconds it took him to stride across the room to Archangel's side, seize his wrist, and block his powers with everything that he had.

Archangel's eyes widened.

"You—" Archangel struggled against his grip, scrabbling to put distance between them. "Get off me!"

"No," he snarled. *No*, to all of it. No, this was done, they were done, deal or no deal. No, because seeing Gabriel hurt killed him, but no – not in the least because Gabriel would never have forgiven him if he gave up the world for him. Gabriel would have rather broken, wouldn't he? No, for him, and for Isaac, and for everyone that Archangel had ignored because he was a telepath and thought he knew better.

No. No. No.

Telepathy was not going to damn well get rid of Isaac right then, and he'd always been physically stronger out of the two of them. He had more reach in his arms. He pushed forwards, trying to force Archangel to the ground, to pin him where he wouldn't hurt or control anyone. He'd never liked the thought of fighting, but he'd damn well learned to do it in his time dead. Some part of him had known, always, that it was better to fight than have no choice in what he was used for. He just had to make sure he kept touching Archangel's skin.

"Stop him now!" Archangel's voice rang with telepathic command.

Sanna's body barrelled into him. Isaac grunted in pain as he hit the floor, their limbs tangling and tumbling before they both froze.

Stop.

Sanna's breath came hard, and her expression twisted with anguish. Tears filled her eyes and splashed down to Isaac's face – the rage, the pain – and then her eyes turned white. Magnified. She inhaled in a ragged breath and went still. Her attention flickered to where her hands were on Isaac, and then her head turned slowly towards Archangel.

"Fine," Archangel said to Isaac, not even looking at Sanna, as if she were nothing more than another tool to be used. "If that's how you want to play it, fine!" He advanced a step closer. "I didn't want it to come to this, but you…you are so desperate to make me the bad guy, aren't you? To make me the *villain*. To be blind."

He looked between them all and Sanna cast her head down to hide her eyes. It might look like shame to the unknowing. Archangel had a terribly disappointed expression on his face as if he had looked into all of their souls and found them utterly lacking. Isaac wanted to spit at him, even as unease and hope warred through him.

Out of the corner of his eye, he saw Morphina and Dahlia enter. They moved with the same stiffness as he did.

"You can't kill them," Gabriel rasped – seeming to guess where his counterpart might be going. "We don't kill people."

Sanna still clutched hold of Isaac's hand.

Archangel's stare snapped to Gabriel.

"I had hoped that telepathy alone would be enough to cure you of your immorality," he said. "I thought I could make you change, genuinely change." His voice grew harsher, more

371

distressed, more *fed up with all of it.* "I thought you could all be saved, with time and patience, I thought you would be able to *see*." He closed his eyes, and his voice grew soft, regretful. "But if you really want me to be the villain, I can be."

Isaac's heart pounded in his chest. Dread clamped cold in the pit of his stomach. He willed Archangel to summon him close enough to touch, but he didn't. Not yet at any rate. Isaac's body stopped about a metre away from him.

"Dahlia," Archangel said, still looking at Gabriel. "Snap everyone but Isaac's neck with your vines—"

He barely had time to finish the sentence before Sanna had stepped forward, buoyed by Isaac's power, and *punched.*

Dahlia's vines dropped as Archangel reeled, hand flying up to his face in shock.

"You should be ashamed of yourself," Sanna hissed. She reached out again, and when she touched Archangel's wrist it gave a sickening crack. Broken.

"You...let go of him!"

Sanna snorted.

"I heal. And he's magnifying me. Fuck you."

It probably wouldn't last – it wasn't like Sanna's powers were mental – but the brain was still a physical organ. Much like Morphina's dreams had made her less tired than the rest of them, now it seemed to offer Sanna some small barrier against the telepathy. And, if healing gave someone the power to move bones and reset them, to close wounds, then maybe with that gift amplified that meant bones could be moved in the other direction too.

"I *defended* you!" Sanna said, and if Archangel's expression was angry than hers was deadly. "Maybe some of your decisions were a bit off, but you were trying to be good.

Trying to help. But you weren't, were you? If you were trying to be good tonight, to do something *good,* it would have been a choice. You wouldn't have – wouldn't have." Her mouth wobbled, and her voice shook with the effort not to cry, but she didn't falter. Her fist curled once more. "I never did *anything* to deserve you hurting me, *killing* me."

For a second, Archangel looked gobsmacked. Like he honestly didn't know what to say to that, and was too surprised to use his telepathy to stop her or attack her again. It wasn't quite regret that crossed his face, he wasn't a creature made for remorse, but if a creature dreamed up without the capacity for remorse could learn such a thing than it was there.

"I – Isaac was fighting me," he began to explain.

"So it was for *the greater good?*" Sanna's voice was acid, and Archangel burnt for it. "I've seen what the greater good can look like. You just reminded me of it with really quite a lot more vividness than I would have wanted."

"They would stop me. Fight me. You think I should just let them do that? Knowing what it would cost?"

Isaac could feel Sanna's hand trembling again where he held her. Whatever pretence that everything was okay, that everything was fine, was gone.

"I think making people good is brilliant," Sanna said, oh so softly. "I think stopping the worst parts of humanity is the most admirable cause you can fight for. I'm not like this lot." She squeezed Isaac's hand. "I don't even care about free will – I've seen what shit people can do with it." She let go of Isaac's hand and stepped towards Archangel.

Isaac opened his mouth to protest, and then closed it. He backtracked, to where Gabriel was still on his knees on the floor, and while Archangel stared at Sanna, he helped Gabriel to his feet. He was careful not to magnify, not yet.

Whatever Archangel saw in Sanna's head made him flinch. The fissures had been there before, growing each time he tried to take on the world, but he had never looked so wrecked. Confused.

"I know you have too," Sanna murmured. She cupped Archangel's face in her hand. "The love of your life killed himself and you just didn't understand, and it wasn't fair. You couldn't understand why someone would do that. You would have done anything if you could have just got in his head… stopped him, made him happy before he did something he couldn't take back…it was the last straw, wasn't it?"

Gabriel squeezed Isaac's hand. Isaac's heart had jumped into his mouth. Their eyes met, and Gabriel nodded.

Isaac let his power go, hearing Gabriel's breath catch as his telepathy amplified.

"I don't think I even cared if you were a good person or not, so long as the end result was good. But this…*this.*" Sanna's voice cracked. "I'm so sorry for that, but this was not fucking good. You felt the pain in this room, and you just…" Her head tilted, like she was trying to understand and couldn't, "*used* it to make people worse. Even knowing how much it would hurt."

She stroked his cheek.

Archangel stared at her, still almost entranced with shock, with the one person he'd thought would always be on his side no matter what, taken utterly for granted, not being there.

"God, I loved you," Sanna said. She leaned in to press a kiss to his forehead and he didn't seem to know what to do or what was happening because nightmares were not programmed to deal with kindness. "But I *really* hate mean people. And there's never an excuse to be the bad guy just because people expect the worst from you."

For a second, Isaac thought that Sanna had got through. Then Archangel's expression hardened, closed off and righteous and so utterly certain that he could never truly be wrong.

"Dahlia—" Archangel began.

"Shut up and don't move," Gabriel said, his voice quiet but steely.

Archangel's mouth snapped shut.

"Now!" Morphina cried.

Isaac had a split second to register her intentions, *their* intentions.

Dahlia's vines whipped around and, in the blink of an eye, snapped Archangel's neck. He crumpled slack and motionless. Dahlia kept going, the vines kept attacking, like she had to be certain that he was well and truly dead. The fear that he would somehow rise, like her sister and the others had rose, had to be obliterated.

Gabriel sagged against him, letting go of Isaac's hand so the telepathy would lessen. He must have heard what Dahlia and Morphina planned, and yet – Isaac's head reeled.

Morphina was the one to move to Dahlia's side, to wrap her arms around the other woman, to tell her that it was okay and that it was done.

Sanna backed away from the body, looking down at her hands.

Isaac simply stared. Perhaps, it should have been him who dealt that killing blow. What was all of his training for except that? But, in the end, he couldn't. Maybe he could understand

375

that in Gabriel – sick to death that the story couldn't end without violence.

Gabriel looked relieved that somebody else had done what he could never do too.

Everything was a mess. None of it was ever supposed to be like this. But, maybe, it was over.

They looked to each other – as if Gabriel was checking that Isaac wasn't already running for the door as much as Isaac was checking that Gabriel wasn't a monster, that he was still there and not mangled on the floor in a motionless tangle of thorns.

"You…" Isaac didn't finish the sentence.

"No more Archangel project," Gabriel said. He tried to smile, reassuring as ever, but it was a sickly and wasted thing. "Possibly could have thought that one out more."

Sanna started to cry then, to properly cry, as everything that had happened washed over her. A dam had broken.

"Hey, hey." Dahlia was at her side in an instant, letting go of Morphina. "I've got you. This is crap, but I've got you. It's over."

"Do you want me to," Gabriel's voice was small. "Mute it? Take it away?"

Sanna glanced at him, and for a second she looked tempted. She said nothing, but Gabriel gave a tiny nod back.

"Okay," he said. "I'm here if you need me. I'm sorry."

Sorry seemed a pathetic word to encompass it all, and Gabriel looked like he knew that.

Isaac eyed the body on the floor and wished he could stop thinking 'what now?'

Nightmares, he knew from last time, did not stay dead so easily as real things did. The fear would always be there lurking beneath the surface, and he was trying to be brave but what if he wasn't strong enough? What if his worst fears crept back on him and on the whole world all over again? What if he, as ever, made things worse?

Morphina whispered something in Dahlia's ear, and then she turned to face them. Nightmares appeared at her sides – the same set from the forest, Gabriel's dead friends ready to attack.

"I'm sorry," she said, sounding like she meant it. "But this can't happen ever again. It just can't."

32 - Gabriel

"Mona—"

"Are you going to lose your shit if I die?" she asked.

Gabriel blinked; he'd expected many outcomes, most of them involving his death or Isaac's, but he hadn't expected that question. His mouth went dry. A horrible sadness swept over him. He'd honestly expected her to attack him.

She smiled, mirthlessly, at the look on his face.

"Your own evil counterpart was going to murder you as a threat to his plans. If that isn't proof that you're not the same, I don't know what it is. Your dreams have changed, Gabriel De Vere." She tapped her head. "And even if I kill you, there'll be someone else, won't there? Something else. Another nightmare." Her hand dropped. "And so long as I'm alive, *he* can come back. He already played me once."

"Is he in your head now?" Gabriel asked, with an odd feeling.

"He's a nightmare," Morphina said. "I don't think he'll ever be gone for me. And I – I can't. So. Please. Are we going to have a repeat of last time?"

Gabriel shook his head.

He'd already helped kill Archangel, and now…no.

378

No, that bit of him wasn't gone. He still didn't want this to end up with someone dead on the floor because they were scared of something they had the potential to do.

"You don't have to die for this," he said. "If you have a responsibility in this, so do I."

He'd never thought he was capable of screwing up so badly, but there it was. He remembered everything. He remembered the desperation, the despair, the awful certainty that it would all happen again and again and unless he did something there would never be an end to any of it. Maybe that was the way she was feeling too. He didn't know, he still couldn't get in her head or stop her nightmares with his powers, without touching Isaac, but maybe he didn't always need telepathy to understand.

"Hell," he continued, "I was the one who forced this to happen. When someone is used as a tool," he glanced at Isaac, "it is not the fault of the tool it is the fault of the person monstrous enough to do the using."

She didn't look entirely convinced.

"I know what it's like feeling like it's all out of your hands." Isaac stepped around him, and Gabriel could feel the sadness and the understanding washing from him too. "Like dying is the only way out because it feels like you can't breathe without making it worse, and it's never going to stop. But if I can learn to control what I can do…so can you." He released a shaking breath. "We all fuck up sometimes, and yeah we gotta own that. But we also don't have to do it alone. You can call me. I've learnt that I can suppress people, not just magnify them. That means I can suppress what you do now too, if you feel it's all going to spin away. I can help. If you let me."

379

He spoke with a confidence, an assurance, that Gabriel hadn't heard before, but he couldn't help but be proud of.

He could feel Sanna wondering if that would be enough, if anything would ever be enough when the bad was always there and ready to rise. How could intentions matter if the best intentions could go so grotesquely wrong as they had? Without telepathic control, there was freedom and choice and that meant the choice to mess everything up. There was uncertainty, and potential, and it scared her. Yet. She'd made her decision when Archangel forced her to confront everything bad that had ever happened to her.

If she didn't make those choices, somebody else would.

Dahlia pressed a kiss to Sanna's head, before she rose to her feet too. She stepped up towards Morphina, and took her hand.

Morphina's gaze startled to her.

"If you go off, I'll kill you," Dahlia said. "Okay? You know I'm capable of it. And I still owe you." It wasn't friendly, but somehow that seemed to reassure Morphina far more than anything that either Gabriel or Isaac had tried to say. "But we didn't go through all of this just to die." Dahlia met Morphina's eyes. "That's just miserable. Feels way too much like letting Archangel win."

"And him?" Morphina asked. She jerked her head at Gabriel. "How are you going to stop him if you have to?"

"With help," Dahlia said. "Morton's just a phone call away, right?"

"Right," Isaac said. Gabriel could feel his trepidation, but he still said it, and right then he seemed to mean it.

An awkward pause followed, strangely anticlimactic.

"So, what now?" Dahlia asked, interrupting them impatiently. "I guess people will start coming to their senses soon, as his telepathy wears off. How long do we have?"

Gabriel hadn't honestly got as far as thinking about after. The stories always skipped to the 'happily ever' part of after. 'After' suddenly seemed very big and dawning rapidly, and not as sweet as 'happily ever'. The world had changed; Archangel had done so much in the space of a few months. It wasn't like they could wake up as if none of it had ever happened. If people had been concerned about registering powered humans before, Gabriel could already tell it would be nothing compared to now. They would be scared, and scared people could do terrible things. He clenched his fists and wished he had an answer. It felt like he was supposed to have an answer, to still always be the one with the answers, but…

The urge to make them all forget rose up in his throat. If they couldn't remember, after all, it couldn't hurt them. Everything would be okay. He shoved the thought away, remembering how it had felt to have his own memories forcibly taken from him.

How could he make the decision for all of them? He wasn't sure he knew how to do that any more, when the weight of everything Archangel had decided loomed over him. He didn't think The Archangel Project had been a complete failure, but it wasn't something that could be forced. It had to be something chosen, something that they all worked towards.

Distress hitched in Dahlia's mind, and in Isaac's, in Sanna's as the silence stretched. All of them wanting, needing; wishing that it could all truly be a bad dream and that it could be as easy as closing their eyes and waking up. No lasting consequences, no harm and no foul. But real life wasn't like that. It even occurred to Isaac that, if this was dreamed up, couldn't they dream it away?

It occurred to Gabriel, then, too, that if he let everyone remember that they might remember him as a monster. He looked like Archangel, after all. He could try 'evil double' but he doubted that was going to swing with everybody. It wasn't like they could punish Archangel for what he had done now, could they? And Gabriel had the same gift, to a lesser extent. He could do again what they feared. What if they decided that he was a good enough alternative to punish? What if they decided to kill Morphina and Isaac and all of them for being a part of this? They couldn't do any of that if they didn't know it had happened.

His stomach churned. He'd never wanted to be the villain, whether that was true or not. Still.

"We can't just turn back the clock and run away from this," Isaac said. "We have to move forward. Most people aren't going to know what exactly happened anyway."

"Sometimes people need to run away," Sanna said. "Sometimes forgetting is a *mercy*. This is going to hurt a lot of people."

"Yes," Gabriel agreed. "But nobody can run forever. And nobody should be *forced* to forget."

Sanna gulped, looking down, but she didn't disagree.

Morphina, he noted, was being quiet where she stood. She was still watching Archangel's body on the ground.

"What do you think?" Gabriel asked her.

Her head shot to him, like she hadn't been expecting to be addressed again. Her eyes narrowed slightly, turning as cool as they had ever been. He saw her gaze drift over Dahlia, saw it shift as she took in the other woman and the resolute set to Dahlia's jaw. It was not, exactly, a look of camaraderie or anything so soft as friendship – not with all those two had done to each other. It was something like understanding. Something like looking at something so impossibly real, so very human, that it couldn't possibly be a dream.

"I..." she faltered for a moment. "We'll be in this together?"

That, they all agreed on. Somehow, despite everything, whatever happened next was something they were going to face together. It was the only way to keep everything from crumpling on them. It was the only way to be accountable.

The world would remember.

"This doesn't ever happen again."

They all agreed on that too, a pact in a ballroom like a fairy-tale, still dressed in the tattered remnants of fancy clothes.

Music drifted in the background.

"Well," Dahlia bared a smile, and went to the buffet to get an unopened bottle. "This is going to be fun."

They had their ending, or maybe, just maybe, they had their start.

33 - Dahlia

D ahlia stood with Sanna, side by side, on the edge of a cliff. The salty sea breeze blustered through her hair, rolling across the grey waters spread out below them. Her fingers tightened on the small pot of Felicity's ashes, not sure she was ready to let go yet. She wasn't sure she ever would be.

It had been months since Fliss, Jack and Lucy had died, but her first priority was a funeral. It was what they had deserved from the start. Some peace. Dahlia didn't know much about grabbing peace for herself, but she could do it for them at the very least. No more walking nightmares.

It was a quiet affair, and swift – she'd wanted to get it done before the world started up a proper uproar about what had happened. Who knew what would happen after that.

"She always said she wanted it like this," Dahlia muttered. "So that she would never be stuck in one place after she was gone." It felt like a useless thing to say aloud, but she didn't know what to say instead.

"You don't want to try bringing her back?" Sanna asked. "We did it with Morphina. We could do it with Felicity."

Dahlia shook her head, fiercely. No. No way. She'd had quite enough of them being brought back. She didn't think she could ever see that again.

Sanna had been the first to offer Dahlia a ride to the coast where she could release the ashes high over the water. She was different without the telepathy in her head. No longer so calm. No longer so ready to be positive and smiley about everything. No longer so ready to drop everything to help other people, without thinking to take time for herself. In a way, Dahlia found herself glad. Sanna deserved to be furious. She'd seen Morton mutter something to her about a counsellor who specialised in PTSD for people with powers – apparently, the ice guy he'd spoken to had recommended them. Him and Isaac had a long conversation.

Gabriel and Isaac had come along also, with Mona piling into the backseat to in a subdued silence. She'd stuck close since Archangel's downfall, and maybe Dahlia didn't mind as much as it felt she should. Felicity would have liked the dreamweaver when she wasn't being murderous, and, besides, for Felicity's sake Dahlia had to keep her promises. She couldn't stop Morphina if she had no idea where she was or what she was doing.

They all stood some way behind her, waiting.

Dahlia didn't look back at them. She brought the pot to her lips and kissed its shell, before releasing a shuddering breath. The pain inside her howled, until it felt like it could drown out anything and everything, until she could break with it. It felt like the world could split with how much it hurt, and how much she wished Felicity would appear truly at her side again. Just for long enough to say goodbye.

Gabriel didn't try and soften it. The grief clanged through her, sharp and clear. It was hers.

He stepped up, once Sanna was ready, placing a hand on her

shoulder. He murmured something into her ear and some of the tension eased from Sanna's face. She leaned into him a little more.

Nobody had much to say on the drive, or when they arrived. Gabriel, Dahlia supposed, could have been holding telepathic conversations. She didn't think so though.

"I'm sorry," Gabriel said, then, to their friends. "I'll do better."

"Be at peace," Sanna added.

They tossed the ashes, but Dahlia still didn't let go yet. Her mind worked through the memories, through all of the places that her sister had told her about. She would go and see them once the dust had settled. She would buy crappy cheap shot glasses and use them to drink orange juice. She would collect dream-catchers. Everything wasn't okay, but it might be.

She'd once thought that the world could have peace once it stopped forcing her to fight. The fight was not over, she knew that, even if Archangel was gone. They had been right about that – there would always be other monsters.

She remembered Morphina's words, down in the dungeons, her tiredness. She remembered the exhausted look on Sanna's face, and the way she had clutched onto mind control for so long because she was just so *tired* too.

Nobody was forcing them to fight, they could have stopped a long time ago. They didn't, neither of them. The nightmares and the pain were always there but they both always chose to keep going in whatever way that they could. They could choose anger, or surrender, or hatred. Or they could choose, as best as they could, to be kind. To not let their worst, most exhausted moments define them.

Maybe their best didn't have to be a literal dream creature

to be worth something.

Dahlia unscrewed the top of Felicity's ashes and tossed her sister to the wind, watching her vanish, carried away above the waves. She allowed herself to be tired then, too, just for a moment. She allowed herself to cry like the world had ended, because the world as she knew it had.

The world would have peace once they'd bloody well finished fighting for it.

34 - Isaac

on't run.

Isaac stiffened at the words. Fear bolted acid up his throat.

Please.

"I just want to talk to you," Gabriel said, aloud, from behind him. "Before you go. Sorry. Old habits."

The sensation on his limbs faded, like Gabriel had drawn back into himself. Isaac turned and studied him. Gabriel looked better now, better rested, more himself. He shifted awkwardly on his feet, looking every inch the gawky teenager desperate to be liked as he had been when they met. Well, maybe not every inch. The years had changed them both, hadn't it?

"I wouldn't have left without saying goodbye," Isaac murmured. Not again. Never again. "I'm not going to vanish, got promises to keep, haven't I?"

Gabriel's throat bobbed as he swallowed, releasing a slightly shaky breath. He shoved his gloved hands deep into his pockets, like pockets were prisons and maybe that was for the best instead of touching.

Isaac had never quite intended that to be the result of everything. He hesitated a moment, before walking over.

The sky was the pale blue of eggshells, speckled with clouds. The first of the spring flowers were beginning to bloom again, bursts of colour and life struggling out of the frozen ground. It had been a difficult and busy month or so as the telepathy on the world faded, full of tears and fury and people who wanted someone to blame. There were new discussions happening about how people with powers could be handled, to avoid any similar situations in future, but nobody quite knew that it was them.

Archangel's face had been around, and people knew of Gabriel, but for the most part...

Somehow, it seemed to have actually worked out. Certainly there were enough tangles to undo that they were hardly the priority of the world. Not everything Archangel had done had been terrible – must have been the Gabriel in him.

Isaac took Gabriel's hand in his gloved own and squeezed, before drawing him close into a fierce hug.

Gabriel unspooled in his arms.

"Are you going to be alright?" Gabriel asked softly, against his shoulder. "Are you going to be happy?"

It was an absurdly childlike question – who could possibly know? – but it made Isaac's stomach flutter all the same. He held Gabriel a little tighter still, and tried for a smile when he pulled back to see his face once more.

"I think I'm going to live." For better or worse, for happiness or sorrow, he was going to learn how to live again. He was not a ghost. He had not died in that university room. He didn't have to die again. He didn't have to be nothing.

The smile flared blinding bright on Gabriel's lips, like a match struck in a dark room. It warmed Isaac up to the bone.

"Good," Gabriel said. "Death never suited you."

Isaac's throat grew tight. He didn't know what to say, but he didn't want to simply leave either, and yet he didn't quite know how to stay. Not yet. One day, maybe. He'd practice. Oh what a mess they'd made of themselves. What could they have been if he wasn't so scared of being too much? If Gabriel wasn't so scared of not being enough? He had a feeling they would finally find out.

"I—" Isaac closed his eyes for a beat. "We both spun a little out of control, didn't we? Got a little lost." It was nothing new, nothing they hadn't said before, but it was without accusation or rancour. People got lost. Then they found the map again.

"It happens," Gabriel said. His hand drifted up to touch Isaac's cheek, before he caught himself, palm trembling an inch away. He didn't touch, even with the glove. "That happens."

Maybe that was what it had always been. Power, yes, but never just. Touch. Connection. Holding the one you loved tight because what else did people do when they were scared and wanted to feel safe for a while? If you made an anchor out of a person, it was easy to become unmoored and just as easy to plummet into the darkness of the ocean floor, too weighed down to find light or air.

Isaac drew Gabriel's hand up again, sliding his glove off, and tipped his head into Gabriel's waiting palm. He released a shaky breath of his own. The contact didn't feel like drowning any more. It was him. It was them, nothing more. It was good. It was complicated.

Gabriel's breath shivered. His eyes stayed his own colour. Isaac didn't magnify. He wouldn't be able to hold it for long, but...

"Still not used to that," Gabriel said. He didn't take his hand away, his thumb stroking Isaac's cheek in an idle hypnosis of warmth lost and found. "Isaac Morton," he murmured, another smile curling his lips. "The man who could turn a super-hero into a god." His other hand rose too, cradling Isaac's head like it was the most precious treasure in the world. "I'm going to bloody miss you, you know."

Always with the saying things like that – things that got too heavy to ever be taken back. Gabriel always offered them up so easily, like they were nothing to give. It was such careless, beautiful, bravery. Isaac had missed it. He was going to miss it even if they weren't saying goodbye forever.

Isaac was going back to his cottage and getting his stuff together. He was clawing out of the grave he'd built for himself. He was figuring who he was, on his own, instead of being someone else's memory or dream.

"You never needed to be a god, Gabriel. I hope you know that," he replied, practising his own weight of words. "You were – are – a perfectly fine mortal too."

Gabriel laughed and shook his head, a touch of colour on his cheeks.

"And I'll see you around," Isaac said. "So don't do the whole dramatic 'I'll miss you' thing on me. Phone call away, remember?" He wouldn't live with Gabriel; he wouldn't be in a relationship with him like the years hadn't happened. He suspected they both needed the space to figure what they were now and certainly Isaac needed to pick Archangel out of his head. But, maybe, one day, no promises. Even after everything, Isaac loved him. He probably always would.

"What about you?" Isaac asked. "Will you be happy? Are you going to be alright?"

"Better. I'm going to save the world."

Isaac had to laugh. And then he had to kiss him. He kissed Gabriel madly, burningly, because he wanted something that wasn't war and wasn't hard and wasn't a weapon or a manipulation. Gabriel's lips were familiar against his own, with all the bitter complexities and sweetness of homecoming. Isaac lost track of his powers then, but though Gabriel's breath caught he didn't flinch or pull away. He didn't seem a million miles away either, he was still with Isaac. He drew Isaac closer to him and they parted breathless, panting.

Gabriel shifted his hands to rest on Isaac's hips, above the thick material of his hoodie. His eyes turned from moonlit white back to brown; to trees, and earth, threaded through with gold in the light.

"I'm going to go back to study, I think," Gabriel said. "Therapy. Counselling. Something like that. Something that focuses on helping people heal, rather than catching the monster." He pressed another gentle kiss to Isaac's lips. "I think I'm done with the glamour of running around playing superhero for a while. I don't think I ever had the right temperament for it."

"As fantastic as you no doubt look in the skintight suit," Isaac said.

Gabriel laughed, surprised.

Isaac smiled back at that, and, when he stepped away, Gabriel let his hands fall without clinging. They were more comfortable than they had been in a long while, if still not completely easy.

They stood together, a little space apart, in the cusp of the seasons. It was time for a change. It was time to finally heal, to move forwards, and stop arguing over whose fault it was.

"Goodbye, Isaac," Gabriel said.

"See you soon, Gabriel."
He walked away freely.

Printed in Poland
by Amazon Fulfillment
Poland Sp. z o.o., Wrocław